INVADERS OF EARTH

Have you looked behind you lately? Is your door firmly bolted—are your windows locked? Well, you may be safe. But then again. . . .

HERE IS A BOOK to curl your hair, to make you wonder if your next-door neighbor is a concealed Martian or the postman a Venusian spy. To you Earth is your home planet, a stepping-off place from which to begin explorations to outer space. But for how many might Earth be a place *to arrive at*? How many from Somewhere Out There are in our midst now?

The 17 spine-chilling and thought-provoking stories (including the famous Orson Welles' broadcast, "Invasion from Mars") are very different, but they have one thing in common: they tell of invaders from other stars or other galaxies, some foes, some friends, all come to Earth for a look around—and sometimes for more.

Groff Conklin, science fiction's most versatile editor, has selected the most imagination-stretching tales of some of science fiction's top writers, all adding up to one question: Are we really alone in the Universe—or are we being watched? What do you think?

TEMPO BOOKS

EDITED BY GROFF CONKLIN

INVADERS
OF EARTH

TEMPO
BOOKS

GROSSET & DUNLAP

NEW YORK

TEMPO BOOKS EDITION, 1962
BY ARRANGEMENT WITH THE VANGUARD PRESS, INC.

FIRST PRINTING, SEPTEMBER 1962

PRINTED IN THE UNITED STATES OF AMERICA

COPYRIGHT ACKNOWLEDGMENTS

CONTENTS

INTRODUCTION   9

PROLOGUE:

The Distant Past   15

Murray Leinster: THIS STAR SHALL BE FREE   16

PART ONE:

The Immediate Past:

It Could Have Happened Already   41

Robert Moore Williams: CASTAWAY   42
Eric Frank Russell: IMPULSE   61
David Grinnell: TOP SECRET   76
William F. Temple: A DATE TO REMEMBER   79
Margaret St. Clair: CHILD OF VOID   97
Theodore Sturgeon: TINY AND THE MONSTER   116
Mack Reynolds: THE DISCORD MAKERS   161
A. E. Van Vogt: NOT ONLY DEAD MEN   176

PART TWO:

The Immediate Future:

It May Happen Yet 205

Howard Koch: INVASION FROM MARS 207

Mildred Clingerman: MINISTER WITHOUT
  PORTFOLIO 236

Fredric Brown: THE WAVERIES 246

Edward Grendon: CRISIS 276

Edgar Pangborn: ANGEL'S EGG 289

William Tenn: "WILL YOU WALK A LITTLE
  FASTER?" 338

Katherine MacLean: PICTURES DON'T LIE 353

EPILOGUE:

The Distant Future 377

Anthony Boucher: THE GREATEST TERTIAN 378

INTRODUCTION

THERE are two ways of looking at the planet Earth from the science-fiction point of view—two ways, that is, that permit sizable scope. One is that Earth is a springboard from which to range other worlds. The other, and in some ways more interesting, way of looking at Earth is that it is a place—to arrive at. Active Man has always liked to consider his own adventures among the stars; contemplative Man is often entranced by the idea of alien star adventurers in our midst. This book is devoted to a number of possible situations in which creatures from out of space have, for any of a multitude of reasons, decided to pay us a visit. As will be noted by the careful reader, these reasons are more likely than not to be uncomfortable from the human point of view, and this is understandable, since the Unknown is always frightening. On the other hand, the Editor's favorite stories are those in which our foreign friends are visiting us purely in a spirit of neighborliness or a reasonably accurate facsimile thereof.

The somewhat minimizing notion that today we are being looked at, used, taken care of, or conquered by alien characters gives rise to a whole new set of speculations. For one thing, our visitants must be more intelligent and scientifically farther advanced than we; otherwise they would not be able to travel in space. We can't, as yet. How, then, will we hold our own against them?

According to the stories in this book, that question can be answered in several ways. We won't be able to. We won't have to. We won't want to. We won't even know that the question exists. You can take your choice. But the one thing you have to accept, if you put any faith at all in the imaginings reflected by these stories, is that Man is not alone. Whether he is the top of the pyramid, the apex, the crown of creation, is something we lack time and space to go into here, but whether he is the only form of intelligent life in the Universe is a question we can answer right off the bat. He probably is not.

Some people will find this idea belittling to their egos; they won't like it. For others, the idea that the Galaxy is inhabited with beings of various types, temperaments, environments, physical structures, and chemical organizations is a pleasing one. These are the Terrans (or, if you prefer, Earthians) who feel less alone because they believe that Man is not unique in the visible Universe. It is to readers of this bent that *Invaders of Earth* should have special appeal. Even those stories in it that reveal inimical life forms in Outer Space still assume that there is life beyond this planet and that—just as on Earth— some forms may be bad for Man and others may be very good indeed for him.

Today the tale of alien invasion has become one of the richest and most varied of all the categories of science fiction, idea-wise. This is a remarkable recent development, stemming most probably from the greatly accelerated advances in electronic communications, rocketry, and atomic energy just before and during World War II.

One important limitation to the types of invasion depicted must be emphasized. The book contains only legitimate and "real" travels through physical space to

Earth. The protagonists may use unusual means of loco-motion, such as hyperspace or telepathy, but they all come from presently existing other worlds. Invaders from the future, time travelers, are a dime a dozen in the current science-fiction magazines, and some of them very wonderful people, too; but none of them class as genuine aliens. They are all paradoxical creatures who really have no business existing, scientifically speaking.

Similarly, creatures from metaphysical parallel worlds are also barred from this volume, since we want nothing to do in this collection with individuals who claim to be occupying the same space as we ourselves are. What if that space is supposed to be in a different kind of time? The idea is still much too confusing. We will have none of it.

We have likewise banned the folks who hail from in-side our Earth, simply because they are subterranean characters and as such cannot take a flyer in space in order to get at us. . . . Ever since the days of Jules Verne, with his *Voyage to the Center of the Earth* (1864), the idea that civilizations of various sorts exist underneath our feet has haunted imaginative writers. There is a good book idea there, too—but not this one. . . .

To sum up, then, our Outlanders, our alien visitors, are exclusively limited to possible beings from the depths of space. Within this scope, the space travelers who in this book are turning their attention upon us provide a rich variety of type, motivation, paraphernalia, and method of approach or attack, as the case may be. One can only marvel at the ingenuity of the writers of the past fifteen years who have invented these miscellaneous peoples, entities, and things, as they may variously be defined. A bright and lively and sometimes startling bunch of characters, full of quips and quiddities. . . .

As for the general purpose, the underlying moral of

this book, it gives the Editor considerable pleasure to announce that, unlike most other books of this nature, this one has not only one—it has two.

It is intended to entertain—and to edify.

It is meant to amuse at the same time that it stretches the unused tentacles of the imagination.

It is planned to help one pass a pleasant hour or so and at the same time insert some uncomfortable queries in the reader's mind about the importance and the wisdom of Man.

For—are we really alone in the Universe? How can we know for sure that we are not being watched? What assurances have we, what defenses, against attack from Outer Space? Or, if not attack, investigation? Or—even worse for the anthropocentric-minded among us—guidance? Maybe this book is true, at least in part. Who can know surely?

GROFF CONKLIN

Invaders of Earth

THE DISTANT PAST: *Prologue*

THE origins of Man and his swift rise to mastery over all that lives on Earth except himself have always been haunting subjects for imaginative writers. In the absence of definite knowledge as to what a few million years may mean in terms of actual evolutionary change through genetic mutation and natural selection, many contemplative penmen have found it convenient to posit some Outside Assistance (non-theological) to speed up the action of the Darwinian-Mendelian mechanisms that have finally produced—us.

After all, why not? Certainly such a presumption is little more imaginative than is the actual theory of the sober scientists themselves: that the primate mammal, Man, developed over a period of a few paltry million years from the creepy-crawly thing he originally had been, whatever that was.

The questions of who, what, why, and when these ancient alien invasions might have been are fascinating, but their scope is, after all, rather narrow. Either there was, or there was not, aid for the developing primate from outside the planet. In view of this limitation, we will represent this idea of inquiry by only one story. This story is . . .

Murray Leinster

THIS STAR SHALL BE FREE

We have had all sorts of stories in the science-fiction canon about alien visitants bringing fire, or the machete, or the wheel, or the bow and arrow to Early Man—or actually bringing Early Man himself in a cocoon-like packet. All these are very interesting, and perhaps not unbelievable.

But there is a really unique invasion story of the ancient past, in which the invaders, bound on a scientific experiment of a fairly ruthless sort, end by believing that they have brought the gift of annihilation to the hopeless savages. It seems, however, that they were slightly mistaken. . . .

THE urge was part of an Antarean experiment in artificial ecological imbalance, though of course the cave folk could not guess that. They were savages with no interest in science or, indeed, in anything much except filling their bellies and satisfying other primal urges. They inhabited a series of caves in a chalk formation above a river that ran through primordial England and France before it joined the Rhine and emptied into the sea.

They did not understand the urge at all—which was natural. It followed the disappearance of the ship from Antares by a full two hours, so they saw no connection between the two. Anyhow, it was just a vague, indefinite desire to move to the eastward—an impulse for which they had no explanation whatever.

16

Tork was spearing fish from a rock out in the river when the ship passed overhead. He was a young man, still gangling and awkward. He wasn't up to a fight with One-Ear yet, and had a bad time in consequence. One-Ear was the boss male of the cave-dwellers' colony in the cliff over the river. He wanted to chase Tork away or kill him, and Tork had to be on guard every second. But he felt safe out on his rock.

He had just speared a fine ganoid when he heard a howl of terror from the shore. He jerked his head around. He saw Bent-Leg, the other adult male, go hobbling in terror toward his own cave mouth, and he saw One-Ear knock two of his wives and three children off the ladder to his cave so he could get in first. The others shrieked and popped into whatever crevice was at hand, including the small opening in which Tork himself slept when he dared. Then there was stillness.

Tork stared blankly. He saw no cause for alarm ashore. He ran his eyes along the top of the cliff. He saw birch and beech and oak, growing above the chalk. His eyes swept the stream. There were old-men's stories of sea monsters coming all the way up from the deep bay (which would some day be the English Channel). But the surface of the river was undisturbed. He scanned the farther shore. There were still a few of the low-browed ogres from whom Tork's people had taken this land, but Tork knew that he could outrun or outswim them. And there were none of them in sight, either.

All was quiet. Tork grew curious and stood up on his rock. Then he saw the ship.

It was an ovoid of polished, silvery metal. It was huge, two hundred feet by three hundred, and it floated tranquilly a hundred yards above the treetops. It moved to the stream and then drifted smoothly in a new direction up the river. It was going to pass directly over Tork's head.

It was so strange as to be unthinkable, and therefore it smote Tork with a terror past expression. He froze into a paralytic stillness, staring up at it. It made no sound. It had no features. Its perfectly reflecting sides presented to Tork's dazed eyes a distorted oval reflection of the river and the stream banks and the cliffs and all the countryside for many miles around. He did not recognize the reflection. To him it seemed that the thing's hide was mottled and that the mottlings shifted in a horrifying fashion.

It floated on, unwavering, as if its mass were too great to be affected by the gentle wind. Tork stood frozen in the ultimate catalepsy of a man faced with terror neither to be fought nor fled from. He did not see the small, spidery frameworks built out from the shining hull. He did not see the tiny tubes moving this way and that, as if peering. He did not see several of the tubes converging upon him. He was numbed, dazed.

Nothing happened. The silver ovoid swam smoothly above the river. Presently the river curved, and the ship from Antares went on tranquilly above the land. A little later it rose to clear a range of low hills. Later still, it vanished behind them.

When he recovered, Tork swam ashore with his fish, shouting vaingloriously that there was nothing to be afraid of. Heads popped timorously into view. Children appeared first, then grownups. One-Ear appeared last of all, with his red-rimmed eyes and whiskery truculence. There were babblings; then they died down. The cave folk could not talk about the thing. They had no words for it. There were no precedents, however farfetched, to compare it with. They babbled of their fright, but they could not talk about its cause.

In an hour, it appeared to have been forgotten. Tork cooked his fish. When his belly was quite full, a young girl named Berry stopped cautiously some yards away from him. She was at once shy and bold.

"You have much fish," she said, with a toss of her head.

"Too much," said Tork complacently. "I need a woman to help eat it."

He looked at her. She was probably One-Ear's daughter, but she was slim and curved and desirable where he was bloated and gross and bad-tempered. An interesting, speculative idea occurred to Tork. He grinned tentatively.

She said, "One-Ear smelled your fish. He sent me to get some. Shall I tell him he is a woman if he eats it?"

Her eyes were intent, not quite mocking. Tork scowled. To let her give such a message would be to challenge One-Ear to mortal combat, and One-Ear was twenty years older and sixty pounds heavier than Tork. He tossed the girl a fish, all cooked and greasy as it was.

"I give you the fish," said Tork grandly. "Eat it or give it to One-Ear. I don't care!"

She caught the fish expertly. Her eyes lingered on him as she turned away. She turned again to peer at him over her shoulder as she climbed the ladder to One-Ear's cave.

At just about that time the urge came to Tork. He suddenly wanted to travel eastward.

Travel, to the cave folk, was peril undiluted. They had clubs and fish spears which were simply sharpened sticks. They had nothing else. Wolves had not yet been taught to fear men. The giant hyena still prowled the wild. There were cave bears and innumerable beasts no man of Tork's people could hope to cope with save by climbing the nearest tree. To want to travel anywhere was folly. To travel eastward, where a sabertooth was rumored to den, was madness. Tork decided not to go.

But the urge remained exactly as strong as before. He summoned pictures of monstrous dangers. The urge did not deny them. It did not combat them. It simply ignored them. Tork wanted to travel to the east. He did not know why.

After half an hour, during which Tork struggled with himself, he saw the girl Berry come out of One-Ear's cave. She began to crack nuts for One-Ear's supper, using two stones. One-Ear's teeth were no longer sound enough to cope with nuts.

Tork looked at her. Presently an astounding idea came to him. He saw that the girl glanced furtively at him sometimes. He made a secret beckoning motion with his hand. After a moment, Berry got up and moved to throw a handful of nutshells into the stream. She stood idly watching them float away. She was only a few feet from Tork.

"I go to the east," said Tork in a low voice, "to look for a better cave than here."

Her eyes flickered sideways to him, but she gave no other sign. She did not move away, either. Tork elaborated: "A fine cave. A deep cave, where there is much game."

She glanced at him again out of the corners of her eyes. Tork's own eyes abruptly burned. He said, greatly daring, "Then I will come and take you to it!"

The girl tossed her head. Among the cave folk, property right to females—even one's own daughters—took precedence over all other forms of possession. Were One-Ear to hear of this invasion of his proprietary rights, there would be war to the death immediately. But the girl did not move away; she did not laugh. Tork felt vast pride and enormous ambition stir within him. After a long, breathless instant the girl turned away from the water and went back to the pounding of nuts for One-Ear. On the way her eyes flickered to Tork. She smiled a faint, almost frightened smile. That was all.

But it was enough to send Tork off within the next half hour with his club in his hand and high romantic dreamings in his heart—and a quite sincere conviction that he was moving eastward to find a cave in which to set up housekeeping.

Because of this, the journey became adventure. Once Tork was treed by a herd of small, piggish animals rather like the modern peccary. Once he fled to the river and dived in because of ominous rustlings which meant he was being stalked by something he didn't wait to identify. And when, near nightfall, he picked a tree to sleep in and started to climb it, he was halfway up to its lowest branch when he saw the ropelike doubling of the thickness of a slightly higher branch. He got down without rousing the great serpent and went shivering for three miles—eastward—before he chose another tree to sleep in. But before he went to sleep he arranged these incidents into quite heroic form, suitable to be recounted to Berry.

Tork went on at sunrise. He paused once to stuff himself with blackberries—and left that spot via nearby trees when something grunting and furry charged him. In midmorning he heard a faraway, earthshaking sound that could come from nothing but sabertooth himself. Then he heard a curious popping noise that he had never heard before, and the snarl ceased abruptly. The hair fairly stood up on Tork's head. But now the urge to move eastward was very strong indeed. It seemed to grow stronger as he traveled. No other creatures seemed to feel it, however. Squirrels frisked in the trees. Once he saw a monstrous elk—the so-called Irish elk—whose antlers had a spread of yards. The monster looked at him with a stately air and did not flee. Tork was the one who gave ground, because the cave folk had no missile weapons save stones thrown by hand. He made a circuit around the great beast.

Then he abruptly ran into tumbled ground, where there were practically no trees but very many rocks. It would be a perfect place for lying in wait. Also, he saw the mouths of several very promising caves. If the urge had not become uncontrollably strong, he would have stopped to investigate them. But he went on. Once his sensitive nostrils smelled carrion, mingled with the musky animal odor of a great carnivore. Mentally he went into gibbering terror. In his mind he fled at top speed. But the urge was incredibly strong. He went on like someone possessed. He had freedom to dodge, to creep stealthily, to take every precaution for silence and to avoid the notice of the animals which had no need to fear one club-armed man. He could even run—provided he fled to eastward. It was no longer possible for him to turn back.

The urge continued to strengthen. After some miles he became an automaton—a blank-faced, gangling figure, sun-bronzed and partly clad in an untanned hide. He carried a club, and in his belt there was a sharpened stick which was his idea of a fish spear. He trudged onward, his eyes unseeing, automatically adjusting his steps to the ground, apathetically moving around great masses of stone in his way. He was, for a time, completely at the mercy of any carnivore that happened to see him.

He did not even falter when he saw the great, silvery ovoid which had passed over his head the day before. He marched toward it with glassy eyes and an expressionless face. Yet the ship was vastly more daunting on the ground than in the air. It was still absolutely mirror-like on its outer surface. It still seemed featureless, because the spidery mounts of its scanning tubes were tiny. But its monstrous size was more evident.

It rested on the ground on its larger, rounded end. Its smaller part pointed upward. It was three hundred feet high—three times the height of the tallest trees about it, some of which had been crushed by its weight as it descended. Their branches projected from beneath it. It was a gigantic silver egg, the height of a thirty-story building and a city block thick. It rested on squashed oak trees in completely enigmatic stillness, with no sign of life or motion anywhere about it.

Tork walked up to it stiffly, seeing nothing and hearing nothing. He moved into the very shadow of the thing. Then he stopped. The urge abruptly ceased.

Pure terror sent him into howling, headlong flight. And instantly the urge returned. Twenty yards from the outward-bulging silvery metal, he crashed to earth. Then he stood up and stiffly retraced his steps toward the ship. Again, compulsion left him and he wailed and fled— and within twenty yards he slowed to a walk, and turned, and came back in blind obedience.

Ten times in all he tried to flee, and each time returned to the shadow of the motionless, mirror-like ovoid. The tenth time he stood still, panting, his eyes wild. He saw his own reflection on the surface of the thing. He croaked at it, thinking that here was another captive. His image made faces at him, but no sound; he could not make it answer. In the end he turned his back upon it sullenly. He stood shivering violently, like any wild thing caught and made helpless.

Half an hour later he saw something moving across the ground toward the great silver egg. There was a faint, faint sound, and a gigantic curved section of the egg opened. Sloshing water poured out and made puddles. There was a smell as of the ocean. The approaching thing, a vehicle, floated nearer, six feet aboveground, with strange shapes upon it and a tawny-striped mass of fur which Tork knew could be nothing but sabertooth. Tork trembled in every limb, but he knew he could not flee.

Just before the vehicle floated into the opening made by the dropped curved plate, two of the shapes descended from it and approached Tork.

He shook like an aspen leaf. He half grasped his club and half raised it, but he was too much unnerved to attack.

The shapes regarded him interestedly. They wore suits of a rubbery fabric bulging as if from liquid within. There were helmets with transparent windows, from which eyes looked out. But the windows were filled with water.

The creatures from Antares halted some paces from Tork. One of them trained a small tube upon him, and immediately he seemed to hear voices.

"We called you here to be kind to you. We saw you yesterday, standing upon a rock."

Tork merely trembled. The second shape trained a tube upon him, and he heard another voice. There was no difference in the timbre, of course, because Tork's own brain was translating direct mental impressions into words; but he knew that the second figure spoke.

"It is an experiment, Man. We come from a far star, mapping out worlds our people may some day need. Yours is a good world, with much water. We do not care for the land. Therefore we do not mind being kind to you who live on the land. . . . You have fire."

Tork found his brain numbly agreeing. He thought of

fire and cookery, and the two creatures seemed to find his thoughts interesting.

"You have intelligence," said the first creature brightly, "and it has occurred to us to make an experiment in ecology. How do you get food?"

Tork grasped only the final sentence. Again, he thought numbly. Gathering nuts. Picking berries. Spearing fish with a sharpened stick. Digging shellfish. Small animals such as rabbits and squirrels, knocked over by lucky stones. He thought also of One-Ear, who had been well fed enough yesterday merely to demand fish. On other occasions he had come bellowing, club in hand, and chased Tork away from the food he had gathered for himself.

"That is bad," said the voice in Tork's mind, but it seemed amused. "We shall show you ways to get much food. All the food you desire. We shall show you defenses against animals. It will be interesting to see what comes of an ecological imbalance so produced. You will wait here."

The two shapes moved away—they floated a little above the ground, Tork noted dazedly—and entered the ship. The curved plate closed behind them. There was a whistling of air somewhere. To men of later millennia, the sound might have suggested a water lock closing, being filled with water so that water-dwelling creatures could swim from it freely into the liquid-filled interior of the ship from Antares. To Tork, it suggested nothing.

Nothing happened for hours. Then, suddenly, Tork saw a great elk moving steadily and hypnotically toward the ship from Antares. It reached a spot less than fifty yards from the ship's side, and seemed suddenly to be released from compulsion. It turned and bounded away; then its flight slackened and stopped. It came back toward the ship. Fifty yards away, again it tried to escape, and again was recaptured.

Tork watched, wide-eyed.

Rabbits appeared, hopping toward the ship. They appeared by dozens and then by hundreds. The steady advance, converging from all directions, came to a halt in milling confusion at a fixed distance from the gigantic, glistening egg.

The curved plate opened again, and again there was a great sloshing of water and the smell of the sea. Four or five shapes emerged, floating above the ground. Even before he saw tubes trained upon him, Tork was aware of fragments of thought-conversation.

"I acknowledge that an experiment on land cannot possibly affect our later use of this planet." Another intonation, indignant: "But it is cruel! Give these creatures unlimited food and the means of defense, and you condemn their descendants to starvation!" Then other voices said disjointedly, "I insist that a new ecological balance of low birth rate will result—" "Land animals are of no concern to us—" "Stability of nature—" "Some new factor will nullify the experiment absolutely—"

Tork was a savage. He was of the cave folk, and he had never in his life come into contact with an abstraction. Because these were thoughts, he perceived them; he even understood them. But they had no reference to any of the other things in his mind or experience. So they lingered only like the fragments of a dream.

The creatures placed a sort of box before him. It seemed to Tork like a stone. There was a pattern of color leaning against it which after laborious study he discovered to be a reduced appearance of a human being. It was the first picture he had ever seen. Actually, it was a picture of him—the key pattern of the urge which had brought him, if the matter were fully understood. But he heeded the mental voices, referring to the box he thought a stone.

"This is a device which projects a desire. Since you are merely a man, we have stabilized the device so that it projects one desire only. That desire is of coming to the place from which the desire is projected. We drew you to this place by tuning the projection to you. It made you wish to come here."

Tork's brain assimilated the information after a fashion. Very patiently, the mental voices corrected his impressions. They went on:

"This device will now project only that desire, but we have left the tuning variable. Any human may change the tuning now. Stand close to the device and think of an animal, and the device will tune to animals of that sort and make them wish to come wherever the device may be."

Tork thought of sabertooth, and cringed. The mental voices were amused.

"Even that is arranged. Here is a picture of a man. Look at it and you will think only of a man, and the device will only call man to you. Here also is a picture of an elk. Place this by the device and look at it, and your thoughts of elk will tune the device, so elk will wish to come to you. Rabbits—"

Tork was frightened. It would be pleasant enough to be able to make squirrels or rabbits—he saw hundreds of rabbits now, out of the corner of his eye—come to be knocked on the head. But an elk? What could a man do with an elk? An elk could trample and toss—

"Naturally," said the voice in his mind, with some dryness, "we give you safety from animals also, if you change your habits to make use of our gifts. We have made spears with points of stone, which you can soon learn to duplicate. With the picture device you can draw animals to you, and with the spears you can kill them. Moreover—"

The voices in his mind went on and on. There were a bow and arrows. There were stone knives. For the purpose of the experiment, each instrument save the hypnotic device itself had been carefully designed to be understood by primitive minds.

"We of Antares seek new worlds for our race to inhabit. We have chosen your world for later use and shall remain upon it for perhaps a hundred of your years, to survey it. We shall be able to see the first results of what we do today. Then we shall go back to our own world, and when we return we will see the final result of our gifts to you. What happens on the land, of course, will not affect our use of the seas."

Another mental voice interrupted, protesting that the man was not given a fair chance to refuse the gifts. The instructor went on dryly, "Your species can now multiply without limit. We think that you will overrun all the land and destroy all other animals for food, and ultimately destroy yourselves. But we are not sure. We are curious to learn. You can refuse the gift if you choose."

Tork blinked. He understood—temporarily. But he was human and a savage. The prospect of unlimited food outweighed all other possible considerations. He was frightened, but he wanted all the food that could be had. Definitely.

Instructions continued. Presently Tork understood the spears, and was naïvely astonished. He understood the bows and arrows, and was amazed. He grew excited. He wanted to use the marvelous new things. He felt that the shapes were amused by him.

The land-suited figures floated back to the water lock of the ship. It closed. He was left alone. He fingered the weapons. Another great plate lowered. But this was not a lock; it was a window. A vast expanse of transparent stuff appeared. Behind it was water, and in the liquid the Antareans—no longer in their rubbery suits—swam within the great metal egg, watching.

Tork, newly instructed, examined the beautifully fashioned stone point of a spear and then lifted the spear as he had been told to do. He remembered sharp-pointed, sharp-edged stones he had seen. He remembered stones breaking when struck together. He knew he could make a point like this. But—

He was a savage. He went to that extraordinary circular confusion where rabbits hopped hypnotically toward the great silver egg and at a certain distance were released and turned to flee, and again became subject to the irresistible urge to approach it. Tork went out to them, his mouth slavering.

He made a monstrous slaughter before it palled on him. Then he saw the elk. Fifty yards from the ship it stopped, stared about it, and bounded away. It turned and came back toward the great ship until suddenly it stopped and stared. . . .

Tork killed it while it marched toward the ship in dazed obedience to the urge. Then he went crazy with triumph. He gorged himself upon the raw flesh and went back to the shadow of the ship—in his triumph he knew no more fear—and squatted down before the device he had been given. He thought of Berry. Inevitably, his thoughts went also to One-Ear and to the other members of the cave by the river. He wished each one of them to see his triumph and his greatness. With a reeking mass of raw meat beside him, he gloated over their admiration of him when they should come. . . .

They came. Berry remembered that Tork had gone to the east. She wished to follow him. One-Ear wished to go to the east. Somehow, in his fumbling brain, the urge became associated with notions of vast quantities of food. The women wished to go east. Seeking unconsciously for a reason, they decided that their children would be safer there. So the colony of cave folk took up the march.

They did not all reach the giant egg. Bent-Leg succumbed to a giant hyena who tried to carry off one of his children. A woman died when she fell behind the others. The rest heard her shriek, but that was all. And there was one small boy missing when, moving like automatons, the rest of the cave people walked with blank faces and empty eyes to within yards of the grinning, triumphant Tork. Then they were released.

There were confusion and panic such as he had felt, until he seized them one by one and held them fast while he boasted and explained. Then they still cringed fearfully for a while—but there was food. One-Ear drooled when Tork thrust a haunch of elk meat upon him. He squatted down and wolfed it, tending to snarl and glare with his wicked, red-rimmed eyes if anyone drew near. But there was food for all. More, there were weapons. Tork shared them, expansively. Small boys killed rabbits. Women used the new stone knives and skinned them.

More humans came. They were not members of Tork's tribe , but fortunately Tork's people were so stuffed with food by the time the strangers came that they felt no inclination to rise and kill them. They howled with laughter at the strangers' release, instant panic and flight, and return and release and panic again. Presently, with vast amusement, they explained and offered food. The strangers stuffed themselves. Behind the great transparent window the Antareans swam and watched. The strangers were shown the new weapons.

They wanted to try them. Tork languidly called more animals to be killed for demonstration—and food.

There was such festival and such feasting as had never before been known in the brief history of Man. By the end of the second day, no fewer than fifty humans either gobbled at more food than they had ever seen before in their lives, or else slept the noisy slumber of repletion, while the Antareans watched.

On the third morning, without any notice, the ship rose quietly from the ground and sped skyward. A thousand feet up, it slanted toward the west, toward the great ocean in which an exploring party from Antares would be most interested.

The humans' first reaction to the departure of the ship was panic. But Tork went to the box—the stone-that-calls-animals—and tried a new picture. He thought of graceful, timid deer. The device called a herd of the spotted creatures, and the cave folk killed them and were reassured.

The feasting might have gone on indefinitely, but that Tork was a savage and therefore like a child. He kept the neighborhood of the camp so crowded with food animals that other creatures came of their own accord to prey on them. When the brutish roaring of the cave bear was heard, terror fell upon the people. They seized the weapons and such food as they could carry, and they fled. Mostly, they scattered.

But Tork's own tribe naturally stayed together. It fled back toward its normal habitation, Tork carrying the stone-that-calls-animals.

Tork and Berry dissuaded the new members of the tribe from looking covetously upon Berry. Berry, in fact, used a spear upon an admirer who was pressing Tork too hard with a club. But nevertheless, when Tork took possession of the one cave that had been empty in the chalk cliff, Berry uttered a purely formal outburst of shrieks as he dragged her inside to begin housekeeping.

Her father, One-Ear, did not go to her rescue. He was stuffed to bursting with deer meat, and he merely cocked a tolerant, sleepy eye when his daughter was thus kidnaped from his very presence. In any case, he knew that she would have used a spear or knife on him or anybody else who interfered, so he merely belched slightly and settled back to slumber.

So Tork and Berry were married. But the end of the Antarean experiment was not yet.

Those who had been called to the shadow of the silver ship and there released spread through the land. Most of them had not joined Tork's tribe. They had new, modern, priceless weapons. Non-possessors of beautiful, up-to-date flint spears tried to do murder for their possession. Their owners did a little murdering on their own. Possessors of spears and arrows which would actually cut and pierce were supermen. And in time it became apparent that a man who practiced and gained skill with the even more scientific bow and arrow was in a still better position to win wives and influence the next generation. So every human who saw or heard of the new weapons craved them passionately.

But, being humans and savages, they did not think of making them for themselves. They tried to get them from Tork and his tribe. At first they journeyed to the chalk-cliff village and asked for the new weapons, naïvely. For a little while, Tork was flattered and open-handed. Then he began to run short of worked flint. He grew stingy; he gave no more away. Then envious men grew desperate. They stole a spear here, an arrowhead there. . . . Tork had to establish a flint curtain, permitting no visitors in his village. He was unquestioned chieftain now. One-Ear had become too fat either to hunt or fight. And then furtive, burning-eyed sneak thieves hung about the village. Some had traveled for weeks through dangers to make the flesh crawl, merely in hope of a chance to steal a spear or flint knife or arrowhead. They developed great adeptness at such sneak thievery.

There came a day when Tork's own personal spear was stolen from the mouth of his own cave. The thief was a youth of an unknown tribe who seemed to appear from nowhere. He dashed to the spear, seized it, and dived overboard with it. He swam underwater, rising only to gasp for breath, until so far offshore as to be out of range of thrown stones. Stone-tipped arrows were far too precious to be fired into the river. He escaped.

Something had to be done. Tork needed that spear. Berry—being now a wife of some months' standing— upbraided him shrilly for his carelessness. Tork went gloomily into the deepest recesses of his cave, to think. The stone-that-calls-animals was there. He regarded it miserably. He thought of the creatures who had given it to him. . . .

And Tork, the cave man, had the inspiration which, in the bumbling, unintentional manner in which men achieve their greatest triumphs, actually determined the future of the human race.

There was a ship from Antares upon Earth. Its crew mapped the Earth's oceans for later colonists. The Antarean civilization was already a hundred thousand years old and very far advanced indeed. Men had just been introduced to flint spears and knives and arrows by the Antareans as an interesting experiment, to see what would happen. But Tork had an inspiration. He thought about the Antareans, while he squatted by the stone-that-calls-animals! It was the greatest single inspiration that any man has ever known. But for it, Earth would be an Antarean colony, and Man— Man would be at best a tolerated animal on the continents the Antareans had no use for.

Tork squatted by the Antarean device and remembered the Antareans in their water-filled suits. Then he thought about them as they had looked in the huge transparent window, paddling in the monster aquarium which was their ship and looking out at the cave folk. The effort made his head hurt.

Presently he called Berry to help him think.

Presently Berry grew impatient. She had housewifely tasks to perform. She told Tork that there should be a picture to look at; then he could keep thinking of them without trouble.

It had long been a pastime of cave children to press one hand against the cave wall and outline the outspread fingers with charcoal. It produced a recognizable picture of a hand. Tork essayed to trace his remembered image of what Antareans looked like, on the wall. The result was extremely crude; but while he worked on it, it was easy to keep thinking about Antareans.

Berry disapproved his drawing. She changed it, making it better. Presently One-Ear, wheezing, came amiably into the cave of his son-in-law and was informed of the enterprise. His sharp, red-rimmed eyes perceived flaws even in Berry's artistry. He was the first human art critic. Other members of the tribe appeared. Some criticized; others attempted drawings of their own. A continuous session of artistic effort began—with everybody thinking about Antareans all the time.

Of course, the Antareans felt the urge. Perhaps at the beginning it was very faint. But the cave-folk's memories of the Antareans grew sharper as they improved their drawings. The tuning of the device improved; and the impulse to move toward the calling device grew stronger. At best, it was nagging. In the end it grew unbearable.

So there came a day when the great silver ovoid appeared in the sky to westward. It came swiftly, undeviatingly, toward the cliff village. It landed on the solid ground above the caves. Instantly it had landed, it was within the space where the call did not operate, and its crew was freed of the urge. The ship took off again, instantly. But instantly it was back in the overwhelming grip of the device the Antareans themselves had made. It returned, took off and returned, and took off and returned. . . .

Presently it settled down solidly on the plateau above the river. Tork went, beaming, to meet the land-suited creatures who came out of the water lock. Two figures floated toward him, menacingly. Voices came in his brain, unreasonably irritated. One said severely, "Man, you should not use the calling device we gave you to call *us!*"

"We need more spears," said Tork, beaming, "and bows and arrows and knives. So we called you to ask you to give them to us."

Crackling, angry thought came into his mind. The Antareans raged. Tork could not understand it. He regarded them blankly. More Antareans came out. He caught comprehensible fragments of other thoughts.

"So long as they think about us, we are helpless to leave! We cannot go beyond the space of freedom. . . ." Another voice said furiously, "We cannot let mere animals call us! We must kill them!" Another voice said reasonably, "Better destroy the device. That will be enough. After all, the experiment—"

Then a dry voice asked, "Where is the device?"

The creatures fretted. Tork stood hopefully, waiting for them to give him spears and knives and arrowheads. He was aware of highly technical conversation. The Antareans located the device. It was deep in the sloping chalk cliff below the ship. But in order for an Antarean to get to it, he would first have to go away from it, to get down the cliff. And he could not go away from it!

A crackling mental voice suggested that they call the humans to them—away from the device. But the same objection applied. In order to approach a similar device inside the ship, the humans in the caves would have to go away from it, and they couldn't do that, either. It was a perfect stalemate. The Antareans were trapped.

They even considered blasting the cliff, to smash the instrument they had presented to Tork. But anything that would smash the device would blow up the ship. The hundred-thousand-year-old Antarean civilization was helpless against the naïve desires of cave men who simply wanted more pieces of worked flint.

"Man," snapped a voice in Tork's mind, "how did you creatures keep your thought steadily upon us so that we were called?"

"We made pictures of you," said Tork happily. "It was not easy to do, but we did it."

He beamed at them. There was pained silence. Then a mental voice said bitterly, "We will give you spears and arrows, Man, if you will destroy every one of the pictures."

"We will do that," promised Tork brightly, "because now we can draw them again when we need you."

He seemed to hear moans inside his head. But the Antareans were civilized, after all. He seemed also to hear wry chucklings. And the dry voice said, inside his skull, "It is agreed. Go down and blot out the pictures of us. We will give you what you wish. Then we can go away.

"And—you will never be able to summon us again, Man! We had intended to stay on this earth for a hundred of your years, and if our experiment seemed too deadly to you, we would have stopped it. But now we will not take that risk. Your species is a land species, and we are of the sea, but we think it best that you disappear. We have given you the means to destroy yourselves. We will depart and let you do so. Now go and blot out the pictures."

Tork went happily down into his cave. He commanded the wiping out of the pictures of Antareans. Within an hour the ship was gone. And this time it rose straight into the sky, as if it weren't coming back.

At first Tork was made happy by a huge new store of worked flint; but within two months disaster fell. The pictures of animals—so needful when using the Antarean device—blew into a cooking fire and burned. Then there was deep mourning, and Tork and Berry and all the tribe tried earnestly to call back the ship to get a fresh supply.

But nothing happened.

This was catastrophe; they could no longer call animals to be killed. But then Berry suggested redrawing the burned pictures on the cave's walls, and again art was attempted, by men working from the motive which has produced most of the great art works of earth—to get something to eat.

The Antarean device worked just as well with pictures of the cave-folk's own drawing as with those the Antareans had provided. But of course the Antareans could not know about it, because they had left the planet altogether. . . .

Tork and Berry lived long lives and had many offspring, all of whom thrived mightily because of the Antarean experiment. Of course, the experiment was not ended. In time, the tribe in the chalk-cliff village had increased so much in numbers that there was lack of room for its members. Colonies were sent out from it, and they thrived, too. And every colony carried with it three distinct results of the Antarean experiment in ecological imbalance.

One was stone weapons, which in time they rather painfully learned to make for themselves. Another was the belief that it was a simple trick to call animals to be killed. The actual Antarean device—being tucked away in the back of Tork's cave—in time was covered over with rubbish and in two generations was forgotten. Since it needed no attention, it got none. In time, when its power grew weaker and its effect less, nobody even thought to uncover and tinker with it. And the third result of the Antarean contact with Tork's tribe was the practice of drawing and painting pictures of animals on cave walls. The art of those Cro-Magnon artists is still admired.

The experiment still went on. Men learned to make weapons. Presently they discovered metal. The spears and arrowheads became bronze, and then iron, and presently gunpowder replaced bowstrings to hurl metal missiles. Later still, there was the atom bomb. In the art line, there were Praxiteles and Rodin and Michelangelo and Picasso. . . . And the consequences of the experiment continued to develop. . . .

A good thirty thousand years after the time of Tork, the Antareans decided that they needed the oceans of Earth for the excess population of several already colonized planets. They prepared a colonizing fleet. The original survey was not complete, but it was good enough to justify a full-scale expedition for settlement.

More than two million Antareans swam in the vessels which launched themselves into space to occupy Earth. It was purely by accident that members of a society of learned Antareans, going over the original survey reports, came upon the record of the experiment. The learned society requested, without much hope, that an effort be made to trace the ancient meddling with the laws of nature and see if any results could be detected.

The Antarean fleet came out of overdrive beyond Jupiter and drove in toward Earth with placid confidence. There was blank amazement on board when small spacecraft hailed the newcomers with some belligerence. The Antareans were almost bewildered. There was no intelligent race here. . . . But they sent out a paralyzing beam to seize one ship and hold it for examination. Unfortunately, the beam was applied too abruptly and tore the Earthship to pieces.

So the many-times-removed great-great-grandchildren of Tork and Berry and the others of the cave-folk tribe —they blasted the Antarean fleet in seconds, and then very carefully examined the wreckage. They got an interstellar drive out of their examination, which well paid for the one lost Earthship. But the Antarean learned society never did learn the results of that experiment in ecological imbalance, started thirty thousand years before.

In fact, the results aren't all in yet.

PART ONE

THE IMMEDIATE PAST:
It Could Have Happened Already

NINETY-NINE per cent of all earth-invasion stories in science fiction are located in a narrow segment of time which flows from a few years in the past, through now, up to a few years in the future. The tales in this section —different though they all are in story line—have one thing in common: they could have happened or may actually be happening now, as you read this. *There is nothing impossible about them. They violate no probabilities and involve no changes in the direction of history* that we know about—*or that are yet obvious. (What suddenly may turn up tomorrow, or a minute from now, as a result of certain doings in these tales is something else again.)*

This type of story has the same sort of hypnotic fascination that many people find in the works of Charles Fort, the Man Who Believed What He Reads in the Papers, or are able to extract from the Great Flying Saucers Mystery. Is they is, or is they ain't? That is the question. All we can say is—make up your own mind. We ourselves don't know.

Robert Moore Williams

CASTAWAY

Our first story of the Immediate Past gently but firmly leads you into the strange position where something you think you know has not happened is, quite obviously, happening. Indeed, it might well be this way, you say: for would not the Outsiders, if they knew of our curiously direct method of dealing with oddities, try to avoid direct contact with us? Such a contact, they will realize if they have studied our reactions with any assiduity, could result in anything from a lynching to an offer of a movie contract. Which fate would seem worse to a sensitive alien we have no way of knowing.

In any event, they must know that the human reaction to something as incredible as galactic visitors would not be likely to be either rational or pleasant. Therefore, all contacts from space have undoubtedly been, whenever possible, secretive, disguised, concealed. As, for instance . . .

"BUT look here," Parker protested into the phone. "You must be mixed up about your dates. I came out of that God-forsaken corner of hell—excuse the profanity, but the description is accurate—only six days ago. I'm not due to relieve Johnson for eight more days, so don't be calling and telling me to report for duty. Huh? What's that?"

It was Hanson's secretary who had called him. Hanson was chief of the Gulf division of the lighthouse service. The girl had made a mistake, he thought.

The phone clicked and the girl's voice was gone. Hanson himself came on the wire, slightly apologetic but with the "duty-is-duty" tone in his voice.

"Parker? Report to the dock immediately. The plane will be ready to take you back to your station by the time you arrive."

"The devil. I mean, sir—"

"I quite appreciate that you are off duty," Hanson said, "but this is an emergency." Parker waited for an explanation. It didn't come.

"What kind of an emergency?" he questioned. "Has something happened to Johnson?"

"Yes. You are to report at once."

"All right, sir. But what happened to Johnson?"

"He fell down the lighthouse steps and broke an arm. We . . . ah . . . had a radio report from him last night. The plane went out for him this morning. I'm sorry to have to ask you to take your turn before your time is up, but we don't have a replacement, and the Navy prefers that we have an observer constantly on duty at your post, as you know. You'll have to finish Johnson's turn and then do your own. By that time, I'll have a new man to take Johnson's place."

"That means I'll spend three weeks out there," Parker grumbled. Then he pointed out: "And if you send a new man, I'll have to stay and break him in. In that time, Johnson should have recovered from his broken arm and be able to take his own turn again. I'm willing to take over his turn, since it's an emergency, but what do you want to send a new man for?"

"Parker, I don't have time to sit here and argue with you about this," Hanson snapped. "I know you're entitled to two full weeks off duty and I also know you've earned every second of it, but I've got to send somebody out to that lighthouse and the only person I can send is you. So cut out this arguing and get down here."

"All right, I'll be down right away," Parker answered.

The old man could be tough at times. This was apparently one of those times. But it seemed to Parker that Hanson was being tougher than circumstances warranted.

Damn Johnson, he thought. Why did the long drink of water have to fall down the stairs and break his arm? And why had he, Parker, ever been big enough fool to enter the lighthouse service? Once it had seemed a rather romantic occupation, taking care of the big lamp, seeing that the lens was clean and the reflectors bright, flashing warnings to ships out in the Gulf. But now Parker had been in the service six years and a lot of romance had vanished. Now he knew that nothing ever happened in a lighthouse.

That was what was wrong with the damned job. Nothing ever happened! You took care of the light, and fished, and made radio reports, and hunted for something to kill the time so the loneliness didn't get you. Two weeks on duty and two weeks off. For two weeks you didn't see another human being.

Hanson was waiting at the landing when Parker arrived. At the end of the wharf a big seaplane was floating, her motors turning over slowly.

"Sorry, Parker," Hanson said, apologizing again, "but the Navy insists that we have trustworthy men at your station, especially with the war in Europe going blue blazes. A sub or two might slip into the Gulf and raise hell with shipping before she could be tracked down, especially if there should be a secret base somewhere around. The patrol boats can't cover everything, you know, and the Navy wants all the eyes it can get on the lookout."

"That's all right," Parker answered rather stiffly. "How's Johnson?"

"Johnson!" Hanson seemed startled. "Oh, I guess he'll be all right. Don't know yet. He's at the hospital now, for observation."

Parker looked at Hanson. The chief had grown gray in the lighthouse service. He looked worried now.

"What is there about a broken arm that calls for observation?" Parker asked.

Hanson had a pair of gimlet eyes that could be used to drill twin holes in a questioner. But he didn't turn the gimlets on the slightly disgruntled young man who was facing him. He studied the seaplane as if he found something of interest in it.

"The arm was pretty badly swollen," he answered, still not looking at Parker. "Take a day or two to get the swelling out so the doctor can set the bone. Well, good luck, lad," he finished, suddenly thrusting out his hand. "Make your reports regularly, and if anything suspicious should turn up, don't hesitate to get in touch with me immediately."

A little startled, Parker took the proffered hand. Hanson didn't usually shake hands with men leaving for a turn of duty. Nor did he usually come down to the landing to see them off.

"Thank you," he said. "If anything turns up, I'll get in touch with you. But nothing will," he added wryly. "Nothing ever does." He walked down the dock toward the plane. Looking back, he saw that Hanson was still watching him.

He got into the plane.

It was a Navy plane, with a crew of two, which was something special in the way of service. Usually the lighthouse service used their own planes, especially in taking men to Parker's station, which was over two hundred miles away on a tiny island near the southern side of the Gulf. But this was an emergency, and perhaps the Navy had been willing to supply transportation, since they were so anxious to have someone on duty all the time.

"Let her roll," Parker said.

There was a lieutenant at the controls. He taxied away from the landing, set her up on the step, and lifted her into the air. Parker was aware that the radio operator was looking at him.

"Too bad about the other chap," the radio operator said.

"Yeah," Parker answered. He was still grumpy at this sudden call to duty. "But he probably fell down the steps and broke his arm on purpose, just so he could go on sick leave."

He knew it wasn't true. Johnson wasn't that kind of guy. Johnson took his duty seriously. But Parker felt grumpy.

"What's that?" the radio operator asked. "He broke his arm?"

"Sure. That's what the old man said. But you ought to know. You brought him in, didn't you?"

The radio operator looked at the lieutenant.

"Yes," the lieutenant said hastily. "We brought him in. It sure was tough, about his arm. You men in that service ought to be very careful. If you suffered a serious accident and couldn't get to the radio, you might die before help was sent."

Parker twisted in his seat. He looked from the lieutenant to the radio operator.

"What do you mean?" he asked. "Are you holding back something? Didn't Johnson have a broken arm?"

"Yes," the lieutenant answered. "That was it. A broken arm. Sure."

A frown settled on Parker's face. But he said nothing more. The plane climbed into the sky, leveled out for flight. He was so busy thinking that almost before he knew it the plane was nosing down again. Far off across the blue water he could see the white tower of the lighthouse rising out of the sea. He was at his station.

The radio operator helped him unload his bags.

"Good luck," the lieutenant said.

Parker watched the plane taxi across the water, watched it rise abruptly into the air. The song of the motors died in the distance. Soon it was as small as a gull. Then it was gone. With it went the only human beings he would see for three weeks.

There was a small frame house beside the lighthouse. The keeper lived there. A boardwalk led from the landing up to the lighthouse. Parker started along the walk. Suddenly he stopped. His eyes ran over the tiny island, over the lighthouse, over the small house beside it, then returned to the boards under his feet.

There were wet splotches on those boards, splotches that were almost dry now. They looked like footprints. Parker stared at them.

"Nuts," he said. "Who do I think I am, Robinson Crusoe, finding a footprint in the sand?"

He went up the walk and into the house, dropped his bags. Automatically, he began a routine tour of inspection. The door of the lighthouse was open. Wet footprints led inside.

Parker looked at them. Standing outside, he ran his eyes up the white wooden walls of the lighthouse tower. He looked at the tracks again. He turned, walked back into the house, took the automatic out of his bag. It was a .45, an Army gun. He clicked a clip of cartridges into place, gently worked the slide to feed a cartridge into the firing chamber. Slipping the gun into his jacket pocket, he went back to the lighthouse. Overhead was a wooden floor. The radio equipment was up there. Much farther up, at the top of the tower, was the light. Steps led up to the radio room through a trap door. The wet footprints went up the steps.

The trap door was open.

He went up very quietly.

"Hello," he said, when his head was above the level of the floor. "What are you doing here?"

The fellow jumped at the sound of Parker's voice. He was in the radio room, staring at the transmitter. He didn't know Parker was near him until the latter spoke.

He was short and squat, built like a battering-ram. Except for a strip of metallic-appearing cloth at his waist, he was naked. He looked at Parker and grinned.

"Hello, Johnson," he said.

The lighthouse keeper's eyes narrowed. He looked the man over. "You're a native, aren't you?" he said. "How does it happen that you speak English?"

The man eyed him. "Speak English?" he parroted. "You not Johnson," he said accusingly.

"No," Parker answered. "I came to take Johnson's place. But how did you get here?"

South America was not too far away, and there were natives there who looked a lot like this fellow. Sometimes storms caught their canoes and drove them far out to sea. Not often, but it had happened.

"Came in boat," the man answered. "Boat got lost. Sink. See light. Swim here. That last dark. Come in. Johnson take care of light. Take care of me, too. Went for swim, come back, Johnson gone. Look for him, not find. Where Johnson go?"

"He went away in a—" Parker hesitated. How could he explain the operation of an airplane to this fellow? "—in a boat that flies through the air, a canoe with wings. I'm taking his place."

The native nodded. The winged canoe did not seem to surprise him. Perhaps he hadn't understood at all.

"You let stay here?" he questioned. He spread his hands in an apologetic gesture. "None other place to go. Big water all around."

"Sure," Parker answered. "Sure. You're welcome, old man. You can stay here until my relief comes, then I'll take you back with me. Maybe I can fix you up on a freighter that will take you back to South America. What's your name, by the way?"

"Name? Name? Oh, name. Bobo."

"Bobo, eh? Well, mine's Parker. What do you say, Bobo, we try to scare up some lunch?"

Parker turned and started down the steps. He looked back. Bobo was staring at him, so he rubbed his stomach and pointed to his mouth. Bobo seemed to get the idea. He came gladly. But he didn't appreciate the food of civilization; he would hardly eat the food Parker set before him.

"Don't you like it, Bobo?" the lighthouse keeper asked.

"Sure," Bobo answered. "Good. Damn good."

"It's rather difficult to manage canned tomatoes with a knife," Parker said, watching the native. "But you'll learn."

"You bet. Learn damned good," Bobo answered, trying to scoop up the tomatoes with the blade of the knife, as Parker was doing. Parker watched him in silence. There were lines of thought at the corners of the lighthouseman's eyes.

That night they slept in adjoining rooms. Lighthouse

keepers never more than cat-napped during the night. The light might go out.

"Good night, Bobo," Parker called, closing the door between the two rooms.

"Good night, Parker," Bobo answered.

Parker didn't go to sleep. He could sleep tomorrow, or next week, or when he was dead. He lay in the darkness, watching the circling light flash through the window. The eternal Gulf wind was blowing. It had found a loose board somewhere on the roof of the house. The board was flapping. There were other sounds, too, sounds that only lonely lighthouse keepers hear, and the lookouts of tall ships, and fishermen. Parker waited. He really wasn't sleepy. The gun under his pillow made a hard lump.

A tiny sound came from the adjoining room. The cot creaked, the way a cot does when a sleeper turns. By and by the outer door creaked. Parker got up. He didn't put on his shoes. He went to the door, the gun in his hand.

There was a full moon overhead. The moon and the light illuminated the tiny island.

A shadow was moving along the walk toward the landing. Bobo. While Parker watched, the native went to the end of the landing and dived into the sea.

Keeping out of sight, the lighthouse keeper slipped down to the edge of the water. Bobo was splashing in the sea, apparently having the very devil of a good time. He dived and swam and turned somersaults in the water with all the grace and agility of a seal.

Parker took the gun out of his pocket. He looked at it thoughtfully, to make certain the safety was off.

Bobo came out of the water. He shook himself like a dog, then strode along the walk and went into the lighthouse tower.

Parker followed. Bobo was in the radio room again.

The trap door was open. There was no light in the radio room except the dim glow coming from the tubes of the transmitter. Bobo had turned on the filament heaters. He was working in the dark, doing something to the transmitter; what it was Parker couldn't see. The native seemed to be making changes in the wave coils. The set operated on a wave length of six hundred meters. Bobo was making changes. He didn't seem to be hesitating about them; he seemed to know what to do and to be able to do it with a deftness that would have amazed the Navy experts who had installed the equipment.

The set was designed for either voice or code. Like all continuous-wave transmitters, it was silent in operation, except for the tapping of the key when code was used. Bobo began to use the key.

Parker knew Morse. He tried to follow the key. Now and then he seemed to catch a letter. It was hard to follow that racing key, so damned hard that Parker eventually knew that Bobo wasn't using Morse. He didn't know what code the native was using, but it certainly wasn't Morse.

Bobo stopped transmitting. Clamping the earphones over his head, he began to twirl the dials of the receiver. Parker watched. The native went back to the transmitter. He examined it carefully and seemed to be making minute changes. Again the key rattled. Again Parker couldn't follow it.

This alternation between transmitter and receiver kept up for perhaps half an hour. Parker, his head just level with the floor, watched. He had the impression that each successive failure sank the native in deeper gloom.

Then Bobo got a reply. He almost danced for joy. He rapped off a hasty answer on the key, listened once, then rapidly began changing the wave coils back to their former frequency values.

Parker went down the steps, went into his room and

waited. Bobo came in, went directly to his room. The cot creaked as he lay down.

He didn't move again all night; Parker stayed awake to make certain. Once Parker got up and went up to the top of the tower to inspect the light. Bobo didn't follow him.

Parker was up with the sun.

"Hey, Bobo," he called. "Lighthouse keepers have to be up early in the morning. Out of it."

Rubbing his eyes, the native came out of his room.

"Sleep good?" Parker asked.

"Sure. Sleep damned good, you bet."

"O.K. I'm going up to turn off the light."

Bobo didn't follow him up the tower. He turned off the light, made notes on the temperature, wind direction, and barometer readings; then, mindful of the Navy's wishes, he picked up the binoculars and swept the surface of the sea. There was no sign of a sub. There was no ripple of a periscope breaking the surface. The Gulf was calm.

He looked down toward the wharf. Bobo was swimming again; he seemed to have almost a mania for the water.

Parker went down to the radio room. By the time he got the transmitter warmed up, Bobo had come up the steps. He shook himself like a dog, and a spray of water flew from his glistening, powerful body.

"What do?" he asked curiously, as Parker picked up the microphone.

"It's time for the regular morning report," the lighthouse keeper answered. "You know, report by radio."

Bobo merely stared at him.

Parker got through to the base station. He reported the temperature, wind direction, barometer reading—dope collected for the weather bureau.

"How's Johnson?" he asked when his report was finished.

"Johnson?" the speaker rattled, after a silence.

"Yes, Johnson. How's his arm coming along? He fell down the stairs and broke it, you know."

"Oh, his arm. Yes. I don't have any dope on it yet this morning, but it's probably doing all right. Anything else?"

Parker hesitated. He glanced sideways at Bobo. The native hadn't moved, but he wasn't watching Parker; he was looking out the window toward the sea.

"No, nothing more," Parker said. He snapped the switches that fed juice into the transmitter, rose to his feet.

"Breakfast, Bobo," he said.

The native jerked around to face him. "Breakfast? You mean eat? Oh, sure, you bet. Eat damned good."

"O.K., you go on down. I'll be down in a minute."

"Go on down? Sure. You bet."

Still dripping water from his recent swim, the native went bounding down the stairs. Parker followed slowly, a thoughtful look on his face. The thoughtful frown was replaced by a look of incredulous amazement the instant he set foot outside the tower.

Bobo was not waiting for him in the house. He was not waiting at all. He was racing along the boardwalk toward the landing, running so rapidly that his legs seemed to blur.

But it was not Bobo's action that stamped the look of incredulous amazement on Parker's face. It was something else, something that was moving across the surface of the sea toward the island and emerging as it moved. It was a round, bulging dome. It threw a long wake behind it.

"A sub!" Parker gasped. "She was lying out there

under the surface all the time. Hey, Bobo!" he yelled. "Don't try to swim out to that thing. Stay away from it. No good. Bad. You hear? Bad!"

The native didn't answer, but kept running along the walk.

"By heaven!" Parker rasped in understanding. "So that's the way it is! So that's why you were sneaking in and using the radio transmitter! You're an educated native, eh? Or maybe you're not a native at all."

"Halt!" he shouted.

Bobo kept running.

The gun seemed to leap into Parker's fist. Its explosion smashed the morning silence into a million pieces. A tiny splash showed where the bullet had struck.

"Halt!" Parker shouted. "The next time I'll shoot to kill."

The native had touched the landing. Never hesitating in his stride, he dived into the water.

Cursing, Parker raced down the walk. In the water, Bobo would be entirely at his mercy. The sub would have to stay well out because of the shoals, and while he didn't know the sub's intentions, as long as he held Bobo, he would have a strong bargaining point. It might easily be a bargaining point on which his life would hinge. That sub would not be likely to leave him here to report its presence. And it would be armed. It could stand off from shore and send a hail of machine-gun bullets smashing over the island. True, America wasn't at war, but no nation seemed to bother much about a declaration of war these days. If he had Bobo, the sub wouldn't dare shell him. Or would it?

A dark shadow was moving through the water. It was Bobo, swimming under the surface. Parker sent a bullet downward. It smacked into the water, but Bobo never halted. Probably the bullet didn't touch him. He was too far under the surface.

"All right, damn you," Parker gritted. "You'll have to come up for air sometime, and when you do—"

The sub was coming closer now. A great bow wave was curling out from it as it drove toward the shore. It was lifting farther and farther out of the water. Men were tumbling out of an opening in the side of the conning tower.

"They'll have a gun in operation in a minute!" Parker thought. "Damn that native! Will he never come up?"

Bobo didn't come up. Parker began to itch, waiting for him. Seconds ticked away. A minute passed. Then two. Three. Parker felt cold. Nobody could stay underwater that long. His eyes followed the shadow that was Bobo. Swimming like a fish, he was moving out toward the sub. Although he was completely under the surface, he was using a kicking stroke that would have made a South Sea islander turn green with envy.

And he wasn't coming up. He was out a hundred yards, then farther. Parker expected his head to break the surface any second. It didn't. The native kept swimming underwater. He was too far out for anything but a lucky shot to get him.

All over his body, Parker's skin seemed to be crawling. He cast a glance at the submarine, at the shadow that was Bobo, then turned and ran toward the lighthouse.

He was expecting a blast of machine-gun fire to let go any instant. Or perhaps a cannon. That sub simply couldn't let its presence here be known. Uncle Sam would raise merry hell about a submarine in the Gulf, merry hell indeed. Hence—machine-gun slugs.

But none came. Yet.

Parker was aware that he was holding his breath as he ran. His back tingled from the bullets he was expecting.

There wasn't a spot of cover where he could hide. All he hoped to do was to reach the radio transmitter in time.

He pounded into the lighthouse and up the steps. With a single bound he was through the trap door and into the room, snapping switches that fed current to the tubes. It took time for the tubes to warm up. It would probably take more time to contact the base station. This wasn't the regular hour for calls. Of course, there would be an operator on duty, but it might take fifteen minutes to raise him. A lot could happen in fifteen minutes.

Through the window Parker had a perfect view of everything that was happening. The sub was still coming in, emerging more and more all the time. Bobo was still swimming toward it. He reached it, was drawn quickly aboard. He had swum underwater all the way to the sub. It was a quarter of a mile at least, probably nearer a half, but Bobo hadn't broken the surface once in all that distance.

"Now it's coming," Parker thought. "Bobo is safely on board. Now it will be my turn."

He leaped to the meter panel. The needles were beginning to wiggle, the transmitter was warming, juice was beginning to flow through it.

"Hurry, damn you, hurry," Parker prayed. "They'll have a machine gun and a landing party on the way in no time."

The meter needles suddenly jumped. Juice was flowing. Parker grabbed the microphone.

"Calling base station lighthouse service, Station 719

calling base station lighthouse service, Station 719 calling base station lighthouse service, calling—"

He switched to the receiver.

No answer.

"Calling—"

Suddenly he stopped. Through the window he could see the submarine. No machine gun had been unlimbered. No ugly-snouted cannon had appeared on the foredeck. The men on the sub were not working with a gun; they were entering the conning tower.

Parker stared.

"Calling base station lighthouse service," he said automatically. He didn't notice what he was saying. He was watching that sub.

It was turning, heading away from the island, heading out to sea. It was going away. It wasn't sending a landing party ashore.

A white wake spread behind it. It was moving faster, still faster. It was going faster than any submarine had ever gone before. *And it was still emerging from the water.*

A low drumming sound, like distant thunder, was beginning to throb in the air.

"Station 719 calling base station light—"

That was as far as he got.

The thunder had grown in volume, had become a roaring torrent of distant sound. More than ever, it sounded like the growling of thunder in a tropic storm.

The sub was still rising out of the water. Jets of fire were appearing along the edges of its hull. It seemed to lift itself on those fire jets; fire spurted from its tail.

It was big, far bigger than any submarine he had ever seen. It had no wings, but in spite of that it was rising into the air. Into the air!

With fascinated eyes, Parker stared at the thing. It

was completely clear of the surface of the sea. Gaining speed, it was rising on a long slant, moving very fast now. The spurts of light from the fire jets were fading into tiny flashes; the drumming thunder was diminishing in the distance.

It went up, up, up. It went out of sight, still going up.

Suddenly Parker sat down. He was weak. Beside the transmitter a pad of yellow paper caught his attention. He stared at it for a long time before he realized what he was seeing. Then slowly his brain began to register the message his eyes were bringing.

The pad of paper had been lying there all the time, but another sheet of paper had been lying on top of it. Somehow, in his haste to get the transmitter into action, he had knocked off the top sheet, revealing what was written on the pad.

> Object much resembling submarine appeared in the sky. Flashes of fire leaped from it and it made a noise like thunder. It glided down to a landing near the island. I saw it first from the light room. After moving across the surface, it stopped for a few minutes, then suddenly submerged. Went out in boat and tried to locate it, but was unable to do so. On returning to island, found I had a visitor who looks like a Carib and calls himself Bobo. He seemed very stupid at first. Couldn't speak English. He began to pick it up from me. From the speed with which he picked it up, I am beginning to doubt that he is a native. I suspect he came here in that strange flying submarine and that he was caught on its deck when it suddenly submerged. Unable to return to his ship, he swam ashore here. He seems very fascinated by our radio equipment, which

is another reason I suspect he is not the wild Carib he seems. No native would grasp the operation of radio apparatus so quickly.

The message had been hastily scribbled. Apparently it was a series of notes made while the events it described were fresh in the observer's mind.

It was in Johnson's handwriting.

Abstractedly, Parker flipped on the receiver.

"Lighthouse service calling Station 719," the speaker squawked, as if the operator had been calling for several minutes and was annoyed because he hadn't received an answer. "Go ahead, Station 719."

"Put Hanson on," said Parker tersely. "Do it fast."

The loud-speaker squawked, and there was a series of clicks. Parker was suddenly sweating; drops of sweat ran down his face. He wiped them away with his hand, stared at his sticky palm.

Hanson came on. "What do you want, Parker?" he demanded.

"I want to report—" Suddenly Parker choked. Sweat was in his eyes. Sweat was all over his body.

"I want to know what happened to Johnson!" he said.

"Johnson? He broke—"

"Skip that part of it," Parker snarled in a tone so savage it startled him. "You can tell that to the Marines. I want to know what really happened to him."

The speaker rattled noisily as Hanson cleared his throat.

"Well, if you must know, he went off the deep end and I had to recall him. He's in a psychopathic hospital for observation. The doctors say there is nothing seriously wrong with him, that when he has a good rest he'll be all right again. I'm arranging a shore job for him."

Parker swallowed. "Then why did you tell me he had a broken arm?"

"For a very good reason," Hanson said exasperatedly. "If I told you the truth, the suggestion might start *you* seeing things, too."

"The devil!" Parker said. "What did he report he saw—a flying submarine?"

"What?" the speaker croaked. "How did you know what he thought he saw? Have you gone off your head, too?" There was suspicion in Hanson's voice.

Parker thought swiftly. Lighthouse-keeper's sickness, they called it. The loneliness caused it. Under different names, sheepherders and forest rangers and lonely trappers suffered from the same illness.

His hands were sticky with sweat. He swallowed.

"Nope," he said.

"Then how did you know what Johnson thought he saw?" Hanson demanded.

"Oh, that," Parker answered. "I ran into some notes he had made, so I thought I would call you and get the truth of the matter."

"Huh? Notes? Then what are you so scared about?"

"I'm not scared," Parker answered stiffly.

"You sound like it."

"Maybe the radio is distorting my voice."

There was a moment of silence. "Maybe that's it," Hanson said. "Oh, well— Are you sure you're all right, lad?"

"Sure. You bet. Sure."

"All right, then. For a minute you had me worried. Is that all you want?"

"Yes," said Parker. "Yes."

"O.K. then."

The speaker snapped into silence. Parker wiped the sweat off his face, then turned off the transmitter. He rose to his feet, looked out the window. A haze was beginning to appear over the Gulf. Far up in the sky white clouds were appearing.

That was all there was in the sky—white clouds and a beginning haze. There was no sound of distant thunder.

Parker looked at the floor. There were still a few wet blotches on the boards where a castaway, who seemed to like water, had stood while he shook himself. The spots were drying rapidly. In a few minutes they would be completely gone.

Eric Frank Russell

IMPULSE

In this story you will learn about a small myriad of nasties from a meteorite—creatures that could well have happened upon us and never been reported on, as you will find out as the story develops.

This is the kind of invasion story that approaches the classic in its perfection; there can be nothing more ghoulish.

IT WAS his receptionist's evening off, and Dr. Blain had to answer the waiting-room buzzer himself. Mentally cursing the prolonged absence of Tod Mercer, his general factotum, he closed the tap of the burette, took the beaker of neutralized liquid from beneath, and set it on a shelf.

Hastily he thrust a folding spatula into a vest pocket, rubbed his hands together, gave a brief glance around the small laboratory. Then he carried his tall, spare form to the waiting room.

The visitor was sprawled in an easy chair. Dr. Blain looked him over and saw a cadaverous individual with mackerel eyes, mottled skin, and pale, bloated hands. The fellow's clothes didn't fit him much better than a sack.

Blain weighed him up as a case of pernicious ulcers, or else a hopeful seller of insurance that he had no intention of buying. In any event, he decided, the man's expression had a weird twist. It gave him the willies.

"Dr. Blain, I believe?" said the man in the chair. His voice gargled slowly, uncannily, and the sound of it grew pimples down Blain's spine.

Without waiting for a reply, and with his dead optics fixed on the standing Blain, the visitor continued. "We are a cadaverous individual with mackerel eyes, mottled skin, and pale, bloated hands."

Sitting down abruptly, Dr. Blain grasped the arms of his chair until his knuckles stood out like blisters. His visitor gargled on slowly and imperturbably.

"Our clothes don't fit us much better than a sack. We are a case of pernicious ulcers, or else a seller of insurance that you have no intention of buying. Our expression has a strange twist, and it gives you the willies."

The speaker rolled a rotting eye which leered, with horrible lack of luster, at the thunderstruck Blain. He added, "Our voice gargles, and the sound of it raises pimples on your spine. We have decaying eyes that leer at you with lack of luster that you consider horrible."

With a mighty effort, Blain leaned forward, red-faced, trembling. His iron-gray hairs were erect on the back of his neck. Before he could open his mouth, his visitor spoke his unuttered words for him: "Good heavens! You've been reading my very thoughts!"

The fellow's cold optics remained riveted to Blain's astounded face while the latter shot to his feet. Then he said briefly, simply, "Be seated."

Blain remained standing. Small globules of perspiration crept through the skin of his brow, trickled down his tired, lined face.

More urgently, warningly, the other gulped, "Be seated!"

His legs strangely weak at the knees, Blain sat. He stared at the ghastly pallor of his visitor's features and stammered, "W-who the devil are you?"

"That!" He tossed Blain a clipping.

A casual look, followed by one far more intent, then Blain protested, "But this is a newspaper report about a corpse being stolen from a morgue."

"Correct," agreed the being opposite.

"But I don't understand." Blain's strained features showed his puzzlement.

"This," said the other, pointing a colorless finger at his sagging vest, "is the corpse."

"What?" For the second time, Blain came to his feet. The clipping dropped from his nerveless fingers, fluttered to the carpet. He towered over the thing in the chair, expelled his breath in a loud hiss, and sought vainly for words.

"This is the body," repeated the claimant. His voice sounded as if it were being bubbled through thick oil. He pointed to the clipping. "You failed to notice the picture. Look at it. Compare the face with the one that we have."

"We?" Blain queried, his mind in a whirl.

"We! There are many of us. We commandeered this body. Sit down."

"But—"

"Sit down!" The creature in the chair slid a cold,

limp hand inside his sloppy jacket, lugged out a big automatic, and pointed it awkwardly. To Blain's view, the weapon's muzzle gaped hugely. He sat down, recovered the clipping, and stared at the picture.

The caption said, "The late James Winstanley Clegg, whose body mysteriously vanished last night from the Simmstown morgue."

Blain looked at his visitor, then at the picture, then at his visitor again. The two were the same; undoubtedly the same. Blood began to pound in his arteries.

The automatic drooped, wavered, lifted up once more. "Your questions are anticipated," slobbered the late James Winstanley Clegg. "No, this is not a case of spontaneous revival of a cataleptic. Your idea is ingenious, but it does not explain the thought reading."

"Then of what is this a case?" demanded Blain with sudden courage.

"Confiscation." His eyes jerked unnaturally. "We have entered into possession. Before you is a man possessed." He permitted himself a ghoulish chuckle. "It seems that in life this brain was endowed with a sense of humor."

"Nevertheless, I can't—"

"Silence!" The gun wagged to emphasize the command. "We shall talk; you will listen. We shall comprehend your thoughts."

"All right." Dr. Blain lay back in his chair, kept a wary eye on the door. He felt convinced that he had to deal with a madman. Yes, a maniac—despite the thought reading, despite that picture on the clipping.

"Two days ago," gargled Clegg, or what once had been Clegg, "a so-called meteor landed outside this town."

"I read about it," Blain admitted. "They looked for it, but failed to find it."

"That phenomenon was actually a space vessel." The automatic sagged in the flabby hand; its holder rested the weapon on his lap. "It was a space vessel that had carried us from our home world of Glantok. The vessel was exceedingly small by your standards—but we, too, are small. Very small. We are submicroscopic, and our number is myriad.

"No, not intelligent germs." The ghastly speaker stole the thought from his listener's mind. "We are less even than those." He paused while he searched around for words more explicit. "In the mass, we resemble a liquid. You might regard us as an intelligent virus."

"Oh!" Blain struggled to calculate the number of jumps necessary to reach the door, and do it without revealing his thoughts.

"We Glantokians are parasitical in the sense that we inhabit and control the bodies of lesser creatures. We came here, to your world, while occupying the body of a small Glantokian mammal." He coughed with a viscous rumble deep down in his gullet, then continued.

"When we landed and emerged, an excited dog chased our creature and caught it. We caught the dog. Our creature died when we deserted it. The dog was useless for our purpose, but it served to transport us into your town and find us this body. We acquired the body. When we left the dog, it lay on its back and died."

The gate creaked with a sudden rasping sound that brought Blain's taut nerves to the snapping point. Light footsteps pit-patted up the asphalt path toward the front door. He waited wtih bated breath, ears alert, eyes wide with apprehension.

"We took this body, liquefied the congealed blood, loosened the rigid joints, softened the dead muscles, and made it walk. It seems that its brain was fairly intelligent in life, and even in death its memories remain recorded. We utilize this dead brain's knowledge to think in human terms and to converse with you after your own fashion."

The approaching footsteps were near, very near. Blain shifted his feet to a solid position on the rug, tightened his grip on the arms of his chair, and fought to keep his thoughts under control. The other took not the slightest notice, but he kept his haggard face turned to Blain and continued slushily to mouth his words.

"Under our control, the body stole these clothes and this weapon. Its own defunct mind recorded the weapon's purpose and told us how it is used. It also told us about you."

"Me?" Startled, Dr. Blain leaned forward, braced his arms, and calculated that his intended spring would barely beat the lift of the opposing automatic. The feet outside had reached the steps.

"It is not wise," warned the creature who claimed to be a corpse. He raised his gun with lethargic hand. "Your thoughts are not only observed but their conclusions anticipated."

Blain relaxed. The feet were tripping up the steps to the front door.

"A dead body is a mere makeshift," the other mouthed. "We must have a live one, with little or no organic disability. As we increase, we must have more bodies. Unfortunately, the susceptibility of nervous systems is in direct proportion to the intelligence of their owners." He gasped, then choked with the same liquid rattle as before.

"We cannot guarantee to occupy the bodies of the intelligently conscious without sending them insane in the process. A disordered brain is less use to us than a recently dead one, and no more use than a wrecked machine would be to you."

The patter of leather ceased; the front door opened, and somebody entered the passage. The door clicked shut. Feet moved along the carpet toward the waiting room.

"Therefore," continued the human who was not human, "we must occupy the intelligent while they are too deeply unconscious to be affected by our permeation, and we must be in complete possession when they awake. We must have the assistance of someone able to treat the intelligent in the manner we desire, and do it without arousing general suspicion. In other words, we require the co-operation of a doctor."

The awful eyes bulged slightly. Their owner added, "Since this inefficient body is beyond even our power to animate much longer, we must have a fresh, live, healthy one as soon as it can be obtained."

The feet in the passage hesitated, stopped. The door opened. At that instant, the dead Clegg stabbed a pallid finger at Blain and burbled, "You will assist us"—the finger swerved toward the door—"and that body will do for the first."

The girl in the doorway was young, fair-haired, pleasingly plump. She posed there, one hand concealing the crimson of her small, half-opened mouth. Her blue eyes were wide with fearful fascination as they gazed at the blanched mask behind the pointing finger.

There was a moment's deep silence, while the digit maintained its fateful gesture. Its owner's features became subject to progressive achromatism, grew more hueless, more ashy. His optics—dead balls in frigid sockets—suddenly glittered with minute specks of light, green light, hellish. He struggled clumsily to his feet, teetered backward and forward on his heels.

The girl gasped. Her eyes lowered, saw the automatic in a hand escaped from the grave. She screamed on a note weak because of its height. She screamed as if she were surrendering her soul to the unknown. Then, as the living dead tottered toward her, she closed her eyes and slumped.

Blain got her just before she hit the floor. He covered the distance in three frantic leaps, caught her smoothly molded body, saved it from bruising contact. He rested her head upon the carpet, patted her cheeks vigorously.

"She's fainted," he growled, in open anger. "She may be a patient or may have come to summon me to a patient. An urgent case, perhaps."

"Enough!" The voice was curt, despite its eerie bubbling. The gun pointed directly at Blain's brow. "We see, from your thoughts, that this fainting condition is a temporary one. Nevertheless, it is opportune. You will take advantage of the situation, place the body under an anesthetic, and we shall claim it for our own."

From his kneeling position beside the girl, Blain looked up and said slowly and deliberately, "I shall see you in hell!"

"No need to have spoken the thought," remarked the creature. He grimaced horribly, took two jerky steps forward. "You may do it yourself, or else we shall do it with the aid of your own knowledge and your own flesh. A bullet through your heart, we take possession of you, repair the wound, and you are ours.

"Damn you!" he cursed, stealing the words from Blain's own lips. "We could use you in any case, but we prefer a live body to a dead one."

Throwing a hopeless glance around the room, Dr. Blain uttered a mental prayer for help—a prayer cut short by the grin of understanding on his opponent's face. Getting up from his knees, he lifted the girl's limp form, carried her through the door, along the passage, and into his surgery. The thing that was the body of Clegg stumbled grotesquely behind him.

Gently lowering the girl to a chair, Blain rubbed her hands and wrists, patted her cheeks again. Faint color crept back to her skin; her eyes fluttered. Blain stepped to a cupboard, slid aside its glass doors, grasped a bottle of *sal volatile*. Something hard prodded him between his shoulder blades. It was the automatic.

"You forget that your mind processes are like an open book. You are trying to revive the body and are playing for time." The sickly countenance behind the weapon forced its facial muscles into a lopsided scowl. "Place the body on that table and anesthetize it."

Unwillingly, Dr. Blain withdrew his hand from the cupboard. He picked up the girl, laid her on the examination table, switched on the powerful lamp that hung directly overhead.

"More meddling!" commented the other. "Turn off that lamp—the one already burning is quite sufficient."

Blain turned off the lamp. His face drawn with agitation, but head erect, his fists bunched, he faced the menacing weapon and said, "Listen to me. I'll make you a proposition."

"Nonsense!" The former Clegg wandered around the table with slow, dragging steps. "As we remarked before, you are playing for time. Your own brain advertises the fact." He stopped abruptly as the recumbent girl murmured vague words and tried to sit up. "Quick! The anesthetic!"

Before either could move, the girl sat up. She came upright and looked straight into a ghastly face that moped and mewed a foot from her own features. She shuddered and said pitifully, "Let me out of here. Let me out. Please!"

A bloated hand reached out to push her. She lay down to avoid contact with the loathsome flesh.

Taking advantage of the slight diversion, Blain slid a hand behind his back, felt for an ornamental poker hanging on the wall. The gun swung up even as his fingers found the impromptu weapon and curled around its cool metal.

"You forget yourself." Pin-point fires sparkled in the other's blotchy orbs. "Mental understanding is not limited in direction. We see you even when these eyes are elsewhere." The gun moved to indicate the girl. "Tie that body down."

Obediently, Dr. Blain found straps, fastened the girl securely to the table. His gray hair was limp, his face moist, as he bent over her and threaded the buckles. He looked at her with courage hardly justified and whispered, "Patience—do not fear." He threw a significant glance at the clock ticking upon the wall. The instrument's hands indicated two minutes before eight.

"So you expect aid," effervesced the tones of a corporate myriad. "Tod Mercer, your handyman, who ought to have been here before now. You think he might be of help, though you have little faith in what few wits he has. In your opinion, he is a dumb ox—too stupid to know his feet from his hands."

"You devil!" swore Dr. Blain at this recital of his thoughts.

"Let this Mercer come. He will be of use—to us! There are enough of us for two bodies—and even a live fool is better than an educated corpse." Anemic lips twisted in a snarl that revealed dry teeth. "Meanwhile, get busy with that body."

"I don't think I have any ether," Blain protested.

"You have something that will do. Your cortex shouts

it! Be speedy, lest we lose patience and take you at the cost of your sanity."

Swallowing hard, Blain opened a drawer and extracted a nasal frame. He clipped on its cotton-gauze pad, placed the frame over the frightened girl's nose. He felt safe in giving her a reassuring wink. A wink is not a thought.

Opening the cupboard once more, Blain stood in front of it, summoned all his faculties, and compelled his mind to recite, "Ether, ether, ether." At the same time, he forced his hand toward a bottle of concentrated sulphuric acid. He made a mighty effort to achieve his dual purpose, urged his fingers nearer and nearer to the bottle. He got it.

Straining every fiber of his being to do one thing while his mind was fixed upon another, he turned around, withdrawing the glass stopper as he turned. Then he stood still, the open bottle in his right hand. The figure of death was immediately in front of him, gun raised.

"Ether," sneered the vocal cords of Clegg. "Your conscious mind yelled 'Ether!' while your subconscious mind whispered 'Acid!' Do you think your inferior intelligence can cope with ours? Do you think you can destroy that which is already dead? You fool!" The gun inched forward. "The anesthetic—without further delay."

Offering no reply, Dr. Blain rammed the stopper into its neck, replaced the bottle whence he had taken it. More deliberately, moving with utmost slowness, he crossed the floor to a smaller cupboard, opened it, took out a small bottle of ether. He placed the bottle on the radiator and started to close the cupboard.

"Take it off!" croaked the uncanny voice with high-pitched urgency. The gun emitted a warning click as

Blain snatched the bottle. "So you hoped the radiator would make the stuff vaporize rapidly enough to burst the bottle, eh?"

Dr. Blain said nothing. Taking as much time as possible, he conveyed the volatile liquid to the table. The girl watched his approach, her eyes wide with apprehension. She gave a low sob. Blain flung a glance at the clock, but, quick as the glance was, his tormentor caught the thought behind it and grinned.

"He is here now."

"Who is here?" demanded Blain.

"Your man, Mercer. He is outside, just about to enter the front door. We perceive the futile wanderings of his sluggish mind. You have not overestimated what little intelligence he does possess."

The front door opened in confirmation of the speaker's prophecy. The girl struggled to raise her head, hope in her eyes.

"Prop her mouth open with something," articulated the voice under alien control. "We shall enter through the mouth." He paused, as heavy feet scuffled on the front door mat. "And call that fool in here. We shall use him also."

His veins bulging on his forehead, Dr. Blain called, "Tod! Come here!" He found a dental gag, toyed with its ratchet.

Excitement thrilled his nerves from head to feet. No gun could shoot two ways at once. If he could wangle the idiotic Mercer into the right position, and put him wise— If he could be on one side and Tod on the other—

"Don't try it," advised the animated Clegg. "Don't even think it. If you do, we shall end up by having you both."

Tod Mercer lumbered into the room, his heavy soles

thumping the rug. He was a big man, with thick shoulders jutting below a plump, moonlike face that sprouted two days' growth. He stopped when he saw the table and the girl. His great, wide, stupid eyes roamed from the girl to the doctor.

"Heck, Doc," he said, with an uneasy fidget, "I got me a puncture and had to change tires on the road."

"Never mind about that," came a sardonic rumble right behind him. "You're in plenty of time."

Tod turned around sluggishly, twisting his boots as if each weighed a ton. He stared at the thing that had been Clegg and said, "Beg pardon, Mister. I didn't know you was there."

His cowlike eyes wandered disinterestedly over the living corpse, over the pointing automatic, then slewed toward the anxious Blain. Tod opened his mouth to say something. He closed the mouth; a look of faint surprise came into his fat features; his eyes swiveled back and found the automatic again.

This time, the look didn't last one tenth of a second. His eyes realized what they saw. He swung a hamlike fist with astounding swiftness, slammed it into the erstwhile Clegg's awful features. The blow was dynamite, sheer dynamite. The cadaver went down with a crash that shook the room.

"Quick!" screamed Dr. Blain. "Get the gun." He vaulted the intervening table—girl and all—landed heavily, made a wild kick at the weapon still gripped in a flabby hand.

Tod Mercer stood abashed, his eyes turning this way and that. The automatic exploded thunderously; its slug nicked the tubular metal edge of the table, ricocheted with a noise like that of a buzz saw, and ripped a foot of plaster from the opposite wall.

Blain kicked frantically at a ghastly wrist, missed it

when its owner jerked it aside. The gun boomed again. Glass tinkled in the farther cupboard. The girl on the table screamed shrilly.

The scream penetrated Mercer's thick skull and brought action. Slamming down a great boot, he imprisoned a rubbery wrist beneath his heel, plucked the automatic from cold fingers. He hefted the weapon, pointed it.

"You can't kill it like that," shouted Blain. He jabbed Tod Mercer to emphasize his words. "Get the girl out of here. Jump to it, man, for heaven's sake!"

Blain's urgency brooked no argument. Mercer handed over the automatic, moved to the table, ripped the straps from the weeping girl. His huge arms plucked her up, bore her from the room.

Down on the floor, the pilfered body writhed and struggled to get up. Its rotting eyes had disappeared. Their sockets were now filled with swirling pools of emerald luminosity. Its mouth gaped as it slowly regurgitated a bright green phosphorescence. The spawn of Glantok was leaving its host!

The body sat up with its back to the wall. Its limbs jerked and twitched in nightmarish postures. It was a fearful travesty of a human being. Green—bright and living green—crept sinuously from its eyes and mouth, formed twisting, swirling snakes and pools upon the floor.

Blain gained the door in one gigantic leap, snatching the ether bottle from the table as he passed. He stood in the doorway, trembling. Then he flung the bottle in the center of the seething green. He flicked his automatic lighter, tossed it after the bottle. The entire room boomed into a mighty blast of flame that immediately became a fiery hell.

The girl clung tightly to Dr. Blain's arm while they

stood by the roadside and watched the house burn. She said, "I came to call you to my kid brother. We think he's got measles."

"I'll be along soon," Blain promised.

A sedan roared up the road, stopped near them with engine still racing. A policeman put his head out and shouted, "What a blaze! We saw the glare a mile back along the road. We've called the fire department."

"They'll be too late, I'm afraid," said Blain.

"Insured?" asked the policeman sympathetically.

"Yes."

"Everybody out of the house?"

Blain nodded an affirmative, and the policeman said, "We happened to be out this way looking for an escaped nut." The sedan rolled forward.

"Hey!" Blain shouted. The sedan stopped again. "Was this madman's name James Winstanley Clegg?"

"Clegg?" came the driver's voice from the other side of the sedan. "Why, that's the fellow whose body walked out of the morgue when the attendant had his back turned for a minute. Funny thing, they found a dead mongrel in the morgue right by where the missing body ought to have been. The reporters are starting to call it a werewolf, but it's still a dog to me."

"Anyway, this fellow isn't Clegg," chimed in the first policeman. "He's Wilson. He's small, but nasty. This is what he looks like." He stretched an arm from the automobile, handed Blain a photograph. Blain studied the picture in the light of rising flames. It bore not the slightest resemblance to his visitor of that evening.

"I'll remember that face," Dr. Blain commented, handing the photograph back.

"Know anything about this Clegg mystery?" inquired the driver.

"I know that he's dead," Blain answered truthfully.

Pensively, Dr. Blain watched flames leap skyward from his home. He turned to the gaping Mercer and said, "What beats me is how you managed to hit that fellow without his anticipating your intention and plugging you where you stood."

"I saw the gun, and I 'it 'im." Mercer spread apologetic hands. "I saw 'e'd got a gun, and I 'it 'im without thinking."

"Without thinking!" murmured Blain.

Dr. Blain chewed his bottom lip, stared at the mounting fire. Roof timbers caved in with a violent crash; a flood of sparks poured upward.

With his mind, but not his ears, he heard faint threnodies of an alien wail that became weaker and weaker, and presently died away.

David Grinnell

TOP SECRET

Personally, the Editor thinks this one is Bible truth. . . .

I CANNOT say whether I am the victim of a very ingenious jest on the part of some of my wackier friends or whether I am just someone accidentally "in" on some top-secret business. But it happened, and it happened to me personally, while visiting Washington recently, just rubbernecking you know, looking at the Capitol and the rest of the big white buildings.

It was summer, fairly hot, Congress was not in session, nothing much was doing, most people vacationing. I was that day aiming to pay a visit to the State Department, not knowing that I couldn't, for there was nothing public to see there unless it's the imposing and rather martial lobby (it used to be the War Department building, I'm told). This I did not find out until I had blithely walked up the marble steps to the entrance, passed the big bronze doors, and wandered about in the huge lobby, wherein a small number of people, doubtless on important business, were passing in and out.

A guard, sitting near the elevators, made as if to start in my direction to find out who and what the deuce I wanted, when one of the elevators came down and a group of men hustled out. There were two men, evidently State Department escorts, neatly clad in gray double-breasted suits, with three other men walking with them. The three men struck me as a little odd; they wore long, black cloaks, big slouch hats with wide brims pulled down over their faces, and carried portfolios. They looked for all the world like cartoon representations of cloak-and-dagger spies. I supposed that they were some sort of foreign diplomats and, as they were coming directly toward me, stood my ground, determined to see who they were.

The floor was marble and highly polished. One of the men nearing me suddenly seemed to lose his balance. He slipped; his feet shot out from under him and he fell. His portfolio slid directly at my feet.

Being closest to him, I scooped up the folio and was the first to help raise him to his feet. Grasping his arm, I hoisted him from the floor—he seemed to be astonishingly weak in the legs; I felt almost that he was about to topple again. His companions stood about rather flustered, helplessly, their faces curiously impassive. And though the man I helped must have received a severe jolt, his face never altered expression.

Just then the two State Department men recovered their poise, rushed about, and, getting between me and the man I had rescued, rudely brushed me aside and rushed their party to the door.

Now what bothers me is not the impression I got that the arm beneath that man's sleeve was curiously wooly, as if he had a fur coat underneath the cloak (and this in a Washington summer!), and it's not the impression that he was wearing a mask (the elastic band of which I distinctly remember seeing amidst the kinky, red, close-cropped hair of his head). No, it's not that at all, which might be merely momentary misconstructions on my part. It's the coin that I picked off the floor where he'd dropped his portfolio.

I've searched through every stamp and coin catalogue I can find or borrow, and I've made inquiries of a dozen language teachers and professors, and nobody can identify that coin or the lettering around its circumference.

It's about the size of a quarter, silvery, very light in weight but also very hard. Besides the lettering on it, which even the Bible Society, which knows a thousand languages and dialects, cannot decipher, there is a picture on one side and a symbol on the other.

The picture is the face of a man, but of a man with very curiously wolfish features: sharp canine teeth parted in what could be a smile; a flattened, broad, and somewhat protruding nose, more like a pug dog's muzzle; sharp, widely spaced, vulpine eyes; and definitely hairy and pointed ears.

The symbol on the other side is a circle with latitude and longitude lines on it. Flanking the circle, one on each side, are two crescent-shaped moons.

I wish I knew just how far those New Mexico rocket experiments have actually gone.

William F. Temple

A DATE TO REMEMBER

Here is an example of one of the most frequently encountered ideas in the science fiction of earthly invasions —the Guidance Theme. In most of these stories we are to assume that, from careful cover that conceals them from all but our hero, kindly and immensely wise Outsiders are leading us forward subtly and nearly unnoticeably to an improved future.

This story tells of Guidance that has been going on for literally thousands of years, and still leads us by the hand. The only unlikely thing about this piece of chronological detective work by Mr. Temple is that the Guiders should be so persistent in their efforts to help out so mulish and suicidally bent a race as ours. This gives his tale a certain air of idealistic unreality.

BELL was ostensibly reading *The Week in Washington* and secretly worrying about something that wasn't in the newspaper at all when the phone rang. He reached out from his armchair and took it.

"Hello. . . . Oh, hello, Mick. Well, I didn't want to go out tonight. Is it really important? Can't wait till the morning? Well, I don't know—hang on a minute."

He clapped his hand over the mouthpiece and looked at his wife who was in the opposite chair. She was knitting calmly.

"Pet," he said, "give me six reasons why I can't go out tonight. Quick."

"There aren't any reasons, and it's no good lying to Mick, anyway," she said. "You know he can read anyone like a book. If he says it's important, you can bet it's important."

"Hey, are you my wife or his? Cooperate, darn you!"

"Just tell him plainly you don't want to go."

Bell grunted and addressed the receiver. "If it's all the same to you, Mick, I'd rather not. You see, any moment, now, something might happen. . . ."

"Nothing's due to happen for three or four days yet," said his wife, joining up a fresh ball of wool.

"All right, Mick," said Bell wearily. "You don't have to keep at me. My wife's on your side, anyway. I'll come right away. 'By."

He went and got his hat and coat. He pulled the window curtain aside and took a peek at the black night.

"Raining like crazy," he said. "Bess, you're a double-crossing, heartless she-cat."

He bent and kissed her hard. "And I love you very much," he added.

He paused at the door for a final injunction: "If anything starts, ring me right away."

The moment Stanley Bell stepped out of the yellow cab, it was as though someone had yanked out the bathtub plug up in heaven. The rain had ceased to a drizzle, but now it came down with a woosh. It bounced up off the sidewalk like rubber. Bell had twenty feet to cover between the cab door and the entrance to the apartment building. He ran, but he might as well have lain full length in the gutter—he could have got no wetter.

"Filthy night," he said to the elevator attendant. "Michael Grahame's apartment—the penthouse."

The attendant slammed the gate and made no answer. He'd been on duty a long time and felt tired. He looked at the fast-growing pool at Bell's feet, knew he'd have to mop it up, and felt more tired.

As the elevator mounted, Bell thought about Michael Grahame.

They'd been friends for twenty years, and all of that time Mick had climbed as steadily as this elevator. From scholarships to college, from college to study in the top-drawer clinics of psychiatry in Vienna, from Vienna to Atlantic City and private practice and authorship—then on to New York, some measure of fame and wealth and this penthouse on upper Fifth Avenue.

Symbolically, Mick was roof garden and Bell was roughly fifth floor, though they'd started together at ground level. But Mick didn't look at it symbolically. His values never changed. That was why their friendship endured. And Stanley Bell prized that friendship as he prized nothing but his wife's love.

Why did he so regard Mick? As the elevator whirred up, he analyzed the feeling. It was because Mick was reassurance. He represented firmness and sanity in the chaos of dying faiths, toppling values, and the growing greeds and fears of this world. The world was going crazy because of the thousand frustrations of a thousand desires.

Mick's sanity and strength lay in the fact that he never seemed to want anything, that he was never frightened to give. If you coveted the Delacroix over his mantel he would give it to you as lightly as he would hand you a cigar.

He never asked for anything himself, never envied anyone, and, because he wanted nothing from the world, it became his friend and lavished wealth and honor on him.

Bell's saga had been different. His rise in the publishing world had been in the teeth of opposition. Had the opposition been of his own creation? Had he assumed, in this highly competitive business, that everyone so engaged was his rival—indeed, his enemy? And had he thus made fresh enemies for himself?

Bell realized now that something like that lay at the root of his own indifferent progress. That he was symptomatic of the current world outlook. That he was a fool among approximately two billion other fools. Suddenly he was blazing mad at himself.

He carried this fury out of the elevator with him, past the ebony plate announcing in gilt, MICHAEL GRAHAME: CONSULTING PSYCHIATRIST, and into Grahame's living room. The tenant was reclining in a saddlebag armchair, slippered feet on a footstool, gazing lazily up at the smoke rising from his cigar.

"Mick," said Bell furiously, "sometime we're going to have one of our long, cozy talks about life and how it should be lived. And I'll be going for your throat because you, knowing better, have allowed me to act like a fool for so long.

"But not tonight. I'm not staying a minute longer than I can help. Now, why in Hades have you dragged me over here on a night like this when you know very well—"

"There's a glass of rum and hot water on the sideboard for you," said Grahame calmly. "Thought you'd need it."

"Thanks," said Bell and went for it.

"Blast!" he said, "I'm leaving wet footprints all over your Kairwan carpet."

"Hang your clothes in the airing chamber. There are slippers here and a dressing gown warming on the radiator."

"I'm *not* staying. I've got to—"

"Get out of those wet things, of course," took up

Grahame. "Or you certainly won't be staying—in this world for long. Bess will have to spare you for half an hour, while your things dry, or she might have to spare you forever."

"Oh, all right," said Bell ungraciously.

As he changed, he said, "What's it all about, anyway?"

Grahame looked at him. Both men were in their forties. Bell was thin, taut, and anxious-looking. Grahame was large, corpulent, relaxed, and radiated serenity.

"About my last book," said Grahame.

"What about it? It's still selling. I'm reprinting it next month."

"I mean my latest book," said Grahame. "That."

He indicated a Florentine leather folder on the table enclosing a thick wad of typescript. Bell went over to it in his drawers.

"You never told me about this. When did you start it?"

"Fifteen years ago," said Grahame.

Bell raised his eyebrows and the cover of the folder simultaneously. The first page said:

THE WHOLE MAN

Book I: Involuntary Hypnosis: Change of Emphasis.
Book II: The Power Complex and Resolution.
Book III: Free Will and Determinism: a Synthesis.
Book IV: Full Integration.

He flipped the pages over. It was very technical. Up till now all Grahame's books had been the wide-selling popular sort—*Master That Inferiority!*, *More Abundant Living*, *The Dynamo in Yourself*. And so on.

Bell donned the dressing gown thoughtfully.

"It'll take a lot of paper, printing, and binding," he said slowly. "Trade conditions are still none too easy."

"You think it won't sell."

There was no note of query in Grahame's voice. He said it flatly, as though he knew exactly what was in Bell's mind.

"It won't sell anything like your usual stuff," said Bell. "It'll be expensive to produce, and I'll have plenty left on my hands. I'd do it out of my regard for you only— well, frankly, Mick, I don't think the firm's finances will stand it.

"We've been shaky for a long time. Your popular psychology stuff has been our mainstay for years. Every other risk I've taken has fallen flat. I'm a rotten businessman."

"Actually," said Grahame, "you're a pretty good businessman. Only you're in the wrong business. Publishing isn't your racket. You've no sense of what the public wants."

"Maybe."

"I'm catching the one A.M. train to Chicago—lecture tour," said Grahame. "I'll be away for a long time. I asked you to come here tonight to hammer a few things into your head. First, *The Whole Man* will be a best seller. You'll make a pile out of it. And I'll make my name out of it."

"You've already made your name."

"Purely marginal fame. *The Whole Man* will make world history. It'll have ten times the influence of *Das Kapital*. Second, there's no time to lose about it. I want you to take it back with you tonight and lay it on the line right away. If it's going to shake the world out of its war hypnosis, it'll have to start doing it pretty darn quick before the radioactive clouds start rolling."

Bell gave a short, harsh bark of laughter which expressed the cynicism of the age. To Grahame, keen prober of mental states, it said a lot.

"So you've written mankind off, Stan?" he said benignly.

"Naturally. It's incurable. We're one of nature's mistakes. We were designed wrong at the start."

"Yet there's a lot worth while in homo saps," said Grahame. "It really would be one of nature's mistakes to scrap him now. I don't think she will."

"Where's your evidence for this optimism?" grunted Bell.

Grahame waved his hand in a circular movement to indicate the adorned walls of the room. The gesture embraced the originals and reproductions of a Delacroix, a Van Eyck, two Corots, Van Gogh's "Champ d'Oliviers," Greuze's "Milkmaid."

It included the loaded bookshelves and the cream of the world's poetry and Tolstoi, Flaubert, Balzac, Dickens, Shaw, Wells. In its orbit came the Ming vase, the Rodin statuette, and the view of the Golden Gate bridge.

"That," he said. "And much, much more. Where's your evidence for your pessimism?"

"That," said Bell, and stabbed a finger at the Sunday newspaper draped over the arm of Grahame's chair.

The paper was dated February 1, 1948. The headlines and subheadings sprang out at one—THE COLD WAR. . .BREAKDOWN OF TALKS. . .WILL CONSCRIPTION COME AGAIN?. . .SCIENTIST SAYS . . .MOLOTOV SAYS. . .BRITAIN SAYS. . .TRUMAN SAYS. . . .

Grahame picked it up and turned to an inner page. "Here's an item of interest, Stan," he said and began to read: " 'Moscow, Saturday. The size—' "

"I'm not interested in what Moscow says," interrupted Bell petulantly. "I'm not interested in what anyone says. It's what they do that matters. Everyone's gabbing about peace and preparing for war. They make me sick."

"They won't face the fact that the causes of war lie neither in economics nor in political history but in psychology," murmured Grahame. "However, for once, this isn't about war. Here, read the thing yourself."

He tossed the paper to Bell. The publisher read it with a frown.

MARTIANS CAME IN 1908
—says Soviet writer

Moscow, Saturday: The size of a hole in the crust of the earth made by a heavenly body on June 30, 1908, has convinced the Soviet writer, A. Kazantsev, that Martians arrived on earth that day in an uranium-propelled spaceship.

Whatever hit the earth that day at Tungus, Siberia, left no fragments of itself behind, Kazantsev stated at the Moscow Planetarium today.

He said it could only have been a Martian ship laden with enough uranium to carry it back to the planet.

"Certain it is," he said, "that no meteorite could have done the damage the Tungus missile did, blasting an area greater than all the Moscow region and sending seismic shocks twice around the world.

"I believe the Martians left the planet in 1907 and arrived in June, 1908, but their ship exploded," he said.

"So what?" asked Bell.

"Have you never wondered why Mars has never sent

us visitors as far as is known? It's an older planet than
Earth and therefore presumably with a more advanced
civilization, technically and morally. Don't you think
they should have sent us explorers, missionaries, ambassadors, or colonists long before this? In fact, long
before 1908?"

"I haven't given it a thought. Maybe the Martians
haven't, either. Maybe there aren't any Martians."

"Maybe," said Grahame. "But there's definitely car-
bon dioxide in the atmosphere of Mars, and the new in-
frared spectrometer shows that the polar caps are certainly solidified water. The temperatures are extreme by
Earthly standards but far from making life impossible—
even Earthly life. The vegetation—"

He went on about the flora and topography of Mars
and was giving the facts of the canal controversy when
Bell interrupted impatiently.

"Look, Mick, at another time I'd be glad to sit at
your feet and hear all about it. I mean that. But I'm not
going to sit here taking lessons in astronomy when I may
be needed at home. You wanted to give me the new
book. Right, I'll take it with me and see if I can get it
out when I've counted the petty cash. If that's all, I'll be
going."

"Wait," said Grahame and produced his checkbook.
He wrote out a check and thrust it on Bell. It was for
a sum that made Bell blink.

"Finance the book with that," said Grahame. "Get a
large edition out quickly. That'll settle your doubts
about losing out on it."

"But—" began Bell.

"You can return it out of the profits when they come
in," said Grahame quickly, anticipating the objection.

"Well—thanks."

"Your clothes will take at least another ten minutes.

Perhaps you can spare me time to air a little fancy of mine?"

"Go ahead, Mick. But don't let it run away with you —about Mars, is it? You think we were visited by Martians in 1908?"

"Perhaps we were. Suppose we were. Suppose they had another try and pulled it off. Suppose they landed tomorrow. What kind of reception do you think they'd get?"

"Depends what kind of mood they were in and what they looked like," said Bell. "If they were mean, like Wells's things, and started flashing heat rays around, I guess they'd soon be nothing but another uranium-made hole in the ground. Unless they had bigger and better bombs than we.

"If they were inoffensive but still looked like Wells's things, they'd probably end up in a zoo. If they were halfway human, I suppose they'd be feted and asked to say a few words over the radio. But I doubt whether they'd be allowed to colonize."

"That's it, Stan. You reflect the current outlook exactly. You see it in terms of power. Two different races, and one's got to get on top of the other. That's the mental sickness my book analyzes. The power complex."

"That's not new."

"No. Far from new. It goes back to the old tribal fear of the stranger. The intolerance of the *difference*. Everyone wants everyone else to accept *his* creed, to be like himself, thus harmless to him. This craving for security, for protection against the different, won't give tolerance and common sense a chance.

"It's the philosophy of dialectic materialism, and people are acting on it more and more, whether they're Marxists or hate Karl's insides, or have simply never heard of him. But all this and much more is in my book."

"O.K., I'll read it religiously and let you know my views," said Bell. "But I don't want to get into a discussion now."

"All right. I just want to make my point. That is, if the Martians came and stayed for any length of time, there would inevitably arise a state of tension and probably conflict between them and Man. Because—and especially if the Martians were a superior race—this increasing fear of the different would pump suspicion into a frenzy in men's minds."

"Surely, if the Martians were more civilized than we, they'd first send missionaries to educate us out of our lowly state," said Bell. "After all, we sent missionaries to Africa and the South Seas to help the natives out."

"And fine juicy steaks the missionaries made until the white man turned up in force, complete with guns, to show said natives who was really top dog.

"Can you imagine proud, intolerant Man, lord of this planet, content to play second fiddle to a crowd of intruding Martians and permitting himself to be bossed around by them? No. He'd soon turn them into juicy steaks. Unless they also had a power complex and slapped his ears down first."

"I see. You think that's the reason why the Martians have never visited us?"

"No. I think they have visited us."

"You mean they tried to in 1908?"

"Doggone, no," said Grahame, stubbing out his cigar. "That was a meteorite and nothing else, despite 'Soviet Science.' I mean long before that."

"Prehistory?"

"No. In recorded history."

"But they're *not* recorded!" said Bell.

"They are. I believe they landed here unseen, went around observing us unseen, and left missionaries to educate us unseen."

"Why unseen? How unseen?"

"Why? Because they didn't want to become steaks. How? How do bird and animal watchers observe unseen? They try to make themselves look like part of the landscape. Which is only a substitute for making themselves look like part of the life they're observing.

"Some of the top deerstalkers actually get themselves up like deer. Those who first studied the Arabs dressed as Arabs, moved among Arabs, and passed for Arabs—even in the sacred enclosure of the Kaaba, where non-Mohammedans were forbidden on pain of death."

"You mean," said Bell slowly, "you think Martians have been moving among us, disguised in some crazy way as human beings? Observing us—and educating us?"

"Yes," said Grahame. "Who are the teachers of mankind?"

"I—er—" hesitated Bell and veered off anxiously, "You haven't put this nutty idea in the book, have you?"

"No. I said this was a fancy of mine."

"Good!" said Bell with relief. "Well, I guess you could say the teachers of mankind are the originals, our really great poets, artists, composers, engineers, scientific men, and so forth. The creators of all this."

And he imitated Grahame's circular gesture at the books and *objets d'art* in the room.

"Exactly. They're the missionaries from Mars. They set the standard. And the rest of mankind tries to reach it when they can turn their thoughts now and again from war making."

"There must have been droves of missionaries coming and going through the ages, then," said Bell.

"Perhaps not so many as you may think. I visualize these people changing their roles, their bodies, sometimes even their subjects over the years to avoid monotony. Being born again—reincarnated. Though perhaps the change-over is gradual. I mean, as life fades out of one body through senile decay, it flourishes gradually in the new body in the form of the child."

Bell regarded the speaker doubtfully. "Think my clothes are dry now," he said and went and got them. He started dressing himself.

" 'Intimations of Immortality,' " murmured Grahame lazily as if meditating aloud. "Wordsworth died in 1850. Robert Louis Stevenson was born in 1850."

"What of it?"

"Byron died in 1824. He was a restless sort. Supposing he wanted to be one of the great physicists for a change? Lord Kelvin was born in 1824.

"Shelley died in 1822. Pasteur was born in 1822. Titian died in 1576, and Robert Burton, of the famous *Anatomy of Melancholy,* was born in 1576. In 1809, Haydn, the father of the symphony, died—and Abe Lincoln was born. In 1828 Schubert died, Tolstoi was born."

Bell fought with his twisted suspenders and said nothing.

"The Martian who played Voltaire from 1694 to 1778 and Sir Humphry Davy, who gave the miners the safety lamp, for one thing, from 1778 to 1829, and Rubinstein from 1829 to 1894 must have had some fun," mused Grahame.

"And where did he go in 1894?" asked Bell gruffly.

Grahame smiled. "Maybe he went back to Mars on furlough."

"In an organized party, perhaps?" Bell tried to make it sound like levity, but underneath was uneasiness about the way Grahame was talking. Grahame had always been common sense personified. But this fantastic stuff . . . if it was meant as a joke it wasn't particularly funny.

And if Grahame were half serious it made one wonder whether the psychiatrist wouldn't soon need a psychiatrist—and whether *The Whole Man* were really valuable property or only something of like quality.

"I doubt whether there were enough of them to make up parties," said Grahame, still smiling. "But there might have been pals who went in pairs. For instance, two great composers, like Liszt and Berlioz, who both died in 1867. Or two great writers, like Mark Twain and Tolstoi, who both died in 1910.

"And the two men who knew more about the soul of humanity than all the others, Cervantes and Shakespeare, both died on the same day—April 23, 1616. On the other hand, Wordsworth and Beethoven were born in the same year, 1770."

"I never could remember dates," said Bell, tying his shoelaces.

"I'm not very good at them myself—these are only odd ones that occur to me," said Grahame carelessly. "But there's one series I know quite well. I'll write it down for you."

"Oh, don't trouble," said Bell, now fully dressed and brushing his coat. But Grahame scribbled a list on the back of an old envelope and held it out to him. Bell took it.

"That—" began Grahame, and was interrupted by the telephone. At the sudden loud tintinnabulation, Bell's stomach seemed to contract to a little lump of pain.

"That may be for me," he said, and licked dry lips.

"It is," said Grahame, who had answered it, holding it out to him. Bell found he was reaching for it with the hand that still clutched the list. He thrust the list impatiently in his pocket and took the phone.

"Hello."

Bess said, "It's started. Sooner than we expected. Don't worry. It'll be some time yet. I'm all packed. The taxi you come back in can take us to the hospital."

"Right. I'm leaving straight away. Make yourself comfortable, pet. Won't be long. 'By."

He dialed the number of a cab rank. When the cab was ordered, he gulped the neat Scotch the understanding Grahame had placed silently at his elbow.

"Thanks. It would happen the one evening I left her. I could murder you, Mick! However, I've no time now."

He snatched his hat.

"Take the book," said Grahame quickly. "Please!"

There was a note in his voice that made Bell, for all his haste, pause to look at him. Grahame was on his feet, a massive figure, standing plumb in the center of his beautiful room, and his attitude was entreaty. Never before had Bell seen Grahame show evidence of wanting anything, a favor least of all. Somehow, it moved him.

"Sure, sure," he muttered. "Can't stop to wrap it, though. Can I borrow the folder?"

"You can keep it," said Grahame.

Bell thrust folder and manuscript under his arm.

Grahame relaxed. He even smiled.

"Don't worry about Bess," he said. "It'll turn out all right. I'd come with you but I'm booked for that train."

"That's all right," said Bell, and they shook hands. "Hope the tour's a hit. When you're back I'll be seeing you."

"Yes," said Grahame, and there passed in his eyes an amused twinkle which Bell was to remember.

The rain had stopped.

As the taxi bore him down the avenue, Bell glanced back through the little rear window at the apartment house. Lighted windows staggered up its tall dark sides to the penthouse, shaped against the night sky. There was a break in the clouds above it, a handful of dim stars just visible.

It was a glimpse into the infinite that one rarely obtained in New York.

And somehow, suddenly, Grahame's fancy about the missionaries from out there seemed—possible. When one was moving, trembling, toward the eternal mystery of the birth of a new part of one's own self—especially if it was your first child and you were the apprehensive sort and you were mad about your wife—then in that borderland of uncertainty and the unprecedented almost anything seemed possible.

He came back to the flat as the shadows were long in the early morning light.

He had a shave and a lonely breakfast. It didn't seem right without Bess at the other side of the little table.

But he was immensely relieved. Things had gone swell. Bess was fine—and he was a father—of a son. Pride glowed steadily within him, as though he were due the credit for arranging everything.

On another morning, the mail's reminder of his precarious business would have worried him.

Now it didn't seem to matter. He even took up the newspaper and glanced over the headlines with a light heart.

Two minutes later he saw an item which knocked

all the cheerfulness out of him, which impelled him to push his plate away, to rest his head in his hands, all his appetite gone.

At a quarter after midnight last night, the cab taking the well-known psychiatrist and author, Michael Grahame, to Grand Central Station had crashed into a streetcar. Grahame had been killed outright.

And Bell, in his empty flat, felt great gulfs of loneliness opening up all around him. The rock of Grahame was gone overnight. And Bess was not here to comfort him. Not that he thought it wise to tell her about Grahame yet.

She was still weak. And she had liked Grahame.

But she had nothing like his own love and hero worship for the man. He recalled his brusque impatience with Mick a few hours back and wished that he'd been more gracious.

He felt a mixture of grief and self-pity. The glory of his fatherhood was somewhat dimmed.

At midday he went to see her again, bearing orchids he couldn't afford.

His son was asleep in the little cot at her bedside.

Bess said, "Well, there he is. Half a day old already. It's just twelve hours since he arrived."

Bell glanced at his watch—12:15.

"That's right," he said. "I ought to know. Shall I ever forget!"

They laughed. But his laughter died before hers because he remembered something: Mick was killed at the same time that their son was born.

Exactly!

Bess sensed his sudden change of mood.

"What's the matter, love?"

He didn't answer. He was fumbling in his pocket.

He drew out the crumpled old envelope Mick had given him and, for the first time, read what his friend had written.

Then he dropped the envelope on the bed and got up to stare unseeing out of the window.

Mick had been forty-four—born in 1904.

Then, as he gazed at the noonday shimmer, his doubts and uncertainties fell away from him. He knew a confidence that he had never known before.

The Whole Man would be all Mick said it would be.

It would make Bell's fortune and lift Grahame's name into the ranks of the great. And there was every chance that it would do what it was primarily designed to do— set mankind's feet firmly on the true path of deliverance.

Best of all, to him, Mick was with him, would always be with him.

Bess looked at him puzzledly, then picked up the envelope.

Her expression of perplexity only deepened as she read.

Michelangelo	—(1474 (1564	*Gainsborough*	—(1727 (1788
Galileo	—(1564 (1642	*Schopenhauer*	—(1788 (1860
Newton	—(1642 (1727	*Chekhov*	—(1860 (1904

"What's it mean, darling?"

He came back, took the envelope, folded it carefully into his wallet.

"Just some notes Mick gave me."

"Oh," she said, "that reminds me. Has it struck you— the boy looks rather like Mick? Don't you think there's something of Mick in him?"

He turned bright eyes on the little red, wrinkled face in the cot.

"Yes," he said, quietly, "I'm sure there's quite a lot of Mick in him."

Margaret St. Clair

CHILD OF VOID

It has been remarked in the Introduction to this book that no Earth invasions through dimensions, parallel worlds, or time were going to be included. But this story is a partial exception. The reason for the word "partial" is that it is literally impossible to decide, after reading the story, where the horrid little aliens actually came from—far places or far times, extrasolar planets or space-time continuum loops. In any event, whether the characters in the blue egg are legally members of the present book's society or strictly extraterrestrial visitants is not really important. They make the reader shake in his shoes, and that, for the moment, is all we want.

ISCHEENAR is his name, and he lives in the big toe of my left foot. He's fairly quiet during the day, except that now and then he makes my foot twitch. But at night he comes out and sits on my knee and says all sorts of hateful things. Once he suggested—

But I didn't mean to tell about Ischeenar yet. I suppose I got off on him thinking about the fire and all that. It was after the fire that he got into my foot. But I want to tell this in order, the way it happened, and I ought to begin at the beginning. I suppose that means telling about how we happened to go to Hidden Valley to live.

Uncle Albert killed himself and left Hidden Valley to Mom in his will. I didn't want to go there. We had visited Hidden Valley once or twice when I was little, and I hated it. It gave me the creeps. It was the kind of place you see articles about in the Sunday supplement—a place where water flows uphill and half the time the laws of gravity don't work, a place where sometimes a rubber ball will weigh three or four pounds and you can look out the upstairs window and see a big blue lake where the vegetable garden ought to be. You never could depend on things being normal and right.

But Mom wanted to go. She said there was a nice little house we could live in, an artesian well with the best water in the world, and good rich soil for growing our own vegetables. There were even a cow and some chickens. Mom said we could be a lot more comfortable there than in the city, and live better. She said we'd get used to the funny things and they wouldn't bother us. And though she didn't say so, I knew she thought I'd be happier away from people, on a farm.

Mom's been awfully good to me. She kept on with the massage and exercises for my back for years after the doctors said it was no use. I wish I could do more for her. Her ideas are usually pretty good, and when I've gone against them I've been sorry. When you think about it, Mom is generally right.

So we went to Hidden Valley, Mom and Donnie (that's my younger brother) and I. It was worse than I had thought it was going to be. The place was still queer enough to scare you purple, but besides that there was something new, a kind of heavy depression in the air.

It was terrible. At first it made you feel like you'd like to put your head up and howl the way a dog does;

then you felt too worn out and miserable and unhappy to have energy left for howling.

It got worse with every hour we stayed there. By the time we'd been in Hidden Valley for two days, Mom and I were looking at each other and wondering which of us would be the first to suggest going back to the city. I kept thinking about how sensible Uncle Albert had been to blow himself up with the dynamite. Even Donnie and his kitten felt the depression; they sat huddled up together in a corner and looked miserable.

Finally Mom said, in a kind of desperate way, "Eddie, why don't you see what you can get on your radio set? It might cheer you up." Mom doesn't give up easily.

I thought it was a silly idea. I've been a ham operator ever since I was fifteen, and it's a lot of fun. I enjoy it more than anything. But when you're feeling as bad as I was then, you don't want to talk to anyone. You just want to sit and wonder about dying and things like that.

My stuff had been dumped down all in a corner of the little beaver-boarded living room. I hadn't felt chipper enough to do anything about getting it set up, though Uncle Albert had put in a private power system and there was electricity in the house. After Mom asked me for the second time, though, I got up and hobbled over to my equipment. And here a funny thing happened. I'd hardly started hunting around for a table to put my stuff on when my depression began to lift.

It was wonderful. It was like being lost in the middle of a dark, choking fog and then having the fog blow away and the bright sun shine out.

The others were affected the same way. Donnie got a piece of string and began playing with the kitten, and the kitten sat back and batted at the string with its paws the way cats do when they're playful. Mom stood watching me for a while, smiling, and then she went out in the kitchen and began to get supper. I could smell the bacon frying and hear her whistling "Onward Christian Soldiers." Mom whistles that way when she's feeling good.

We didn't go back to feeling depressed again, either. The funny things about Hidden Valley stopped bothering us, and we all enjoyed ourselves. We had fresh eggs, and milk so rich you could hardly drink it, and lettuce and peas and tomatoes and everything. It was a dry year, but we had plenty of water for irrigation. We lived off the fat of the land; you'd have to have a hundred dollars a week to live like that in the city.

Donnie liked school (he walked about a mile to the school bus) better than he had in the city because the kids were more friendly, and Mom got a big bang out of taking care of the cow and the chickens. I was outside all day long, working in the garden, and I got a fine tan and put on some weight. Mom said I never looked so well. She went into town in the jalopy twice a month to get me books from the county library, and I had all kinds of interesting things to read.

The only thing that bothered me—and it didn't really *bother* me, at that—was that I couldn't contact any other hams with my station. I never got a single signal from anyone. I don't know what the trouble was, really —what it looked like was that radio waves couldn't get into or out of the valley. I did everything I could to soup up my equipment. I had Mom get me a dozen books from the county library, and I stayed up half the night studying them. I tore my equipment down and built it up again eight or ten times and put in all sorts of fancy stuff. Nothing helped. I might as well have held a rock to my ear and listened to it.

But outside of that, as I say, I thought Hidden Valley was wonderful. I was glad Mom had made me and Donnie go there. Everything was doing fine, until Donnie fell in the cave.

It happened when he went out after lunch to hunt his kitten—it was Saturday—and he didn't come back and he didn't come back. At last Mom, getting worried, sent me out to look for him.

I went to all the usual places first, and then, not finding him, went farther away. At last, high up on a hillside, I found a big, fresh-looking hole. It was about five feet across, and from the look of the grass on the edges, the earth had just recently caved in. It seemed to be six or seven feet deep. Could Donnie be down in there? If there's a hole to fall in, a kid will fall in it.

I put my ear over the edge and listened. I couldn't see anything when I looked. After a moment I heard a sound like sobbing, pretty much muffled.

"Donnie!" I yelled. "Oh, Donnie!" There wasn't any answer, but the sobbing seemed to get louder. I figured if he was down there, he was either hurt or too scared to answer my call.

I hobbled back to the house as quick as I could and got a stepladder. I didn't tell Mom—no use in worrying her any more. I managed to get the ladder to the hole and down inside. Then I went down myself. I've got lots of strength in my arms.

Donnie wasn't at the bottom. Some light was coming in at the top, and I could see that the cave went on sloping down. I listened carefully and heard the crying again.

The slope was pretty steep, about twenty degrees. I went forward carefully, feeling my way along the side and listening. Everything was as dark as the inside of a cow. Now and then I'd yell Donnie's name.

The crying got louder. It did sound like Donnie's voice. Pretty soon I heard a faint "Eddie!" from ahead.

And almost at the same moment I saw a faint gleam.

When I got up to it, Donnie was there. I could just make him out silhouetted against the dim yellowish glow. When I said his name this time, he gulped and swallowed. He crawled up to me as quick as he could and threw his arms around my legs.

"Ooooh, Eddie," he said, "I'm so glad you came! I fell in and hurt myself. I didn't know how to get out. I crawled away down here. I've been awful scared."

I put my arms around him and patted him. I certainly was glad to see him. But my attention wasn't all on him. Part of it was fixed on the egg.

It wasn't really an egg, of course. Even at the time I knew that. But it looked like a reptile's egg, somehow, a huge, big egg. It was about the size of a cardboard packing box, oval-shaped, and it seemed to be covered over with a tough and yet gelatinous skin. It glowed faintly with a pale orange light, as if it were translucent and the light were coming through it from behind. Shadows moved slowly inside.

Donnie was holding onto my legs so tightly I was afraid he'd stop the circulation. I could feel his heart pounding against me, and when I patted him his face was wet with tears. "I'm awful glad you came, Eddie," he said again. "You know that ol' egg there? It's been making me see all sorts of things. I was awful scared."

Donnie never lies. "It's all right now, kid," I said, looking at the egg. "We won't let it show you any more bad things."

"Oh, they weren't bad!" Donnie drew away from me. "The egg's bad, but the things weren't! They were awful nice."

I knew I ought to get him out, but I was curious. I was so curious I couldn't stand it. I said, "What kind of things, Quack-quack?" (That's his pet name, because his name is Donald.)

"Oh . . ." Donnie's voice was dreamy. His heartbeat was calming down. "Books and toys and candy. A great big Erector set. A toy farm and fire truck and a cowboy suit. And ice cream—I wish you could have some of the ice cream, Eddie. I had sodas and malteds and Eskimo bars and Cokes. Oh, and I won first prize in the spelling contest. Mom was awful glad."

"You mean—the egg let you have all these things?" I asked, feeling dazed.

"Naw." Donnie's tone held disgust. "But I could have 'em, all that and a lot more, if I'd do what the egg wanted."

"Oh."

"But I wouldn't do it." Donnie's voice was virtuous. "I said no to 'em. That egg's bad."

"What did the egg want you to do?"

"Aw, they wouldn't tell me." Donnie's tone was full of antagonism. "They never did say. C'm on, let's get out of here. You help me, I don't like it here."

I didn't answer. I didn't move. I couldn't. The egg . . . was showing me things.

What sort of things? The things I wanted most, just as it had with Donnie. Things I wanted so much I wouldn't even admit to wanting them. I saw myself healthy and normal and strong, with a straight back and powerful limbs. I was going to college, I was captain of the football team. I made the touchdown that won the big game. I was graduated with honors while Mom and my girl friend—such a pretty, jolly girl—looked on, their faces bright with pride. I got an important research job in radio. And so on—foolish ambitions, impossible hopes. Crazy dreams.

But they weren't dreams when the egg was showing

them to me. They were real, they weren't something I had to hide or laugh at any longer. And all the time a voice inside my brain was saying, "You can have this. You can have all this.

"Won't you help us, won't you please help us? We're harmless, we're trapped and hurt. We came here from our own place to colonize, and we can't get out and we can't get back.

"It would be easy for you to help us. And we'll be grateful. We'll give you all you saw. And more. All you have to do . . ."

I took a step forward. Of course I wanted what they had shown me. I wanted them very much. And besides, I felt sorry for the things, the harmless things imprisoned in the egg. I've known what it is to feel helpless and trapped.

Donnie was beating on my thigh with his fists and screaming. I tried to shake him off so I could go on listening to the other voice. He hung on, pummeling me, and finally, in desperation, grabbed at my hand and bit it hard with his sharp little teeth. "Eddie, Eddie, Eddie! Come out of it, please come out of it!"

That roused me. I looked at him, dazed and resentful. Why wouldn't he let me listen so I could help the poor things in the egg? "Be quiet, Quack-quack," I mumbled to him.

"You gotta listen, Eddie! Don't let them get you! 'Member what happened to Uncle Albert? 'Member how we felt when we first came to the farm?"

The words penetrated. My normal caution was waking up. "But they say they don't mean us any harm," I argued weakly. I was talking to Donnie just like he was grown up.

"Aw, they're big liars. They can't help hurting us. It's something they put into the air, like, by just being alive. They can stop it for a while, if they try hard. But that's the way they really are. Like poison oak or a rattlesnake. 'Sides, I think they like it. They like being the way they are."

Poison oak and rattlers, I translated to myself, aren't consciously evil. They don't will their nature. But it's their nature to be poisonous. If Donnie was right in thinking that the things in the egg gave out, as a part of their metabolism, a vibration which was hostile to human life . . . Uncle Albert had committed suicide by blowing himself up with dynamite.

"We'd better get rid of the egg, Quack-quack," I said.

"Yes, Eddie."

I helped him up the shaft to the mouth of the cave. He'd sprained his ankle. On the way I asked, "What are the things in the egg like, Donnie?" I had an idea, but I wanted to check it with him. I felt his young mind and senses were keener and more reliable in this than mine.

"Like radio. Or 'lectricity."

"Where did they come from?"

"Another—not like where we live. Everything's different. It's not like here. It's right here beside us. An' it's a long way off."

I nodded. I helped him up the ladder and left him sitting on the hillside. Then I went back to the house for my .22 and a can of kerosene.

Donnie watched me anxiously as I went down with them. I don't mind admitting I was pretty nervous myself.

A .22 isn't an elephant gun. Still, at a two-foot range it ought to have some penetrating power. It didn't. The bullets just bounced off from the side of the egg. I could hear them spatting against the walls of the cave. I used three clips before I gave up.

That left the kerosene. There hadn't been any more

attempts to show me pictures or bring me around. In a silence that seemed bitterly hostile I poured kerosene all over the egg. I used plenty. Then I stood back and tossed a match at it.

Heat boiled up. It got so hot I retreated nearly to where Donnie had fallen in. But when it cooled off enough so that I could go back, I found the egg sitting there as good as new. There wasn't even any soot on it.

I was beaten. I couldn't think of anything more to do. I went up the ladder with the empty kerosene can and my gun. Donnie seemed to know I'd failed. He was crying when I came up to him. "Don't tell Mom," I said, and he nodded dutifully.

Would the egg let it go at that? I didn't think so. After supper I said to Mom, "You know, sometimes I think it would be nice to go back to the city for a while."

She looked at me as if she couldn't believe her ears. "Are you crazy, Eddie? We never had it so good before." Her eyes narrowed and she began to get worried. "What's the matter, honey? Aren't you feeling well?"

I couldn't tell her. I knew she'd believe me; that was just the trouble. If she knew there was a chance I could be cured, be made healthy and strong the way she wanted me to be, she'd make a dicker with the things in the egg, come hell or high water. It wouldn't make any difference to her whether they were good or bad, if she thought they could help *me*. Mom's like that.

"Oh, I feel fine," I said as heartily as I could. "It was just an idea. How's for seconds on the strawberry short-cake? It's even better than usual, Mom."

Her face relaxed. But I didn't sleep much that night.

The breakfast Mom cooked next morning was punk. I wasn't hungry, but I couldn't help noticing. The toast was burned, the eggs were leathery and cold, the coffee was the color of tea. There was even a fly in the pitcher of orange juice. I thought she must be worried about Donnie. I had bandaged his foot according to the picture in the first-aid book, but the ankle had swelled up like a balloon, and it looked sore and bad.

After breakfast Mom said, "Eddie, you seem worn out. I think carrying Donnie so far was bad for you. I don't want you to do any work today. You just sit around and rest."

"I don't feel like resting," I objected.

"Well—" Her face brightened. "I know," she said, sounding pleased. "Why don't you see what you can get on your radio set? The cord's long enough you could take it out on the side porch and be out in the fresh air. It's been a long time since you worked with it. Maybe you could get some of the stations you used to get."

She sounded so pleased with herself for having thought of the radio that I didn't have the heart to argue with her. She helped me move the table and the equipment outside, and I sat down and began to fiddle with it. It was nice and cool out on the porch.

I didn't get any signals, of course. Pretty soon Donnie came limping out. He was supposed to stay on the couch in the living room, but it's hard for a kid to keep still.

"What's the matter, Donnie?" I asked, looking at him. He was frowning, and his face was puckered up and serious. "Foot hurt?"

"Oh, some. . . . But Eddie . . . you know that old egg?"

I picked up my headphones and turned them a bit. "Um," I said.

"Well, I don't think you should'a built that fire around it. It was a bad thing to do."

I put the headphones down. I wanted to tell Donnie to shut up and not bother me; I know that was because

I didn't like what he was saying. "Why was it bad?" I asked.

"Because it stirred the things in the egg up. I kin feel it. It's like you have a station with more juice, you can get farther. The fire gave them more juice."

I didn't know what to say. I figured he was right, and I felt scared. After a minute I made myself laugh. "Nothing to worry about, Quack-quack," I said. "We can lick any old egg."

His face relaxed a little. "I guess so," he said. He sat down in the porch swing.

Mom stuck her head around the edge of the door. "Did you get anything on your radio, Eddie?" she asked.

"No," I said a little shortly.

"That's too bad." She went back in the kitchen and hung her apron up, and then she came out on the porch. She was rubbing her forehead with the back of her hand as if her head ached.

To please her, I put on my headphones and twiddled the dials. No dice, of course. Mom frowned. She went around to the other side of the table and stood looking at the wiring, something I'd never seen her do before. "How would it be if you moved this from here to here?" she said. Her voice was a little high.

I leaned over to see what she was pointing at. "That would just burn out the tubes."

"Oh." She stood there for a moment. Then her hand darted out, and before I could stop her, before I even had any idea what she was up to, she moved the wire she'd been talking about.

"Hey!" I squawked, "stop that!" I said it too late. There was a crackle and a flash and all the tubes burned out. My station was completely dead.

Mom rubbed her forehead and looked at me. "I don't know what made me do that, Eddie," she said apologetically. "It was just like something moved my hand! I'm awfully sorry, son."

"Oh, that's o.k.," I said. "Don't worry about it. The station wasn't good for anything."

"I know, but . . . My head's been feeling queer all morning. I think it must be the weather. Doesn't the air feel heavy and oppressive to you?"

The air did have a thick, discouraging feel, but I hadn't noticed it before she burned out the radio tubes. I opened my mouth to say something, but before I could say it, Donnie yelled, "Look at Fluffie! She's walking on the air!"

We both jerked around. There Fluffie was, about ten feet up, making motions with her paws as if she were trying to walk. She was mewing a blue streak. Now and then she'd slip down three or four feet and then go up to the former level, just as if a hand had caught at her. Her fur was standing up all over, and her tail was three times its usual size. Finally she went up about twenty feet and then came sailing down in a long curve. She landed on the ground with a thump. And that was the beginning of all the phenomena.

It wasn't so much that we felt depressed at first, though we certainly did. But we could stand it; the depression wasn't as bad as it had been when we first came to Hidden Valley. I guess that was because the things in the egg were more spread out now. Whether that was the reason or not, most of the phenomena were physical.

You could hardly get into the living room. It was like pushing your way through big wet bladders to go into it. If you sat on the sofa you had a sense of being crowded and pushed, and pretty soon you'd find yourself down at the far end of it, squeezed into a corner. When Mom struck matches to make a fire for lunch, the matches were twitched out of her hand and went sailing around the room. We had to eat cold things; she was afraid of burning down the place.

At first Mom tried to pretend there was nothing wrong; after all, you couldn't *see* anything. But I went out in the kitchen at suppertime and found her crying quietly. She said it was because she'd been trying to cut bread for sandwiches and the knife in her hand kept rising up toward her throat. I knew that if Mom was crying it had been pretty bad. So I told her about the egg in the cave and all that.

"They're out of the egg now," she said unhappily when I had finished. "My burning out the tubes this morning let them out. We've got to go back to the city, Eddie. It's the only thing to do."

"And leave them loose?" I said sharply. "We can't do that. If it was just a case of deserting the valley and having them stay here, it would be all right. But they won't stay here. They came to Earth to colonize. That means they'll increase and spread out.

"Remember how it was when we came here? Remember how we felt? Suppose it was like that over most of the Earth!"

Mom shook her head till her gray curls bobbed. "This can't be real, Eddie," she said in a sort of wail. "We must be having hallucinations or something. I keep telling myself, this can't be real."

Donnie, outside, gave a sudden horrible shriek. Mom turned as white as a ghost. Then she darted out, with me after her.

Donnie was standing over Fluffie's body, crying with rage. He was so mad and so miserable he could hardly talk. "They killed her! They killed her!" he said at last. "She was way up in the air, and they pushed her down hard and she squashed when she hit the ground. She's all mashed flat!"

There wasn't anything to say. I left Mom to try to comfort Donnie, and went off by myself to try to think.

I didn't get anywhere with my thinking. How do you fight anything you can't see or understand? The things from the egg were immaterial but could produce material phenomena; Donnie had said they were like electricity or radio. Even if that were true, how did it help? I thought up a dozen fragmentary schemes, each with some major flaw, for getting rid of them, and in the end I had to give up.

None of us went to bed that night. We stayed up in the kitchen huddled together for comfort and protection, while the house went crazy around us. The things that happened were ridiculous and horrible. They made you feel mentally outraged. It was like being lowered down into a well filled with craziness.

About three o'clock the light in the kitchen went slowly out. The house calmed down and everything got quiet. I guess the things from the egg had revenged themselves on us enough for having tried to get rid of them, and now they were going about their own business, perhaps beginning to increase. Because from then on the feeling of depression got worse. It was worse than it had ever been before.

It seemed like years and years until four o'clock. I sat there in the dark, holding Mom's and Donnie's hands and wondering how much longer I could stand it. I had a vision of life, then, that people in asylums must have, an expanse filled with unbearable horror and pain and misery.

By the time it was getting light I couldn't stand it any longer. There was a way out; I didn't have to go on seeing Hell opening in front of me. I pulled my hands from Mom's and Donnie's and stood up. I knew where Uncle Albert had kept the dynamite. I was going to kill myself.

Donnie's eyes opened and he looked at me. I'd known he wasn't asleep. "Don't do it, Eddie," he said in a thread of a voice. "It'll only give them more juice."

Part of my mind knew dimly what he meant. The things from the egg weren't driving me to suicide deliberately; they didn't care enough about me for that. But my death—or any human's death—would be a nice little event, a tidbit, for them. Life is electrical. My death would release a little juice.

It didn't matter, it wasn't important. I knew what I was going to do.

Mom hadn't moved or looked at me. Her face was drawn and gray and blotched. I knew, somehow, that what she was enduring was worse than what I had endured. Her vision was darker than mine had been. She was too deep in it to be able to think or speak or move.

The dynamite was in a box in the shed. I hunted around until I found the detonator and the fuse. I stuffed the waxy, candlelike sticks inside the waistband of my trousers and picked up the other things. I was going to kill myself, but part of me felt a certain compunction at the thought of blowing up Mom and Donnie. I went outside and began to walk uphill.

The sun was coming up in a blaze of red and gold and there was a soft little breeze. I could smell wood smoke a long way off. It was going to be a fine day. I looked around me critically for a good place to blow myself up.

They say suicides are often very particular; I know I was. This spot was too open and that one was too enclosed; there was too much grass here and not quite enough at the other place. It wasn't that I had cold feet. I hadn't. But I wanted everything to go off smoothly and well, without any hitches or fuss. I kept wandering around and looking, and pretty soon, without realizing it, I was near the hillside with the cave.

For a moment I thought of going down in the cave to do what I had to do. I decided against it. The explosion, in that confined space, might blow up the whole valley. I moved on. And suddenly I felt a tug at my mind.

It wasn't all around, like the feeling of depression was, something that seemed to be broadcast generally into the air. And it wasn't like the voice inside my head I'd heard in the cave. The best way I can express the feeling is by saying that it was like walking past a furnace with your eyes shut.

I hesitated. I was still feeling suicidal; I never wavered in that. But I felt a faint curiosity and something a lot fainter that you might call, if you exaggerated, the first beginnings of hope.

I went to the mouth of the cave and let myself down through the opening.

The egg, when I reached it, was different from the way I remembered it. It was bigger and the edges were misty. But the chief difference was that it was rotating around its long axis at a really fancy rate of speed. It reminded me of the rotation of a generator. The sensation I felt was coming out from it.

Watching the thing's luminous, mazy whirling, I got the idea that it and the things which had come out of it represented opposite poles. It was as alive as they were, though in an opposite way, and its motion provided the energy for them to operate.

I pulled the sticks of dynamite out of my belt and began setting them up. There really wasn't much danger of blowing up the valley, and as long as I was going to do away with myself, I might as well take the egg with me, or try to. That was the way I looked at it.

No attempt was made to stop me. This may have been because the things from the egg weren't interested in human beings, except spasmodically, but I think it more likely was because they, being polar opposites from the egg, had to keep their distance from it. Anyhow, I got my connections made without interference. I stood back a foot or two.

I closed the switch.

The next thing I knew, my head was on Mom's lap. She was shaking me desperately by the shoulders and crying something about fire.

Now, I don't see how I could have been responsible for the fire. The earthquake, possibly. Apparently when the dynamite exploded, the egg tried to absorb the energy. (That's why I wasn't hurt more.) It got an overload. And the overload, somehow, blew it clean out of our space. I got a glimpse of the space it was blown into, I think, just before my head hit the rock. But anyhow, a thing like that might possibly have caused an earthquake. All the country around Hidden Valley is over a fault.

Anyhow, there'd been earthquakes, several of them. Mom and Donnie had gone out hunting me as soon as the worst shocks were over, and found me lying at the mouth of the cave. They got me up somehow; I don't weigh much. Mom was nearly crazy with worry because I was still unconscious. For the last two hours or so she'd been smelling the smoke and hearing the crackling of the fire.

Some camper up in the mountains, I guess, started it. It was an awfully dry year. Anyhow, by the time I was conscious and on my feet again, it was too late to think about running. We didn't even have time to grab a suitcase. Mom and Donnie and I went down the flume.

That was some trip. When we got to Portsmouth, we found the whole town ready to pick up and leave, the fire was that close. They got it out in time, though. And then we found out that we were refugees.

There were pieces about the three of us in the city papers, with scareheads and everything. The photographers took pictures of all of us, even me, and they tried to make out we were heroes because we'd gone down the flume and hadn't got burned up in the fire. That was a lot of foolishness; there isn't anything heroic in saving your own life. And Mom hated those pictures. She said they made her look like she was in her seventies and heading for the grave.

One of the papers took up a collection for us, and we got a couple of hundred dollars out of it. It was a big help to us, because all we had in the world was the clothes we were standing in. After all, though, we hadn't really expected to live. And we'd got rid of the things from the egg.

As Mom says, we have a lot to be thankful for.

I could be more thankful, though, if I didn't have Ischeenar. I've tried and tried to figure out why he didn't die when the rest of the things did, when the egg was blown into another space. The only thing I can think of is that maybe, having been born here on Earth, he's different from the rest of them. Anyhow, he's here with us. I've managed to keep Mom from finding out, but, as I say, he lives in my big toe.

Sometimes I feel almost sorry for him. He's little and helpless, and alone in a big and hostile world. He's different from everything around him. Like us, he's a refugee.

But I wish I could get rid of him. He's not so bad now while he's young. He's really not dangerous. But I wish to *God* I could get rid of him.

He's going to be a stinker when he grows up.

Theodore Sturgeon

TINY AND THE MONSTER

The problem presented to the Monster must at first have seemed to be nearly insuperable. Its solution would result in the joyous "disinvading" of Earth by a strictly impromptu visiting alien with no desire to be where he is, but in desperate need of a tungsten casting to go elsewhere. However, tungsten cannot be cast; and, furthermore, the Monster cannot communicate with human beings without being immediately threatened with violent elimination. And yet the problem is solved. How it is solved makes for one of the most ingenious pieces of "zoological" science fiction (shaggy-dog zoology) in the whole literature of fantasy.

Of course, the Forsythe Formulas have not yet been announced, but you may be sure they will be any day now.

SHE *had* to find out about Tiny—*everything* about Tiny.

They were bound to call him Tiny. The name was good for a laugh when he was a pup, and many times afterward.

He was a Great Dane, unfashionable with his long tail, smooth and glossy in the brown coat which fit so snugly over his heavily muscled shoulders and chest. His eyes were big and brown and his feet were big and black; he had a voice like thunder and a heart ten times his own great size.

He was born in the Virgin Islands, on St. Croix,

which is a land of palm trees and sugar, of soft winds and luxuriant undergrowth whispering with the stealthy passage of pheasant and mongoose. There were rats in the ruins of the ancient estate houses that stood among the foothills—ruins with slave-built walls forty inches thick and great arches of weathered stone. There was pasture land where the field mice ran, and brooks asparkle with gaudy blue minnows.

But—where in St. Croix had he learned to be so strange?

When Tiny was a puppy, all feet and ears, he learned many things. Most of these things were kinds of respect. He learned to respect that swift, vengeful piece of utter engineering called a scorpion, when one of them whipped its barbed tail into his inquiring nose. He learned to respect the heavy deadness of the air about him that preceded a hurricane, for he knew that it meant hurry and hammering and utmost obedience from every creature on the estate. He learned to respect the justice of sharing, for he was pulled from the teat and from the trough when he crowded the others of his litter. He was the largest.

These things, all of them, he learned as respects. He was never struck, and although he learned caution he never learned fear. The pain he suffered from the scorpion—it happened only once—the strong but gentle hands which curbed his greed, the frightful violence of the hurricane that followed the tense preparations—all these things and many more taught him the justice of respect. He half understood a basic ethic: namely, that he would never be asked to do something, or to refrain from doing something, unless there was a good reason for it. His obedience, then, was a thing implicit, for it was half reasoned; and since it was not based on fear, but on justice, it could not interfere with his resourcefulness.

All of which, along with his blood, explained why he was such a splendid animal. It did not explain how he learned to read. It did not explain why Alec was compelled to sell him—not only to sell him but to search out Alistair Forsythe and sell him to her.

She *had* to find out. The whole thing was crazy. She hadn't wanted a dog. If she had wanted a dog, it wouldn't have been a Great Dane. And if it had been a Great Dane, it wouldn't have been Tiny, for he was a Crucian dog and had to be shipped all the way to Scarsdale, New York, by air.

The series of letters she sent to Alec were as full of wondering persuasion as his had been when he sold her the dog. It was through these letters that she learned about the scorpion and the hurricane, about Tiny's puppyhood and the way Alec brought up his dogs. If she learned something about Alec as well, that was understandable. Alec and Alistair Forsythe had never met, but through Tiny they shared a greater secret than many people who have grown up together.

"As for why I wrote you, of all people," Alec wrote in answer to her direct question, "I can't say I chose you at all. It was Tiny. One of the cruise-boat people mentioned your name at my place, over cocktails one afternoon. It was, as I remember, a Dr. Schwellenbach. Nice old fellow. As soon as your name was mentioned, Tiny's head came up as if I had called him. He got up from his station by the door and lolloped over to the doctor with his ears up and his nose quivering. I thought for a minute that the old fellow was offering him food, but no—he must have wanted to hear Schwellenbach say your name again. So I asked about you. A day or so later I was telling a couple of friends about it, and when I mentioned the name again, Tiny came snuffling over and shoved his nose into my hand. He was shivering. That got me. I wrote to a friend in New York who got your name and address in the phone book. You know the rest. I just wanted to tell you about it at first, but something made me suggest a sale. Somehow, it didn't seem right to have something like this going on and not have you meet Tiny. When you wrote that you couldn't get away from New York, there didn't seem to be anything else to do but send Tiny to you. And now— I don't know if I'm too happy about it. Judging from those pages and pages of questions you keep sending me, I get the idea that you are more than a little troubled by this crazy business."

She answered: *"Please* don't think I'm troubled about this! I'm not. I'm interested, and curious, and more than a little excited; but there is nothing about the situation that frightens me. I can't stress that enough. There's something around Tiny—sometimes I have the feeling it's something outside Tiny—that is infinitely comforting. I feel protected, in a strange way, and it's a different and greater thing than the protection I could expect from a large and intelligent dog. It's strange, and it's mysterious enough; but it isn't at all frightening.

"I have some more questions. Can you remember exactly what it was that Dr. Schwellenbach said the first time he mentioned my name and Tiny acted strangely? Was there ever any time that you can remember when Tiny was under some influence other than your own— something which might have given him these strange traits? What about his diet as a puppy? How many times did he get . . ." and so on.

And Alec answered, in part: "It was so long ago now that I can't remember exactly; but it seems to me Dr. Schwellenbach was talking about his work. As you know, he's a professor of metallurgy. He mentioned Professor Nowland as the greatest alloy specialist of his time —said Nowland could alloy anything with anything. Then he went on about Nowland's assistant. Said the assistant was very highly qualified, having been one of these Science Search products and something of a prodigy; in spite of which she was completely feminine and as beautiful a redhead as had ever exchanged heaven for earth. Then he said her name was Alistair Forsythe. (I hope you're not blushing, Miss Forsythe; you asked for this!) And then it was that Tiny ran over to the doctor in that extraordinary way.

"The only time I can think of when Tiny was off the estate and possibly under some influence was the day old Debbil disappeared for a whole day with the pup when he was about three months old. Debbil is one of the characters who hang around here. He's a Crucian about sixty years old, a piratical-looking old gent with one eye and elephantiasis. He shuffles around the grounds running odd errands for anyone who will give him tobacco or a shot of white rum. Well, one morning I sent him over the hill to see if there was a leak in the water line that runs from the reservoir. It would only take a couple of hours, so I told him to take Tiny for a run.

"They were gone for the whole day. I was short-handed and busy as a squirrel in a nuthouse and didn't have a chance to send anyone after him. But he drifted in toward evening. I bawled him out thoroughly. It was no use asking him where he had been; he's only about quarter-witted anyway. He just claimed he couldn't remember, which is pretty usual for him. But for the next three days I was busy with Tiny. He wouldn't eat, and he hardly slept at all. He just kept staring out over the cane fields at the hill. He didn't seem to want to go there at all. I went out to have a look. There's nothing out that way but the reservoir and the old ruins of the governor's palace, which have been rotting out there in the sun for the last century and a half. Nothing left now but an overgrown mound and a couple of arches, but it's supposed to be haunted. I forgot about it after that because Tiny got back to normal. As a matter of fact, he seemed to be better than ever, although, from then on, he would sometimes freeze and watch the hill as if he were listening to something. I haven't attached much importance to it until now. I still don't. Maybe he got chased by some mongoose's mother. Maybe he chewed up some ganjaweed—marijuana to you. But I doubt that it has anything to do with the way he acts now, any more than that business of the compasses that pointed west might have something to do with it. Did you hear about that, by the way? Craziest thing I ever heard of. It was right after I shipped Tiny off to you last fall, as I remember. Every ship and boat and plane from here to Sandy Hook reported that its compass began to indicate due west instead of a magnetic north! Fortunately the effect only lasted a couple of hours so there were no serious difficulties. One cruise steamer ran aground, and there were a couple of Miami fishing-boat mishaps. I only bring it up to remind both of us that Tiny's behavior may be odd, but not exclusively so in a world where such things as the crazy compasses occur."

And in her next, she wrote: "You're quite the philosopher, aren't you? Be careful of that Fortean attitude, my tropical friend. It tends to accept the idea of the unexplainable to an extent where explaining, or even investigating, begins to look useless. As far as that crazy compass episode is concerned, I remember it well indeed. My boss, Dr. Nowland—yes, it's true, he can alloy anything with anything!—has been up to his ears in that fantastic happenstance. So have most of his colleagues in half a dozen sciences. They're able to explain it quite satisfactorily, too. It was simply the presence of some quasi-magnetic phenomenon that created a resultant field at right angles to the Earth's own magnetic influences. That solution sent the pure theorists home happy. Of course, the practical ones—Nowland and his associates in metallurgy, for example—have only to figure out what caused the field. Science is a wonderful thing.

"By the way, you will notice my change of address. I have wanted for a long time to have a little house of my own, and I was lucky enough to get this one from a friend. It's up the Hudson from New York, quite countrified, but convenient enough to the city to be practical. I'm bringing Mother here from upstate. She'll love it. And besides—as if you didn't know the most important reason when you saw it!—it gives Tiny a place to run. He's no city dog. . . . I'd tell you that he found the house for me, too, if I didn't think that, these days, I'm crediting him with even more than his remarkable powers. Gregg and Marie Weems, the couple who had the cottage before, began to be haunted. So they said, anyway. Some indescribably horrible monster that both of them caught glimpses of, inside the house and out of it. Marie finally got the screaming meemies about it and insisted on Gregg's selling the place, housing shortage or no. They came straight to me. Why? Because they—Marie, anyway; she's a mystic little thing—had the idea that someone with a large dog would be safe in that house. The odd part of that was that neither of them knew I had recently acquired a Great Dane. As soon as they saw Tiny they threw themselves on my neck and begged me to take the place. Marie couldn't explain the feeling she had; what she and Gregg came to my place for was to ask me to buy a big dog and take the house.

Why me? Well, she just felt I would like it, that was all. It seemed the right kind of place for me. And my having the dog clinched it. Anyway, you can put that down in your notebook of unexplainables."

So it went for the better part of a year. The letters were long and frequent, and, as sometimes happens, Alec and Alistair grew very close indeed. Almost by accident, they found themselves writing letters that did not mention Tiny at all, although there were others that concerned nothing else. And, of course, Tiny was not always in the role of *canis superior*. He was a dog—all dog—and acted accordingly. His strangeness only came out at particular intervals. At first it had been at times when Alistair was most susceptible to being astonished by it—in other words, when it was least expected. Later, he would perform his odd feat when she was ready for him to do it, and under exactly the right circumstances. Later still, he became the superdog only when she asked him to. . . .

The cottage was on a hillside, such a very steep hillside that the view over the river overlooked the railroad, and the trains were a secret rumble and never a sight at all. There was a wild and clean air about the place— a perpetual tingle of expectancy, as though someone coming into New York for the very first time on one of the trains had thrown his joyous anticipation high in the air and the cottage had caught it and breathed it and kept it forever.

Up the hairpin driveway to the house, one spring afternoon, toiled a miniature automobile in its lowest gear. Its little motor grunted and moaned as it took the last steep grade, a miniature Old Faithful appearing around its radiator cap. At the foot of the brownstone porch steps it stopped, and a miniature lady slid out from under the wheel. But for the facts that she was wearing an aviation mechanic's coveralls, and that her very first remark—an earthy epithet directed at the steaming radiator—was neither ladylike nor miniature, she might have been a model for the more precious variety of Mother's Day greeting card.

Fuming, she reached into the car and pressed the horn button. The quavering ululation that resulted had its desired effect. It was answered instantly by the mighty howl of a Great Dane at the peak of aural agony. The door of the house crashed open and a girl rushed out on the porch, to stand with her russet hair ablaze in the sunlight, her lips parted, and her long eyes squinting against the light reflected from the river. "What— Mother! Mother, darling . . . is that you? Already? Tiny!" she rapped as the dog bolted out of the open door and down the steps. "Come back here!"

The dog stopped. Mrs. Forsythe scooped a crescent wrench from the ledge behind the driver's seat and brandished it. "Let him come, Alistair," she said grimly. "In the name of sense, girl, what are you doing with a monster like that? I thought you said you had a dog, not a Shetland pony with fangs. If he messes with me, I'll separate him from a couple of those twelve-pound feet and bring him down to my weight. Where do you keep his saddle? I thought there was a meat shortage in this part of the country. Whatever possessed you to take up your abode with that carnivorous dromedary, anyway? And what's the idea of buying a barn like this, thirty miles from nowhere and perched on a precipice to boot, with a stepladder for a driveway and an altitude fit to boil water at eighty degrees Centigrade? It must take you forever to make breakfast. Twenty-minute eggs, and then they're raw. I'm hungry. If that Danish basilisk hasn't eaten everything in sight, I'd like to nibble on about eight sandwiches. Salami on whole wheat. Your flowers are gorgeous, child. So are you. You always were, of course. Pity you have brains. If you had no brains, you'd get married. A lovely view, honey, lovely. I like it here. Glad you bought it. Come here, you," she said to Tiny.

He approached this small specimen of volubility with his head a little low and his tail down. She extended a hand and held it still to let him sniff it before she thumped him on the withers. He waved his unfashionable tail in acceptance and then went to join the laughing Alistair, who was coming down the steps.

"Mother, you're marvelous. And you haven't changed a bit." She bent and kissed her. "What on earth made that awful noise?"

"Noise? Oh—the horn." Mrs. Forsythe busily went about lifting the hood of the car. "I have a friend in the shoelace business. Wanted to stimulate trade for him. Fixed this up to make people jump out of their shoes. When they jump they break the laces. Leave their shoes in the street. Thousands of people walking about in their stocking feet. More people ought to, anyway. Good for the arches." She pointed. There were four big air-driven horns mounted on and around the little motor. Over the mouth of each was a shutter, so arranged that it revolved about an axle set at right angles to the horn, so that the bell was opened and closed by four small DC motors. "That's what gives it the warble. As for the beat-note, the four of them are tuned a sixteenth-tone apart. Pretty?"

"Pretty," Alistair conceded with sincerity. "No—please don't demonstrate it again, Mother! You almost wrenched poor Tiny's ears off the first time."

"Oh—did I?" Contritely, she went to the dog. "I didn't mean to, honey-poodle, really I didn't." The honey-poodle looked up at her with somber brown eyes and thumped his tail on the ground. "I like him," said Mrs. Forsythe decisively. She put out a fearless hand and pulled affectionately at the loose flesh of Tiny's upper lip. "Will you look at those tusks! Great day in the morning, dog, reel in some of that tongue or you'll turn yourself inside out. Why aren't you married yet, chicken?"

"Why aren't you?" Alistair countered.

Mrs. Forsythe stretched, "I've *been* married," she said, and Alistair knew now her casualness was forced. "A married season with the likes of Dan Forsythe sticks with you." Her voice softened. "Your daddy was all kinds of good people, baby." She shook herself. "Let's eat. I want to hear about Tiny. Your driblets and drablets of information about that dog are as tantalizing as Chapter Eleven of a movie serial. Who's this Alec creature in St. Croix? Some kind of native—cannibal, or something? He sounds nice. I wonder if you know how nice *you* think he is? Good heavens, the girl's blushing! I only know what I read in your letters, darling, and I never knew you to quote anyone by the paragraph before but that old scoundrel Nowland, and that was all about ductility and permeability and melting points. Metallurgy! A girl like you mucking about with molybs and durals instead of heartbeats and hope chests!"

"Mother, sweetheart, hasn't it occurred to you at all that I don't *want* to get married? Not yet, anyway."

"Of course it has! That doesn't alter the fact that a woman is only forty per cent a woman until someone loves her, and only eighty per cent a woman until she has children. As for you and your precious career, I seem to remember something about a certain Marie Sklodowska who didn't mind marrying a fellow called Curie, science or no science."

"Darling," said Alistair a little tiredly as they mounted the steps and went into the cool house, "once and for all, get this straight. The career, as such, doesn't matter at all. The work does. I like it. I don't see the sense in being married purely for the sake of being married."

"Oh, for heaven's sake, child, neither do I!" said Mrs. Forsythe quickly. Then, casting a critical eye over her daughter, she sighed, "But it's such a waste!"

"What do you mean?"

Her mother shook her head. "If you don't get it, it's because there's something wrong with your sense of values; in which case, there's no point in arguing. I love your furniture. Now, for pity's sake feed me and tell me about this canine Carnera of yours."

Moving deftly about the kitchen while her mother perched like a bright-eyed bird on a utility ladder, Alistair told the story of her letters from Alec and Tiny's arrival.

"At first he was just a dog. A very wonderful dog, of course, and extremely well trained. We got along beautifully. There was nothing remarkable about him but his history, as far as I could see, and certainly no indication of . . . of anything. I mean, he might have responded to my name the way he did because the syllabic content pleased him."

"It should," said her mother complacently. "Dan and I spent weeks at a sound laboratory graphing a suitable name for you. Alistair Forsythe. Has a beat, you know. Keep that in mind when you change it."

"Mother!"

"All right, dear. Go on with the story."

"For all I knew, the whole thing was a crazy coincidence. Tiny didn't respond particularly to the sound of my name after he got here. He seemed to take a perfectly normal, doggy pleasure in sticking around, that was all.

"Then one evening after he had been with me about a month, I found out he could read."

"Read!" Mrs. Forsythe toppled, clutched the edge of the sink, and righted herself.

"Well, practically that. I used to study a lot in the evenings, and Tiny used to stretch out in front of the fire with his nose between his paws and watch me. I was tickled by that. I even got the habit of talking to him while I studied. I mean, about the work. He always seemed to be paying very close attention, which, of course, was silly. And maybe it was my imagination, but the times he'd get up and nuzzle me always seemed to be the times when my mind was wandering or when I would quit working and go on to something else.

"This particular evening I was working on the permeability mathematics of certain of the rare-earth group. I put down my pencil and reached for my *Handbook of Chemistry and Physics* and found nothing but a big hole in the bookcase. The book wasn't on the desk, either. So I swung around to Tiny and said, just for something to say, 'Tiny, what have you done with my handbook?'

"He went *whuff!* in the most startled tone of voice, leaped to his feet, and went over to his bed. He turned up the mattress with his paw and scooped out the book. He picked it up in his jaws—I wonder what he would have done if he were a Scotty? That's a chunky piece of literature!—and brought it to me.

"I just didn't know what to do. I took the book and riffled it. It was pretty well shoved around. Apparently he had been trying to leaf through it with those big splay feet of his. I put the book down and took him by the muzzle. I called him nine kinds of a rascal and asked him what he was looking for." She paused, building a sandwich.

"Well?"

"Oh," said Alistair, as if coming back from a far distance. "He didn't say."

There was a thoughtful silence. Finally, Mrs. Forsythe looked up with her odd birdlike glance and said, "You're kidding. That dog isn't shaggy enough."

"You don't believe me." It wasn't a question.

The older woman got up to put a hand on the girl's shoulder. "Honey-lamb, your daddy used to say that the only things worth believing were things you learned from people you trusted. Of course I believe you. Thing is—do *you* believe you?"

"I'm not—sick, Mum, if that's what you mean. Let me tell you the rest of it."

"You mean there's more?"

"Plenty more." She put the stack of sandwiches on the sideboard where her mother could reach it. Mrs. Forsythe fell to with a will. "Tiny has been goading me to do research. A particular kind of research."

"Hut hine uffefa?"

"Mother! I didn't give you those sandwiches only to feed you. The idea was to soundproof you a bit, too, while I talked."

"Hohay!" said her mother cheerfully.

"Well, Tiny won't let me work on any other project but the one he's interested in. Mum, I can't talk if you're going to gape like that! No . . . I can't say he won't let me do *any* work. But there's a certain line of endeavor that he approves. If I do anything else, he snuffles around, joggles my elbow, grunts, whimpers, and generally carries on until I lose my temper and tell him to go away. Then he'll walk over to the fireplace and flop down and sulk. Never takes his eyes off me. So, of course, I get all softhearted and repentant and apologize to him and get on with what he wants done."

Mrs. Forsythe swallowed, coughed, gulped some milk, and exploded, *"Wait* a minute! You're away too fast for me! What is it that he wants done? How do you know he wants it? Can he read, or can't he? Make some sense, child!"

Alistair laughed richly. "Poor Mum! I don't blame you, darling. No, I don't think he can really read. He shows no interest at all in books or pictures. The episode with the handbook seemed to be an experiment that didn't bring any results. *But*—he knows the difference between my books, even books that are bound alike, even when I shift them around in the bookcase. Tiny!"

The Great Dane scrambled to his feet from the corner of the kitchen, his paws skidding on the waxed linoleum. "Get me Hoag's *Basic Radio,* old feller, will you?"

Tiny turned and padded out. They heard him going up the stairs. "I was afraid he wouldn't do it while you were here," she said. "He generally warns me not to say anything about his powers. He growls. He did that when Dr. Nowland dropped out for lunch one Saturday. I started to talk about Tiny and just couldn't. He acted disgracefully. First he growled and then he barked. It was the first time I've ever known him to bark in the house. Poor Dr. Nowland! He was scared half out of his wits!"

Tiny thudded down the stairs and entered the kitchen. "Give it to Mum," said Alistair. Tiny walked sedately over to the stool and stood before the astonished Mrs. Forsythe. She took the volume from his jaws.

"Basic Radio," she breathed.

"I asked him for that because I have a whole row of technical books up there, all from the same publisher, all the same color and about the same size," said Alistair calmly.

"But . . . but . . . how does he do it?"

Alistair shrugged. "*I* don't know! He doesn't read the titles. That I'm sure of. He can't read anything. I've tried to get him to do it a dozen different ways. I've lettered instructions on pieces of paper and shown them to him . . . you know . . . 'Go to the door' and 'Give me a kiss' and so on. He just looks at them and wags his tail. But if I read them first—"

"You mean, read them aloud?"

"No. Oh . . . he'll do anything I ask him to, sure. But I don't have to say it. Just read it, and he turns and does it. That's the way he makes me study what he wants studied."

"Are you telling me that that behemoth can read your mind?"

"What do you think? Here—I'll show you. Give me the book."

Tiny's ears went up. "There's something in here about the electrical flux in supercooled copper that I don't quite remember. Let's see if Tiny's interested."

She sat on the kitchen table and began to leaf through the book. Tiny came and sat in front of her, his tongue lolling out, his big brown eyes fixed on her face. There was silence as she turned pages, read a little, turned some more. And suddenly Tiny whimpered urgently.

"See what I mean, Mum? All right, Tiny. I'll read it over."

Silence again, while Alistair's long green eyes traveled over the page. All at once Tiny stood up and nuzzled her leg.

"Hm-m-m? The reference? Want me to go back?"

Tiny sat again, expectantly. "There's a reference here to a passage in the first section on basic electric theory that he wants," she explained. She looked up. "Mother! You read it to him!" She jumped off the table, handed the book over. "Here, Section 45. Tiny! Go listen to Mum. Go on!" and she shoved him toward Mrs. Forsythe, who said in an awed voice, "When I was a little girl, I used to read bedtime stories to my dolls. I thought I'd quit that kind of thing altogether, and now I'm reading technical literature to this . . . this canine catastrophe here. Shall I read aloud?"

"No—don't. See if he gets it."

But Mrs. Forsythe didn't get the chance. Before she had read two lines Tiny was frantic. He ran to Mrs. Forsythe and back to Alistair. He reared up like a frightened horse, rolled his eyes, and panted. He whimpered. He growled a little.

"For pity's sake, what's wrong?"

"I guess he can't get it from you," said Alistair. "I've had the idea before that he's tuned to me in more ways than one, and this clinches it. All right, then, give me back the—"

But before she could ask him, Tiny had bounded to Mrs. Forsythe, taken the book gently out of her hands, and carried it to his mistress. Alistair smiled at her paling mother, took the book, and read until Tiny suddenly seemed to lose interest. He went back to his station by the kitchen cabinet and lay down, yawning.

"That's that," said Alistair, closing the book. "In other words, class dismissed. Well, Mum?"

Mrs. Forsythe opened her mouth, closed it again, and shook her head. Alistair loosed a peal of laughter.

"Oh, Mum, Mum," she gurgled through her laughter. "History has been made. Mum, darling, you're speechless!"

"I am not," said Mrs. Forsythe gruffly. "I . . . I think . . . well, what do you know! You're right! I *am!*"

When they had their breath back—yes, Mrs. Forsythe joined in, for Alistair's statement was indeed true—Alistair picked up the book and said, "Now look, Mum, it's almost time for my session with Tiny. Oh, yes; it's a regular thing, and he certainly is leading me into some fascinating byways."

"Like what?"

"Like the old impossible problem of casting tungsten, for example. You know, there is a way to do it."

"You don't say! What do you cast it in—a play?"

Alistair wrinkled her straight nose. "Did you ever hear of pressure ice? Water compressed until it forms a solid at what is usually its boiling point?"

"I remember some such."

"Well, all you need is enough pressure, and a chamber that can take that kind of pressure, and a couple of details like a high-intensity field of umpteen megacycles phased with . . . I forget the figures; anyhow, that's the way to go about it."

" 'If we had some eggs we could have some ham and eggs if we had some ham,' " quoted Mrs. Forsythe. "And besides, I seem to remember something about that pressure ice melting pretty much right now, like so," and she snapped her fingers. "How do you know your molded tungsten—that's what it would be, not cast at all —wouldn't change state the same way?"

"That's what I'm working on now," said Alistair calmly. "Come along, Tiny. Mum, you can find your way around all right, can't you? If you need anything, just sing out. This isn't a séance, you know."

"Isn't it, though?" muttered Mrs. Forsythe as her lithe daughter and the dog bounded up the stairs. She shook her head, went into the kitchen, drew a bucket of water, and carried it down to her car, which had cooled to a simmer. She was dashing careful handfuls of it onto the radiator, before beginning to pour, when her quick ear caught the scrunching of boots on the steep drive.

She looked up to see a young man trudging wearily in the mid-morning heat. He wore an old sharkskin suit and carried his coat. In spite of his wilted appearance, his step was firm and his golden hair was crisp in the sunlight. He swung up to Mrs. Forsythe and gave her a grin, all deep-blue eyes and good teeth. "Forsythe's?" he asked in a resonant baritone.

"That's right," said Mrs. Forsythe, finding that she had to turn her head from side to side to see both of his shoulders. And yet she and he could swap belts. "You must feel like the Blue Kangaroo here," she added, slapping her miniature mount on its broiling flank. "Boiled dry."

"You cahl de cyah de Blue Kangaroo?" he repeated, draping his coat over the door and mopping his forehead with what seemed, to Mrs. Forsythe's discerning eye, a pure linen handkerchief.

"I do," she replied, forcing herself not to comment on the young man's slight but strange accent. "It's strictly a dry-clutch job and acts like a castellated one. Let the pedal out, she races. Let it out three thirty-seconds of an inch more, and you're gone from there. Always stopping to walk back and pick up your head. Snaps right off, you know. Carry a bottle of collodion and a couple of splints to put your head back on. Starve to death without a head to eat with. What brings you here?"

In answer he held out a yellow envelope, looking solemnly at her head and neck, then at the car, his face quiet, his eyes crinkling with a huge enjoyment.

Mrs. Forsythe glanced at the envelope. "Oh. Telegram. She's inside. I'll give it to her. Come on in and have a drink. It's hotter than the hinges of Hail Colum-

bia, Happy Land. Don't go wiping your feet like that!
By jeepers, that's enough to give you an inferiority complex! Invite a man in, invite the dust on his feet, too.
It's good, honest dirt and we don't run to white broad-
looms here. Are you afraid of dogs?"

The young man laughed. "Dahgs talk to me, ma'am."

She glanced at him sharply, opened her mouth to tell
him he might just be taken at his word around here, then
thought better of it. "Sit down," she ordered. She bustled
up a foaming glass of beer and set it beside him. "I'll
get her down to sign for the wire," she said. The man
half lowered the glass into which he had been jowls-
deep, began to speak, found he was alone in the room,
laughed suddenly and richly, wiped off the mustache of
suds, and dove down for a new one.

Mrs. Forsythe grinned and shook her head as she
heard the laughter, and went straight to Alistair's study.
"Alistair!"

"Stop pushing me about the ductility of tungsten,
Tiny! You know better than that. Figures are figures,
and facts are facts. I think I see what you're trying to
lead me to. All I can say is that if such a thing is possible, I never heard of any equipment that could handle
it. Stick around a few years and I'll hire you a nuclear
power plant. Until then, I'm afraid that—"

"Alistair!"

"—there just isn't . . . hm-m-m? Yes, Mother?"

"Telegram."

"Oh. Who from?"

"I don't know, being only one fortieth of one per cent
as psychic as that doghouse Dunninger you have there.
In other words, I didn't open it."

"Oh, Mum, you're silly! Of course you could have
. . . oh, well, let's have it."

"I haven't got it. It's downstairs with Discobolus

Junior, who brought it. No one," she said ecstatically, "has a right to be so tanned with hair that color."

"What *are* you talking about?"

"Go on down and sign for the telegram and see for yourself. You will find the maiden's dream with his golden head in a bucket of suds, all hot and sweaty from his noble efforts in attaining this peak without spikes or alpenstock, with nothing but his pure heart and Western Union to guide him."

"This maiden's dream happens to be tungsten treatment," said Alistair with some irritation. She looked longingly at her work sheet, put down her pencil, and rose. "Stay here, Tiny. I'll be right back as soon as I have successfully resisted my conniving mother's latest scheme to drag my red hairing across some young buck's path to matrimony." She paused at the door. "Aren't you staying up here, Mum?"

"Get that hair away from your face," said her mother grimly. "I am not. I wouldn't miss this for the world. And don't pun in front of that young man. It's practically the only thing in the world I consider vulgar."

Alistair led the way down the stairs and through the corridor to the kitchen, with her mother crowding her heels, once fluffing out her daughter's blazing hair, once taking a swift tuck in the back of the girl's halter. They spilled through the door almost together. Alistair stopped and frankly stared.

For the young man had risen and, still with the traces of beer foam on his modeled lips, stood with his jaws stupidly open, his head a little back, his eyes partly closed as if against a bright light. And it seemed as if everyone in the room forgot to breathe for a moment.

"Well!" Mrs. Forsythe exploded after a moment. "Honey, you've made a conquest. Hey—*you!* Chin up! Chest out!"

"I beg your humble pardon," muttered the young man; and the phrase seemed more a colloquialism than an affectation.

Alistair, visibly pulling herself together, said, "Mother! Please!" and drifted forward to pick up the telegram that lay on the kitchen table. Her mother knew her well enough to realize that her hands and her eyes were steady only by a powerful effort. Whether the effort was in control of annoyance, embarrassment, or out-and-out biochemistry was a matter for later thought. At the moment she was enjoying it tremendously.

"Please wait," said Alistair coolly. "There may be an answer to this." The young man simply bobbed his head. He was still a little walleyed with the impact of seeing Alistair, as many a young man had been before. But there were the beginnings of his astonishing smile around his lips as he watched her rip the envelope open.

"Mother! Listen!

"ARRIVED THIS MORNING AND HOPE I CAN CATCH YOU AT HOME. OLD DEBBIL KILLED IN ACCIDENT BUT FOUND HIS MEMORY BEFORE HE DIED. HAVE INFORMATION WHICH MAY CLEAR UP MYSTERY—OR DEEPEN IT. HOPE I CAN SEE YOU FOR I DON'T KNOW WHAT TO THINK.

                                        ALEC."

"How old is this tropical savage?" asked Mrs. Forsythe.

"He's not a savage and I don't know how old he is and I can't see what that has to do with it. I think he's about my age or a little older." She looked up, and her eyes were shining.

"Deadly rival," said Mrs. Forsythe to the messenger consolingly. "Rotten timing here, somewhere."

"I—" said the young man.

"Mother, we've got to fix something to eat. Do you

suppose he'll be able to stay over? Where's my green dress with the . . . oh, you wouldn't know. It's new."

"Then the letters weren't all about the dog," said Mrs. Forsythe, with a Cheshire grin.

"Mum, you're impossible! This is . . . is important. Alec is . . . is . . ."

Her mother nodded. "Important. That's all I was pointing out."

The young man said, "I—"

Alistair turned to him. "I do hope you don't think we're totally mad. I'm sorry you had such a climb." She went to the sideboard and took a quarter out of a sugar bowl. He took it gravely.

"Thank you, ma'am. If you don't min', I'll keep this piece of silver for the rest o' my everlahstin'."

"You're wel— *What?*"

The young man seemed to get even taller. "I greatly appreciate your hospitality, Mrs. Forsythe. I have you at a disadvantage, ma'am, and one I shall correct." He put a crooked forefinger between his lips and blew out an incredible blast of sound.

"Tiny!" he roared. "Here to me, dahg, an' mek me known!"

There was a roar from upstairs, and Tiny came tumbling down, scrabbling wildly as he took the turn at the foot of the stairs and hurtled over the slick flooring to crash joyfully into the young man.

"Ah, you beast," crooned the man, cuffing the dog happily. His accent thickened. "You thrive yourself here wid de lady-dem, you grayyut styoupid harse. You glad me, mon, you glad me." He grinned at the two astonished women. "Forgive me," he said as he pummeled Tiny, pulled his ears, shoved him away, and caught him by the jaws. "For true, I couldn't get in the first word with Mrs. Forsythe, and after I couldn't help meself.

Alec my name is, and the telegram I took from the true messenger, finding him sighing and sweating at the sight of the hill there."

Alistair covered her face with her hands and said "Oooh." Mrs. Forsythe whooped with laughter. She found her voice and demanded, "Young man, what is your last name?"

"Sundersen, ma'am."

"Mother! Why did you ask him that?"

"For reasons of euphony," said Mrs. Forsythe with a twinkle. Alexander Sundersen. Very good. Alistair—"

"Stop! Mum, don't you dare—"

"I was going to say, Alistair, if you and our guest will excuse me, I'll have to get back to my knitting." She went to the door.

Alistair threw an appalled look at Alec and cried, "Mother! What are you knitting?"

"My brows, darling. See you later." Mrs. Forsythe chuckled and went out.

It took almost a week for Alec to get caught up with the latest developments in Tiny, for he got the story in the most meticulous detail. There never seemed to be enough time to get in an explanation or an anecdote, so swiftly did the time fly when he and Alistair were together. Some of these days he went into the city with Alistair in the morning and spent the day buying tools and equipment for his estate. New York was a wonder city to him—he had been there only once before—and Alistair found herself getting quite possessive about the place, showing it off like the contents of a jewel box. And then Alec stayed at the house a couple of days. He endeared himself forever to Mrs. Forsythe by removing, cleaning, and refacing the clutch on the Blue Kangaroo, simplifying the controls on the gas refrigerator so it could be defrosted without a major operation, and putting a building jack under the corner of the porch that threatened to sag.

And the sessions with Tiny were resumed and intensified. At first, he seemed a little uneasy when Alec joined one of them, but within half an hour he relaxed. Thereafter, more and more he would interrupt Alistair to turn to Alec. Although he apparently could not understand Alec's thoughts at all, he seemed to comprehend perfectly when Alec spoke to Alistair. And within a few days she learned to accept these interruptions, for they speeded up the research they were doing. Alec was almost totally ignorant of the advanced theory with which Alistair worked, but his mind was clear, quick, and very direct. He was no theorist, and that was good. He was one of those rare grease-monkey geniuses, with a grasp that amounted to intuition concerning the laws of cause and effect. Tiny's reaction to this seemed to be approved. At any rate, the occasions when Alistair lost the track of what Tiny was after happened less and less frequently. Alec instinctively knew just how far to go back, and then how to spot the turning at which they had gone astray. And, bit by bit, they began to identify what it was that Tiny was after. As to why—and how—he was after it, Alec's experience with old Debbil seemed a clue. It certainly was sufficient to keep Alec plugging away at a possible solution to the strange animal's stranger need.

"It was down at the sugar mill," he told Alistair, after he had become fully acquainted with the incredible dog's action and they were trying to determine the why and the how. "He called me over to the chute where cane is loaded into the conveyors.

" 'Bahss,' he told me, 'dat t'ing dere, it not safe, sah.' And he pointed through the guard over the bull gears that drove the conveyor. Great big everlahstin' teeth it has, Miss Alistair, a full ten inches long, and it whirlin' to the drive pinion. It's old, but strong for good. Debbil, what he saw was a bit o' play on the pinion shaf'.

" 'Now, you're an old fool,' I told him.

" 'No, Bahss,' he says. 'Look now, sah, de t'ing wit' de teet'—dem, it not safe, sah. I mek you see,' and before I could move meself or let a thought trickle, he *opens* the guard up and thrus' his han' inside! Bull gear, it run right up his arm and nip it off, neat as ever, at the shoulder. I humbly beg your pardon, Miss Alistair."

"G-go on," said Alistair, through her handkerchief.

"Well, sir, old Debbil was an idiot for true, and he only died the way he lived, rest him. He was old and he was all eaten out with malaria and elephantiasis and the like, that not even Dr. Thetford could save him. But a strange thing happened. As he lay dyin', with the entire village gathered roun' the door whisperin' plans for the wake, he sent to tell me come quickly. Down I run, and for the smile on his face I glad him when I cross the doorstep."

As Alec spoke, he was back in the Spanish-wall hut, with the air close under the palm-thatch roof and the glare of the pressure lantern set on the tiny window ledge to give the old man light to die by. Alec's accent deepened. " 'How you feel, mon?' I ahsk him. 'Bahss, I'm a dead man now, but I got a light in mah hey-yud.'

" 'Tell me, then, Debbil.'

" 'Bahss, de folk-dem say, ol' Debbil, him cyahn't remembah de taste of a mango as he t'row away de skin. Him cyahn't remembah his own house do he stay away t'ree day.'

" 'Loose talk, Debbil.'

" 'True talk, Bahss. Foh de Lahd give me a leaky pot fo' hol' ma brains. But Bahss, I do recall one t'ing now, bright an' clear, and you must know. Bahss, de day I go up the wahtah line, I see a great jumbee in de stones of de Gov'nor Palace dere.' "

"What's a jumbee?" asked Mrs. Forsythe.

"A ghost, ma'am. The Crucians carry a crawlin' heap of superstitions. Tiny! What eats you, mon?"

Tiny growled again. Alec and Alistair exchanged a look. "He doesn't want you to go on."

"Listen carefully. I want him to get this. I am his friend. I want to help you help him. I realize that he wants as few people as possible to find out about this thing. I will say nothing to anybody unless and until I have his permission."

"Well, Tiny?"

The dog stood restlessly, swinging his great head from Alistair to Alec. Finally he made a sound like an audible shrug, then turned to Mrs. Forsythe.

"Mother's part of me," said Alistair firmly. "That's the way it's got to be. No alternative." She leaned forward. "You can't talk to us. You can only indicate what you want said and done. I think Alec's story will help us to understand what you want and help you to get it more quickly. Understand?"

Tiny gazed at her for a long moment, said *"Whuff!"* and lay down with his nose between his paws and his eyes fixed on Alec.

"I think that's the green light," said Mrs. Forsythe, "and I might add that most of it was due to my daughter's conviction that you're a wonderful fellow."

"Mother!"

"Well, pare me down and call me Spud! They're *both* blushing!" said Mrs. Forsythe blatantly.

"Go on, Alec," choked Alistair.

"Thank you. Old Debbil told me a fine tale of the things he had seen at the ruins. A great beast, mind you, with no shape at all, and a face ugly to drive you mad.

And about the beast was what he called a 'feelin' good.' He said it was a miracle, but he feared nothing. 'Wet it was, Bahss, like a slug, an' de eye it have is whirlin' an' shakin', an' I standin' dar feelin' like a bride at de altar step an' no fear in me.' Well, I thought the old man's mind was wandering, for I knew he was touched. But the story he told was *that* clear, and never a simple second did he stop to think. Out it all came like a true thing.

"He said that Tiny walked to the beast and that it curved over him like an ocean wave. It closed over the dog, and Debbil was rooted there the livelong day, still without fear, and feelin' no smallest desire to move. He had no surprise at all, even at the thing he saw restin' in the thicket among the old stones.

"He said it was a submarine, a mighty one as great as the estate house and with no break nor mar in its surface but for the glass part let in where the mouth is on a shark.

"And then when the sun begun to dip, the beast gave a shudderin' heave and rolled back, and out walked Tiny. He stepped up to Debbil and stood. Then the beast begun to quiver and shake, and Debbil said the air aroun' him heavied with the work the monster was doing, tryin' to talk. A cloud formed in his brain, and a voice swept over him. 'Not a livin' word, Bahss, nor a sound at all. But it said to forget. It said to leave dis place and forget, sah.' And the last thing old Debbil saw as he turned away was the beast slumping down, seeming all but dead from the work it had done to speak at all. 'An' de cloud leave in mah hey-yud, Bahss, f'om dat time onward. I'm a dead man now, Bahss, but de cloud gone and Debbil know de story.' " Alec leaned back and looked at his hands. "That was all. This must have happened about fifteen months pahst, just before Tiny began to show his strange stripe." He drew a deep breath and looked up. "Maybe I'm gullible. But I knew the old man too well. He never in this life could invent such a tale. I troubled myself to go up to the Governor's Palace after the buryin'. I might have been mistaken, but something big had lain in the deepest thicket, for it was crushed into a great hollow place near a hundred foot long. Well, there you are. For what it's worth, you have the story of a superstitious an' illiterate old man, at the point of death by violence and many years sick to boot."

There was a long silence, and at last Alistair threw her lucent hair back and said, "It isn't Tiny at all. It's a . . . a thing outside Tiny." She looked at the dog, her eyes wide. "And I don't even mind."

"Neither did Debbil, when he saw it," said Alec gravely.

Mrs. Forsythe snapped, "What are we sitting gawking at each other for? Don't answer; I'll tell you. All of us can think up a story to fit the facts, and we're all too self-conscious to come out with it. Any story that fit those facts would really be a killer."

"Well said." Alec grinned. "Would you like to tell us your idea?"

"Silly boy," muttered Alistair.

"Don't be impertinent, child. Of course I'd like to tell you, Alec. I think that the good Lord, in His infinite wisdom, has decided that it was about time for Alistair to come to her senses, and, knowing that it would take a quasi-scientific miracle to do it, dreamed up this—"

"Some day," said Alistair icily, "I'm going to pry you loose from your verbosity and your sense of humor in one fell swoop."

Mrs. Forsythe grinned. "There is a time for jocularity, kidlet, and this is it. I hate solemn people solemnly sitting around being awed by things. What do you make of all this, Alec?"

Alec pulled his ear and said, "I vote we leave it up to Tiny. It's his show. Let's get on with the work and just keep in mind what we already know."

And to their astonishment, Tiny stumped over to Alec and licked his hand.

The blowoff came six weeks after Alec's arrival. (Oh, yes! He stayed six weeks, and longer! It took some fiendish cogitation for him to think of enough legitimate estate business that had to be done in New York to keep him that long; but after that he was so much one of the family that he needed no excuse.) He had devised a code system for Tiny, so that Tiny could add something to their conversations. His point: "Here he sits, ma'am, like a fly on the wall, seeing everything and hearing everything and saying not a word. Picture it for yourself, and you in such a position, full entranced as you are with the talk you hear." And for Mrs. Forsythe particularly, the mental picture was altogether too vivid! It was so well presented that Tiny's research went by the board for four days while they devised the code. They had to give up the idea of a glove with a pencil pocket in it, with which Tiny might write a little, or any similar device. The dog was simply not deft enough for such meticulous work; and besides, he showed absolutely no signs of understanding any written or printed symbolism. Unless, of course, Alistair thought about it. . . .

Alec's plan was simple. He cut some wooden forms— a disk, a square, a triangle to begin with. The disk signified "yes" or any other affirmation, depending on the context. The square was "no" or any negation; and the triangle indicated a question or a change in subject. The amount of information Tiny was able to impart by moving from one to another of these forms was astonishing. Once a subject for discussion was established, Tiny would take a stand between the disk and the square, so that all he had to do was to swing his head to one side or the other to indicate a "yes" or a "no." No longer were there those exasperating sessions in which the track of his research was lost while they back-trailed to discover where they had gone astray. The conversations ran like this:

"Tiny, I have a question. Hope you won't think it too personal. May I ask it?" That was Alec, always infinitely polite to dogs. He had always recognized their innate dignity.

Yes, the answer would come, as Tiny swung his head over the disk.

"Are we right in assuming that you, the dog, are not communicating with us: that you are the medium?"

Tiny went to the triangle. "You want to change the subject?"

Tiny hesitated, then went to the square. *No.*

Alistair said, "He obviously wants something from us before he will discuss the question. Right, Tiny?"

Yes.

Mrs. Forsythe said, "He's had his dinner, and he doesn't smoke. I think he wants us to assure him that we'll keep his secret."

Yes.

"Good. Alec, you're wonderful," said Alistair. "Mother, stop beaming! I only meant—"

"Leave it at that, child! Any qualification will spoil it for the man!"

"Thank you, ma'am," said Alec gravely, with that deep twinkle of amusement around his eyes. Then he turned back to Tiny. "Well, what about it, sah? Are you a superdog?"

No.

"Who . . . no, he can't answer that. Let's go back a bit. Was old Debbil's story true?"

Yes.

"Ah." They exchanged glances. "Where is this— monster? Still in St. Croix?"

No.

"Here?"

Yes.

"You mean here, in this room or in the house?"

No.

"Nearby, though?"

Yes.

"How can we find out just where, without mentioning the countryside item by item?" asked Alistair.

"I know," said Mrs. Forsythe. "Alec, according to Debbil, that 'submarine' thing was pretty big, wasn't it?"

"That it was, ma'am."

"Good. Tiny, does he . . . it . . . have the ship here, too?"

Yes.

Mrs. Forsythe spread her hands. "That's it, then. There's only one place around here where you could hide such an object." She nodded her head at the west wall of the house.

"The river!" cried Alistair. "That right, Tiny?"

Yes. And Tiny went immediately to the triangle.

"Wait!" said Alec. "Tiny, beggin' your pardon, but there's one more question. Shortly after you took passage to New York, there was a business with compasses, where they all pointed to the west. Was that the ship?"

Yes.

"In the water?"

No.

"Why," said Alistair, "this is pure science fiction! Alec, do you ever get science fiction in the tropics?"

"Ah, Miss Alistair, not often enough, for true. But well I know it. The spaceships are Old Mother Goose to me. But there's a difference here. For in all the stories I've read, when a beast comes here from space, it's to kill and conquer; and yet—and I don't know why—I know that this one wants nothing of the sort. More, he's out to do us good."

"I feel the same way," said Mrs. Forsythe thoughtfully. "It's sort of a protective cloud which seems to surround us. Does that make sense to you, Alistair?"

"I know it from 'way back," said Alistair with conviction. She looked at the dog thoughtfully. "I wonder why he . . . it . . . won't show itself. And why it can communicate only through me. And why me?"

"I'd say, Miss Alistair, that you were chosen because of your metallurgy. As to why we never see the beast— Well, it knows best. Its reason must be a good one."

Day after day, and bit by bit, they got and gave information. Many things remained mysteries; but, strangely, there seemed no real need to question Tiny too closely. The atmosphere of confidence, of good will that surrounded them made questions seem not only unnecessary but downright rude.

And day by day, and little by little, a drawing began to take shape under Alec's skilled hands. It was a casting, with a simple enough external contour, but inside it contained a series of baffles and a chamber. It was designed, apparently, to support and house a carballoy shaft. There were no openings into the central chamber except those taken by the shaft. The shaft turned; *something* within the chamber apparently drove it. There was plenty of discussion about it.

"Why the baffles?" moaned Alistair, palming all the neatness out of her flaming hair. "Why carballoy? And in the name of Nemo, why tungsten?"

Alec stared at the drawing for a long moment, then suddenly clapped a hand to his head. "Tiny! Is there radiation inside that housing? I mean, hard stuff?"

Yes.

"There you are, then," said Alec. "Tungsten to shield the radiation. A casting for uniformity. The baffles to make a meander out of the shaft openings—see, the shaft has plates turned on it to fit between the baffles."

"And nowhere for anything to go in, nowhere for anything to come out—except the shaft, of course—and besides, you can't cast tungsten that way! Maybe Tiny's monster can, but we can't. Maybe with the right flux and with enough power—but that's silly. Tungsten won't cast."

"And we cahn't build a spaceship. There must be a way!"

"Not with today's facilities, and not with tungsten," said Alistair. "Tiny's ordering it from us the way we would order a wedding cake at the corner bakery."

"What made you say 'wedding cake'?"

"You, too, Alec? Don't I get enough of that from Mother?" But she smiled all the same. "But about the casting—it seems to me that our mysterious friend is in the position of a radio fiend who understands every part of his set, how it's made, how and why it works. Then a tube blows, and he finds he can't buy one. He has to make one if he gets one at all. Apparently old Debbil's beast is in that kind of spot. What about it, Tiny? Is your friend short a part which he understands but has never built before?"

Yes.

"And he needs it to get away from Earth?"

Yes.

Alec asked, "What's the trouble? Can't get escape velocity?"

Tiny hesitated, then went to the triangle. "Either he doesn't want to talk about it or the question doesn't quite fit the situation," said Alistair. "It doesn't matter. Our main problem is the casting. It just can't be done. Not by anyone on this planet, as far as I know; and I think I know. It has to be tungsten, Tiny?"

Yes.

"Tungsten, for what?" asked Alec. "Radiation shield?"

Yes.

He turned to Alistair. "Isn't there something just as good?"

She mused, staring at his drawing. "Yes, several things," she said thoughtfully. Tiny watched her, motionless. He seemed to slump as she shrugged dispiritedly and said, "But not anything with walls as thin as that. A yard or so of lead might do it, and have something like the mechanical strength he seems to want, but it would obviously be too big. Beryllium—" At the word, Tiny went and stood right on top of the square—a most emphatic *no.*

"How about an alloy?" Alec asked.

"Well, Tiny?"

Tiny went to the triangle. Alistair nodded. "You don't know. I can't think of one. I'll take it up with Dr. Nowland. Maybe—"

The following day Alec stayed home and spent the day arguing cheerfully with Mrs. Forsythe and building a grape arbor. It was a radiant Alistair who came home that evening. "Got it! Got it!" she caroled as she danced in. "Alec! Tiny—come on!"

They flew upstairs to the study. Without removing the green "beanie" with the orange feather that so nearly matched her hair, Alistair hauled out four reference books and began talking animatedly. "Auric molybdenum, Tiny! What about that? Gold and molyb III should do it! Listen!" And she launched forth into a spatter of absorption data, Greek-letter formulas, and strength-of-materials comparisons that quite made Alec's head swim. He sat watching her without listening. Increasingly, this was his greatest pleasure.

When Alistair was quite through, Tiny walked away from her and lay down, gazing off into space.

"Well, strike me!" said Alec. "Look yonder, Miss Alistair. The very first time I ever saw him thinking something over."

"Sh-h! Don't disturb him, then. If that *is* the answer, and if he never thought of it before, it will take some figuring out. There's no knowing what fantastic kind of science he's comparing it with."

"I see the point. Like . . . well, suppose we crashed a plane in the Brazilian jungle and needed a new hydraulic cylinder on the landing gear. Now, then, one of the natives shows us ironwood, and it's up to us to figure out if we can make it serve."

"That's about it," breathed Alistair. "I—" She was interrupted by Tiny, who suddenly leaped up and ran to her, kissing her hands, committing the forbidding enormity of putting his paws on her shoulders, running back to the wooden forms and nudging the disk, the *yes* symbol. His tail was going like a metronome without its pendulum. Mrs. Forsythe came in in the midst of all this rowdiness and demanded:

"What goes on? Who made a dervish out of Tiny? What have you been feeding him? Don't tell me. Let me . . . you don't mean you've solved his problem for him? What are you going to do—buy him a pogo stick?"

"Oh, Mum! We've got it! An alloy of molybdenum and gold! I can get it alloyed and cast in no time!"

"Good, honey—good. You going to cast the whole thing?" She pointed to the drawing.

"Why, yes."

"Humph!"

"Mother! Why, if I may ask, do you 'humph' in that tone of voice?"

"You may ask. Chicken, who's going to pay for it?"

"Why, that will . . . I—oh. *Oh!*" she said, aghast, and ran to the drawing. Alec came and looked over her shoulder. She figured in the corner of the drawing, ohed once again, and sat down weakly.

"How much?" asked Alec.

"I'll get an estimate in the morning," she said faintly. "I know plenty of people. I can get it at cost—maybe." She looked at Tiny despairingly. He came and laid his head against her knee, and she pulled at his ears. "I won't let you down, darling," she whispered.

She got the estimate the next day. It was a little over thirteen thousand dollars.

Alistair and Alec stared blankly at each other and then at the dog.

"Maybe you can tell us where we can raise that much money?" said Alistair, as if she expected Tiny to whip out a wallet.

Tiny whimpered, licked Alistair's hand, looked at Alec, and then lay down.

"Now what?" mused Alec.

"Now we go and fix something to eat," said Mrs. Forsythe, moving toward the door. The others were about to follow, when Tiny leaped to his feet and ran in front of them. He stood in the doorway and whimpered. When they came closer, he barked.

"Sh-h! What is it, Tiny? Want us to stay here a while?"

"Say! Who's the boss around here?" Mrs. Forsythe wanted to know.

"He is," said Alec, and he knew he was speaking for all of them. They sat down, Mrs. Forsythe on the studio couch, Alistair at her desk, Alec at the drawing table. But Tiny seemed not to approve of the arrangement. He became vastly excited, running to Alec, nudging him hard, dashing to Alistair, taking her wrist very gently in his jaws and pulling gently toward Alec.

"What is it, fellow?"

"Seems like matchmaking to me," remarked Mrs. Forsythe.

"Nonsense, Mum!" said Alistair, coloring. "He wants Alec and me to change places, that's all."

Alec said, "Oh!" and went to sit beside Mrs. Forsythe. Alistair sat at the drawing table. Tiny put a paw up on it, poked at the large tablet of paper. Alistair looked at him curiously, then tore off the top sheet. Tiny nudged a pencil with his nose.

Then they waited. Somehow, no one wanted to speak. Perhaps no one could, but there seemed to be no reason to try. And gradually a tension built up in the room. Tiny stood stiff and rapt in the center of the room. His eyes glazed, and when he finally keeled over limply, no one went to him.

Alistair picked up the pencil slowly. Watching her hand, Alec was reminded of the movement of the pointer on a ouija board. The pencil traveled steadily, in small surges, to the very top of the paper and hung there. Alistair's face was quite blank.

After that no one could say what happened, exactly. It was as if their eyes had done what their voices had done. They could see, but they did not care to. And

Alistair's pencil began to move. Something, somewhere, was directing her mind—not her hand. Faster and faster her pencil flew, and it wrote what was later to be known as the Forsythe Formulas.

There was no sign then, of course, of the furor that they would cause, of the millions of words of conjecture that were written when it was discovered that the girl who wrote them could not possibly have had the mathematical background to have written them. They were understood by no one at first, and by very few people ever. Alistair certainly did not know what they meant.

An editorial in a popular magazine came startlingly close to the true nature of the formulas when it said: "The Forsythe Formulas, which describe what the Sunday supplements call the 'Something-for-Nothing Clutch,' and the drawing that accompanies them, signify little to the layman. As far as can be determined, the formulas are the description and working principles of a device. It appears to be a power plant of sorts, and if it is ever understood, atomic power will go the way of gas lights.

"A sphere of energy is enclosed in a shell made of neutron-absorbing material. This sphere has inner and outer 'layers.' A shaft passes through the sphere. Apparently a magnetic field must be rotated about the outer casing of the device. The sphere of energy aligns itself with this field. The inner sphere rotates with the outer one and has the ability to turn the shaft. Unless the mathematics used are disproved—and no one seems to have come anywhere near doing that, unorthodox as they are—the aligning effect between the rotating field and the two concentric spheres, as well as the shaft, is quite independent of any load. In other words, if the original magnetic field rotates at 3000 r.p.m., the shaft will rotate at 3000 r.p.m., even if there is only a sixteenth horsepower turning the field while there is a 10,000 braking stress on the shaft.

"Ridiculous? Perhaps. And perhaps it is no more so than the apparent impossibility of 15 watts of energy pouring into the antenna of a radio station, and nothing coming down. The key to the whole problem is in the nature of those self-contained spheres of force inside the shell. Their power is apparently inherent, and consists of an ability to align, just as the useful property of steam is an ability to expand. If, as is suggested by Reinhardt in his 'Usage of the Symbol B in the Forsythe Formulas,' these spheres are nothing but stable concentrations of pure binding energy, we have here a source of power beyond the wildest dreams of mankind. And whether or not we succeed in building such devices, it cannot be denied that whatever their mysterious source, the Forsythe Formulas are an epochal gift to several sciences, including, if you like, the art of philosophy."

After it was over, and the formulas written, the terrible tension lifted. The three humans sat in their happy coma, and the dog lay senseless on the rug. Mrs. Forsythe was the first to move, standing up abruptly. "Well!" she said.

It seemed to break a spell. Everything was quite normal. No hangovers, no sense of strangeness, no fear. They stood looking wonderingly at the mass of minute figures.

"I don't know," murmured Alistair, and the phrase covered a world of meaning. Then, "Alec—that casting. We've got to get it done. We've just *got* to, no matter what it costs us!"

"I'd like to," said Alec. "Why do we *have* to?"

She waved toward the drawing table. "We've been given that."

"You don't say!" said Mrs. Forsythe. "And what is *that?*"

Alistair put her hand to her head, and a strange, unfocused look came into her eyes. That look was the only part of the whole affair that ever really bothered Alec. It was a place she had gone to, a little bit; and he knew that no matter whatever happened, he would never be able to go there with her.

She said, "He's been . . . talking to me, you know. You do know that, don't you? I'm not guessing, Alec—Mum."

"I believe you, chicken," her mother said softly. "What are you trying to say?"

"I got it in concepts. It isn't a thing you can repeat, really. But the idea is that he couldn't give us any *thing*. His ship is completely functional, and there isn't anything he can exchange for what he wants us to do. But he has given us something of great value—" Her voice trailed off; she seemed to listen to something for a moment. "Of value in several ways. A new science, a new approach to attack the science. New tools, new mathematics."

"But what is it? What can it do? And how is it going to help us pay for the casting?" asked Mrs. Forsythe.

"It can't, immediately," said Alistair decisively. "It's too big. We don't even know what it is. Why are you arguing? Can't you understand that he can't give us any gadgetry? That we haven't his techniques, materials, and tools, and so we couldn't make any actual machine he suggested? He's done the only thing he can; he's given us a new science, and tools to take it apart."

"That I know," said Alec gravely. "Well, indeed. I felt that. And I . . . I trust him. Do you, ma'am?"

"Yes, of course. I think he's—people. I think he has a sense of humor and a sense of justice," said Mrs. Forsythe firmly. "Let's get our heads together. We ought to be able to scrape it up some way. And why shouldn't we? Haven't we three got something to talk about for the rest of our lives?"

And their heads went together.

This is the letter that arrived two months later in St. Croix.

Honey-lamb,
Hold on to your seat. It's all over.

The casting arrived. I missed you more than ever, but when you have to go—and you know I'm glad you went! Anyway, I did as you indicated, through Tiny, before you left. The men who rented me the boat and ran it for me thought I was crazy, and said so. Do you know that once we were out on the river with the casting, and Tiny started whuffing and whimpering to tell me we were on the right spot, and I told the men to tip the casting over the side, they had the colossal nerve to insist on opening the crate? Got quite nasty about it. Didn't want to be a party to any dirty work. It was against my principles, but I let them, just to expedite matters. They were certain there was a body in the box! When they saw what it was, I was going to bend my umbrelly over their silly heads, but they looked so funny! I couldn't do a thing but roar with laughter. That was when the man said I was crazy.

Anyhow, over the side it went, into the river. Made a lovely splash. And about a minute later I got the loveliest feeling—I wish I could describe it to you. I was sort of overwhelmed by a feeling of utter satisfaction, and gratitude, and . . . oh, I don't know. I just felt *good,* all over. I looked at Tiny, and he was trembling. I think he felt it, too. I'd call it a thank you, on a grand psychic scale. I think you can rest assured that Tiny's monster got what it wanted.

But that wasn't the end of it. I paid off the boatmen and started up the bank. Something made me stop, and wait, and then go back to the water's edge.

It was early evening, and very still. I was under some sort of compulsion—not an unpleasant thing, but an unbreakable one. I sat down on the river wall and watched the water. There was no one around—the boat had left—except one of those snazzy Sunlounge cruisers anchored a few yards out. I remember how still it was, because there was a little girl playing on the deck of the yacht, and I could hear her footsteps as she ran about.

Suddenly I noticed something in the water. I suppose I should have been frightened, but somehow I wasn't at all. Whatever the thing was, it was big and gray and slimy and quite shapeless. And somehow, it seemed to be the source of this aura of well-being and protectiveness that I felt. It was staring at me. I knew it was before I saw that it had an eye—a big one, with something whirling inside of it. . . . I don't know. I wish I could write. I wish I had the power to tell you what it was like. I know that it was, by human standards, infinitely revolting. If this was Tiny's monster, I could understand its being sensitive to the revulsion it might cause. And wrongly, for I felt to the core that the creature was good.

It winked at me. I don't mean blinked. It winked. And then everything happened at once.

The creature was gone, and in seconds there was a disturbance in the water by the yacht. Something gray and wet reached up out of the river, and I saw it was going for that little girl. Only a tyke—about three, she was. Red hair just like yours. And it thumped that child in the small of the back just enough to knock her over—into the river.

And can you believe it? I just sat there watching and said never a word! It didn't seem right to me that that baby could be struggling in the water. *But it didn't seem wrong, either!*

Well, before I could get my wits together, Tiny was off the wall like a hairy bullet and streaking through the water. I have often wondered why his feet are so big; I never will again. The hound is built like the lower half of a paddle wheel! In two shakes he had the baby by the scruff of the neck and was bringing her back to me. No one had seen that child get pushed, Alistair! No one but me. But there was a man on the yacht who must have seen her fall. He was all over the deck, roaring orders and getting in the way of things, and by the time he had his wherry in the water, Tiny had reached me with the little girl. She wasn't frightened, either—she thought it was a grand joke! Wonderful youngster.

So the man came ashore, all gratitude and tears, and wanted to goldplate Tiny or something. Then he saw me. "That your dog?" I said it was my daughter's. She was in St. Croix on her honeymoon. Before I could stop him, he had a checkbook out and was scratching away at it. He said he knew my kind. Said he knew I'd never accept a thing for myself, but wouldn't refuse something for my daughter. I enclose the check. Why he picked a sum like thirteen thousand, I'll never know. Anyhow, I know it'll be a help to you. Since the money really comes from Tiny's monster, I suppose I can confess that getting Alec to put up the money—even though he would have to clean out his savings and mortgage his estate—would be a good idea if he were one of the family, because then he'd have you to help him make it all back again—that was all my idea. Sometimes, though, watching you, I wonder if I really had to work so all-fired hard to get you nice people married to each other.

Well, I imagine that closes the business of Tiny's monster. There are a lot of things we'll probably never know. I can guess some things, though. It could communicate with a dog but not with a human, unless it half killed itself trying. Apparently a dog is telepathic with humans to a degree, though it probably doesn't understand a lot of what it gets. I don't speak French, but I could probably transcribe French phonetically well enough so a Frenchman could read it. Tiny was transcribing that way. The monster could "send" through him and control him completely. It no doubt indoctrinated the dog—if I can use the term—the day old Debbil took him up the waterline. And when the monster caught, through Tiny, the mental picture of you when Dr. Schwellenbach mentioned you, it went to work through the dog to get you working on its problem. Mental pictures—that's probably what the monster used. That's how Tiny could tell one book from another without being able to read. You visualize everything you think about. What do you think? *I* think that mine's as good a guess as any.

You might be amused to learn that last night all the compasses in this neighborhood pointed west for a couple of hours! 'By, now, chillun. Keep on being happy.

> Love and love, and a kiss for Alec,
> Mum.

P.S. Is St. Croix really a nice place to honeymoon? Jack—he's the fellow who signed the check—is getting very sentimental. He's very like your father. A widower, and—Oh, I don't know. Says fate, or something, brought us together. Said he hadn't planned to take a trip upriver with the baby, but something drove him to it. He can't imagine why he anchored just there. Seemed a good idea at the time. Maybe it was fate. He is very sweet. I wish I could forget that wink I saw in the water.

Mack Reynolds

THE DISCORD MAKERS

There are Those Who Guide, as in William Temple's "A Date to Remember" earlier in this book. And there are Those Who Take Over, as here. This theme, which is commonly known as the "we're property" idea, is very frequently used in mass-produced science fiction, since it is easy to work up some unsubtle shudders over the notion of Things that secretly surmount us.

"The Discord Makers" is included in this book as the only compleat exemplar of this theme—and a very effective one, because it is so uncomfortably circumstantial in its approach. Change a few names, and who can say for sure that this is not a situation that exists? It would certainly be an easy way to explain some of the insanities that beset the Earth.

HARVEY TODD, Director of the Department of Security, initialed two papers, put them aside, and reached for another report. He didn't bother to look up. "Wish you'd make this brief as possible, Ross. I'm up to my ears."

"Chief," Ross Wooley said hesitantly, "suppose I wanted to investigate something on my own, follow up a hunch?"

His superior shot a quizzical look at the undersized agent. "What d'ya have in mind?"

"It's something screwy," the other answered. "Something that'll sound like I'm around the corner."

Harvey Todd put down his pen and grinned at his best operative. "You must have a lulu this time, Ross, but your reputation's good and your hunches've been so far. What is it?"

Wooley scratched his chin with a thumbnail. "Chief," he said slowly, not sure how his words would be received, "I've got reasons to suspect there might be aliens in the United States."

The Department of Security head scowled at him. "Of course there're aliens here. What of it? That's not our jurisdiction."

"I mean aliens from space, some other planet, maybe."

"Are you drunk?"

"No, sir."

Harvey Todd stared at him for a long time without saying anything. Finally he muttered, "Let's hear it."

"I'd like permission to investigate. If I can't have it, I'd like leave of absence to probe around on my own. If I can't have that, I'll submit my resignation so that I'll be free to look into this as a private citizen." The little agent's eyes blinked rapidly behind his shell-rimmed glasses.

Todd glanced down at the pile of letters on his desk and sighed. He brushed them aside, reached into a drawer of his desk, and brought out a prehistoric brier and a can of tobacco. He didn't speak again until the pipe was filled and lit and he was leaning back in his chair, puffing at it. Then he said, "This seems to mean quite a bit to you. What d'ya have?"

The agent stirred uncomfortably. "Not enough to

make sense, chief. An article here, a news item there, some quotations from obscure scientists; more hunch than anything else. What I'd like is enough time to make a preliminary investigation. If I get anything definite, I'll report. Then it's up to you."

Harvey Todd let smoke trickle through his nostrils and squinted worriedly through it. "Give me more than that, Ross. I can't assign an agent to go around searching for characters out of Buck Rogers without having some idea what he's working on."

"You said my reputation was good."

Todd picked up his pen and doodled a series of cubes on a pad before him. "It's bad for the department to be held up to ridicule, Ross. We've been under fire several times this past year. I can think of several congressmen who'd like to know we assign agents to tail men from Mars."

"Then you'd prefer my resignation?" The dynamic little agent's voice was tight.

His chief grunted disgustedly, then suddenly made up his mind. "No, damn it! Make your investigation. But, for heaven's sake, keep it quiet. If it gets into the papers, I'll have you counting your toes on Alcatraz before I'm through with you, Ross."

Ross Wooley grinned. "Thanks. Er . . . I'll have to do some traveling."

"See Smith about it on your way out. Now beat it. I think you're crazy." Harvey Todd took up his pen and another stack of letters, sighed, and went back to work.

A maid ushered him into the study. He gave the room a quick once-over and gained an impression of endless shelves of books, several comfortable chairs, good lighting, two well-conceived oils on the walls, a small portable bar. A scholar's room but, at the same time, a man's.

Professor André Dumar looked up from his chair with a frown, then squinted at the card in his hand again. "Mr. Ross Wooley?"

"That's right." The agent turned and looked at the maid. She left the room, closing the heavy door behind her.

"Sit down, Mr. Wooley," the professor said. "You don't look the way Hollywood leads us to believe a Security agent does."

Ross Wooley didn't smile. He'd heard the equivalent too often before. "My strong point as an operative, Professor."

Dumar said, "About thirty years ago, while I was still an undergraduate, I recall writing a paper for my anthropology class entitled 'Primitive Communism among the Amerindians.' Otherwise, I can't think of anything in my life that would call for a visit from a Department of Security man."

Wooley grinned and selected a chair. "I came for information, Professor. You seem to be an authority on several obscure subjects; sort of an *off-trail* specialist."

"That sounds as though it needs amplification."

"You confine your research to subjects many men of science, fearing ridicule, deliberately avoid. Mental telepathy and clairvoyance, for instance; you were a pioneer in their early study."

The professor nodded. "Actually out of my line, but a fascinating investigation. Now the ice is broken, more capable specialists than I are doing yeoman work in ESP."

Ross Wooley ran his left hand nervously over his chin. "Before we go further, Professor, I'd like you to understand that no matter how strange the things I ask you, the department requests that you not discuss them, even with family members."

Professor Dumar scowled and studied Ross Wooley's card again. "This says you're a government agent. Prove it, please."

Wooley smiled. "A sensible precaution, sir." He drew his wallet from his pocket and held it over for the other's inspection.

The professor went over the credentials carefully, then picked up the telephone and dialed the operator. "Give me the Department of Security, please. . . . Hello. This is Professor André Dumar. Here in my study is a man claiming to be Ross Wooley. Have you an agent of that name? . . . Thank you. Will you now describe him? Thank you very much. Good-by."

The professor returned the wallet and relaxed in his chair. "You seem to be what you claim. What are your questions?"

Ross Wooley framed the first carefully. "Professor, is there life in the Universe besides that found on Earth?"

Dumar removed his pince-nez glasses and stared. "Life?"

"Yes. Alien life."

The scientist considered for a moment, then said slowly, "We are quite positive that at least vegetation exists on Mars, but it's unlikely any of the other planets have life forms."

"How about other star systems?"

"Of course, the authorities differ considerably . . ."

"I'm asking *your* opinion, Professor," Wooley said.

The other shifted in his chair, as though the agent's questions irritated him. "Given the multitude of stars in our Universe, it is likely that the conditions applying in our Solar System are duplicated elsewhere. In such case, I should say that life is probably also duplicated."

"Intelligent life?" Wooley pursued.

"Possibly."

"Now this is the important question, Professor. Granting that life does exist elsewhere, could representatives of it have made their way to Earth?"

Professor Dumar flicked a fingernail against the gold rim of his glasses. "Who informed you of my research into this subject?" he snapped.

Pay dirt, the agent breathed. Then, even more earnestly, "Nobody, Professor. It was a strike in the dark. Please tell me what you can."

Dumar got to his feet and went over to his portable bar. "Drink?" he asked over his shoulder.

"No, thanks." This was the first break in the investigation. The little agent was stimulated enough without alcohol.

"If you don't mind, I'll have one." The professor mixed himself whisky and water and returned to his chair. He took half the drink down in a gulp, then launched into his subject.

"I became aware about three years ago that there were unnatural life forms on Earth. They had seemingly been here for a lengthy period, but, nevertheless, something was wrong about them. My first clue was the fact that they seemed to revolt other animals, including Man."

Wooley injected. "How do you mean, *revolt?*"

The professor ran a hand through his hair in irritation, as though it were difficult to explain. "Take the spider, for instance, or the snake; there's an instinctive loathing that nine out of ten persons feel at the sight of either. I believe it's because we know they don't *belong.* They're alien to Earth, and, subconsciously, we realize it and our flesh crawls. To this list you might also add the rat and the cockroach."

Ross Wooley scratched his chin with a thumbnail. "I've always thought the fear of the snake and spider was instinctive, handed down from primitive Man. They're poisonous, after all."

The professor shook his head. "That doesn't answer it. For one thing, few snakes and fewer spiders are poisonous. For another, it's more than just fear—it's absolute revulsion we feel. Besides, predatory animals killed more of primitive Man than did the snake or spider. Why don't we feel this instinctive fear when we see lions, bears, or wolves? In addition, you'll find we have somewhat the same loathing, though not so strong for some reason, of rats and cockroaches, though they aren't poisonous."

The agent grimaced. "But how did they get here? Surely, you don't suggest that snakes, or spiders, or even rats have the ability to construct spaceships."

"Frankly, that's been the greatest obstacle to my theory. I have two possible answers; neither quite satisfies me."

"Do you mind explaining them?"

"One possibility is that a spaceship arrived here a considerable time ago and crashed. The alien life forms it carried were forced to remain. However, the conditions on Terra were different from those on their home planet and they weren't completely successful in adapting themselves. They degenerated until now they are on a par with unintelligent life forms."

Ross Wooley was unsatisfied. "What led you to that theory?"

"For one thing, I note indications that the rat once held a higher stage on the scale of evolution. You'll find that the rat sometimes decorates its nest with broken pieces of colored glass or shiny bits of metal. Could it have the remnants of an aesthetic sense?"

"Or the beginnings of one?" Wooley suggested.

"Possibly. I'm not too strong for this theory. The theory I like best is that they're guinea pigs," the professor said.

"Guinea pigs?"

"That's right. Suppose some other planet wanted room for expansion and saw Earth as a prospective colony. Rather than risk unknown diseases, or other deadly possibilities, they would simply land a number of inferior life forms from their planet. If the snake, spider, and rat could adapt themselves, without harm, to the Earth, then these aliens could take over."

Ross Wooley blinked. "Professor, it seems to me that the weakest point in these theories of yours is the fact that these forms of life have been on Earth indefinitely. The cockroach, for instance; it seems to me I've read that it's one of Earth's oldest inhabitants. And all of them, snake, spider, rat, have been here since far back in the most primitive periods."

Dumar sipped his drink thoughtfully. "We don't know that the aliens are in any particular hurry. They might be willing to wait hundreds of thousands of years to be sure Earth is suitable for their species. To a young civilization like ours, a few thousand years seems an endless time, but to a culture that might be many millions of years in age, it's a short period indeed."

"Then, to sum it up, you believe there is other intelligent life in the Universe and that, for one reason or other, they've landed alien life forms on Earth."

The professor nodded. "That's about it."

The next name took him across the continent to San Francisco; he'd have hesitated before expending the time and money involved if it hadn't been for the renewed interest Dumar had inspired.

First saying, "This comes from one of your recent lectures," the agent took a news clipping from an envelope and read aloud. ". . . In fact, so chaotic are Man's affairs, so unbelievable is it he could thus be his own worst enemy, that one is led to believe aliens from space, enemies for some unknown reason, are in our midst and sabotaging our efforts toward progress. . . ."

Wooley looked up. "I assume the quotation is correct?"

The nationally known lecturer and commentator, in whose office they sat, frowned but nodded. "Substantially."

"What did you mean by it?"

Morton Harrison ran an irritated hand through his famous snow-white hair. "I didn't mean anything by it. What in the world are you driving at?"

Ross Wooley returned the clipping to his pocket. "Where did you get the idea that there is a possibility of aliens from space being in our midst?"

The other began to laugh. Finally, "Good heavens, man, has the Department of Security finally reached the point where it's investigating characters out of science fiction? That illustration meant nothing; I thought of it out of a clear sky."

Wooley had pulled another blank. He sighed in resignation and leaned back in his chair. "All right, Mr. Harrison. But now I'm here, and just for the record, what were you illustrating when you used that example?"

The other rose to his feet and flicked his right arm in the gesture so well known to his audiences. Unthinkingly, his voice and movements took on his platform mannerisms. "I was only pointing out that Man is his own enemy to such an extent that it seems unbelievable."

"Such as what?" Ross asked.

Morton Harrison tugged at his right ear. "I could give a score of examples, but let me suggest just one or two.

"First, have you ever noticed that persons and organizations that strive for Man's advancement are usually either given the silent treatment or laughed to scorn? Take our pacifists, for instance. Most people think of them as crackpots. They're made light of in peace, and in times of war, thrown into concentration camps or jail. Almost everyone claims he is against war; why, then, this contempt for the persons who work hardest to end it?"

Ross Wooley ran a thumbnail over his chin reflectively. "Never thought of it that way," he admitted.

"Let me use another example," Harrison continued. "In this country we like to speak of our freedoms, but, actually, there are few places where we find more intolerance and persecution. In our Southern states, the example is obvious; and throughout the nation we have anti-Semitism. But that's only the beginning. On the West Coast we have discrimination against those of Japanese descent in some areas, those of Mexican descent in others. In central California there is discrimination against those of Portuguese descent. In the Northern Great Lakes area, the Finns are the butt; in the Southwest, the American Indian.

"Nor is the practice limited to our nation. When we Americans go abroad we often find cutting indication that we are scorned, disliked, considered *pushers* and moneygrabbers by other nationalities. It's amusing. America, England, France, and the other United Nations sneered at the German and Japanese claims to being supermen, *herrenvolk;* but, actually, we all practice the same delusion."

Wooley stirred as though to protest at least part of the lecture he was being given, but the other held up a restraining hand and went on.

"The point is that instead of encouraging and fighting for such things as the end of war, a better social system, for an end to intolerance and racial discrimination, the average person is actually led to revile, or at least be disdainful of, those who work to those ends. We seem to be deliberately fighting against the very things we want most."

Ross Wooley returned his note pad to his pocket and got to his feet. "I suppose I see your point. I don't agree with you entirely, but at least I get what you meant in your reference to visitors from space." He held out his hand to be shaken.

The Harrison interview had been disappointing, and only one other name remained on the list he'd compiled. He scowled at it, not liking a Los Angeles address even when the man's name was followed by a Ph.D. The City of Angels, home of the crackpot, he told himself. The guy'd probably claim he had a whole cellar full of Martians.

However, Dr. Kenneth Keith, President of the Western Rocket Society and a leading member of a Fortean group, was too near not to see. Ross Wooley took a plane to L.A. and a cab to the home of the man who had written an article on the possibilities of space travel.

It took him five minutes to convince Mrs. Keith he wasn't a science-fiction fan, trying to meet the President of the Rocket Society for the purpose of arguing over the desirability of using nitric acid and aniline for fuel, instead of nitric acid and vinyl ethyl, in the first Moon rocket.

When he finally found himself in the doctor's study,

he hesitated before beginning. He'd had so many rebuffs.

The doctor took the initiative. "You're probably here about my article in which I mentioned the presence of beings from other plants on Terra."

Ross Wooley blinked at him. "How . . ."

Dr. Keith grinned and held up two hands in an expressive shrug. "It's been suggested, even proven, a score of times. It's only recently come to my attention just why the proof has been ignored, and I think it about time the situation is exposed. That's why I emphasized that although Man is on the verge of discovering space travel, he is not the first to utilize it."

Wooley leaned forward excitedly. "Before we go any further, you say that the fact of space travel has been proven a score of times. Name one."

Kenneth Keith rose and strode over to one of the bookcases that lined the walls. He returned with a volume that he tossed into the lap of the Department of Security agent. "There's proof," he said.

Ross Wooley took it up eagerly, read the title, and then snorted in disgust. "*Lo!* by Charles Fort."

Keith shot a finger out at him. "That's what I'm talking about. Why were you disgusted when you saw the *proof* I offered?"

The little agent tossed the book contemptuously to a coffee table which sat before him. "I'm afraid Fort isn't exactly acceptable as proof. He's commonly thought of as a crack—" He stopped, suddenly remembering what Morton Harrison had told him. Those persons who were foremost in fighting Man's battle of progress were scorned as crackpots, nuts, lunatics. So was Fort.

"All right," he said. "I'm listening. Tell me things."

Dr. Kenneth Keith beamed and launched happily into his subject. "In the past century it's been established a score of times that there's travel to this planet from others. Fort, among others, proves it quite conclusively in his books. I've been aware of this for years, and I've been puzzled because the fact hasn't been widely accepted. I've recently found the reason."

"And what is that reason?" asked Wooley, now tensed in expectation.

"We who have suspected the existence of these visitors have always thought of them as merely that— *visitors.* Most of us supposed they didn't reveal themselves to us openly because they thought of Man as a backward creature and not ready for intercourse with more advanced life forms."

Ross Wooley stirred. "But what is it you've discovered?"

The rocket authority stared seriously into the agent's face. "They aren't *visitors,* they're *conquerors.* Possibly we're already property, as Charles Fort suggested, but I'm inclined to think that our potential masters thus far haven't assimilated Terra."

Ross Wooley fingered the skin on his throat, as though he'd just finished shaving and was checking to find whether he'd done a good job. "I'm afraid I don't follow you."

The other jabbed out a finger again to emphasize his point. "No conqueror ever bothers to take over a worthless desert or an uninhabited mountain range. Before it's worth acquiring an area, it has to be populated by those you can exploit. For hundreds and thousands of years these aliens have visited Terra. We weren't ready for conquest as yet, but they were interested in watching us develop along the lines they thought best; sometimes they even helped.

"As we finally approached an advanced civilization, they increasingly took control of our destiny. They wanted us to progress along a certain route and made sure we did. Among other things: long after war has become ridiculous, they see to it that we remain warlike; they nurture our superstitions and our intolerances; they keep us divided into nations, classes, races, different religious groups.

"We've finally almost reached the point where we have space travel ourselves, and it's at this period they grow more evident. Obviously, they're about ready to assume their role as rulers."

"But why . . ."

Keith jumped to his feet and paced the room impatiently. "Perhaps they have bred us for soldiers to be used in their interplanetary or interstellar wars. Perhaps we are to be slaves. All I know is that they are beginning to take over. They're assuming positions of power in our governments, our communication centers, our educational systems. In this manner they've been able to laugh Fort, and other farseeing humans of his type, to scorn."

He broke off his tirade and sat down again to face the undersized agent. "The proof, Mr. Wooley, is endless. Take the recent flying saucers . . ."

Harvey Todd, Director of the Department of Security, finally looked up from the papers before him, removed his pipe—long since gone out—from his mouth, and said, "This is quite a report, Ross." His expression was quizzical.

The agent had been sitting to one side, nervously fingering his chin, while his chief read the score or more pages he'd typed up. "Yes, sir," he said.

"I'd like to have your own summation, since you were the one who secured the material. What's your opinion?"

Ross Wooley ran his thumbnail back and forth over his chin. "Briefly this, sir. A helluva long time ago, when Earth was in its infancy, the first explorers from other planets arrived. They left various life forms here from their own world to see whether they would survive. The snake and spider are examples. Then, as Man evolved, they assumed a certain amount of direction of his development. The way they directed us is an indication that they aren't exactly benevolent. Nobody could call it that. Never.

"We've finally reached a point where it's to their interest to take a more active part in our affairs. I think they're on the verge of assimilating us. It's been suggested that some of them have already infiltrated high positions in Man's educational system, government, and so forth."

The chief smiled broadly. "You really believe that, eh?"

Ross Wooley flushed. "Yes, sir," he said stubbornly.

"That there's an alien underground—perhaps I should call it an *overhead* since they come from the stars—working within the framework of our government?"

Ross Wooley blinked rapidly behind his heavy glasses and nodded. "Yes, sir. And I believe that the most important thing in the world today is to expose these enemies of the human race; root them out, de—"

Harvey Todd interrupted. "Suppose I tell you to drop it, that it's a lot of nonsense?"

"In that case, sir, I'd resign from the department and continue the investigation on my own."

The Department of Security head looked at him for a long moment. Finally, "O.K., Ross. Sorry." He pressed a button on his desk and a section of the wall slid back silently. Two strangely clad figures stepped out of the passage behind it. They weren't human—not exactly.

The chief eyed his agent laconically. "You were right in believing we of Aldebaran—it's Aldebaran, not Mars or Venus—have assumed positions of power in your fantastic Earth governments."

He turned to the first of the strangers, who had covered Wooley with an ugly weapon. "Dispose of him in the usual way."

Ross Wooley's hand streaked for his left shoulder. A pale light gleamed momentarily; he dropped his gun, stiffened, and began to slump forward. The two aliens grabbed him as he fell and began to drag his body to the passageway.

"Just a moment," Harvey Todd called. "Take along this report. There're several names on it that'll call for a visit from us, a Professor Dumar and a Dr. Keith, in particular."

He glanced at the pile of papers on his desk and sighed. "Now get out of here. I'm up to my ears in work."

A. E. Van Vogt

NOT ONLY DEAD MEN

In this last tale from the Immediate Past, some sort of saurian visitants are in trouble and land their spaceship on Earth, near a whaling vessel peacefully pursuing its maritime affairs. The spaceship is fleeing from another sort of alien, a true monster that is a threat to both human and saurian.

The solution to this fantastic three-way struggle is one that—in the final paragraph or so of the story—provides one with a dizzying expansion of horizon that suddenly becomes Galaxy-wide in scope. Curiously enough, this enormous change is somehow comforting to the human animal, who until now has felt his bitter aloneness in the Cosmos.

For we are not alone, this story says; we are not alone. . . .

WHALESHIP FOUND
  BATTERED DERELICT OFF
    NORTHERN ALASKA

June 29, 1942—Smashed in every timber, and with no trace of the crew, the whaleship *Albatross* was found today by an American patrol ship in the Bering Strait. Naval authorities are mystified by reports that the deck and sides of the schooner were staved in as by gigantic blows not caused "by bombs, torpedoes, shellfire, or other enemy action," according to the word received. The galley stoves were said to be still warm, and, as there have been no storms in this region for three weeks, no explanation has been forthcoming.

The *Albatross* sailed from a West Coast American port early in March, with Captain Frank Wardell and a crew of eighteen, all of whom are missing.

Captain Wardell, of the whaleship *Albatross,* was thinking so darkly of the three long whaleless months just past that he had started to edge the schooner through the narrows before he saw the submarine lying near the shore in the sheltered waters of that far-northern bay of Alaska.

His mind did a spinning dive into blankness. When he came up for air, his reflexes were already working. The engine-room indicator stood at REVERSE FULL SPEED. And his immediate plan was as clear as it was simple.

He parted his lips to shout at the wheelman, then closed them again, made for the wheel, and, as the ship began to go backward, guided her deftly behind the line of shoals and the headland of trees. The anchor went down with a rattle and a splash that echoed strangely in the windless morning.

Silence settled where the man-made sound had been; and there was only the quiet ripple of that remote northern sea, the restless waters lapping gently against the *Albatross,* washing more sullenly over the shoals behind which she lay, and occasionally letting out a roar as a great wave smashed with a white fury at a projecting rock.

Wardell, back on the small bridge, stood very still, letting his mind absorb impressions, and—listening.

But no alien sound came to disturb his straining ears, no Diesel engines raging into life, no fainter hum of powerful electric motors. He began to breathe more steadily. He saw that his first mate, Preedy, had slipped softly up beside him.

Preedy said in a low voice, "I don't think they saw us, sir. There was not a soul in sight. And, besides, they're obviously not fit to go to sea."

"Why not?"

"Didn't you notice, sir—they haven't got a conning tower? It must have been shot away."

Wardell was silent, shocked at himself for not having noticed. The vague admiration that had begun to grow inside him at the cool way in which he handled the ship deflated a little.

Another thought came into his mind; and he scowled with a dark reluctance at the very idea of revealing a further deficiency in his observation. But he began grudgingly:

"Funny how your mind accepts the presence of things that aren't there." He hesitated; then, "I didn't even notice whether or not their deck gun was damaged."

It was the mate who was silent now. Wardell gave a swift glance at the man's long face, realized that the mate was undergoing a private case of shock and annoyance, and said quickly, "Mr. Preedy, call the men forward."

Conscious again of superiority, Wardell went down to the deck. With great deliberateness he began examining the antisub gun beside the whale gun. He could hear the men gathering behind him, but he did not turn until feet began to shuffle restlessly.

He looked them over then, glancing from face to rough, tough, leatherbeaten face. Fifteen men and a boy, not counting the engineer and his assistant—and every one of them looking revitalized, torn out of the glumness that had been the stock expression around the ship for three months.

Wardell's mind flashed back over the long years some of these men had been with him; he nodded, his heavy face dark with satisfaction, and began, "Looks like we've got a disabled Jap sub cornered in there, men. Our duty's clear. The navy gave us a three-inch gun and four machine guns before we sailed, and—"

He stopped, frowned at one of the older men. "What's the matter, Kenniston?"

"Begging your pardon, cap'n, that thing in there isn't a sub. I was in the service in '18, and I can tell one at a glance, conning tower bombed off or not.

"Why, that vessel in there has metal walls like dark scales—didn't you notice? We've got *something* cornered in there, sir, but it isn't a sub."

From where he lay with his little expedition, behind the line of rock ledge, Wardell studied the strange vessel. The long, astoundingly hard walk to reach this vantage point had taken more than an hour. And now that he was here, what about it?

Through his binoculars, the—ship—showed as a streamlined, cigar-shaped, dead metal that lay motionless in the tiny pattern of waves that shimmered atop the waters of the bay. There was no other sign of life. Nevertheless—

Wardell suddenly stiffened, with a sharp consciousness of his responsibilities—all these men, six here with him, carrying two of the precious machine guns, and the other men on the schooner.

The alienness of the vessel, with its dark, scaly metal walls, its great length, struck him with a sudden chill. Behind him somebody said into the silence of that bleak, rocky landscape, "If only we had a radio sending set! What a bomber could do to that target! I—"

Wardell was only dimly aware of the way the man's voice sank queerly out of audibility. He was thinking heavily: two machine guns against *that*. Or, rather—even the mental admission of greater strength came unwillingly—four machine guns and a three-incher. After all, the weapons back on the *Albatross* had to be included, even though the schooner seemed dangerously far away. He—

His mind went dead slowly. With a start, he saw that the flat, dark reach of deck below was showing movement; a large metal plate turning, then jerking open as if springs had snapped at it with irresistible strength. Through the hatchway thus created, a figure was coming.

A figure—a *beast*. The thing reared up on horny, gleaming legs, and its scales shone in the late morning sun. Of its four arms, one was clutching a flat, crystalline structure, a second held a small, blunt object that showed faintly crimson in the dazzling sunbeams. The other two arms were at ease.

The monster stood there under Earth's warm sun,

NOT ONLY DEAD MEN

silhouetted against the background of limpid, blue-green sea; stood there arrogantly, its beast head flung back on its short neck with such pride and confidence that Wardell felt a tingle at the nape of his neck.

"For Heaven's sake," a man whispered hoarsely, "put some bullets in it."

The sound, more than the words, reached into the region of Wardell's brain that controlled his muscles.

"Shoot!" he rasped. "Frost! Withers!"

Chat-chat-chat! The two machine guns yammered into life, wakening a thousand echoes in the virgin silence of the cove.

The figure, which had started striding briskly along the curving deck in the direction away from shore, its webbed feet showing plainly at each step, stopped short, turned—and looked up.

Eyes as green and fiery as a cat's at night blazed at —seemingly straight at—Wardell's face. The captain felt the muscles of his body constrict; his impulse was to jerk back behind the ledge, out of sight, but he couldn't have moved to save his life.

The mind-twisting emotion must have been evoked in every man present. For the machine guns ceased their stammering; and there was unnatural silence.

The yellow-green reptile moved first. It started to run, back toward the hatch. Reaching the opening, it stooped and seemed about to leap down headfirst, as if it couldn't get in too quickly.

Instead of going down, however, it handed the crystalline object that it had held in one hand to somebody below; then it straightened.

There was a clang as the hatch banged shut—and the reptile stood alone on the deck, cut off from escape.

The scene froze like that for a fraction of a second, a tableau of rigid figures against a framework of quiet

sea and dark, almost barren land. The beast stood absolutely still, its head flung back, its blazing eyes fixed on
the men behind the ledge.

Wardell had not thought of its posture as a crouching
one, but abruptly it straightened visibly and bounced
upward and sideways, like a frog leaping or a diver jack-
knifing. Water and beast met with a faint splash. When
the shimmering veil of agitated water subsided, the beast
was gone.

They waited.

"What goes down," Wardell said finally in a voice
that had in it the faintest shiver, "must come up. Heaven
only knows what it is, but hold your guns ready."

The minutes dragged. The shadow of a breeze that
had been titillating the surface of the bay died completely; and the water took on a flat, glassy sheen that
was broken only far out near the narrow outlet to the
rougher sea beyond.

After ten minutes, Wardell was twisting uneasily, dis-
satisfied with his position. At the end of twenty minutes
he stood up.

"We've got to get back to the ship," he said tensely.
"This thing is too big for us."

They were edging along the shore five minutes later
when the clamor started: a distant shouting, then a long,
sharp rattle of machine-gun fire, then—silence.

It had come from where the schooner lay, out of their
line of vision behind the bank of trees half a mile across
the bay.

Wardell grunted as he ran. It had been hard enough
walking—earlier. Now he was in an agony of jolts and
half stumbles. Twice, during the first few minutes, he
fell heavily.

The second time he got up very slowly and waited for
his panting men to catch up with him. There was no

more running because—it struck him with piercing sharpness—what had happened on the ship *had* happened.

Gingerly, Wardell led the way over the rock-strewn shore, with its wilderness of chasms. He kept cursing softly under his breath in a sweat of fury with himself for having left the *Albatross*. And there was a special rage at the very idea that he had automatically set his fragile wooden ship against an armored sub.

Even though, as it had turned out, it wasn't a sub.

His brain stalled before the bare contemplation of what it might be.

For a moment he tried, mentally tried, to picture himself here, struggling over the barren shore of this rocky inlet in order to see what a—lizard—had done to his ship. And he couldn't. The picture wouldn't piece together. It was not woven even remotely of the same cloth as all that life of quiet days and evenings he had spent on the bridges of ships, just sitting or smoking his pipe, mindlessly contemplating the sea.

Even more dim and unconnectable was the civilization of back-room poker games and loud-laughing, bold-eyed women who made up his life during those brief months when he was in harbor—that curious, aimless life that he always gave up so willingly when the time came to put to sea again.

Wardell pushed the gray, futile memory from him and said, "Frost, take Blakeman and McCann and pick up one drum of water. Danny ought to have them all filled by now. No, keep your machine gun. I want you to stay with the remaining drums till I send some more men. We're going to get that water and then get out of here."

Wardell felt the better for his definite decision. He would head south for the naval base; and then others, better equipped and trained, would tackle the alien ship.

If only his ship were still there, intact—just what he feared he wasn't certain. He was conscious of the queasiest thrill of relief as he topped the final and steepest hill —and there she was. Through his glasses he made out the figures of men on the deck. And the last sodden weight of anxiety in him yielded to the fact that, barring accidents to individuals, everything was all right.

Something had happened, of course. In minutes he would know—

For a time it seemed as if he would never get the story. The men crowded around him as he clambered aboard, more weary than he cared to admit. The babble of voices that raged at him, the blazing excitement of everyone, did not help.

Words came through about a beast "like a man-sized frog" that had come aboard. There was something about the engine room, and incomprehensibility about the engineer and his assistant waking up, and—

Wardell's voice, stung into a bass blare by the confusion, brought an end to the madness. The captain said crisply, "Mr. Preedy, any damage?"

"None," the mate replied, "though Rutherford and Cressy are still shaky."

The reference to the engineer and his assistant was obscure, but Wardell ignored it. "Mr. Preedy, dispatch six men ashore to help bring the water aboard. Then come to the bridge."

A few minutes later, Preedy was giving Wardell a complete account of what had happened. At the end of the machine-gun fire from Wardell's party, all the men had crowded to port side of the ship and had stayed there.

The watery tracks left by the creature showed that it had used the opportunity to climb aboard the starboard side and had gone below. It was first seen standing at the fo'c'sle hatchway, coolly looking over the forward deck where the guns were.

The thing actually started boldly forward under the full weight of nine pairs of eyes, apparently heading straight for the guns; abruptly, however, it turned and made a running dive overboard. Then the machine guns started.

"I don't think we hit him," Preedy confessed.

Wardell was thoughtful. "I'm not sure," he said, "that it's bothered by bullets. It—" He stopped himself. "What the devil am I saying? It runs every time we fire. But go on."

"We went through the ship and that's when we found Rutherford and Cressy. They were out cold, and they don't remember a thing. There's no damage, though, engineer says; and, well, that's all."

It was enough, Wardell thought, but he said nothing. He stood for a while, picturing the reality of a green-and-yellow lizard climbing aboard his ship. He shuddered. What could the damned thing have wanted?

The sun was high in the middle heavens to the south when the last drum of water was hoisted aboard and the whaler began to move.

Up on the bridge, Wardell heaved a sigh of relief as the ship nosed well clear of the white-crested shoals and headed into deep water. He was pushing the engine-room indicator to FULL SPEED AHEAD when the thud of the Diesels below became a cough that—ended.

The *Albatross* coasted along from momentum, swishing softly from side to side. In the dimly lighted region that was the engine room, Wardell found Rutherford on the floor, laboriously trying to light a little pool of oil with a match.

The action was so mad that the captain stopped, stared, and then stood there speechless and intent.

For the oil wouldn't take fire. Four matches joined the burned ends on the floor beside the golden puddle. Then:

"Hell's bells!" said Wardell, "you mean that *thing* put something in our oil that—"

He couldn't go on; and there was no immediate answer. But finally, without looking up, the engineer said thickly, "Skipper, I've been tryin' ta think. Wha' for would a bunch of lizards be wantin' us to lay to here?"

Wardell went back on deck without replying. He was conscious of hunger. But he had no illusions about the empty feeling inside him. No craving for food had ever made him feel like that.

Wardell ate, scarcely noticing his food, and came out into the open feeling logy and sleepy. The climb to the bridge took all his strength and will. He stood for a moment looking out across the narrows that led into the bay.

He made a discovery. In the brief minutes that the Diesels had operated on the untainted oil in the pipes, the *Albatross* had moved to a point where the dark vessel in the distance was now visible across the bows.

Wardell studied the silent alien ship sleepily, then gazed along the shore line through his glasses. Finally he turned his attention to the deck in front of him. And nearly jumped out of his skin.

The *thing* was there, calmly bending over the whale gun, its scaly body shining like the wet hide of a big lizard. Water formed in little dark pools at its feet, spread damply to where Gunner Art Zote lay face downward, looking very dead.

If the interloper had been a man, Wardell was sure he could have forced his paralyzed muscles to draw the revolver that hung from his belt. Or even if the thing had been as far away as when he had first seen it.

But he was standing there less than twenty-five feet from it, staring down at that glistening, reptilian monstrosity with its four arms and its scale-armored legs; and the knowledge in the back of his mind that machine-gun bullets hadn't hurt it before, and—

With a cool disregard for possible watching eyes, the reptile began to tug at the harpoon where it protruded from the snout of the whale gun. It gave up after a second and went around to the breech of the gun. It was fumbling there, the crimson thing it held flashing with spasmodic incarnadine brilliance, when a wave of laughter and voices shattered the silence of the afternoon.

The next second the galley door burst open and a dozen men debouched upon the deck. The solid wooden structure that was the entrance to the fo'c'sle hid the beast from their sight.

They stood for a moment, their ribald laughter echoing to the skies above that perpetually cold sea. As from a vast distance, Wardell found himself listening to the rough jokes, the rougher cursing; and he was thinking: like children, they are. Already, the knowledge that the strangest creatures in all creation had marooned them here on a fuelless ship must seem a dim thing in their minds. Or they wouldn't be standing like mindless fools while—

Wardell stopped the thought, astounded that he had allowed it to distract him for a single second. With a gasp, he snatched at his revolver and took aim at the exposed back of the lizard where it was now bending over the strong, dark cable that attached the harpoon to the ship.

Curiously, the shot brought a moment of complete silence. The lizard straightened slowly and turned half in annoyance. And then—

Men shouted. The machine gun in the crow's-nest began to yelp with short, excited bursts that missed the deck and the reptile but made a white foam in the water beyond the ship's bows.

Wardell was conscious of a frantic irritation at the damned fool up there. In the fury of his annoyance he turned his head upward and yelled at the fellow to learn to aim properly. When he looked again at the deck, the beast wasn't there.

The sound of a faint splash permeated through a dozen other noises; and, simultaneously, there was a stampede for the rails as the crew peered down into the water. Over their heads, Wardell thought he caught the yellow-green flash in the depths, but the color merged too swiftly, too easily, with the shifting blue-green-gray of the northern sea.

Wardell stood very still; there was a coldness in the region of his heart, an empty sense of unnormal things. His gun hadn't wavered. The bullet couldn't have missed. Yet nothing had happened.

The clammy tightness inside him eased as he saw Art Zote getting up shakily from the deck, not dead, not dead after all. Abruptly, Wardell was trembling in every muscle. Good old Art. It took more than a scoundrelly lizard to kill a man like that.

"Art!" Wardell yelled in a blaze of his tremendous excitement, "Art, turn the three-incher on that sub. Sink the damn thing. We'll teach those skunks to—"

The first shell was too short. It made a pretty spray a hundred yards from that distant metal hull. The second one was too far; it exploded futilely, stirring a hump of grayish rock on the shore into a brief furious life.

The third smashed squarely on the target. And so did the next ten. It was beautiful shooting, but at the end of it Wardell called down uneasily, "Better stop. The shells don't seem to be penetrating—I can't see any holes.

We'd better save our ammunition for point-blank range, if it comes to that. Besides—"

He fell silent, reluctant to express the thought that had come to his mind, the fact that so far the creatures on that mysterious vessel had done them no harm and that it was the *Albatross* and its crew that were doing all the shooting. There was, of course, that business of their oil being rendered useless and the curious affair just now: the thing coming aboard for the single purpose of studying the harpoon gun. But nevertheless—

He and Preedy talked about it in low, baffled tones during the foggy afternoon and the cold evening, decided finally to padlock all the hatches from inside and put a man with a gun in the crow's-nest.

Wardell wakened to the sound of excited yelling. The sun was just streaking over the horizon when he tumbled out onto the deck, half dressed. He noticed, as he went through the door, that the padlock had been neatly sliced out.

Grim, he joined the little group of men gathered around the guns. It was Art Zote, the gunner, who querulously pointed out the damage. "Look, cap'n, the dirty beggars have cut our harpoon cable. And they've left us some measly copper wire or something in its place. Look at the junk."

Wardell took the extended wire blankly. The whole affair seemed senseless. He was conscious of the gunner's voice continuing to beat at him:

"And the damn stuff's all over the place, too. There's two other harpoon sets, and each set is braced like a bloomin' masthead. They bored holes in the deck and ran the wires through and lashed them to the backbone of the ship. It wouldn't be so bad if the stuff was any good, but that thin wire—Hell!"

"Get me a wire cutter," Wardell soothed. "We'll start clearing it away and—"

Amazingly, it wouldn't cut. He strained with his great strength, but the wire only looked vaguely shiny, and even that might have been a trick of light. Behind him, somebody said in a queer voice, "I think maybe we got a bargain. But what kind of a whale are they getting us ready for?"

Wardell stood very still, startled by the odd phrasing of the words: *What . . . are they getting us ready for?*

He straightened, cold with decision. "Men," he said resonantly, "get your breakfasts. We're going to get to the bottom of this if it's the last thing we ever do."

The oarlocks creaked; the water whispered gently against the side of the rowboat—and every minute Wardell liked his position less.

It struck him, after a moment, that the boat was not heading directly at the vessel, and that their angle of approach was making for a side view of the object he had already noticed at the front of the stranger's metal deck.

He raised his glasses; and then he just sat there too amazed even to exclaim. It was a weapon, all right— *a harpoon gun.*

There was no mistaking it. They hadn't even changed the design, the length of the harpoon, or—Wait a minute! What about the line?

He could make out a toy-sized roller beside the gun, and there was a coppery gleam coming from it that told a complete story.

"They've given us," he thought, "a cable as good as their own, something that will hold—anything." Once again, the chill struck through him, and the words that one of his crew had used: *What kind of a whale—*

"Closer!" he said hoarsely.

He was only dimly conscious that this kind of bold-ness was utterly rash. Careful, he thought, there were too many damn fools in Hell already. Foolhardiness was—

"Closer!" he urged.

At fifty feet, the long, dark hull of the ship, even a part of what was under water, showed plainly; and there wasn't a scratch to indicate where the shells from the three-incher had exploded, not a sign of damage any-where.

Wardell was parting his lips to speak again, his mind hard on his determination to climb aboard under cover of the point-blank range of the machine gun—when there was a thunder of sound.

It was a cataclysmic sound, like whole series of mon-strous guns firing one after the other. The roar echoed hugely from the barren hills and spat backward and for-ward across the natural hollow made by the almost completely landlocked bay.

The long, torpedo-shaped ship began to move. Faster, faster—it made a great half circle, a wave of fiery flashes pouring into the water from its rear; and then, having avoided the rowboat completely, headed for the narrows that led to the open sea.

Suddenly, a shell splashed beside it, then another and a third; Wardell could see the muzzle flame of the three-incher on the distant deck of the *Albatross*. There was no doubt that Art Zote and Preedy thought the hour of crisis was at hand.

But the stranger heeded not. Straight for the narrows it thundered, along the gantlet made by the shallows and then out into the deep water. It rumbled a full mile past the schooner, and then the fiery explosions ceased. The skies emptied of the rolling roar on roar of sound. The ship coasted on momentum, then stopped.

And lay there, silent, lifeless as before, a dark shape protruding out of the restless waters. Somewhere along its course, Art Zote had had the sense to stop his useless firing.

In the silence, Wardell could hear the heavy breathing of the men laboring at the oars. The rowboat shuddered at each thrust and kept twisting as the still turbulent waters of the bay churned against its sides.

Back on the whaler, Wardell called Preedy into his cabin. He poured out two stiff drinks, swallowed his own portion with a single, huge gulp, and said, "My plan is this: We'll fit up the small boat with grub and water and send three men down the coast for help. It's obvious we can't go on playing this game of hide-and-seek without even knowing what the game is about. It shouldn't take three good men more than a week to get to, say, the police station on the Tip, maybe sooner. What do you think?"

What Preedy thought was lost in the clattering of boots. The door burst open. The man who unceremoniously pushed into the room held up two dark objects and yelled, "Look, cap'n, what one of them beasts just threw on board: a flat, metal plate and a bag of something. He got away before we even saw him."

It was the metal board that snatched Wardell's attention, because it seemed to have no purpose. It was half an inch thick by ten inches long by eight wide. It was a silvery, metallic color on one side and black on the other.

That was all. He saw then that Preedy had picked up the bag and opened it. The mate gasped, "Skipper, look! There's a photograph in here of the engine room, with a pointer pointing at a fuel tank—and some gray powder. *It must be to fix up the oil."*

Wardell lowered the metal plate, started to grab for the bag. And stopped himself with a jerk as an abnormality about the—black—of the metal board struck him with all the force of a blow.

It was—three-dimensional. It started at an incredible depth inside the plate, and reached to his eyes. Curious, needle-sharp, intensely bright points of light peered out of the velvety, dead blackness.

As Wardell stared at it, it changed. Something floated onto the upper edge, came nearer, and showed itself against the blackness as a tiny animal.

Wardell thought: "A photograph, by heaven; a moving photograph of some kind."

The thought shredded. A photograph of *what?*

The animal looked tiny, but it was the damnedest horror his eyes had ever gazed on, a monstrous, many-legged, long-bodied, long-snouted, hideous miniature, a very caricature of abnormal life, a mad creation of an insane imagination.

Wardell jumped—for the thing grew huge. It filled half that fantastic plate, and still it looked as if the picture was being taken from a distance.

"What is it?" he heard Preedy gasp over his shoulder.

Wardell did not answer—for the story was unfolding before their eyes.

The fight in space had begun in the only way a devil-Blal was ever contacted: unexpectedly. Violent energies flashed; the inertialess police ship spun desperately as the automatics flared with incandescent destruction— too late.

The monster showed high on the forward visiplate, a thin, orange radiance breaking out from its thick head.

Commander Ral Dorno groaned as he saw the orange radiance hold off the white fire of the patrol vessel—just long enough to ruin the ship.

"Space!" he yelled, "we didn't get his Sensitives in time. We didn't—"

The small ship shuddered from stem to stern. Lights blinked and went out; the communicator huzzaed with alien noise, then went dead. The atomic motors stuttered from their soundless, potent jiving to a hoarse, throbby ratcheting. And stopped.

The spaceship began to fall.

Somewhere behind Dorno, a voice—Senna's—yelled in relief, "Its Sensitives are turning black. We did get it. It's falling, too."

Dorno made no reply. Four scaly arms held out in front of him, he fumbled his way from the useless visiplate and peered grimly through the nearest porthole.

It was hard to see against the strong light of the sun of this planetary system, but finally he made out the hundred-foot-long, bullet-shaped monstrosity. The vicious ten-foot snout of the thing was opening and closing like the steel traps of a steam shovel. The armored legs pawed and clawed at the empty space; the long, heavy body writhed in a stupendous working of muscles.

Dorno grew aware of somebody slipping up beside him. Without turning, he said tautly, "We've knocked out its Sensitives, all right. But it's still alive. The pressure of the atmosphere of that planet below will slow it down sufficiently so that the fall will only stun it. We've got to try to use our rockets, so that we don't land within five hundred *negs* of that thing. We'll need at least a hundred *lan*-periods for repair, and—"

"Commander . . . what is it?"

The words were almost a gasp, so faint they were.

Dorno recognized the whisper as coming from the novitiate, Carliss, his ship wife.

It was still a little strange to him, having a wife other than Yarosan. And it took a moment in this crisis to realize that that veteran of many voyages was not with him. But Yarosan had exercised the privilege of patrol women.

"I'm getting to the age where I want some children," she had said, "and as, legally, only one of them can be yours, I want you, Ral, to find yourself a pretty trainee and marry her for two voyages—"

Dorno turned slowly, vaguely irritated by the thought that there was somebody aboard who didn't automatically know everything. He said curtly, "It's a devil-Blal, a wild beast with an I.Q. of ten that haunts these outer, unexplored systems, where it hasn't yet been exterminated. It's abnormally ferocious. It has in its head what is called a sensitive area, where it organically manufactures enormous energies.

"The natural purpose of those energies is to provide it with a means of transportation. Unfortunately, when that thing is on the move, any machine in the vicinity that operates on forces below the molecular level is saturated with that—organic—force. It's a long, slow job draining it off, but it has to be done before a single atomic or electronic machine will function again.

"Our automatics managed to destroy the Blal's Sensitives at the same time it got us. We now have to destroy its body, but we can't do that till we get our energy weapons into operation again. Everything clear?"

Beside him, Carliss, the female Sahfid, nodded hesitantly. She said finally, "Suppose it lives on the planet below? And there are others there? What then?"

Dorno sighed. "My dear," he said, "there is a regulation that every crew member should familiarize himself or herself with data about any system which his ship happens to be approaching, passing, or—"

"But we only saw this sun half a *lan* ago."

"It's been registering on the multiboard for three *lans*—but never mind that. The planet below is the only one in this system that is inhabited. Its land area being one twentieth or more of the whole, it was colonized by the warm-blooded human beings of Wodesk. It is called Earth by its people, and has yet to develop space travel.

"I could give you some astrogeographical technical information, including the fact that the devil-Blal wouldn't willingly go near such a planet, because it most violently doesn't like an eight-*der* gravity or the oxygen in the atmosphere. Unfortunately, it will live in spite of this physical and chemical irreconcilability; and that is the enormous, indeed, the absolutely mortal, danger.

"It has a one-track mind. We have destroyed its main organic energy source, but actually its entire nervous system is a reservoir of sensitive forces. In its hunting, it has to project itself through space in pursuit of meteorites traveling many miles per second; to enable it to keep track of them ages ago it developed an ability to attune itself to any material body.

"Because of the pain we have caused it, it has been attuned to us from the first energy exchange; therefore, as soon as it lands, it will start for us, no matter how far away we are. We must make sure it doesn't get to us before we have a disintegrator ready. Otherwise—"

"Surely it can't damage a metalite spaceship."

"Not only can, but will. Its teeth are not just teeth. They project thin beams of energy that will dissolve any metal, however hard. And when it's through with us, just imagine the incalculable damage it will do on Earth before the patrol discovers what has happened—all this not counting the fact that it is considered an absolute catastrophe by galactic psychologists when a planet learns before it should that there is an enormously superior galactic civilization."

"I know." Carliss nodded vigorously. "The regulation is that if any inhabitant of such a planet so much as glimpses us, we must kill him or her forthwith."

Dorno made a somber sound of agreement, summarized grimly, "Our problem accordingly is to land far enough from the beast to protect ourselves, destroy it before it can do any harm, and finally make certain that no human being sees us."

He finished: "And now I suggest that you observe how Senna uses the rocket tubes to bring us down safely in this emergency landing. He—"

A gas light flickered outside the door of the control room. The Sahfid who came in was bigger, even, than the powerful Dorno. He carried a globe that burned mistily and shed a strong white light.

"I have bad news," said Senna. "You will recall we used rocket fuel chasing the Kjev outlaws and have not yet had the opportunity of replacing it. We shall have to land with a minimum of maneuvering."

Even after Senna went out, Dorno had nothing to say. There was nothing to say—for here was disaster.

They labored—Dorno and Carliss, Senna and Degel, his wife—with a quiet, relentless fury. After four *lans,* all the drainers were in position, and there was nothing to do but wait drearily while the electronic structures normalized in their agonizingly slow way. Dorno said:

"Some of the smaller motors, and the useless hand weapons, and the power tools in the machine shop will be in operation before the devil-Blal arrives. But nothing of value. It will require four day-and-night periods of this planet before the drive motors and the disintegrators are working again—and that makes it rather hopeless.

"I suppose we could fashion some kind of reaction gun, using the remnants of our rocket fuel as a propellant. But they would only enrage the beast."

He shrugged. "I'm afraid it's useless. According to our final observations, the monster will have landed about a hundred *negs* north of us, and so it will be here some time tomorrow. We—"

There was a clang as the molecular alarms went off. A few moments later, they watched the schooner creep through the narrows, then hastily back out again. Dorno's unwinking, lidless eyes watched thoughtfully until the whaler was out of sight.

He did not speak immediately, but spent some time examining the automatic photographs, which were entirely chemical in their operation and therefore unaffected by the catastrophe that had struck the rest of the ship. He said finally, slowly, "I'm not sure, but I think we're in luck. The enlargers show that that ship has two guns aboard, and one of those guns has a hooked thing protruding from it. That gives me an idea. We must, if necessary, use our remaining rocket fuel to stay near the vessel until I have been aboard and investigated."

"Be careful!" said Carliss anxiously.

"My transparent armor," Dorno told her, "will protect me from all except the most sustained gunfire."

A warm sun blazed down on the bay, and that made utterly surprising the bitter cold of the water. The icy feel of it in his gills was purest agony—but even the brief examination of the harpoon gun from the fo'c'sle hatchway told him that here was the answer.

"A most remarkable weapon," he told his companions when he returned to the patrol ship. "It will require a stronger explosive to drive it into the Blal and, of course, better metal in every phase of its construction. I shall have to go back for measurements and later to install the new equipment. But that will be simple. I succeeded in negating their fuel."

He ended, "That will have to be rectified at the proper time. They must be able to maneuver when the Blal arrives."

"But will they fight?" asked Carliss.

Dorno smiled mirthlessly. "My dear," he said, "that is something that we shall not leave to chance. A scopeograph film will tell them the rather appalling story. As for the rest, we shall simply keep their ship between ourselves and the devil-Blal. The beast will sense life force aboard their vessel and, in its stupid way, connect them with us. Yes, I can guarantee that they'll fight."

Carliss said, "The Blal might even save us the trouble of having to kill them later."

Dorno looked at her thoughtfully. "Oh, yes," he said, "the regulations! I assure you that we shall carry them out to the letter."

He smiled. "Some day, Carliss, you must read them all. The great ones who prepared them for us to administer made them comprehensive. Very comprehensive."

Wardell's fingers whitened on his binoculars as he studied the great, bulging back that glinted darkly in the swell half a mile to the north, bearing straight down on the ship. The monster left a gleaming trail in the sea as it swam with enormous power.

In a way, the part of it that was visible looked like nothing other than a large whale. Wardell clutched at the wild hope and then—

A spume of water sprayed the sea, and his illusion smashed like a bulletproof jacket before a cannon ball.

Because no whale on God's wide oceans had ever retched water in such a formidable fashion. Wardell had a brief, vivid mental picture of ten-foot jaws convulsively working under the waves and spreading water like a bellows.

For a moment, he felt violent anger at himself that he should have imagined, even for a second, it was a whale. Rage died as it struck him that the thought was not really a wasted one. For it was a reminder that he had all his years played a game where fear was not a factor.

Very slowly, very carefully, he straightened. He called in a calm, resonant voice, "Men, we're in this whether we like it or not. So let's take it in our stride, like the damnedest best whalers in the business—"

All the damage to the *Albatross* was done in the first two minutes after the harpoon belched forth from Art Zote's gun.

At that cruel blow, a nightmare, eyeless head, champing tons of water, reared up; and the attack was a flailing thing of armored legs that stamped as madly at the sea as at the frantically backing schooner.

She was clear at last; and Wardell, clambering shakily out of the ruin of the bridge, grew aware for the first time of the thunderous engines of the lizard's ship and of a second harpoon sticking in the side of the monster— the harpoon's gleaming coppery tail extending tenuous and taut back to the scale-armored vessel.

Four more harpoons lashed forth, two from each ship; and then they had the thing stretched between them.

For a solid hour Art Zote pumped the remnants of their shells into a body that writhed with an agonized but unkillable ferocity.

And then, for three long days and nights, they hung

on, while a beast that wouldn't die twisted and fought with a senseless and endless fury. . . .

It was the fourth morning.

From the shattered deck of his ship, Wardell watched the scene on the other vessel. Two lizards were setting up a curious, glittering structure that began to glow with a gray, misty light.

The almost palpable mist poured onto the beast in the sea; and where it struck was—change—that became—nothingness.

There was not a sound now, not a movement, aboard the *Albatross*. Men stood where they were and stared in a semiparalyzed fascination as a one-hundred-ton monster yielded its elements before the transcendental force that was tearing at it.

A long half hour passed before that hard and terrible body was dissolved. . . .

The glittering disintegrator was withdrawn then, and for a while there was—deadness. A thin fog appeared on the horizon to the north and blew over the two ships. Wardell waited with his men, tense and cold and—wondering.

"Let's get out of here," somebody said. "I don't trust those scoundrels even after we helped them."

Wardell shrugged helplessly. "What can we do? That bag of chemical powder they threw aboard, along with the motion-picture machine, released only one fuel tank, and that the half-empty one. We've used all except a few gallons in maneuvering. We. . . ."

"Damn those scum!" another man moaned. "It's the mysterious way they did it all that I don't like. Why, if they wanted our help, didn't they come and ask us?"

Wardell hadn't realized how great his own tension was. The sailor's words brought a wave of rage.

"Oh, sure," he said scathingly, "I can just picture it.

I can just see us rolling out the welcome mat—with a blast from our three-incher.

"And if they ever did get to tell us that they wanted to take the measurements of our harpoon gun, so they could build one of their own, and would we let them fix ours so that it would hold twenty whales at once, and would we please hang around here until that hellish thing arrived— Oh, yes, we would have stayed. Like hell we would!

"But they weren't as big saps as all that. It's the damnedest cold-blooded thing I ever saw pulled off, but we stayed because we had to, and no please or thank you about it. The thing that worries me is the fact that we've never seen their kind before, or heard of them. That might only prove that dead men have told no tales, but . . ."

His voice faded, for there was life again on the lizard ship, another structure being set up: smaller, duller in appearance than the first and equipped with odd, gunlike projectors.

Wardell went rigid, then his bellow echoed across the deck:

"That can only be for us. Art, you've still got three shells. Stand by, ready to fire. . . ."

A puff of silver-shining smoke cut off his words, his thoughts, his consciousness—instantaneously.

Dorno's soft, hissing voice made a quiet design of sound against the silence of the spaceship cabin:

"The regulations are designed to protect the moral continuity of civilization and to prevent a too literal interpretation of basic laws by time-calloused or thoughtless administrators. It is right that low-degree planets should be protected from contact, so vitally right that death is a justifiable measure against those who glimpse the truth, BUT—"

Dorno smiled, said, "When important assistance has been rendered a galactic citizen or official, no matter what the circumstances, it is morally necessary to the continuity of civilized conduct that other means be taken to prevent the tale from spreading.

"There are precedents, of course," Dorno added quietly. "Accordingly, I have been plotting our new course. It will take us past the distant sun of Wodesk, from whose green and wonderful planets Earth was originally colonized.

"It will not be necessary to keep our guests in a cataleptic state. As soon as they recover from the effects of the silver gas, let them . . . experience the journey."

PART TWO

THE IMMEDIATE FUTURE:

It May Happen Yet

NOW let imagination rage and horrors flit around! For we are, in this section, freed from the necessity of having to assume that our stories may actually have happened. Here our only concern is that the tales tell of things that are not too impossible.

With no holds barred, it would be easy to turn this section into a horrendous mess of invincible monsters, telepathic Things, or invisible spirits that blithely, openly, take us over and that's that. There have been hundreds of such stories published during the past couple of decades; next to the space opera, the "borax" invasion story is probably the most oft encountered form of science fiction in the pulps.

In this section, however, an effort has been made to keep the BEMS (bug-eyed monsters) down to a minimum and the overwhelming catastrophes within the realm of at least superreason. Not *every* story ends with the possible, probable, or actual elimination of the human race. Some, indeed, assume that the human race itself is going places and that those places are not up in smoke.

But we must have one or two tales of attempted or actually completed conquest of the human race. The section opens with one of the most famous of all tales of attempted conquest of Earth. Farther on you will find mankind in various stages of submission, slavery, or camaraderie, with or to, odd creatures or forces from outer space. Very appetizing futures to look forward to, indeed—all of them!

Howard Koch

INVASION FROM MARS

There should be no need to introduce this piece, probably the most famous radio script ever written. For this is the document that started off the astonishing scare, back in 1938, when its broadcast convinced several hundred thousand otherwise sane New Jerseyites, New Yorkers, Connecticutians, and Pennsylvanians that the jig was up and the Martians were actually trying to take over.

The by-line above gives credit to the brilliant writer of the script, but two other people must also be asked to take a bow at this time, if just due is to be given.

First and foremost, H. G. Wells, from whose superb novel, The War of the Worlds *(first published, believe it or not, in 1895), the script was adapted. Wells is still the greatest science-fiction novelist of them all, and it is a pleasure to give his departed ghost a big hand.*

And then—Orson Welles, on whose Mercury Theatre radio program the script was presented, whose actors and sound-effects men performed to such telling effect, and who was himself as surprised as anyone else at unwittingly giving the Earth its first rehearsal of invasion from space. Applause to the Welles with the "e" for producing a terrifyingly real piece of business out of purely imaginary—nay, fantastic—material!

The radio-script version of H. G. Wells's famous novel, *The War of the Worlds,* freely adapted by Howard Koch and presented by Orson Welles

and his Mercury Theatre on the Air over the
Columbia Broadcasting System, October 30,
1938.

NARRATOR: We know now that in the early years of
the twentieth century this world was being watched
closely by intelligences greater than man's and yet as
mortal as his own. We know now that as human beings
busied themselves about their various concerns they
were scrutinized and studied, perhaps almost as nar-
rowly as a man with a microscope might scrutinize the
transient creatures that swarm and multiply in a drop
of water. With infinite complacence people went to and
fro over the Earth about their little affairs, serene in the
assurance of their dominion over this small, spinning
fragment of solar driftwood which by chance or design
man has inherited out of the dark mystery of Time and
Space. Yet across an immense ethereal gulf, minds that
are to our minds as ours are to the beasts in the jungle,
intellects vast, cool, and unsympathetic, regarded this
Earth with envious eyes and slowly and surely drew
their plans against us. In the thirty-ninth year of the
twentieth century came the great disillusionment.

It was near the end of October. Business was better.
The war scare was over. More men were back at work.
Sales were picking up. On this particular evening, October 30, the Crossley service estimated that thirty-two
million people were listening in on radios.

ANNOUNCER CUE: . . . for the next twenty-four hours
not much change in temperature. A slight atmospheric
disturbance of undetermined origin is reported over
Nova Scotia, causing a low-pressure area to move down
rather rapidly over the northeastern states, bringing a
forecast of rain, accompanied by winds of light gale

force. Maximum temperature 66; minimum 48. This weather report comes to you from the Government Weather Bureau.

ANNOUNCER TWO: We now take you to the Meridian Room in the Hotel Park Plaza in downtown New York, where you will be entertained by the music of Ramon Raquello and his orchestra.

(*Spanish theme song . . . Fades*)

ANNOUNCER THREE: Good evening, ladies and gentlemen. From the Meridian Room in the Park Plaza in New York City, we bring you the music of Ramon Raquello and his orchestra. With a touch of the Spanish, Ramon Raquello leads off with "La Cumparsita."

(*Piece starts playing*)

ANNOUNCER TWO: Ladies and gentlemen, we interrupt our program of dance music to bring you a special bulletin from the Intercontinental Radio News. At twenty minutes before eight, central time, Professor Farrell of the Mount Jennings Observatory, Chicago, Illinois, reports observing several explosions of incandescent gas, occurring at regular intervals on the planet Mars.

The spectroscope indicates the gas to be hydrogen and moving toward the earth with enormous velocity. Professor Pierson of the observatory at Princeton confirms Farrell's observation, and describes the phenomenon as (quote) like a jet of blue flame shot from a gun (unquote). We now return you to the music of Ramon Raquello, playing for you in the Meridian Room of the Park Plaza Hotel, situated in downtown New York.

(*Music plays for a few moments until piece ends . . . Sound of applause*)

Now a tune that never loses favor, the ever popular "Star Dust." Ramon Raquello and his orchestra . . .

(*Music*)

ANNOUNCER TWO: Ladies and gentlemen, following on the news given in our bulletin a moment ago, the Government Meteorological Bureau has requested the large observatories of the country to keep an astronomical watch on any other disturbances occurring on the planet Mars. Due to the unusual nature of this occurrence, we have arranged an interview with the noted astronomer, Professor Pierson, who will give us his views on this event. In a few moments we will take you to the Princeton Observatory at Princeton, New Jersey. We return you until then to the music of Ramon Raquello and his orchestra.

(*Music*)

ANNOUNCER TWO: We are ready now to take you to the Princeton Observatory at Princeton, where Carl Phillips, our commentator, will interview Professor Richard Pierson, famous astronomer. We take you now to Princeton, New Jersey.

(*Echo chamber*)

PHILLIPS: Good evening, ladies and gentlemen. This is Carl Phillips, speaking to you from the observatory at Princeton. I am standing in a large semicircular room, pitch-black except for an oblong split in the ceiling. Through this opening I can see a sprinkling of stars that cast a kind of frosty glow over the intricate mechanism of the huge telescope. The ticking sound you hear is the vibration of the clockwork. Professor Pierson stands directly above me on a small platform, peering through the giant lens. I ask you to be patient, ladies and gentlemen, during any delay that may arise during our interview. Besides his ceaseless watch of the heavens, Professor Pierson may be interrupted by telephone or other communications. During this period he is in constant touch with the astronomical centers of the world— Professor, may I begin our questions?

PIERSON: At any time, Mr. Phillips.

PHILLIPS: Professor, would you please tell our radio audience exactly what you see as you observe the planet Mars through your telescope?

PIERSON: Nothing unusual at the moment, Mr. Phillips. A red disk swimming in a blue sea. Transverse stripes across the disk. Quite distinct now because Mars happens to be at the point nearest the earth—in opposition, as we call it.

PHILLIPS: In your opinion, what do these transverse stripes signify, Professor Pierson?

PIERSON: Not canals, I can assure you, Mr. Phillips, although that's the popular conjecture of those who imagine Mars to be inhabited. From a scientific viewpoint the stripes are merely the result of atmospheric conditions peculiar to the planet.

PHILLIPS: Then you're quite convinced as a scientist that living intelligence as we know it does not exist on Mars?

PIERSON: I should say the chances against it are a thousand to one.

PHILLIPS: And yet, how do you account for these gas eruptions occurring on the surface of the planet at regular intervals?

PIERSON: Mr. Phillips, I cannot account for it.

PHILLIPS: By the way, Professor, for the benefit of our listeners, how far is Mars from the earth?

PIERSON: Approximately forty million miles.

PHILLIPS: Well, that seems a safe enough distance—

Just a moment, ladies and gentlemen, someone has just handed Professor Pierson a message. While he reads it, let me remind you we are speaking to you from the observatory in Princeton, New Jersey, where we are interviewing the world-famous astronomer, Professor Pierson. . . . One moment, please. Professor Pierson has passed me a message which he has just received. Professor, may I read the message to the listening audience?

PIERSON: Certainly, Mr. Phillips.

PHILLIPS: Ladies and gentlemen, I shall read you a wire addressed to Professor Pierson from Dr. Gray of the National History Museum, New York. "9:15 P.M. Eastern standard time. Seismograph registered shock of almost earthquake intensity occurring within a radius of twenty miles of Princeton. Please investigate. Signed, Lloyd Gray, Chief of Astronomical Division." Professor Pierson, could this occurrence possibly have something to do with the disturbances observed on the planet Mars?

PIERSON: Hardly, Mr. Phillips. This is probably a meteorite of unusual size, and its arrival at this particular time is merely a coincidence. However, we shall conduct a search, as soon as daylight permits.

PHILLIPS: Thank you, Professor. Ladies and gentlemen, for the past ten minutes we've been speaking to you from the observatory at Princeton, bringing you a special interview with Professor Pierson, noted astronomer. This is Carl Phillips speaking. We now return you to our New York studio.

(*Fade in piano playing*)

ANNOUNCER TWO: Ladies and gentlemen, here is the latest bulletin from the Intercontinental Radio News. Toronto, Canada: Professor Morse of Macmillan University reports observing a total of three explosions on the planet Mars, between the hours of 7:45 P.M. and 9:20 P.M., Eastern standard time. This confirms earlier reports received from American observatories. Now, nearer home, comes a special announcement from Trenton, New Jersey. It is reported that at 8:50 P.M. a huge, flaming object, believed to be a meteorite, fell on a farm in the neighborhood of Grovers Mill, New Jersey, twenty-two miles from Trenton. The flash in the sky was visible within a radius of several hundred miles and the noise of the impact was heard as far north as Elizabeth.

We have dispatched a special mobile unit to the scene, and will have our commentator, Mr. Phillips, give you a word description as soon as he can reach there from Princeton. In the meantime, we take you to the Hotel Martinet in Brooklyn, where Bobby Millette and his orchestra are offering a program of dance music.

(*Swing band for 20 seconds . . . Then cut*)

ANNOUNCER TWO: We take you now to Grovers Mill, New Jersey.

(*Crowd noises . . . Police sirens*)

PHILLIPS: Ladies and gentlemen, this is Carl Phillips again, at the Wilmuth farm, Grovers Mill, New Jersey. Professor Pierson and myself made the eleven miles from Princeton in ten minutes. Well, I—I hardly know where to begin, to paint for you a word picture of the strange scene before my eyes, like something out of a modern *Arabian Nights*. Well, I just got here. I haven't had a chance to look around yet. I guess that's it. Yes, I guess that's the—thing, directly in front of me, half buried in a vast pit. Must have struck with terrific force. The ground is covered with splinters of a tree it must have struck on its way down. What I can see of the—

object itself doesn't look very much like a meteor, at least not the meteors I've seen. It looks more like a huge cylinder. It has a diameter of—what would you say, Professor Pierson?

PIERSON (*off*): About thirty yards.

PHILLIPS: About thirty yards— The metal on the sheath is—well, I've never seen anything like it. The color is sort of yellowish-white. Curious spectators now are pressing close to the object in spite of the efforts of the police to keep them back. They're getting in front of my line of vision. Would you mind standing on one side, please?

POLICEMAN: One side, there, one side.

PHILLIPS: While the policemen are pushing the crowd back, here's Mr. Wilmuth, owner of the farm here. He may have some interesting facts to add. Mr. Wilmuth, would you please tell the radio audience as much as you remember of this rather unusual visitor that dropped in your back yard? Step closer, please. Ladies and gentlemen, this is Mr. Wilmuth.

WILMUTH: I was listenin' to the radio—

PHILLIPS: Closer and louder, please.

WILMUTH: Pardon me!

PHILLIPS: Louder, please, and closer.

WILMUTH: Yes, sir—while I was listening to the radio and kinda drowsin', that Professor fellow was talkin' about Mars, so I was half dozin' and half—

PHILLIPS: Yes, yes, Mr. Wilmuth. And then what happened?

WILMUTH: As I was sayin', I was listenin' to the radio kinda halfways—

PHILLIPS: Yes, Mr. Wilmuth, and then you saw something?

WILMUTH: Not first off. I heard something.

PHILLIPS: And what did you hear?

WILMUTH: A hissing sound. Like this: sssssssss—kinda like a Fourt' of July rocket.

PHILLIPS: Then what?

WILMUTH: Turned my head out the window and would have swore I was to sleep and dreamin'.

PHILLIPS: Yes?

WILMUTH: I seen a kinda greenish streak and then zingo! Somethin' smacked the ground. Knocked me clear out of my chair!

PHILLIPS: Well, were you frightened, Mr. Wilmuth?

WILMUTH: Well, I—I ain't quite sure. I reckon I—I was kinda riled.

PHILLIPS: Thank you, Mr. Wilmuth. Thank you.

WILMUTH: Want me to tell you some more?

PHILLIPS: No—that's quite all right, that's plenty—Ladies and gentlemen, you've just heard Mr. Wilmuth, owner of the farm where this thing has fallen. I wish I could convey the atmosphere—the background of this—fantastic scene. Hundreds of cars are parked in a field in back of us. Police are trying to rope off the roadway leading into the farm. But it's no use. They're breaking right through. Their headlights throw an enormous spot on the pit where the object's half buried. Some of the more daring souls are venturing near the edge. Their silhouettes stand out against the metal sheen.

(Faint humming sound)

One man wants to touch the thing—he's having an argument with a policeman. The policeman wins—Now, ladies and gentlemen, there's something I haven't mentioned in all this excitement, but it's becoming more distinct. Perhaps you've caught it already on your radio. Listen *(Long pause)* . . . Do you hear it? It's a curious humming sound that seems to come from inside the object. I'll move the microphone nearer. Here. *(Pause)*

Now we're not more than twenty-five feet away. Can you hear it now? Oh, Professor Pierson!

PIERSON: Yes, Mr. Phillips?

PHILLIPS: Can you tell us the meaning of that scraping noise inside the thing?

PIERSON: Possibly the unequal cooling of its surface.

PHILLIPS: Do you think it's a meteor, Professor?

PIERSON: I don't know what to think. The metal casing is definitely extraterrestrial—not found on this Earth. Friction with the Earth's atmosphere usually tears holes in a meteorite. This thing is smooth and, as you can see, of cylindrical shape.

PHILLIPS: Just a minute! Something's happening! Ladies and gentlemen, this is terrific! This end of the thing is beginning to flake off! The top is beginning to rotate like a screw! The thing must be hollow!

VOICES: She's a-movin'!

Look, the darn thing's unscrewing!

Keep back, there! Keep back, I tell you.

Maybe there's men in it trying to escape!

It's red-hot, they'll burn to a cinder!

Keep back there! Keep those idiots back!

(*Suddenly the clanking sound of a huge piece of falling metal*)

VOICES: She's off! The top's loose!

Look out there! Stand back!

PHILLIPS: Ladies and gentlemen, this is the most terrifying thing I have ever witnessed— Wait a minute! Someone's crawling out of the hollow top. Someone or —something. I can see peering out of that black hole two luminous disks—are they eyes? It might be a face. It might be—

(*Shout of awe from the crowd*)

Good heavens, something's wriggling out of the shadow like a gray snake. Now it's another one, and another. They look like tentacles to me. There, I can see the thing's body. It's large as a bear and glistens like wet leather. But that face. It—it's indescribable. I can hardly force myself to keep looking at it. The eyes are black and gleam like a serpent. The mouth is V-shaped with saliva dripping from its rimless lips that seem to quiver and pulsate. The monster or whatever it is can hardly move. It seems weighed down by—possibly gravity or something. The thing's raising up. The crowd falls back. They've seen enough. This is the most extraordinary experience. I can't find words—I'm pulling this microphone with me as I talk. I'll have to stop the description until I've taken a new position. Hold on, will you please, I'll be back in a minute.

(*Fade into piano*)

ANNOUNCER TWO: We are bringing you an eyewitness account of what's happening on the Wilmuth farm, Grovers Mill, New Jersey.

(*More piano*)

We now return you to Carl Phillips at Grovers Mill.

PHILLIPS: Ladies and gentlemen (Am I on?)—ladies and gentlemen, here I am, back of a stone wall that adjoins Mr. Wilmuth's garden. From here I get a sweep of the whole scene. I'll give you every detail as long as I can talk. As long as I can see. More State Police have arrived. They're drawing up a cordon in front of the pit, about thirty of them. No need to push the crowd back now. They're willing to keep their distance. The captain is conferring with someone. We can't quite see who. Oh, yes, I believe it's Professor Pierson. Yes, it is. Now they've parted. The professor moves around one side, studying the object, while the captain and two police-men advance with something in their hands. I can see it now. It's a white handkerchief tied to a pole—a flag of truce. If those creatures know what that means—what anything means! . . . *Wait!* Something's happening!

(*Hissing sound followed by a humming that increases in intensity*)

A humped shape is rising out of the pit. I can make out a small beam of light against a mirror. What's that? There's a jet of flame springing from that mirror, and it leaps right at the advancing men. It strikes them head on! Good Lord, they're turning into flame!

(*Screams and unearthly shrieks*)

Now the whole field's caught fire. (*Explosion*) The woods—the barns, the gas tanks of automobiles—it's spreading everywhere. It's coming this way. About twenty yards to my right—

(*Crash of microphone . . . Then dead silence . . .*)

ANNOUNCER TWO: Ladies and gentlemen, due to cir-cumstances beyond our control, we are unable to con-tinue the broadcast from Grovers Mill. Evidently there's some difficulty with our field transmission. However, we will return to that point at the earliest opportunity. In the meantime, we have a late bulletin from San Diego, California. Professor Indellkoffer, speaking at a dinner of the California Astronomical Society, expressed the opinion that the explosions on Mars are undoubtedly nothing more than severe volcanic disturbances on the surface of the planet. We continue now with our piano interlude.

(*Piano . . . Then cut*)

Ladies and gentlemen, I have just been handed a message that came in from Grovers Mill by telephone. Just a moment. At least forty people, including six State Troopers, lie dead in a field east of the village of Grovers Mill, their bodies burned and distorted beyond all possible recognition. The next voice you hear will be that of Brigadier General Montgomery Smith, commander of the State Militia at Trenton, New Jersey.

SMITH: I have been requested by the Governor of New Jersey to place the counties of Mercer and Middlesex as far west as Princeton, and east to Jamesburg, under martial law. No one will be permitted to enter this area except by special pass issued by state or military authorities. Four companies of State Militia are proceeding from Trenton to Grovers Mill and will aid in the evacuation of homes within the range of military operations. Thank you.

ANNOUNCER: You have just been listening to General Montgomery Smith, commanding the State Militia at Trenton. In the meantime, further details of the catastrophe at Grovers Mill are coming in. The strange creatures, after unleashing their deadly assault, crawled back in their pit and made no attempt to prevent the efforts of the firemen to recover the bodies and extinguish the fire. Combined fire departments of Mercer County are fighting the flames, which menace the entire countryside.

We have been unable to establish any contact with our mobile unit at Grovers Mill, but we hope to be able to return you there at the earliest possible moment. In the meantime we take you—uh, just one moment please.

(*Long pause . . . Whisper*)

Ladies and gentlemen, I have just been informed that we have finally established communication with an eyewitness of the tragedy. Professor Pierson has been located at a farmhouse near Grovers Mill, where he has established an emergency observation post. As a scientist, he will give you his explanation of the calamity. The next voice you hear will be that of Professor Pierson, brought to you by direct wire. Professor Pierson.

PIERSON: Of the creatures in the rocket cylinder at Grovers Mill, I can give you no authoritative information—either as to their nature, their origin, or their purposes here on Earth. Of their destructive instrument I might venture some conjectural explanation. For want of a better term, I shall refer to the mysterious weapon as a heat-ray. It's all too evident that these creatures have scientific knowledge far in advance of our own. It is my guess that in some way they are able to generate an intense heat in a chamber of practically absolute nonconductivity. This intense heat they project in a parallel beam against any object they choose, by means of a polished parabolic mirror of unknown composition, much as the mirror of a lighthouse projects a beam of light. That is my conjecture of the origin of the heat-ray. ·

ANNOUNCER TWO: Thank you, Professor Pierson. Ladies and gentlemen, here is a bulletin from Trenton. It is a brief statement informing us that the charred body of Carl Phillips, the radio commentator, has been identified in a Trenton hospital. Now here's another bulletin from Washington, D.C.

Office of the director of the National Red Cross reports ten units of Red Cross emergency workers have been assigned to the headquarters of the State Militia stationed outside of Grovers Mill, New Jersey. Here's a bulletin from State Police, Princeton Junction: The fires at Grovers Mill and vicinity now under control. Scouts report all quiet in the pit, and no sign of life appearing from the mouth of the cylinder. And now, ladies and gentlemen, we have a special statement from Mr. Harry McDonald, vice-president in charge of operations.

MC DONALD: We have received a request from the militia at Trenton to place at their disposal our entire broadcasting facilities. In view of the gravity of the situation, and believing that radio has a definite responsibility to serve in the public interest at all times, we are turning over our facilities to the State Militia at Trenton.

ANNOUNCER: We take you now to the field headquarters of the State Militia near Grovers Mill, New Jersey.

CAPTAIN: This is Captain Lansing of the Signal Corps, attached to the State Militia now engaged in military operations in the vicinity of Grovers Mill. Situation arising from the reported presence of certain individuals of unidentified nature is now under complete control.

The cylindrical object which lies in a pit directly below our position is surrounded on all sides by eight battalions of infantry, without heavy fieldpieces, but adequately armed with rifles and machine guns. All cause for alarm, if such cause ever existed, is now entirely unjustified. The things, whatever they are, do not even venture to poke their heads above the pit. I can see their hiding place plainly in the glare of the searchlights here. With all their reported resources, these creatures can scarcely stand up against heavy machine-gun fire. Anyway, it's an interesting outing for the troops. I can make out their khaki uniforms, crossing back and forth in front of the lights. It looks almost like a real war. There appears to be some slight smoke in the woods bordering the Millstone River. Probably fire started by campers. Well, we ought to see some action soon. One of the companies is deploying on the left flank. A quick thrust and it will all be over. Now wait a minute! I see something on top of the cylinder. No, it's nothing but a shadow. Now the troops are on the edge of the Wilmuth farm. Seven thousand armed men closing in on an old metal tube. Wait, that wasn't a shadow! It's something moving—solid metal—kind of a shieldlike affair rising up out of the cylinder— It's going higher and higher. Why, it's standing on legs—actually rearing up on a sort of metal framework. Now it's reaching above the trees and the searchlights are on it! Hold on!

(*Silence*)

ANNOUNCER TWO: Ladies and gentlemen, I have a grave announcement to make. Incredible as it may seem, both the observations of science and the evidence of our eyes lead to the inescapable assumption that those strange beings who landed in the Jersey farmlands tonight are the vanguard of an invading army from the planet Mars. The battle which took place tonight at Grovers Mill has ended in one of the most startling defeats ever suffered by an army in modern times; seven thousand men armed with rifles and machine guns pitted against a single fighting machine of the invaders from Mars. One hundred and twenty known survivors. The rest strewn over the battle area from Grovers Mill to Plainsboro, crushed and trampled to death under the metal feet of the monster, or burned to cinders by its heat-ray. The monster is now in control of the middle section of New Jersey and has effectively cut the state through its center. Communication lines are down from Pennsylvania to the Atlantic Ocean. Railroad tracks are torn, and service from New York to Philadelphia discontinued except routing some of the trains through Allentown and Phoenixville. Highways to the north, south, and west are clogged with frantic human traffic. Police and Army reserves are unable to control the mad flight. By morning the fugitives will have swelled Philadelphia, Camden, and Trenton, it is estimated, to twice their normal population.

At this time martial law prevails throughout New Jersey and eastern Pennsylvania. We take you now to Washington for a special broadcast on the National Emergency. . . . The Secretary of the Interior—

SECRETARY: Citizens of the nation: I shall not try to conceal the gravity of the situation that confronts the country, nor the concern of your government in protecting the lives and property of its people. However, I wish to impress upon you—private citizens and public officials, all of you—the urgent need of calm and resourceful action. Fortunately, this formidable enemy is still confined to a comparatively small area, and we may place our faith in the military forces to keep them there. In the meantime, placing our faith in God, we must continue the performance of our duties each and every one of us, so that we may confront this destructive adversary with a nation united, courageous, and consecrated to the preservation of human supremacy on this earth. I thank you.

ANNOUNCER: You have just heard the Secretary of the Interior speaking from Washington. Bulletins too numerous to read are piling up in the studio here. We are informed that the central portion of New Jersey is blacked out from radio communication due to the effect of the heat-ray upon power lines and electrical equipment. Here is a special bulletin from New York. Cables received from English, French, German scientific bodies offering assistance. Astronomers report continued gas outbursts at regular intervals on planet Mars. Majority voice opinion that enemy will be reinforced by additional rocket machines. Attempts made to locate Professor Pierson of Princeton, who has observed Martians at close range. It is feared he was lost in recent battle.

Langham Field, Virginia: Scouting planes report three Martian machines visible above treetops, moving north toward Somerville with population fleeing ahead of them. Heat-ray not in use; although advancing at express-train speed, invaders pick their way carefully. They seem to be making conscious effort to avoid destruction of cities and countryside. However, they stop to uproot power lines, bridges, and railroad tracks. Their apparent objective is to crush resistance, paralyze communication, and disorganize human society.

Here is a bulletin from Basking Ridge, New Jersey: Coon hunters have stumbled on a second cylinder similar to the first embedded in the great swamp twenty miles south of Morristown. U.S. Army fieldpieces are proceeding from Newark to blow up second invading unit before cylinder can be opened and the fighting machine rigged. They are taking up position in the foothills of Watchung Mountains. Another bulletin from Langham Field, Virginia: Scouting planes report enemy machines now, three in number, increasing speed northward, kicking over houses and trees in their evident haste to form a conjunction with their allies south of Morristown. Machines also sighted by telephone operator east of Middlesex within ten miles of Plainfield. Here's a bulletin from Winston Field, Long Island: Fleet of Army bombers carrying heavy explosives flying north in pursuit of enemy. Scouting planes act as guides. They keep speeding enemy in sight. Just a moment please. Ladies and gentlemen, we've run special wires to the artillery line in adjacent villages to give you direct reports in the zone of the advancing enemy. First we take you to the battery of the twenty-second Field Artillery, located in the Watchung Mountains.

OFFICER: Range—thirty-two meters.

GUNNER: Thirty-two meters.

OFFICER: Projection, thirty-nine degrees.

GUNNER: Thirty-nine degrees.

OFFICER: Fire!

(*Boom of heavy gun . . . Pause*)

OBSERVER: One hundred and forty yards to the right, sir.

OFFICER: Shift range—thirty-one meters.

GUNNER: Thirty-one meters.

OFFICER: Projection—thirty-seven degrees.

GUNNER: Thirty-seven degrees.

OFFICER: Fire!

(*Boom of heavy gun . . . Pause*)

OBSERVER: A hit, sir! We got the tripod of one of them. They've stopped. The others are trying to repair it.

OFFICER: Quick, get the range! Shift fifty thirty meters.

GUNNER: Thirty meters.

OFFICER: Projection—twenty-seven degrees.

GUNNER: Twenty-seven degrees.

OFFICER: Fire!

(*Boom of heavy gun . . . Pause*)

OBSERVER: Can't see the shell land, sir. They're letting off a smoke.

OFFICER: What is it?

OBSERVER: A black smoke, sir. Moving this way. Lying close to the ground. It's moving fast.

OFFICER: Put on gas masks. (*Pause*) Get ready to fire. Shift to twenty-four meters.

GUNNER: Twenty-four meters.

OFFICER: Projection, twenty-four degrees.

GUNNER: Twenty-four degrees.

OFFICER: Fire! (*Boom*)

OBSERVER: I still can't see, sir. The smoke's coming nearer.

OFFICER: Get the range. (*Coughs*)

OBSERVER: Twenty-three meters. (*Coughs*)

OFFICER: Twenty-three meters. (*Cough*)

OBSERVER: Projection—twenty-two degrees. (*Coughing*)

OFFICER: Twenty-two degrees. (*Fade in coughing*)

(*Fading in . . . sound of airplane motor*)

COMMANDER: Army bombing plane, V-8-43 off Bayonne, New Jersey, Lieutenant Voght, commanding eight bombers. Reporting to Commander Fairfax, Langham Field— This is Voght, reporting to Commander Fairfax, Langham Field— Enemy tripod machines now in sight. Reinforced by three machines from the Morristown cylinder. Six altogether. One machine partially crippled. Believed hit by shell from Army gun in Watchung Mountains. Guns now appear silent. A heavy black fog hanging close to the Earth—of extreme density, nature unknown. No sign of heat-ray. Enemy now turns east, crossing Passaic River into Jersey marshes. Another straddles the Pulaski Skyway. Evident objective is New York City. They're pushing down a high-tension power station. The machines are close together now, and we're ready to attack. Planes circling, ready to strike. A thousand yards and we'll be over the first—eight hundred yards . . . six hundred . . . four hundred . . . two hundred . . . There they go! The giant arm raised— Green flash! They're spraying us with flame! Two thousand feet. Engines are giving out. No chance to release bombs. Only one thing left—drop on them, plane and all. We're diving on the first one. Now the engine's gone! Eight—

OPERATOR ONE: This is Bayonne, New Jersey, calling Langham Field— This is Bayonne, New Jersey, calling Langham Field— Come in, please— Come in, please—

OPERATOR TWO: This is Langham Field—go ahead—

OPERATOR ONE: Eight Army bombers in engagement with enemy tripod machines over Jersey flats. Engines incapacitated by heat-ray. All crashed. One enemy machine destroyed. Enemy now discharging heavy black smoke in direction of—

OPERATOR THREE: This is Newark, New Jersey— This is Newark, New Jersey— Warning! Poisonous black smoke pouring in from Jersey marshes. Reaches South Street. Gas masks useless. Urge population to move into open spaces—automobiles use routes 7, 23, 24—avoid congested areas. Smoke now spreading over Raymond Boulevard—

OPERATOR FOUR: 2X2L—calling CQ— 2X2L—calling CQ— 2X2L calling 8X3R—

OPERATOR FIVE: This is 8X3R—coming back at 2X2L.

OPERATOR FOUR: How's reception? How's the reception? K, please. Where are you, 8X3R? What's the matter? Where are you?

(*Bells ringing over city, gradually diminishing*)

ANNOUNCER: I'm speaking from the roof of Broadcasting Building, New York City. The bells you hear are ringing to warn the people to evacuate the city as the Martians approach. Estimated in last two hours three million people have moved out along the roads to the north, Hutchinson River Parkway still kept open for motor traffic. Avoid bridges to Long Island—hopelessly jammed. All communication with Jersey shore closed ten minutes ago. No more defenses. Our army wiped out

—artillery, Air Force, everything wiped out. This may be the last broadcast. We'll stay here to the end. People are holding service below us—in the cathedral.

(*Voices singing hymn*)

Now I look down the harbor. All manner of boats, overloaded with fleeing population, pulling out from docks.

(*Sound of boat whistles*)

Streets are all jammed. Noise in crowds like New Year's Eve in city. Wait a minute— Enemy now in sight above the Palisades. Five great machines. First one is crossing river. I can see it from here, wading the Hudson like a man wading through a brook— A bulletin's handed me—Martian cylinders are falling all over the country. One outside Buffalo, one in Chicago, St. Louis —seems to be timed and spaced— Now the first machine reaches the shore. He stands watching, looking over the city. His steel, cowlish head is even with the skyscrapers. He waits for the others. They rise like a line of new towers on the city's west side— Now they're lifting their metal hands. This is the end now. Smoke comes out—black smoke, drifting over the city. People in the streets see it now. They're running toward the East River—thousands of them, dropping in like rats. Now the smoke's spreading faster. It's reached Times Square. People are trying to run away from it, but it's no use. They're falling like flies. Now the smoke's crossing Sixth Avenue— Fifth Avenue— a hundred yards away— it's fifty feet—

OPERATOR FOUR: 2X2L calling CQ— 2X2L calling CQ— 2X2L calling CQ— New York— Isn't there anyone on the air? Isn't there anyone—2X2L—

II

PIERSON: As I set down these notes on paper, I'm obsessed by the thought that I may be the last living man on Earth. I have been hiding in this empty house near Grovers Mill—a small island of daylight cut off by the black smoke from the rest of the world. All that happened before the arrival of these monstrous creatures in the world now seems part of another life—a life that has no continuity with the present, furtive existence of the lonely derelict who pencils these words on the back of some astronomical notes bearing the signature of Richard Pierson. I look down at my blackened hands, my torn shoes, my tattered clothes, and I try to connect them with a professor who lives at Princeton and who, on the night of October 30, glimpsed through his telescope an orange splash of light on a distant planet. My wife, my colleagues, my students, my books, my observatory, my—my world—where are they? Did they ever exist? Am I Richard Pierson? What day is it? Do days exist without calendars? Does time pass when there are no human hands left to wind the clocks? In writing down my daily life I tell myself I shall preserve human history between the dark covers of this little book that was meant to record the movements of the stars. But to write I must live, and to live I must eat— I find moldy bread in the kitchen, and an orange not too spoiled to swallow. I keep watch at the window. From time to time I catch sight of a Martian above the black smoke.

The smoke still holds the house in its black coil— But at length there is a hissing sound and suddenly I see a Martian mounted on his machine, spraying the air with a jet of steam, as if to dissipate the smoke. I watch in a corner as his huge metal legs nearly brush against the house. Exhausted by terror, I fall asleep.

It's morning. Sun streams in the window. The black cloud of gas has lifted, and the scorched meadows to the north look as though a black snowstorm had passed over them. I venture from the house. I make my way to a road. No traffic. Here and there a wrecked car, baggage overturned, a blackened skeleton. I push on north. For some reason I feel safer trailing these monsters than running away from them. And I keep a careful watch. I have seen the Martians feed. Should one of their machines appear over the top of trees, I am ready to fling myself flat on the earth. I come to a chestnut tree. October, chestnuts are ripe. I fill my pockets. I must keep alive. Two days I wander in a vague northerly direction through a desolate world. Finally I notice a living creature—a small red squirrel in a beech tree. I stare at him and wonder. He stares back at me. I believe at that moment the animal and I shared the same emotion—the joy of finding another living being— I push on north. I find dead cows in a brackish field. Beyond, the charred ruins of a dairy. The silo remains standing guard over the wasteland like a lighthouse deserted by the sea. Astride the silo perches a weathercock. The arrow points north.

Next day I came to a city vaguely familiar in its contours, yet its buildings strangely dwarfed and leveled off as if a giant had sliced off its highest towers with a capricious sweep of his hand. I reached the outskirts. I found Newark, undemolished, but humbled by some whim of the advancing Martians. Presently, with an odd feeling of being watched, I caught sight of something crouching in a doorway. I made a step toward it, and it rose up and became a man—a man, armed with a large knife.

STRANGER: Stop—Where did you come from?

PIERSON: I come from—many places. A long time ago from Princeton.

STRANGER: Princeton, huh? That's near Grovers Mill!

PIERSON: Yes.

STRANGER: Grovers Mill— (*Laughs as at a great joke*) There's no food here. This is my country—all this end of town down to the river. There's only food for one—Which way are you going?

PIERSON: I don't know. I guess I'm looking for—for people.

STRANGER: (*nervously*) What was that? Did you hear something just then?

PIERSON: Only a bird—a live bird!

STRANGER: You get to know that birds have shadows these days— Say, we're in the open here. Let's crawl into this doorway and talk.

PIERSON: Have you seen any Martians?

STRANGER: They've gone over to New York. At night the sky is alive with their lights. Just as if people were still living in it. By daylight you can't see them. Five days ago a couple of them carried something big across the flats from the airport. I believe they're learning how to fly.

PIERSON: Fly!

STRANGER: Yeah, fly.

PIERSON: Then it's all over with humanity. Stranger, there's still you and I. Two of us left.

STRANGER: They got themselves in solid; they wrecked the greatest country in the world. Those green stars, they're probably falling somewhere every night. They've only lost one machine. There isn't anything to do. We're done. We're licked.

PIERSON: Where were you? You're in uniform.

STRANGER: What's left of it. I was in the militia—

National Guard. That's good! Wasn't any war any more than there's war between men and ants.

PIERSON: And we're eatable ants. I found that out. What will they do to us?

STRANGER: I've thought it all out. Right now we're caught as we're wanted. The Martian only has to go a few miles to get a crowd on the run. But they won't keep doing that. They'll begin catching us systematic like— keeping the best and storing us in cages and things. They haven't begun on us yet!

PIERSON: Not begun!

STRANGER: Not begun. All that's happened so far is because we don't have sense enough to keep quiet— bothering them with guns and such stuff and losing our heads and rushing off in crowds. Now instead of our rushing around blind, we've got to fix ourselves up according to the way things are now. Cities, nations, civilization, progress—

PIERSON: But if that's so, what is there to live for?

STRANGER: There won't be any more concerts for a million years or so, and no nice little dinners at restaurants. If it's amusement you're after, I guess the game's up.

PIERSON: And what is there left?

STRANGER: Life—that's what! I want to live. And so do you! We're not going to be exterminated. And I don't mean to be caught, either, and tamed, and fattened, and bred like an ox.

PIERSON: What are you going to do?

STRANGER: I'm going on—right under their feet. I gotta plan. We men, as men, are finished. We don't know enough. We gotta learn plenty before we've got a chance. And we've got to live and keep free while we learn. I've thought it all out, see.

PIERSON: Tell me the rest.

STRANGER: Well, it isn't all of us that are made for wild beasts, and that's what it's got to be. That's why I watched you. All these little office workers that used to live in these houses—they'd be no good. They haven't any stuff to 'em. They just used to run off to work. I've seen hundreds of 'em, running wild to catch their commuters' train in the morning for fear that they'd get canned if they didn't; running back at night afraid they won't be in time for dinner. Lives insured and a little invested in case of accidents. And on Sundays, worried about the hereafter. The Martians will be a godsend for these guys. Nice roomy cages, good food, careful breeding, no worries. After a week or so chasing about the fields on empty stomachs, they'll come and be glad to be caught.

PIERSON: You've thought it all out, haven't you?

STRANGER: You bet I have! And that isn't all. These Martians will make pets of some of them, train 'em to do tricks. Who knows? Get sentimental over the pet boy who grew up and had to be killed. And some, maybe, they'll train to hunt us.

PIERSON: No, that's impossible. No human beings—

STRANGER: Yes, they will. There's men who'll do it, gladly. If one of them ever comes after me—

PIERSON: In the meantime, you and I and others like us—where are we to live when the Martians own the Earth?

STRANGER: I've got it all figured out. We'll live underground. I've been thinking about the sewers. Under New York are miles and miles of 'em. The main ones are big enough for anybody. Then there's cellars, vaults, underground storerooms, railway tunnels, subways. You begin to see, eh? And we'll get a bunch of strong men together. No weak ones, that rubbish, out.

PIERSON: And you meant me to go?

STRANGER: Well, I gave you a chance, didn't I?

PIERSON: We won't quarrel about that. Go on.

STRANGER: And we've got to make safe places for us to stay in, see, and get all the books we can—science books. That's where men like you come in, see? We'll raid the museums, we'll even spy on the Martians. It may not be so much we have to learn before—just imagine this: Four or five of their own fighting machines suddenly start off—heat-rays right and left and not a Martian in 'em. Not a Martian in 'em! But men—men who have learned the way how. It may even be in our time. Gee! Imagine having one of them lovely things with its heat-ray wide and free! We'd turn it on Martians, we'd turn it on men. We'd bring everybody down to their knees.

PIERSON: That's your plan?

STRANGER: You and me and a few more of us, we'd own the world.

PIERSON: I see.

STRANGER: Say, what's the matter? Where are you going?

PIERSON: Not to *your* world. Good-by, stranger. . . . After parting with the artilleryman, I came at last to the Holland Tunnel. I entered that silent tube anxious to know the fate of the great city on the other side of the Hudson. Cautiously I came out of the tunnel and made my way up Canal Street.

I reached Fourteenth Street, and there again were black powder and several bodies, and an evil, ominous smell from the gratings of the cellars of some of the houses. I wandered up through the Thirties and Forties; I stood alone on Times Square. I caught sight of a lean dog running down Seventh Avenue with a piece of dark-brown meat in his jaws, and a pack of starving mongrels at his heels. He made a wide circle around me, as though he feared I might prove a fresh competitor. I walked up Broadway in the direction of that strange powder—past silent shop windows, displaying their mute wares to empty sidewalks—past the Capitol Theater, silent, dark—past a shooting-gallery, where a row of empty guns faced an arrested line of wooden ducks. Near Columbus Circle I noticed models of 1939 motorcars in the showrooms facing empty streets. From over the top of the General Motors Building I watched a flock of black birds circling in the sky. I hurried on. Suddenly, I caught sight of the hood of a Martian machine, standing somewhere in Central Park, gleaming in the late afternoon sun. An insane idea! I rushed recklessly across Columbus Circle and into the Park. I climbed a small hill above the pond at Sixtieth Street. From there I could see, standing in a silent row along the Mall, nineteen of those great metal Titans, their cowls empty, their steel arms hanging listlessly by their sides. I looked in vain for the monsters that inhabit those machines.

Suddenly, my eyes were attracted to the immense flock of black birds that hovered directly below me. They circled to the ground, and there before my eyes, stark and silent, lay the Martians, with the hungry birds pecking and tearing brown shreds of flesh from their dead bodies. Later, when their bodies were examined in laboratories, it was found that they were killed by the putrefactive and disease bacteria against which their systems were unprepared—slain, after all Man's defenses had failed, by the humblest thing that God in His wisdom put upon this Earth.

Before the cylinder fell, there was a general persuasion that through all the deep of space no life existed beyond the petty surface of our minute sphere. Now we see farther. Dim and wonderful is the vision I have conjured up in my mind of life spreading slowly from this little seedbed of the Solar System throughout the inanimate vastness of sidereal space. But that is a remote dream. It may be that the destruction of the Martians is only a reprieve. To them, and not to us, is the future ordained, perhaps.

Strange it now seems to sit in my peaceful study at Princeton writing down the last chapter of the record begun at a deserted farm in Grovers Mill. Strange to see from my window the university spires dim and blue through an April haze. Strange to watch children playing in the streets. Strange to see young people strolling on the green, where the new spring grass heals the last black scars of a bruised Earth. Strange to watch the sightseers enter the museum where the disassembled parts of a Martian machine are kept on public view. Strange when I recall the time I first saw it, bright and clean-cut, hard and silent, under the dawn of that last great day.

Mildred Clingerman

MINISTER WITHOUT PORTFOLIO

Here, on the other hand, is an invasion story so quiet, so unmelodramatic, and so unassuming that at first sight it seems almost mousy—until you reach the ending. Now, under ordinary circumstances the trick ending is not a particularly desirable fictional technique; too often it is only a bad pun or something of that nature. In this instance, however, the trick is so convincing and the interaction between human and aliens is based on such sympathetic understanding that the combination is hard to resist. A bit short on science-fiction background, the story nevertheless has a science-fiction theme—in this case a charming one.

This story, the first one published by the authoress, was called to the Editor's attention by Anthony Boucher some months before it appeared in the Magazine of Fantasy and Science Fiction.

MRS. CHRISWELL's little roadster came to a shuddering halt. Here was the perfect spot. Only one sagging wire fence to step over, and not a cow in sight. Mrs. Chriswell was terrified of cows, and if the truth were told, only a little less afraid of her daughter-in-law, Clara. It was all Clara's idea that her mother-in-law should now be lurking in meadows peering at birds. Clara had been delighted with the bird-watching idea, but, frankly, Mrs. Chriswell was bored with birds. They *flew* so much. And as for their colors, it was useless for her to speculate. Mrs. Chriswell was one of those rare women who are quite, quite color-blind.

"But Clara," Mrs. Chriswell had pleaded, "what's the point if I can't tell what color they are?"

"Well, but darling," Clara had said crisply, "how much cleverer if you get to know them just from the distinctive markings!"

Mrs. Chriswell, sighing a little as she recalled the firm look of Clara's chin, maneuvered herself and her burdens over the sagging wire fence. She successfully juggled the binoculars, the heavy bird book, and her purse, and thought how ghastly it was at sixty to be considered so useless that she must be provided with harmless, genteel occupations to keep her out of the way.

Since Mr. Chriswell's death she had moved in with her son and his wife, to face a life of enforced idleness. The servants resented her presence in the kitchen, so cooking was out. Clara and the snooty nursemaid would brook no interference with the nursery routine, so Mrs. Chriswell had virtually nothing to do. Even her crocheted doilies disappeared magically soon after their presentation to Clara and the modern furniture.

Mrs. Chriswell shifted the bird book and considered rebelling. The sun was hot and her load was heavy. As she toiled on across the field, she thought she saw the glint of sun on water. She would sit and crochet in the shade nearby and remove the big straw cartwheel hat Clara had termed "just the thing."

Arrived at the trees, Mrs. Chriswell dropped her burdens and flung the hat away from her. Ugly, ridiculous thing. She glanced around for the water she thought she'd seen, but there was no sign of it. She leaned back against a tree trunk and sighed blissfully. A little breeze had sprung up and was cooling the damp tendrils on her forehead. She opened her big purse and scrambled through the muddle of contents for her crochet hook and the ball of thread attached to a half-finished doily. In her search she came across the snapshots of her granddaughters—they were in color, but unfortunately Mrs. Chriswell saw them only as various shades of gray. The breeze was getting stronger now, very pleasant, but the dratted old cartwheel monstrosity was rolling merrily down the slight grade to the tangle of berry bushes a few yards away. Well, it would catch on the brambles. But it didn't. The wind flirted it right around the bushes, and the hat disappeared.

"Fiddle!" Mrs. Chriswell dared not face Clara without the hat. Still hanging on to the bulky purse, she got up to give chase. Rounding the tangle of bushes, she ran smack into a tall young man in uniform.

"Oh!" Mrs. Chriswell said. "Have you seen my hat?"

The young man smiled and pointed down the hill.

Mrs. Chriswell was surprised to see her hat being passed from hand to hand among three other tall young men in uniform. They were laughing at it, and she didn't much blame them. They were standing beside a low, silvery aircraft of some unusual design. Mrs. Chriswell studied it a moment, but really she knew nothing about such things. The sun glinted on it, and she realized this was what she had thought was water. The young man beside her touched her arm. She turned toward him and saw that he had put a rather lovely little metal hat on his head. He offered her one with grave courtesy. Mrs. Chriswell smiled up at him and nodded. The young man fitted the hat carefully, adjusting various little ornamental knobs on its top.

"Now we can talk," he said. "Do you hear well?"

"My dear boy," Mrs. Chriswell said, "of course I do. I'm not so old as all that." She found a smooth stone and sat down to chat. This was much nicer than birdwatching, or even crochet.

The tall young man grinned and signaled excitedly to his companions. They, too, put on little metal hats and came bounding up the hill. Still laughing, they deposited the cartwheel in Mrs. Chriswell's lap. She patted the stone by way of invitation, and the youngest-looking one of the four dropped down beside her.

"What is your name, Mother?" he asked.

"Ida Chriswell," she said. "What's yours?"

"My name is Jord," the boy said.

Mrs. Chriswell patted his hand. "That's a nice, unusual name." The boy grabbed Mrs. Chriswell's hand and rubbed it against the smoothness of his cheek.

"You are like my mother's mother," the boy explained, "whom I have not seen in too long." The other young men laughed, and the boy looked abashed and stealthily wiped at a tear that slid down his nose.

Mrs. Chriswell frowned warningly at the laughter and handed him her clean pocket handkerchief, scented with lavender. Jord turned it over and over in his hands and then tentatively sniffed at it.

"It's all right," Mrs. Chriswell said. "Use it. I have another." But Jord only breathed more deeply of the faint perfume in its folds.

"This is only the thinnest thread of melody," he said, "but, Mother Ida, it is very like one note from the Harmony Hills of home!" He passed the handkerchief all around the circle, and the young men sniffed at it and smiled.

Mrs. Chriswell tried to remember if she had ever read of the Harmony Hills, but Mr. Chriswell had always told her she was lamentably weak in geography, and she supposed that this was one of her blank spots, like where on earth was Timbuktu? Or the Hellandgone people were always talking about? But it was rude not to make some comment. Wars shifted people about such a lot, and these boys must be homesick and weary of being strangers, longing to talk of home. She was proud of herself for realizing that they were strangers. But there was something . . . Hard to say, really. The way they had bounded up the hill? Mountain people, perhaps, to whom hills were mere springboards to heights beyond.

"Tell me about your hills," she said.

"Wait," Jord said. "I will show you." He glanced at his leader as if for approval. The young man who had fitted her hat nodded. Jord drew a fingernail across the breast of his uniform. Mrs. Chriswell was surprised to see a pocket opening where no pocket had been before. Really, the Air Force did amazing things with its uniforms, though, frankly, Mrs. Chriswell thought the cut of these a bit extreme.

Carefully, Jord lifted out a packet of gossamer material. He gently pressed the center of the packet, and it blossomed out into voluminous clouds of featherweight threads held together loosely in a weave like a giant spider web. To Mrs. Chriswell's eyes, the mesh of threads was the color of fog and almost as insubstantial.

"Do not be afraid," Jord said softly, stepping closer to her. "Bend your head, close your eyes, and you shall hear the Harmony Hills of home."

There was one quick-drawn breath of almost fear, but before she shut her eyes Mrs. Chriswell saw the love in Jord's, and in that moment she knew how rarely she had seen this look, anywhere . . . any time. If Jord had asked it of her, it was all right. She closed her eyes and bowed her head, and in that attitude of prayer she felt a soft weightlessness descend upon her. It was as if twilight had come down to drape itself around her shoulders. And then the music began. Behind the darkness of her eyes it rose in majesty and power, in colors she had never seen, never guessed. It blossomed like flowers —giant forests of them. Their scents were intoxicating and filled her with joy. She could not tell if the blending perfumes made the music or if the music itself created the flowers and the perfumes that poured forth from them. She did not care. She wanted only to go on listening forever to all this color. It seemed odd to be listening to color, perhaps, but after all, she told herself, it would seem just as odd to me to *see* it.

She sat blinking at the circle of young men. The music was finished. Jord was putting away the gossamer threads in the secret pocket and laughing aloud at her astonishment.

"Did you like it, Mother Ida?" He dropped down beside her again and patted her wrinkled face, still pink with excitement.

"Oh, Jord," she said, "how lovely. . . . Tell me . . ."

But the leader was calling them to order. "I'm sorry, Mother Ida, we must hurry about our business. Will you answer some questions? It is very important."

"Of course," Mrs. Chriswell said. She was still feeling a bit dazed. "If I can. . . . If it's like the quizzes on the radio, though, I'm not very good at it."

The young man shook his head. "We have been instructed," he said, "to investigate and report on the true conditions of this . . . of the world." He pointed at the aircraft glittering in the sunlight. "We have—traveled all around in that slow machine, and our observations have been accurate . . ." He hesitated, drew a deep breath, and continued, ". . . and perhaps we shall be forced to give an unfavorable report, but this depends a great deal on the outcome of our talk with you. We are glad you stumbled upon us. We were about to set out on a foray to secure some individual for questioning. It is our last task." He smiled. "And Jord, here, will not be sorry. He is sick for home and loved ones." He sighed, and all the other young men echoed the sigh.

"Every night," Mrs. Chriswell said, "I pray for peace on earth. I cannot bear to think of boys like you fighting and dying, and the folks at home waiting and waiting . . ." She glanced at their listening faces. "And I'll tell you something else," she said. "I find I can't really hate anybody, even the enemy." Around the circle, the young men nodded at one another. "Now ask me your questions." She fumbled in her purse for her crochet work and found it.

Beside her, Jord exclaimed with pleasure at the sight of the half-finished doily. Mrs. Chriswell warmed to him even more.

The tall young man began his grave questioning. They were very simple questions, and Mrs. Chriswell answered them without hesitation. Did she believe in God? Did she believe in the dignity of Man? Did she truly abhor war? Did she believe that Man was capable of love for his neighbor? The questions went on and on, and Mrs. Chriswell crocheted while she gave her answers.

At last, when the young man had quite run out of questions and Mrs. Chriswell had finished the doily, Jord broke the sun-lazy silence that had fallen upon them.

"May I have it, Mother?" He pointed to the doily. Mrs. Chriswell bestowed it upon him with great pleasure, and Jord, like a very small boy, stuffed it greedily into another secret pocket. He pointed at her purse.

"May I look, Mother?"

Mrs. Chriswell indulgently passed him her purse. He opened it and poured the litter of contents on the ground between them. The snapshots of Mrs. Chriswell's grandchildren stared up at him. Jord smiled at the pretty little-girl faces. He groped in the chest pocket and drew out snapshots of his own. "These," he told Mrs. Chriswell proudly, "are my little sisters. Are they not like these little girls of yours? Let us exchange, because soon I will be at home with them and there will be no need for pictures."

Mrs. Chriswell would have given Jord the entire contents of the purse if he had asked for them. She took the snapshots he offered and looked with pleasure at the sweet-faced children. Jord still stirred at the pile of things from Mrs. Chriswell's purse. By the time she was ready to leave, he had talked her out of three illustrated recipes torn from magazines, some swatches of material, and two pieces of peppermint candy.

The young leader helped Mrs. Chriswell remove the pretty little hat when she indicated he should. She would have liked to keep it, but she didn't believe Clara would approve. She clapped the straw monstrosity on her head, kissed Jord's cheek, waved good-by to the rest, and groped her way around the berry bushes. She had to grope because her eyes were tear-filled: all the young men had saluted her so grandly as she turned to go.

Clara's usually sedate household was in an uproar when Mrs. Chriswell returned. All the radios in the house were blaring. Even Clara sat huddled over the one in the library. Mrs. Chriswell heard a boy in the street crying "EXTRA, EXTRA," and the upstairs maid almost knocked her down getting out the front door to buy one. Mrs. Chriswell, sleepy and somewhat sunburned, supposed it was something about the awful war.

She was just turning up the stairs to her room when the snooty nursemaid came rushing down, to disappear kitchenwards with another newspaper in hand. Good, the children were alone. She'd stop in to see them. Suddenly she heard the raised voices from the back of the house. The cook was yelling at somebody, "I tell you, I saw it! I took out some garbage and there it was, right over me!" Mrs. Chriswell lingered at the foot of the stairway, puzzled by all the confusion. The housemaid came rushing in with the Extra edition. Mrs. Chriswell quietly reached out and took it.

"Thank you, Nadine," she said. The housemaid was still staring at her as she climbed the stairs.

Edna and Evelyn were sitting on the nursery floor, a candy box between them, and shrieking at each other when their grandmother opened the door. They were cramming candy into their mouths between shrieks. Their faces and pinafores were smeared with chocolate. Edna suddenly yanked Evelyn's hair, hard. "Pig!" she shouted. "You got three more than I did!"

"Children! Children! Not fighting?" Mrs. Chriswell

was delighted. Here was something she could cope with. She led them firmly to the bathroom and washed their faces. "Change your frocks," she said, "and I'll tell you my adventure."

There were only hissing accusals and whispered countercharges behind her as she turned her back on the children to scan the newspaper. Grandmothers, she told herself, have a calming effect on children. The headlines leaped up at her.

"FLYING SAUCERS APPEAR OVER CITY." "Mysterious Broadcast Interrupts Programs on All Wave Lengths." "Unknown Woman Saves World Say Men from Space." "ONE SANE HUMAN FOUND ON EARTH. TOTAL DESTRUCTION OF WORLD AVERTED." "Useful, Busy Females Hope of Future." "Cooking, Needlework, Home, and Religious Interests Sway Space Judges." Every column of the paper was crowded with the same unintelligible nonsense. Mrs. Chriswell folded it neatly, deposited it on a table, and turned to tie her granddaughters' sashes and tell her adventure.

". . . And then he gave me some lovely photographs. In color, he said . . . Good little girls, just like Edna and Evelyn. Would you like to see them?"

Edna made a rude noise with her mouth pursed. Evelyn's face grew saintlike in retaliation. "Yes, show us," she said.

Mrs. Chriswell passed them the snapshots, and the children drew close together for a moment, before Evelyn dropped the pictures as if they were blazing. She stared hard at her grandmother while Edna made a gagging noise.

"Green!" Edna gurgled. "Gaaaa . . . green skins!"

"Grandmother!" Evelyn was tearful. "Those children are frog-colored!"

Mrs. Chriswell bent over to pick up the pictures. "Now, now, children," she murmured absently. "We don't worry about the color of people's skins. Red . . . yellow . . . black . . . we're all God's children. Asia or Africa, make no difference . . ." But before she could finish her thought, the nursemaid loomed disapprovingly in the doorway. Mrs. Chriswell hurried out to her own room, while some tiny worry nagged at her mind. "Red, yellow, black, white," she murmured over and over, "and brown . . . but green . . . ?" Geography had always been her weak point. Green . . . Now where on earth . . . ?

Fredric Brown

THE WAVERIES

Take a deep breath, shake yourself vigorously a couple of times, and try to imagine, before you begin this story, what the "Waveries" might be. Ten thousand to one you won't be able to!

Certainly, this is one of the most unique invasion stories of the last couple of decades. There have been two or three others that have more or less played around with the same general idea, but none which carried it relentlessly through to its ultimate consequence—the complete "conquest" of humanity.

The "conquest," however, is far from malign. Perhaps we could use some Waveries in actuality, for the end result of their activity might force us to greater self-reliance, relaxation from tension, and a return to some of the less mechanized pleasures that our grandparents knew.

DEFINITIONS from school-abridged Webster-Hamlin Dictionary, 2088 edition:

wavery (WĀ-ver-ĭ) *n.* a vader—*slang*
vader (VĀ-dêr) *n.* inorgan of the class Radio
inorgan (ĭn-ÔR-găn) *n.* noncorporeal ens, a vader
radio (RĀ-dĭ-ōh, ră-DĒ-ōh) *n.* 1. Class of inorgans.
2. Etheric frequency between light and electricity. 3. (obsolete) Method of communication used up to 1971.

The opening guns of invasion were not at all loud, although they were heard by many people. George Bailey was one of the many; I choose George Bailey because he was the only one who came within a googol of light-years of guessing what they were.

George Bailey was drunk, and under the circumstances one can't blame him. He was listening to radio advertisements of the most verbose and annoying kind. Not because he *wanted* to listen to them, but because he'd been told to listen by his boss, J. R. McGee, of the MID network.

George Bailey wrote advertising for the radio. The only thing he hated worse than advertising was radio. And here, on his own time in the late evening, he was listening to fulsome and saccharine drippings on a rival network, at J. R. McGee's suggestion—which George very rightly took for an order.

"Bailey, you should be more familiar with what others are doing. Particularly those of our own accounts which use several networks. I'd suggest that—"

One doesn't quarrel with suggestions and keep a hundred-and-fifty-dollar-a-week job. But one can drink whisky sours while listening. One George Bailey did.

Also, one could play gin rummy with Maisie Hetterman, a cute little redheaded typist from the studio. One could do no more than that, but Maisie was worth just looking at across a card table. It was Maisie's apartment and Maisie's radio, but George had brought the liquor.

"—only the best tobaccos," said the radio, "go *dit-dit-dit*—the nation's favorite cigarettes—"

George glanced at the radio. "Marconi," he said.

He meant Morse, naturally, but the whisky sours had muddled him a bit, so he was nearer right than most people who heard that dit-dit-dit. It *was* Marconi, in a way; in, as it turned out, a very peculiar way.

"Marconi?" asked Maisie.

George Bailey, who hated to talk while a radio was going, leaned over and switched it off.

"I mean Morse," he said. "Morse, as in Boy Scouts or the Signal Corps. I used to be a Boy Scout once."

"You don't look it."

George sighed. "Somebody going to catch hell," he said, "broadcasting code on that wave length."

"What did it mean?"

"Mean? Oh, you mean what did it mean. Uh . . . S, letter S. *Dit-dit-dit.* SOS *is dit-dit-dit, dah-dah-dah, dit-dit-dit.*"

"O is *dah-dah-dah?*"

George grinned. "Say it again, Maisie. I like it. I think 'oo is *dah-dah-dah,* too."

"George! Maybe it's really an SOS message. Turn it back on, please."

He turned it back on. The tobacco ad was still going. "—gentlemen of the most . . . *dit-dit-dit* . . . ing taste prefer the finer taste of Golden Harvest . . . *dit-dit-dit* . . . arettes. In the new package that keeps them . . . *dit-dit-dit* . . . and ultrafresh—"

"It's just S-S-S-S," said George. "Like a teakettle.

Or maybe somebody s-s-stutters. But the Golden Harvest people are going to raise— Say—"

"What, George?"

"Maybe it's deliberate, an advertising gag like L.S. M.F.T. used to be. Just a minute till I—"

He reached over and turned the dial of the radio a bit to the right, then a bit to the left, and an incredulous look came over his face. He turned the dial to the extreme right, as far as it would go. There wasn't any station there—not even the hum of a carrier wave.

"*Dit-dit-dit*," said the radio, "*—dit-dit-dit.*"

George turned it to the other end of the dial. "*Dit-dit-dit*," said the radio.

He switched it off and stared at Maisie, without even seeing her, which was hard to do.

"Something wrong, George?"

"I hope so," said George Bailey. "I certainly hope so."

He started to reach for another drink, then changed his mind. He had a sudden hunch that something big was happening, and wanted to sober up to appreciate it.

He didn't have the faintest idea *how* big it was.

"George, what do you mean?"

"I don't know. But Maisie, let's take a run down to the studio, huh? There ought to be some excitement."

April 5, 1947; that was the night the waveries came.

It was a gay night, except for radio technicians. New York was at its best and gayest, and the main stem, which is Broadway, running high, wide, and expensive. The streets were full of uniforms, mostly uniforms of men already demobilized, due to recent reduction in the armies of occupation—so recently demobilized that they hadn't taken time to buy civvies. Discharge pay burning in their pockets, they wanted Broadway and they took Broadway; or Broadway took them. Fresh shiploads of them daily.

The gaiety was hectic, but it was a surface gaiety, even greater than that of the boom years of 1928 and '29. Workers dead weary from overtime in the reconverted factories trying to supply the peak demand for automobiles and radios and jukeboxes and pinball games left the factories for a hasty meal, then went out in their automobiles—with car radios blaring—and spent their overtime pay in the jukeboxes and pinball machines. Which, of course, increased the demand for those commodities, which increased the overtime of the factories, which increased the overtime pay, which increased the spending and the demand and— Well, you see what I mean.

It was a vicious circle that would eventually have bitten itself.

But the waveries bit first.

April 5, 1947; that was the night the waveries came.

George and Maisie tried in vain to get a cab and took the subway instead. Oh, yes, the subways were still running then. It took them within a block of the MID Network Building.

It was a madhouse. George, grinning, strolled through the lobby with Maisie on his arm, took the elevator to five, and for no reason at all gave the elevator boy a dollar. He'd never before in his life tipped an elevator operator.

The boy grinned. "Better stay away from the big shots, Mr. Bailey," he said. "They're ready to chew off anybody's ears that looks at 'em cockeyed."

"Swell," said George. He left the elevator and headed straight for the office of J. R. McGee, himself. There were strident voices behind the glass door.

"But George," protested Maisie, "you'll be fired!"

"'When in the course of human events,'" said George. "Oh, well, it's worth it. I got money saved up."

"But what are you going to do, George?"

"Stand back away from that door, honey." Gently, but firmly, he moved her to a safe position.

"But what *are* you—"

"This," said George Bailey soberly.

The frantic voices stopped as he opened the glass door a bit. All eyes turned as he stuck his head in through the crack of the door.

"Dit-dit-dit," he said. *"Dit-dit-dit."*

He ducked back and to one side just in time to escape the flying glass, as a paperweight and an inkwell came through the pane.

He grabbed Maisie and ran for the stairs.

"Now we get a drink," he told her.

The bar across from the Network Building was crowded, but it was a strangely silent crowd. Most of them were bunched around the big cabinet radio at one end of the bar.

"Dit," said the cabinet radio. *"dit-dah-d'dah-dit-dahditditdah . . . d'd'dahditdddititdah—"*

Somebody fiddled with the dial. Somebody asked, "What band is that?" and somebody said, "Police." Somebody said, "Try the foreign band," and somebody did. "This ought to be Buenos Aires," somebody said. The radio said, *"dit-dit-dahditititdditah."*

George squeezed Maisie's arm.

"Lovely," he said. Maybe he meant her and maybe not; it didn't matter at the moment.

Somebody ran fingers through his hair and yelled, "Shut that thing off." Somebody did. Somebody else turned it back on.

George grinned and led the way to a back booth

where he'd spotted Pete Mulvaney sitting alone with a tall bottle in front of him.

George seated Maisie and himself across from Pete Mulvaney.

"Hello," he said gravely.

"Hello," said Pete, who was head of the technical research staff of the MID.

"A beautiful night, Mulvaney. Did you see the moon riding high in the fleecy clouds like a golden galleon tossed upon silver-crested whitecaps in a stormy—"

"Shut up," said Pete. "I'm thinking."

"Whisky sours," said George to the waiter. He turned back to the brooding man across the table. "Think out loud," he said. "We sit at your feet. But first, how did you escape the looney bin?"

"I'm bounced, fired, discharged."

"Shake," said George, "and then explain."

"I told them what I thought it was, and they said I was crazy."

"Are you?"

"Yes," said Mulvaney.

"Good," said George. "I don't care what it is, as long as it's nothing trivial. But what the devil *is* it?"

"I don't know. Space, I think. Space is warped."

"Good old space," said George Bailey.

"George," said Maisie, "please shut up. I want to hear this."

"Space is also finite. You go far enough in any direction, and you get back where you started." Pete Mulvaney poured himself another drink. "Like an ant crawling around an apple."

"Make it an orange," said George.

"All right, an orange. Suppose the first radio waves ever sent out have just made the round trip. In forty-six years."

"Forty-six years? But I thought radio waves traveled at the speed of light. In forty-six years they could go only forty-six light-years, and *that* can't be around the Universe, because there are Galaxies known to be thousands of light-years away, or maybe millions; I don't know. But more than forty-six, Pete."

Pete Mulvaney sighed deeply. "We," he said, "are in the middle of a super-Galaxy that is two million light-years in diameter. That is just one Galaxy, a medium-sized one, they tell us. Yes, it's more than forty-six light-years around the orange."

"But—"

"But listen to that stuff. Can you read code?"

"Nope, not that fast, anyway."

"Well, I can. That's early American ham. Lingo and all. That's the kind of stuff the air was full of before *broadcasting*. It's the lingo, the abbreviations, the barnyard-to-attic chitchat of amateurs with keys, with Marconi coherers or Fessenden barreters—and you can listen for a violin solo pretty soon now. And you know what the first phonograph record ever broadcast was? Handel's *Largo* sent out by Fessenden from Brant Rock in 1906. You'll hear his CQ-CQ any minute now. Bet you a drink."

"Sure, but what was the *dit-dit-dit* that started what's turned into hash since?"

Mulvaney grinned and then his face went blank. He said, "Marconi, George. What was the first *powerful* signal ever broadcast, and by whom and when?"

"Marconi? *Dit-dit-dit*? Forty-six years ago?"

"Head of the class. The first transatlantic signal on December 12, 1901. For three hours Marconi's big station at Poldhu with two-hundred-foot masts sent out an intermittent S . . . *dit-dit-dit* . . . while Marconi and two assistants at St. Johns in Newfoundland got a kite-borne aerial four hundred feet in the air and finally got the signal. Across the Atlantic, George, with sparks jumping from the big Leyden jars at Poldhu and 20,000-volt juice jumping off the tremendous aerials—"

"Wait a minute, Pete, you're off the beam. If that was in 1901 and the first broadcast about 1906, it'll be five years before the Fessenden stuff gets here, on the same route. Even if there's a forty-six-light-year short cut across space, and even if those signals didn't get so weak en route that we couldn't hear them. It's crazy."

"I told you I was crazy," said Mulvaney. "Those signals should be so infinitesimal you couldn't hear them with the best set on Earth. Furthermore, they're all over the band on everything from microwave to ten kilocycles, and equally strong on each. Furthermore, we've come five years in two hours, which isn't possible. I told you I was crazy."

"But—"

"Listen," said Pete.

A blurred but unmistakably human voice was coming from the radio, mingling with the cracklings of code. And then music, faint and scratchy and punctuated by *dit-dah*, but nevertheless music. Handel's *Largo*.

Only it suddenly climbed in pitch, as though modulating from key to key, until it became so horribly shrill as to hurt the ear, like an orchestra made up of nothing but piccolos. And kept on going, past the high limit of audibility, until they could hear it no more.

Somebody said, "Shut that thing off." Somebody did, and this time nobody turned the thing back on.

George and Maisie looked at Pete Mulvaney, and Pete Mulvaney looked back at them.

"But it can't be," said Pete Mulvaney. "There must

be some other explanation. The more I think of it, now, the more I think I'm wrong."

He was right; he was wrong.

"Preposterous," said Mr. Ogilvie. He took off his glasses, frowned fiercely, and put them back on again. He looked through them at the several sheets of copy paper in his hand and tossed them contemptuously to the top of his desk. They slid to rest against the triangular name plate that read:

B. R. Ogilvie
Editor-in-Chief

"Preposterous," he said again.

Casey Blair, his star reporter, blew a smoke ring and poked his index finger through it. "Why?" he asked.

"Because . . . why, it's preposterous!"

Casey Blair said, "It is now three o'clock in the morning. The radio interference has gone on for five hours and has reached the point where not a single current program is getting through. Every major broadcasting station in the world has gone off the air.

"For two reasons. One: It wasn't doing a bit of good to stay on the air and waste current, no matter what wave length they were on. Two: The communications bureaus of their respective governments requested them to get off to aid their campaigns with the direction finders. For five hours now—since the first note of interference—they've been working with everything they've got. And what have they got?"

"Preposterous," said the editor.

"Exactly. Greenwich at eleven P.M.—New York time —got a bearing in about the direction of Miami. It shifted northward until at two o'clock the direction was approximately that of Richmond, Virginia. Now, San

Francisco at eleven got a bearing in about the direction of Denver; three hours later it shifted southward toward Tucson. Southern hemisphere: bearings from Capetown, South Africa, shifted from approximate direction of Buenos Aires to direction of Montevideo, a thousand miles north. New York had trouble with direction finders; weak indications at eleven were toward Madrid; by two o'clock they could get no bearings at all." He blew another smoke ring. "Maybe because the loop antennas they use turn only on a horizontal plane."

"Absurd," said Mr. Ogilvie.

Casey said. "I liked 'preposterous' better, Mr. Ogilvie. It's not absurd; I'm scared stiff. Those lines converge on about the constellation Leo, if you take them as straight lines instead of curving them around the surface. I did it with a little globe and a star map." He leaned forward and tapped a forefinger on the top copy page. "Stations directly under that point in the sky get no bearings at all. Stations on, as it were, the perimeter of the Earth get strong bearings in the horizontal plane."

"But the Heaviside layer, Blair—isn't that supposed to stop all radio waves—bounce 'em back, or something?"

"Uh-huh. It does. But maybe it leaks. Maybe some waves got through. It isn't a solid wall."

"But—"

"I know; it's preposterous. But there it is. Only there's an hour before press time and you ought to turn the observatories on it and get it more accurately. Get *them* to extend those bearing lines. I did it by rule of thumb. Further, I didn't have the data for checking planet positions. Leo's on the ecliptic; a planet could be in line between here and there. Like Mars, maybe."

Mr. Ogilvie's eyes brightened, then clouded again.

He said, "We'll be the laughingstock of the world, Blair, if we're wrong."

"And if I'm right?"

Ogilvie picked up the phone and snapped an order that sent every rewrite man into his office for orders.

April 6th headline of the New York *Morning Messenger,* final (5 A.M.) edition:

RADIO INTERFERENCE COMES FROM SPACE: ORIGINATES IN LEO, SAY SCIENTISTS

May Be Attempt at Communication by Beings Outside Solar System!

All Broadcasting Suspended

RKO and Radio Corporation stocks, having closed the previous day at 10¼ and 11½ respectively, opened at 9¾ and 9½ and dropped sharply. By noon they were off four and five points respectively, when a moderate buying rally brought each of them back a fraction over two points.

Public action was mixed; people who had no radios rushed out to buy them, and there was a boom market in portable and table-top receivers. Those who had radios listened as long as their curiosity enabled them to stand it, and then turned them off. Extraterrestrial or not, the programs were a horrible hash.

Oh, there were flashes—times when, for several seconds at a time, a listener could recognize the voices of Will Rogers or Geraldine Farrar or could catch a scrap of the Dempsey-Carpentier fight. But things worth hearing—even for seconds at a time—were rare. Mostly it was a jumble of soap opera, advertising, and off-key snatches of what had once been music. It was utterly indiscriminate and utterly unbearable for any length of time.

But curiosity is a powerful motive. There *was* a brief boom in radio sets that morning.

There were other booms, less explicable, less capable of analysis. Reminiscent of the Wells-Welles Martian scare was a sudden upswing in the sale of shotguns and sidearms. Bibles sold as readily as books on astronomy —and books on astronomy sold like hot cakes. One section of the country showed a sudden interest in lightning rods—builders were deluged with orders for immediate demonstration.

For some reason which has never been clearly ascertained, there was a run on fishhooks in Mobile, Alabama; every hardware and sporting-goods store in that city was sold out of them before noon.

The public libraries had a run on books on astrology and books on Mars. Yes, on Mars—despite the fact that Mars was at the moment on the other side of the Sun and that every newspaper article on the subject stressed the fact that *no* planet was between Earth and the constellation Leo.

And not a radio station on Earth was on the air that morning.

Newspapers were passed from hand to hand because the presses couldn't keep up with the demand. *No news on the radio*—and something big was happening. People waited, in mobs, outside the newspaper offices for each new edition to appear. Circulation managers went quietly mad.

People gathered in curious little knots about the broadcasting studios. MID Network doors were locked, although there was a doorman on duty to admit technicians, who were trying to find an answer to the unprecedented difficulty. Some, who had been on duty the previous day, had now spent twenty-four hours without sleep.

George Bailey woke at noon, with only a slight headache. He turned on his radio and turned it off again quickly.

He shaved and showered, went out and drank a light breakfast, and was himself again. He bought early editions of the afternoon papers, read them, and grinned. His hunch had been right; whatever was wrong with radio, it was nothing trivial.

But *what* was wrong?

The later editions of the evening papers had it.

EARTH INVADED, SAYS SCIENTIST

Thirty-six line type was the biggest they had; they used it. Not a home-edition copy of a newspaper was delivered that evening. Newsboys starting on their routes were practically mobbed. They sold papers instead of delivering them; the smart ones got a quarter apiece for them. The foolish ones who didn't want to sell, because the papers had been bought for their routes, lost them anyway; people grabbed them.

The later home editions and the finals changed the heading only slightly—from a typographical viewpoint. But it was a big change, just the same:

EARTH INVADED, SAY SCIENTISTS

Funny what moving an S from the ending of a verb to the ending of a noun can do.

Carnegie Hall shattered precedents that evening with a lecture given at midnight. An unscheduled and unadvertised lecture. Professor Helmetz had stepped off the train at eleven-thirty, and a mob of reporters had been waiting for him. Helmetz, of Harvard, had been the scientist—singular—who had made the first headlines.

Harvey Ambers, Director of the Board of Carnegie Hall, had pushed his way through the mob. He arrived minus glasses, hat, and breath, but got hold of Helmetz's arm and hung on until he could talk again. "We want you to talk at Carnegie, Professor," he shouted into Helmetz's ear. "Thousand bucks for a lecture on the 'vaders!"

"Certainly. Tomorrow afternoon?"

"Now! I've got a cab waiting. Come on."

"But . . . but . . ."

"We'll get you an audience. Hurry!" He turned to the mob. "Let us through! You can't hear the professor here. Come to Carnegie and he'll talk to you. Spread the word."

The word spread so well that Carnegie Hall was jammed by midnight, when the professor began to speak. By twelve-thirty, they'd rigged a loud-speaker system so that people outside could hear. By one o'clock in the morning the streets were jammed for blocks around.

There wasn't a sponsor on Earth with a million dollars to his name who wouldn't have given a million dollars to sponsor the broadcasting of that lecture—but it was not broadcast on the radio.

The line was busy.

"Questions?" asked Professor Helmetz.

A reporter in the front row made it first. "Professor," he asked, "have *all* direction-finding stations on Earth confirmed your statement as to the change this afternoon?"

"Yes, absolutely. At about noon, the directional indications began to grow weaker. At 2:47 o'clock, New York time, they ceased completely. Until then, the radio waves emanated from the sky, constantly changing direction with reference to the Earth's surface, but *constant* with reference to the point in the constellation Leo."

"What star in Leo?"

"No star. Merely a point in the sky coinciding exactly with the position of no visible star on the most minute charts. At 2:47 o'clock all direction finders went dead, but the signals persisted. They came from *all sides* equally. The invaders were here. There is no other conclusion to be drawn. Earth is now surrounded, completely blanketed, by radio waves which have *no point of origin,* which travel ceaselessly around the Earth in all directions, changing shape at will—which at the moment seems to be in imitation of the Earth-origin signals that attracted their attention, that brought them here."

"From nowhere? From just a point in space?"

"Why not, sir? They are creatures of *ether,* not of matter. Ether permeates space uniformly. They were, until they were attracted here, at a point in space not greater than twenty-three light-years away. Our first indication of their arrival—rather, the arrival of the first ones, if you want to put it that way—came with a repetition of Marconi's S-S-S transatlantic broadcast of forty-six years ago. Apparently that was the first Earth broadcast of sufficient power to send signals that they could perceive at that distance. They started for Earth then, presumably. It took twenty-three years for those waves to reach them and twenty-three years for them to reach us. The first to arrive had formed themselves, imitatively, to duplicate the shape, as it were, of the signals that attracted them. Later arrivals were in the form of other waves that they had met, or passed, or absorbed, on their way to Earth. There are now fragments of programs broadcast as recently as a few days ago . . . uh . . . wandering about the ether. Undoubtedly, also, there are fragments of the very last programs to be broadcast, but they have not yet been identified."

"Professor, can you *describe* one of the invaders?"

"No more than one can describe a radio wave. They *are* radio waves, in effect, although they emanate from no broadcasting station. They are a form of life dependent upon the movement of ether, as life as we know it is dependent upon the vibration of matter. Life is movement—or at least, life is contingent upon movement."

"They are different sizes?"

"Yes—in two senses of the word size. Radio waves are measured from crest to crest, which measurement is known as the wave length. Since the invaders cover the entire dials of our receiving sets, obviously they can—in imitation, undoubtedly, of the waves of ours that they have met—adjust themselves to any frequency, or crest-to-crest wave length.

"But that is only a crest-to-crest length. The actual length of a radio wave is much greater. If a broadcasting station sends out a program of one second's duration, the length of the wave carrying that program is one light-second, or 186,270 miles. A half-hour program is on a continuous wave, as it were, one-half light-hour long, and so on.

"On that basis, the individual . . . uh . . . invaders vary in length from a hundred thousand miles long—less than a second in duration—to about five million miles long—almost half a minute in duration. Each is in constant movement at the speed of light, and presumably that movement is now in a circle about the surface of the Earth. Each wave, as it were, extends many times, or many thousands of times, around the Earth."

"How can that be told?"

"By the length of the . . . ah . . . excerpts from various programs. None are under half a second in duration, none over half a minute."

"But why assume, Professor Helmetz, that these . . . these waves are living things? Why not just inanimate waves?"

"An inanimate wave . . . as you call it . . . would follow certain laws. Just as inanimate matter follows certain laws. An animal can climb uphill, however, or run in circles, or . . . uh . . . climb a tree. A stone can do none of these unless impelled by some outside force. It is the same with these invaders. They are living things because they show volition, because they are not limited in direction of travel, because they can change their form—because they *retain their identity;* two signals never come together on the same radio or conflict with one another. They follow one another but do not come simultaneously. They do not blend or heterodyne as signals on the same wave length would ordinarily do. They follow laws and rules of their own. They are *not* merely radio waves."

"But, Professor, are they intelligent beings?"

Professor Helmetz took off his glasses and polished them thoughtfully. He said finally, "I doubt if we shall ever know. The intelligence of such things, if any, would be on such a completely different plane from ours that there would be no common point from which we could start intercourse. We are material; they are immaterial. I do not think there can ever be common ground between us."

"But if they are intelligent at all, Professor—"

"Ants are intelligent, after a fashion. Even if one calls it instinct that enables them to do such marvelous things, still instinct is a form of intelligence. Yet we cannot communicate with ants; we shall be less likely to communicate with the invaders. The difference in type between ant intelligence and ours would be nothing to the difference in type between the intelligence of the invaders and our own. What *could* we have to say to one another?"

The professor must have had something there. Communication with the vaders—a clipped form, of course, of "invaders"—was never established.

Radio stocks stabilized on the Exchange. Until, a day after the midnight lecture, someone asked Dr. Helmetz the sixty-four-dollar question and the newspapers published his answer:

"Resume broadcasting? I don't know. Not until the invaders go away, and why should they? Unless, of course, radio communication is perfected on some other planet in some other Galaxy, and they're attracted there."

"And if they did go away—?"

"Oh, they'd be back when we started to broadcast again."

Radio stocks dropped to practically zero in an hour. There wasn't any frenzied scene on the Exchange, however; no frenzied selling, because there was no buying, frenzied or otherwise. No radio stocks exchanged hands.

Radio musicians took jobs in theaters, taverns, and the like. And failed completely to fulfill the increased demand for talent. With radio out, other forms of entertainment boomed.

Magazine sales boomed. Movies boomed. Vaudeville was coming back. Everything boomed except radio.

"One down," said George Bailey. The bartender asked what he meant.

"I dunno, Hank. I got a hunch."

"What kind of hunch?"

"I don't even know that. Shake me up one more of those, and I'll go home."

The electric shaker wouldn't work, and Hank had to shake it up by hand.

"Exercise; that's what you need," said George. "Take some of that fat off you."

Hank grunted and the ice tinkled merrily as he tilted the shaker to pour out the drink.

George Bailey drank it leisurely and strolled out into an April thundershower. He stood under the awning and watched for a taxi. An old man was standing in front of him.

"Some weather," George said.

The old man grinned at him. "You noticed it?"

"Huh? Noticed what?"

"Just watch a while, mister. Just watch a while."

The old man moved on. George stood there quite a while—for no cab went by empty—before he got it. His jaw dropped a trifle, and then he closed his mouth and went back into the tavern. He went into a phone booth and called Pete Mulvaney.

He got three wrong numbers and lost four nickels before he got Pete. Pete's voice said "Yeah?"

"George Bailey, Pete. Listen, the weather. Notice it?"

"Yes. What's it mean, you want to know. So do I. You tell me. I think it's—" A crackling sound on the wire blurred it out.

"Hey, Pete! You there?"

The sound of a violin. Pete Mulvaney didn't play the violin.

"Hey, Pete! What in—"

Pete's voice again. "Come on over, George. This isn't going to last long. Bring—" A buzzing noise and then a voice that was not Pete's said, "—come to Carnegie

Hall. The best tunes of all come to Carnegie Hall. Yes, the best tunes of all come to Car—"

George slammed down the receiver.

He walked through the rain to Pete's place. On the way he bought a bottle of Scotch. Pete had started to tell him to bring something, and maybe, he figured, that was what it was.

It was.

They poured a drink apiece and lifted them. The lights flickered briefly, went out, and then on again.

"No lightning," said George. "No lightning and pretty soon no lighting. They're taking over the telephone. What do they do with lightning, though?"

"Eat it, maybe."

"No lightning," said George. "I can get by without a telephone, and candles and oil lamps aren't bad for lights, but I'm going to miss lightning. I *like* lightning."

Pete Mulvaney leaned back in his chair. He said, "Electric lights, electric toasters, electric hair curlers, vacuum cleaners. Electric power, and—automobiles and airplanes and Diesel-engined boats. George, do you know no gasoline engine can work without electricity?"

"Huh? For a starter, sure, but can't it be cranked by hand?"

"Yes, but the *spark*."

"Yes, the spark. Hey, how about these new rocket planes? Those, too?"

"Those, too."

"Movies?"

"Definitely, movies. You couldn't work a projector with an oil lamp. You need concentrated light for that. And sound tracks—well, that's electricity *per se*."

George Bailey shook his head slowly. "All right, scratch movies. Streetcars. Trucks, tanks, toasters— See what it all means, Pete?"

Pete poured another drink. "It means we're going back to the original source of horsepower. Horses. If you want to invest, buy horses. Particularly mares; mares are going to be worth their weight in gold."

"Hey, though, there are steam engines. Locomotives."

Pete Mulvaney nodded. "The iron horse. We'll be back to it for the long hauls, and back to Dobbin for the short ones. Can you ride?"

George sipped his drink slowly. "Used to when I was a kid. Guess I can learn again. Say, it'll be fun. And say—"

"What?"

"Used to play the cornet when I was a kid. Think I'll get one and learn again. That'll be fun, too. And maybe I'll hole in somewhere and write that nov— Say, what about printing?"

"They printed books long before electricity. Take a while to readjust the printing industry, but there'll be books and magazines, all right."

George Bailey grinned and got up. He walked over to the window and looked out and down into the storm. A streetcar was stalled in the middle of the block outside. Behind him, the lights flickered again. An automobile stopped, then started more slowly, stopped again.

A neon light across the way suddenly went dark.

He looked up at the sky and sipped his drink.

"No lightning," he said. He was going to *miss* the lightning.

The change-over, for a wonder, went smoothly.

The government, having had experience of a multiplicity of divided authorities, created one board with practically unlimited authority, and under it three subsidiary boards. The main board, called the Economic Readjustment Bureau, had only seven members, and its job was to coordinate the efforts of the three subsidiary boards and to decide, quickly and without delay, any jurisdictional disputes among them.

First of the three subsidiary boards was the Transportation Bureau. It immediately took over, temporarily, the railroads. It ordered Diesel engines run on sidings and left there, organized use of the steam locomotives, and solved the problems of railroading sans telegraphy and electric signals. It dictated, then, what should be transported, food coming first, coal and fuel oil second, and essential manufactured articles in the order of their relative importance. Carload after carload of new radios, electric stoves, refrigerators and such useless articles were dumped unceremoniously alongside the tracks, to be salvaged for scrap metal later.

All horses were declared wards of the government, graded according to capabilities, and put to work or to stud. Draft horses were used for only the most essential kinds of hauling. The breeding program was given the fullest possible emphasis; the bureau estimated that the equine population would double in two years, quadruple in three, and that within six or seven years there would be a horse in every garage in the country.

Farmers, deprived temporarily of their horses, and with their tractors rusting in the fields, were instructed how to use cattle for plowing and other work about the farm, including light hauling.

The second board, the Manpower Relocation Bureau, functioned just as one would deduce from its title. It handled unemployment benefits for the millions thrown temporarily out of work and helped relocate them—not too difficult a task, considering the tremendously increased demand for hand labor in many fields. In May of 1947, thirty-five million employables were out of work; in October, fifteen million; by May of 1948, five million. By 1949 the situation was completely in hand and competitive demand was already beginning to raise wages.

The third board had the most difficult job of the three. It was called the Factory Readjustment Bureau. It coped with the stupendous task of converting factories, filled with electrically operated machinery and, for the most part, tooled for the production of other electrically operated machinery, over to the production, without electricity, of essential nonelectrical articles.

The few available stationary steam engines worked twenty-four-hour shifts in those early days, and the first thing they were given to do was to run stampers and planers and millers turning out more stationary steam engines, of all sizes. These, in turn, were first put to work making still more steam engines. The number of steam engines grew by squares and cubes, as did the number of horses put to stud. The principle was the same. One might—and many did—refer to those early steam engines as stud horses. At any rate, there was no lack of metal for them. The factories were filled with nonconvertible machinery waiting to be melted down.

Only when steam engines—the basis of the new factory economy—were in full production were they assigned to running machinery for the manufacture of other articles: oil lamps, clothing, coal stoves, oil stoves, bathtubs, and bedsteads.

Not quite all the big factories were converted. For, while the conversion period went on, individual handicrafts sprang up in thousands of places. Little one- and two-man shops made and repaired furniture, shoes, candles, all sorts of things that *could* be made without complex machinery. At first these small shops made small fortunes because they had no competition from heavy industry. Later, they bought small steam engines to run small machines, and held their own, growing with the boom that came with a return to normal employment and buying power, increasing gradually in size until many of them rivaled the bigger factories in output and beat them in quality.

There *was* suffering, during the period of economic readjustment, but less than there had been during the great depression of the early 1930's. And the recovery was quicker.

The reason was obvious: In combating the depression, the government was working in the dark. They didn't know its cause—rather, they knew a thousand conflicting theories of its cause—and they didn't know the cure. They were hampered by the idea that the thing was temporary and would cure itself if left alone. Briefly and frankly, they didn't know what it was all about, and while they experimented, it snowballed.

But the situation that faced the country—and all other countries—in 1947 was clear-cut and obvious. No more electricity. Readjust for steam and horsepower.

As simple and clear as that, and no ifs or ands or buts. And the whole people—except for the usual scattering of cranks—back of them.

By 1951—

It was a rainy day in April, and George Bailey was waiting under the sheltering roof of the little railroad station at Blakestown, Connecticut, to see who might come in on the 3:14.

It chugged in at 3:25 and came to a panting stop: three coaches and a baggage car. The baggage-car door opened and a sack of mail was handed out and the door closed again. No luggage, so probably no passengers would—

Then at the sight of a tall, dark man swinging down from the platform of the rear coach, George Bailey let out a yip of delight. "Pete! Pete Mulvaney! What the devil—"

"Bailey, by all that's holy! What are you doing here?"

George was wringing his hand. "Me? I live here. Two years now. I bought the Blakestown *Weekly* in '49, for a song, and I run it—editor, reporter, and janitor. Got one printer to help me out with that end, and Maisie does the social items. She's—"

"Maisie? Maisie Hetterman?"

"Maisie Bailey now. We got married same time I bought the paper and moved here. What are you doing here, Pete?"

"Business. Just here overnight. See a man named Wilcox."

"Oh, Wilcox. Our local screwball—but don't get me wrong; he's a smart guy, all right. Well, you can see him tomorrow. You're coming home with me now for dinner and to stay overnight. Maisie'll be glad to see you. Come on, my buggy's over here."

"Sure. Finished whatever you were here for?"

"Yep, just to pick up the news on who came in on the train. And *you* came in, so here we go."

They got in the buggy, and George picked up the reins and said, "Giddap, Bessie," to the mare. Then, "What are you doing now, Pete?"

"Research. For a gas-supply company. Been working on a more efficient mantle, one that'll give more light and be less destructible. This fellow Wilcox wrote us he had something along that line; the company sent me up to look it over. If it's what he claims, I'll take him back to New York with me and let the company lawyers dicker with him."

"How's business, otherwise?"

"Great, George. *Gas;* that's the coming thing. Every

new home's being piped for it, and plenty of the old ones. How about you?"

"We got it. Luckily we had one of the old linotypes that ran the metal pot off a gas burner, so it was already piped in. And our home is right over the office and print shop, so all we had to do was pipe it up a flight. Great stuff, gas. How's New York?"

"Fine, George. Down to its last million people, and stabilizing there. No crowding, and plenty of room for everybody. The *air*—why, it's better than Atlantic City, without gasoline fumes."

"Enough horses to go around yet?"

"Almost. But bicycling's the craze; the factories can't turn out enough to meet the demand. There's a cycling club in almost every block, and all the able-bodied cycle to and from work. Doing 'em good, too; a few more years, and the doctors will go on short rations."

"You got a bike?"

"Sure, a pre-vader one. Average five miles a day on it, and I eat like a horse."

George Bailey chuckled. "I'll have Maisie include some hay in the dinner. Well, here we are. Whoa, Bessie."

An upstairs window went up, and Maisie looked out and down. She called out, "Hi, Pete!"

"Extra plate, Maisie," George called. "We'll be up soon as I put the horse away and show Pete around downstairs."

He led Pete from the barn into the back door of the newspaper shop. "Our linotype!" he announced proudly, pointing.

"How's it work? Where's your steam engine?"

George grinned. "Doesn't work yet; we still handset the type. I could get only one steamer and had to use that on the press. But I've got one on order for the lino and coming up in a month or so. When we get it, Pop Jenkins, my printer, is going to put himself out of a job by teaching me to run it. With the linotype going, I can handle the whole thing myself."

"Kind of rough on Pop?"

George shook his head. "Pop eagerly awaits the day. He's sixty-nine and wants to retire. He's just staying on until I can do without him. Here's the press—a honey of a little Miehle; we do some job work on it, too. And this is the office, in front. Messy, but efficient."

Mulvaney looked around and grinned. "George, I believe you've found your niche. You were cut out for a small-town editor."

"Cut out for it? I'm crazy about it. I have more fun than everybody. Believe it or not, I work like a dog and like it. Come on upstairs."

On the stairs, Pete asked, "And the novel you were going to write?"

"Half done, and it isn't bad. But it isn't the novel I was going to write; I was a cynic then. Now—"

"George, I think the waveries were your best friends."

"Waveries?"

"Lord, how long does it take slang to get from New York out to the sticks? The vaders, of course. Some professor who specializes in studying them described one as a wavery place in the ether, and 'wavery' stuck. . . . Hello there, Maisie, my girl. You look like a million."

They ate leisurely. Almost apologetically, George brought out beer, in cold bottles. "Sorry, Pete, haven't anything stronger to offer you. But I haven't been drinking lately. Guess—"

"*You* on the wagon, George?"

"Not on the wagon, exactly. Didn't swear off or anything, but haven't had a drink of strong liquor in almost a year. I don't know why, but—"

"I do," said Pete Mulvaney. "I know exactly why you don't—because I don't drink much either, for the same reason. We don't drink because we don't *have* to. . . . Say, isn't that a *radio* over there?"

George chuckled. "A souvenir. Wouldn't sell it for a fortune. Once in a while I like to look at it and think of the awful guff I used to sweat out for it. And then I go over and click the switch and nothing happens. Just silence. Silence is the most wonderful thing in the world sometimes, Pete. Of course, I couldn't do that if there was any juice, because I'd get vaders then. I suppose they're still doing business at the same old stand?"

"Yep, the Research Bureau checks daily. They try to get up current with a little generator run by a steam turbine. But no dice; the vaders suck it up as fast as it's generated."

"Suppose they'll ever go away?"

Mulvaney shrugged. "Helmetz thinks not. He thinks they propagate in proportion to the available electricity. Even if the development of radio broadcasting some- where else in the Universe would attract them there, some would stay here—and multiply like flies the minute we tried to use electricity again. And meanwhile, they'll live on the static electricity in the air. What do you do evenings up here?"

"Do? Read, write, visit with one another, go to the amateur groups—Maisie's chairman of the Blakestown Players, and I play bit parts in it. With the movies out, everybody goes in for theatricals, and we've found some real talent. And there's the chess-and-checker club, and cycle trips and picnics. . . . There isn't time enough. Not to mention music. Everybody plays an instrument, or is trying to."

"You?"

"Sure, cornet. First cornet in the Silver Concert Band,

with solo parts. And— Good heavens! Tonight's rehearsal, and we're giving a concert Sunday afternoon. I hate to desert you but—"

"Can't I come around and sit in? I've got my flute in the brief case here and—"

"Flute? We're short on flutes. Bring that around and Si Perkins, our director, will practically shanghai you into staying over for the concert Sunday—and it's only three days, so why not? And get it out now; we'll play a few old-timers to warm up. Hey, Maisie, skip those dishes and come on in to the piano!"

While Pete Mulvaney went to the guest room to get his flute from the brief case, George Bailey picked up his cornet from the top of the piano and blew a soft, plaintive little minor run on it. Clear as a bell; his lip was in good shape tonight.

And with the shining silver thing in his hand he wandered over to the window and stood looking out into the night. It was dusk, and the rain had stopped.

A high-stepping horse *clop-clopped* by, and the bell of a bicycle jangled. Somebody across the street was strumming a guitar and singing. He took a deep breath and let it out slowly.

The scent of spring was soft and sweet in the moist air.

Peace and dusk and distant rolling thunder. Thunder, but— "I wish," he said softly, "there was a bit of lightning. I *miss* the lightning."

Edward Grendon

CRISIS

Well, you have had the invasion for Conquest by Force, the invasion for Conquest by Infiltration, the invasion for Guidance, the accidental invasion for repairs or other succor, the invasion for . . . oh, lots of other things.

Here you have an invasion that has none of these motives. It is a formal invasion, full of panoply and protocol, small in size (ambassadorial rather than military), but most impressive, and complete with creatures that are at least quasi-BEMS even though their eyes don't bug out. And Earth is fully prepared to receive them.

What all these efforts and preparations lead to, you will have to find out for yourself. We suspect you will feel pretty savagely cut down to size by the time you have come to the tale's ending.

BY 1980 the balance had shifted. The progress of the physical sciences had by no means stopped, but it had slowed considerably. The social sciences, on the other hand, had moved ahead with unexpected speed. The integration between academic and therapeutic psychology had been the first step; the rest followed quickly. When the final *rapprochement* between psychoanalysis and neurology was made, there existed, for the first time, a comprehensive theory of behavior, not only of human beings and animals but of other— so far theoretical—nervous systems as well. Just as the mathematicians were able to postulate geometries that existed in no known Universe when they were first devised, the psychologists were now able to postulate non-Terran behavior systems.— Saevolies, John. *The History of Thought in the Modern World,* World Press, 1998.

Woodward looked at his graphs for the last time. They eliminated a few possibilities and indicated a good probability that three were valid. Some fifty-seven other vectors were possible but not probable, and in a very few minutes he had to recommend a definite course of action on the basis of them. A recommendation that was almost certain to be accepted.

Briefly, he considered going over the protocols again and discarded the idea. If he had been able to get no more conclusive results with the aid of his entire staff, he would get none now. If only he had proof to back up the certainty he felt! Intuitively, he was positive which possibility was the correct one; scientifically, he could prove nothing. He stood up, placed a file envelope under his arm, and walked out to the coffee bar.

The council chairman called the meeting to order and waited until the four hundred delegates became quiet. When he spoke it was in a tired, quiet voice.

"At this special meeting, gentlemen, we will dispense with the minutes and the usual formalities. You all know our subject. We are here to consider the 'Voice,' as the aliens have come to be known. To recapitulate briefly, we first heard of them when most radio communication was interrupted thirty-six days ago. A voice speaking good English with a rather high-pitched tone broke in. It introduced itself as a visitor from a nearby star system, without giving a precise location. It stated that, with our permission, an ambassador was to be sent to Earth to see if we were developed enough for intercourse with other highly developed races. It asked that this ambassador be allowed a visit of three weeks with a typical Earth family rather than be shown over the whole planet. Specifications were given as to the type of signal we should set up for landing purposes and the date of landing, if we wished to accede. That date is now two weeks off.

"We have had three separate teams working on an analysis of the message. The chief of each team will now tell you his recommendation. They are Mr. Woodward, of the International Psychological Association team; Mr. Jelfiffe, of the team of the Society of Human Engineers; and Mr. Dever, of the team of the Federation of Social Sciences. We recognize the difficulty of their task and the speculative nature of their results which are, however, the best we have. Mr. Dever."

The gangling, weary man with the sensitive scholar's face stood up at the right of the president.

"All we can make is a good guess. We believe the alien to possess a nervous system of Cantor's Class 4 type. This means an organism who acts warily, plans far in advance, and is too rigid to do anything but retreat quickly or strike out spasmodically when its predictions are inaccurate. It would tend to have a strong ethical system applied to the ingroup, and no concern with organisms not members of the ingroup. If frustrations imposed on it are expected, it retreats; if unexpected, it attacks. Since it will be unable to predict clearly the course of development of human beings, it is more than liable to feel frustration and to become hostile and aggressive. We recommend refusal of permission to land and signaling that we will not be ready for relations with extraterrestrial groups for at least one hundred years. The aliens almost certainly see this as a possible reply and are most likely to withdraw for that time. At the end of that period we can re-evaluate the situation."

He sat down and buried his face in his hands. Those who knew him realized what he had lost. Dever, who had sought after knowledge from childhood, who had spent his life at research, who had the most insatiable of all desires, the hunger to know, had foregone the vast store of ideas and concepts the aliens would have provided. He had followed the logic of his science to its inexorable end, and the result was bitter for him.

After a long minute the president said, "Mr. Jelfiffe," and Eli Jelfiffe stood up—a serious, intent man who had made great contributions in the application of social science to the social system. A good speaker, his voice was clear and carried through the hall without the need for the microphone.

"We essentially agree with Mr. Dever. Further, we suggest a marked increase for research and training in both the physical and social sciences for the next fifty years. Class 4 organisms are very unlikely to get along well with human beings who are Class 9. Neither is basically stable enough when their plans are thwarted. Contact between the two will result in frequent lapses of communication, which must end in violent collision. Eventual contact is certain. Let us arm ourselves against that day."

Some men need freedom and peace, for themselves and for others. They work for it all their lives. Jelfiffe was such a man, and the knowledge that he was urging preparation for war rested more heavily on him than on any of his hearers. His poise had been good and his speaking technique excellent, but his face was gray.

Woodward rose without waiting for an introduction.

"We agree in general with the findings of the other two teams, but our recommendations are quite different."

He paused and waited for the murmur of surprise to die down. Jelfiffe and Dever were staring at him, and the entire group waited tensely.

"We think we have detected slight variations from the Class 4 pattern, which lead us to believe that the alien is much more rigid and inflexible than would appear from usual techniques of message analysis. We believe him to be an organism that lays long-range plans, checks them against empirical data a few times, and then must follow them through. In other words, if predictions are demonstrated valid in two or three checks, the alien is no longer structurally capable of abandoning the plan. However, if the empirical data do not fit prediction curves, the alien will withdraw from the situation and feel real emotional blockage to attacking this particular problem again.

"Before going into the details of this, let me sketch the broad outlines of my recommendation. We let them land at a country estate we prepare. A family is there—a rather typical one—and a staff of servants. We have been going over psychographs for family and staff and submit, as recommendations, Mr. Dever for gardener, Mr. Jelfiffe and his wife as the family, myself as cook. We also have other recommendations, but this is a matter of detail.

"In effect, then, this is a Class 4 organism with several major differences. As Mr. Dever stated, it is probably empathic and cooperative with its ingroup, rather hostile with others. It makes plans far in advance, sets up prediction curves with a margin for error, and checks those curves. If there is agreement with the data, it must follow through. Further, we believe its purpose here to be aggressive and probably exploitative in nature. There seems little chance that aliens and humans could get along together without violent clashes and probably war. We can, however, possibly turn this situation into a not unprofitable course. Now as to the details. . . ."

The estate in Florida consisted of a large, low, rambling house built around three sides of a court. The fourth side was a lawn that sloped down to a small lake some three hundred yards away. Beyond the lake, open fields stretched for nearly two miles. Some of the fields were newly planted and beginning to grow. Cows and sheep grazed in others. One very large field, about a mile from the house, was of hard-packed earth that was torn up in several places as if small bombs had landed there. A tremendous target, with the outermost circle fifty yards in diameter, was whitewashed on the ground. A steel needle twenty feet long, with fins on the large end, lay in the target. Beyond this field the hills began.

Behind the house were roads with a two-lane cement highway coming within a hundred yards of the house. A single-track railroad paralleled the road and had a turntable at the end nearest the house. Off to the right stood barns, stables, and servant quarters. The estate entirely filled the small but beautiful valley. It had stood for many years, and there were now no signs of the furious labor that had gone into it in the past two weeks. The army of technicians had installed their equipment, tested it, and gone home. Only a "typical family" awaited the alien's ambassador.

The small sphere had detached itself from the large cylinder under the close scrutiny of various cameras, spectroscopes, telescopes, and other instruments. With no evidence showing of what was keeping it up, it floated and circled slowly down to the far end of the lawn.

Once there, it opened up like a flower and became a flat platform on the ground. Two beings walked off the platform, the sides of it curled up, and the reshaped sphere rose into the air and headed upward toward the cylinder.

They had the general body shape and size of Shetland ponies. A heavy bone carapace covered the neck and back. The head had a large brain case which changed the looks of the entire face. It had a human quality which probably came from both the bulging skull and the intelligent-looking mobility of the face. A long, flexible tentacle emerging from the base of the neck lay curled passively on the carapace of each. They stood quietly on the lawn looking toward the house, obviously waiting to be received.

Eli and Wendy Jelfiffe had come out of the house when the vehicle landed. They watched until the sphere was quite out of sight, and then Eli lifted his wrist and spoke into a small radio. Several minutes later a sleigh pulled by three oxen appeared from behind the barn. Driving it was Mr. Dever. In a few minutes Dever and the Jelfiffes had driven up to the ambassadors and dismounted from the sleigh. Behind them the tracks made by the heavy oak runners of the sleigh stretched across the lawn. Eli Jelfiffe moved forward and spoke. "It is a pleasure to welcome you. I am Jon Parsons, and this is my wife. This is my gardener, Mr. Spencer. We have a place for you and are very glad you are staying with us. We have instructions to continue living as we normally do. You will be our guests. We have further instructions to answer no technical questions but to allow you to inspect anything on the estate. Is that satisfactory?"

The heavier of the two aliens replied in the same formal tone, "My name is Inot and this is Kcid. We believe that the arrangement you state will be entirely acceptable. Food will be landed for us every three of your days, and we do not require to eat oftener than that."

Jelfiffe raised his wrist to his mouth and spoke into it, "Cook, the aliens do not require food; you may discontinue preparations." Noticing the aliens' eyes on him, he smiled and said, "Not knowing exactly what you ate, we were preparing a wide variety of foods for you to choose from. Our cook, Mr. Wis, was making lists of the chemical constituents of each to help you decide." He took the reins, gestured his guests onto the broad, flat back of the sleigh, and turned the oxen back to the house.

Although it was only late afternoon, the sky was gray and a chill had begun to creep into the air. The house was brightly lit, the tall chimneys of the kerosene lamps blazed with a warm glow. Jelfiffe showed his guests to two large, bare chambers on the ground floor. "If you will describe the furniture you would like in here, I can have it made and shipped in by rocket plane within a few hours. You can control the temperature in these rooms by means of those levers, which connect with the atomic pile we use for heating. The small wheel at the base of each kerosene lamp controls the amount of illumination it gives off."

Kcid, who had been fingering with his tentacle the various controls mentioned, looked up from the kerosene lamp. "Why do you not use other power than this for light?"

Jelfiffe thought a moment. "I'm afraid that comes under the heading of technical questions. Now if you would care to look over the rest of the house? Oh, I forgot—furniture. We can transmit the designs to the factory as fast as you make or describe them."

"We will need some large heavy cloths—blankets or

suchlike—and you probably have enough of them here. We prefer to sleep on them rather than anything else. We would like to see the house. Tell me—we had understood most families have children. We do not mean to be personal, but do you and your wife have any, and where are they?"

"We have two boys of nineteen and twenty-two years," replied Jelfiffe. "Neither has been here for some time. The younger one is away at college. He should get his degree in electronics next year. The older is serving as a mercenary abroad—as a captain in a company of lancers. If his campaign goes well, he may get a short furlough and be permitted to come here and see you. But tell me, how did you learn English?"

Inot smiled. "Your radio waves are powerful and can be heard a good deal farther than you probably imagine. Once we figured out that you were broadcasting in several languages, we were able to analyze the most prevalent one. We could learn your language from it but get no consistent picture of your world. So many different kinds of people—so many different techniques and motivations. So we came here to learn more about you."

"We are glad you came and within the limits of our instructions will help you as much as we can. Now let us show you around. Then we will eat. You may watch us, rest here, look through our library, or watch our television. There are various programs, and our butler will show you how to work the set."

While family and servants ate together, Jelfiffe and his wife at the upper table and the servants at the lower one below the salt, the aliens wandered around the house. They watched the eating for a while, motionless through the long grace, listened to the harpist play from his corner for a brief period, and then went into the living room. They found five channels of the television operating; one showed a film about pirates, another a First World War battle. The third showed *Ben Hur,* the fourth a Dr. Kildare film, and the fifth a science fantasy. In the manner typical of films, all apparently were set in the present. Occasional commercials featured such articles as electric razors, crossbows, aspirin, home permanent kits, and magic love charms.

In the morning Jelfiffe and his wife told their guests their usual daily routine. "We generally do a little farming in the morning and sports in the afternoon, then a siesta and supper."

The aliens watched the routine for two weeks. Sometimes the gardener would sit on the terrace and operate the remote-controlled farming machinery while Jelfiffe sweated with scythe or hoe in the fields. Sometimes Jelfiffe would sit at the small control box while the servants worked with rake or shovel. They saw Woodward open frozen-food containers and cook the foods on a wood-burning range. Once a day the mail truck came speeding up the road, its jet leaving a long roar behind it. Every other day the supplies came in on the railroad behind the tiny, chugging steam engine that had been resurrected from the Smithsonian Institution. Sometimes, in the afternoon, Jelfiffe and his staff would dress in light mail armor and, mounted on armored horses, practice with lances at targets. The small, electric-powered planes would swoop and dive about the field while the horsemen thundered after them, occasionally catching one on the end of a spear, at which time the others would shout in triumph. On other days they would have contests with slings or simply throw stones by hand at straw-filled dummies. Other sports included skeet shooting, midget-automobile racing, fencing, discus throwing, and sailing races in small catboats on the lake.

Several times Dever brought out small vehicles with an elaborate covered apparatus on the hood. Each had levers, dials, and a telescopic sight. One of the humans would get into each vehicle and aim the sights at the great needle lying on its target in the distant field. He would manipulate the controls, and presently the needle would rise into the air some sixty or seventy feet. It would then fall, point first, onto the target. As far as the aliens could tell, the object of the game was to drop the needle in the exact center of the target. They asked no questions about the energies used in the game, and no information was volunteered.

Evenings, they listened to the harpist or watched groups of players put on short skits in the living room. The humans looked at television, listened to a crystal set, played chess, go, dominoes, and checkers, read, talked, and occasionally got drunk.

At the end of the second week the two aliens suddenly announced that they had to leave and asked Jelfiffe to signal their ship. They refused to give reasons, and two hours later the sphere closed around them and slowly floated up to the cylinder. Several hours later the cylinder gathered speed and moved rapidly out into space.

Woodward again faced the general council, Dever and Jelfiffe at each side of him. This time the atmosphere was much more cheerful. Woodward was smiling as he continued.

". . . It was not too difficult, once we made the analysis of the message. We were taking a terrific chance, of course, but a chance of some sort had to be taken. We were in a corner and had to do something. The fact that they left early proves we were right.

"They had obviously been listening to our radio programs. That was the most likely way they would have learned English. The programs concern all kinds of people and all types of adventures.

"Our best analyses were that they were rigid, somewhat hostile organisms who had probably made an analysis of us on the basis of our planetary conditions and our radio programs. They seemed to be making a check on their predictions when they sent us ambassadors. On the basis of *our* analyses, we felt that they would check their predictions once or twice and then act on them. If their predictions failed in unexpected ways, they would probably withdraw and find real emotional difficulty in reattacking the problem. This should mean, we hope, that we will not see them again until *we* are ready to make contact.

"This, of course, is not ideal. Trade and information exchange would be much better. But neither race is now ready for contact; we both need more maturing. In particular, now when we are in a hopelessly inferior position scientifically, contact between us would certainly lead to our being badly exploited. In the future, if we can catch up—and the evidence is that we will catch up—things may be different. When we finish analyzing all our new information—everything that was said by *anyone* on the estate was, of course, picked up on hidden microphones and recorded—we shall have an excellent store of knowledge about the aliens, their personality structure, and even some of their science.

"The estate was rigged so that they could form no picture of us. The human inhabitants apparently followed a routine, but the things they did were taken from every age and every culture. We even faked one technique so they would be further hampered in judging us. We buried large coils in the ground, rigged so that a heavy electrical charge flowing through them would throw the needle high in the air, and then it would fall back point first. It looked as though those contraptions mounted on the little cars made the needle go up into the air. In reality, of course, underground wires led out of the valley, and our technicians there were tipped off by signals given off when the driver fiddled with the dials.

"In short, gentlemen, we have come through a major crisis and learned much from it. When we meet the aliens next time, it will be on much more even terms." He sat down to thunderous applause.

As their ship went into overdrive, Inot and Kcid were just finishing their report. "In conclusion," said Inot into the recorder while the entire crew listened, "this is an essentially primitive life class too unsure of its young sciences to meet us openly. They know of only aggressive, hostile organisms and had never observed a peaceful, friendly form of life and so could not conceive of one. Doubtless, they projected their own rigidity and hostilities onto us and so saw our advanced science as dangerous to them.

"They therefore attempted to trick us, using cultural techniques from many of their past ages. Naturally, they did not realize that if our physical sciences were more advanced than theirs, our social sciences would be similarly advanced, and it was no difficult trick to analyze them through the screens they attempted to throw up.

"We were careful what we said near their recording instruments and made sure they learned a good deal that they can use in advancing both their physical and social sciences. When we accomplished our purpose, we left.

"When we next make contact they should be more mature. We will then be able to treat them as we wish to, as equals and colleagues. They will be wiser, more advanced, and, in short, when we next meet these aliens, it will be on much more even terms."

Edgar Pangborn

ANGEL'S EGG

The highly advanced far-planet civilization is one of the more common concepts of modern science fiction. Many authors refuse to assume that mankind is the apex, the point of the pyramid, the tip of the top. In some of their tales, as in the preceding item in this collection, we find that members of some alien civilizations are so far ahead of us that we are beneath their notice. When they find out what we are, they simply consign us to our fate and take off for other, more promising, parts of the Galaxy.

On the other hand, some authors take it for granted that the creatures from space will be friendly even though they are a few thousand years ahead of us, eager to help us even though most of us would blindly and savagely strike them down if we could, and willing to work painstakingly with the few humans who have imagination and ability to learn, even though, in doing so, the aliens might become permanent exiles from their home planet.

"Angel's Egg" is a beautifully conceived and grace-fully written story of this type, and the author's first published science fiction, as well.

LETTER OF RECORD, BLAINE TO MC CARRAN, DATED
AUGUST 10, 1951

Mr. Cleveland McCarran
Federal Bureau of Investigation
Washington, D.C.

Dear Sir:

In compliance with your request I enclose herewith a
transcript of the pertinent sections of the journal of Dr.
David Bannerman, deceased. The original document is
being held at this office until proper disposition can be
determined.

Our investigation has shown no connection between
Dr. Bannerman and any organization, subversive or
otherwise. So far as we can learn, he was exactly what
he seemed, an inoffensive summer resident, retired, with
a small independent income—a recluse to some extent,
but well spoken of by local tradesmen and other neighbors. A connection between Dr. Bannerman and the
type of activity that concerns your Department would
seem most unlikely.

The following information is summarized from the
earlier parts of Dr. Bannerman's journal, and tallies with
the results of our own limited inquiry. He was born in
1898 at Springfield, Massachusetts, attended public
school there, and was graduated from Harvard College
in 1922, his studies having been interrupted by two
years' military service. He was wounded in action in
Argonne, receiving a spinal injury. He earned a doctor-
ate in biology in 1926. Delayed aftereffects of his war
injury necessitated hospitalization, 1927–28. From 1929
to 1948 he taught elementary sciences in a private
school in Boston. He published two textbooks in introductory biology, 1929 and 1937. In 1948 he retired

from teaching: a pension and a modest income from textbook royalties evidently made this possible. Aside from the spinal deformity, which caused him to walk with a stoop, his health is said to have been fair. Autopsy findings suggested that the spinal condition must have given him considerable pain; he is not known to have mentioned this to anyone, not even to his physician, Dr. Lester Morse. There is no evidence whatever of drug addiction or alcoholism.

At one point early in his journal Dr. Bannerman describes himself as "a naturalist of the puttering type—I would rather sit on a log than write monographs: it pays off better." Dr. Morse, and others who knew Dr. Bannerman personally, tell me that this conveys a hint of his personality.

I am not qualified to comment on the material of this journal, except to say I have no evidence to support (or to contradict) Dr. Bannerman's statements. The journal has been studied only by my immediate superiors, by Dr. Morse, and by myself. I take it for granted you will hold the matter in strictest confidence.

With the journal I am also enclosing a statement by Dr. Morse, writing at my request for our records and for your information. You will note that he says, with some qualifications, that "death was not inconsistent with an embolism." He has signed a death certificate on that basis. You will recall from my letter of August 5 that it was Dr. Morse who discovered Dr. Bannerman's body. Because he was a close personal friend of the deceased, Dr. Morse did not feel able to perform the autopsy himself. It was done by a Dr. Stephen Clyde of this city, and was virtually negative as regards cause of death, neither confirming nor contradicting Dr. Morse's original tentative diagnosis. If you wish to read the autopsy report in full I shall be glad to forward a copy.

Dr. Morse tells me that so far as he knows, Dr. Bannerman had no near relatives. He never married. For the last twelve summers he occupied a small cottage on a back road about twenty-five miles from this city, and had few visitors. The neighbor, Steele, mentioned in the journal is a farmer, age 68, of good character, who tells me he "never got really acquainted with Dr. Bannerman."

At this office we feel that unless new information comes to light, further active investigation is hardly justified.

Respectfully yours,
Garrison Blaine
Capt., State Police
Augusta, Me.

Encl: Extract from Journal of David Bannerman, dec'd.
Statement by Lester Morse, M.D.

LIBRARIAN'S NOTE: The following document, originally attached as an unofficial "rider" to the foregoing letter, was donated to this institution in 1994 through the courtesy of Mrs. Helen McCarran, widow of the martyred first President of the World Federation. Other personal and state papers of President McCarran, many of them dating from the early period when he was employed by the FBI, are accessible to public view at the Institute of World History, Copenhagen.

PERSONAL NOTE, BLAINE TO MC CARRAN, DATED AUGUST 10, 1951

Dear Cleve:
Guess I didn't make it clear in my other letter that that bastard Clyde was responsible for my having to drag you into this. He is something to handle with tongs.

Happened thusly— When he came in to heave the autopsy report at me, he was already having pups just because it was so completely negative (he does have certain types of honesty), and he caught sight of a page or two of the journal on my desk. Doc Morse was with me at the time. I fear we both got upstage with him (Clyde has that effect, and we were both in a State of Mind anyway), so right away the old drip thinks he smells something subversive. Belongs to the atomize-'em-NOW-WOW-WOW school of thought—nuf sed? He went into a grand whuff-whuff about referring to Higher Authority, and I knew that meant your hive, so I wanted to get ahead of the letter I knew he'd write. I suppose his literary effort couldn't be just sort of quietly transferred to File 13, otherwise known as the Appropriate Receptacle?

He can say what he likes about my character, if any, but even I never supposed he'd take a sideswipe at his professional colleague. Doc Morse is the best of the best and would not dream of suppressing any evidence important to us, as you say Clyde's letter hints. What Doc did do was to tell Clyde, pleasantly, in the privacy of my office, to go take a flying this-and-that at the moon. I only wish I'd thought of the expression myself. So Clyde rushes off to tell teacher. See what I mean about the tongs? However (knock on wood) I don't think Clyde saw enough of the journal to get any notion of what it's all about.

As for that journal, damn it, Cleve, I don't know. If you have any ideas I want them, of course. I'm afraid I believe in angels, myself. But when I think of the effect on local opinion if the story ever gets out—brother! Here was this old Bannerman living alone with a female angel and they wuzn't even common-law married. Aw, gee. . . . And the flood of phone calls from other crackpots anxious to explain it all to me. Experts in the care and feeding of angels. Methods of angel-proofing. Angels right outside the window a minute ago. Make Angels a Profitable Enterprise in Your Spare Time!!!

When do I see you? You said you might have a week clear in October. If we could get together maybe we could make sense where there is none. I hear the cider promises to be good this year. Try and make it. My best to Ginny and the other young fry, and Helen of course.

> Respeckfully yourn,
> Garry

P.S. If you do see any angels down your way, and they aren't willing to wait for a Republican Administration, by all means have them investigated by the Senate—then we'll *know* we're all nuts.

> G.

EXTRACT FROM JOURNAL OF DAVID BANNERMAN, JUNE 1–JULY 29, 1951

June 1

It must have been at least three weeks ago when we had that flying saucer flurry. Observers the other side of Katahdin saw it come down this side; observers this side saw it come down the other. Size anywhere from six inches to sixty feet in diameter (or was it cigar-shaped?) and speed whatever you please. Seem to recall the witnesses agreed on a rosy-pink light. There was the inevitable gobbledegookery of official explanation designed to leave everyone impressed, soothed, and disappointed. I paid scant attention to the excitement and less to the explanations—naturally, I thought it was just a flying saucer. But now Camilla has hatched out an angel.

It would have to be Camilla. Perhaps I haven't mentioned my hens enough. In the last day or two it has dawned on me that this journal may be of importance to other eyes than mine, not merely a lonely man's plaything to blunt the edge of mortality: an angel in the house makes a difference. I had better show consideration for possible readers.

I have eight hens, all yearlings except Camilla: this is her third spring. I boarded her two winters at my neighbor Steele's farm when I closed this shack and shuffled my chilly bones off to Florida, because even as a pullet she had a manner which overbore me. I could never have eaten Camilla: if she had looked at the ax with that same expression of rancid disapproval (and she would), I should have felt I was beheading a favorite aunt. Her only concession to sentiment is the annual rush of maternity to the brain—normal, for a case-hardened White Plymouth Rock.

This year she stole a nest successfully in a tangle of blackberry. By the time I located it, I estimated I was about two weeks too late. I had to outwit her by watching from a window—she is far too acute to be openly trailed from feeding ground to nest. When I had bled and pruned my way to her hideout she was sitting on nine eggs and hating my guts. They could not be fertile, since I keep no rooster, and I was about to rob her when I saw the ninth egg was nothing of hers. It was a deep blue and transparent, with flecks of inner light that made me think of the first stars in a clear evening. It was the same size as Camilla's own. There was an embryo, but I could make nothing of it. I returned the egg to Camilla's bare and fevered breastbone and went back to the house for a long, cool drink.

That was ten days ago. I know I ought to have kept a record; I examined the blue egg every day, watching how some nameless life grew within it. The angel has been out of the shell three days now. This is the first time I have felt equal to facing pen and ink.

I have been experiencing a sort of mental lassitude unfamiliar to me. Wrong word: not so much lassitude as a preoccupation, with no sure clue to what it is that preoccupies me. By reputation I am a scientist of sorts. Right now I have no impulse to look for data; I want to sit quiet and let truth come to a relaxed mind if it will. Could be merely a part of growing older, but I doubt that. The broken pieces of the wonderful blue shell are on my desk. I have been peering at them—into them— for the last ten minutes or more. Can't call it study: my thought wanders into their blue, learning nothing I can retain in words. It does not convey much to say I have gone into a vision of open sky—and of peace, if such a thing there be.

The angel chipped the shell deftly in two parts. This was evidently done with the aid of small horny out-growths on her elbows; these growths were sloughed off on the second day. I wish I had seen her break the shell, but when I visited the blackberry tangle three days ago she was already out. She poked her exquisite head through Camilla's neck feathers, smiled sleepily, and snuggled back into darkness to finish drying off. So what could I do, more than save the broken shell and wriggle my clumsy self out of there? I had removed Camilla's own eggs the day before—Camilla was only moderately annoyed. I was nervous about disposing of them, even though they were obviously Camilla's, but no harm was done. I cracked each one to be sure. Very frankly rotten eggs and nothing more.

In the evening of that day I thought of rats and weasels, as I should have done earlier. I prepared a box in the kitchen and brought the two in, the angel quiet in my closed hand. They are there now. I think they are comfortable.

Three days after hatching, the angel is the length of my forefinger, say three inches tall, with about the relative proportions of a six-year-old girl. Except for head, hands, and probably the soles of her feet, she is clothed in down the color of ivory; what can be seen of her skin is a glowing pink—I do mean glowing, like the inside of certain sea shells. Just above the small of her back are two stubs which I take to be infantile wings. They do not suggest an extra pair of specialized forelimbs. I think they are wholly differentiated organs; perhaps they will be like the wings of an insect. Somehow, I never thought of angels buzzing. Maybe she won't. I know very little about angels. At present the stubs are covered with some dull tissue, no doubt a protective sheath to be discarded when the membranes (if they are membranes) are ready to grow. Between the stubs is a not very prominent ridge—special musculature, I suppose. Otherwise her shape is quite human, even to a pair of minuscule mammalian buttons just visible under the down; how that can make sense in an egg-laying organism is beyond my comprehension. (Just for the record, so is a Corot landscape; so is Schubert's *Unfinished;* so is the flight of a hummingbird, or the other-world of frost on a window pane.) The down on her head has grown visibly in three days and is of different quality from the body down—later it may resemble human hair, as a diamond resembles a chunk of granite. . . .

A curious thing has happened. I went to Camilla's box after writing that. Judy* was already lying in front

* Dr. Bannerman's dog, mentioned often earlier in the journal. A nine-year-old English setter. According to an entry of May 15, 1951, she was then beginning to go blind.

—BLAINE.

of it, unexcited. The angel's head was out from under
the feathers, and I thought—with more verbal distinct-
ness than such thoughts commonly take, "So here I am,
a naturalist of middle years and cold sober, observing a
three-inch oviparous mammal with down and wings."
The thing is—she giggled. Now, it might have been only
amusement at my appearance, which to her must be
enormously gross and comic. But another thought
formed unspoken: "I am no longer lonely." And her
face (hardly bigger than a dime) immediately changed
from laughter to a brooding and friendly thoughtfulness.

Judy and Camilla are old friends. Judy seems untroubled by the angel. I have no worries about leaving
them alone together. I must sleep.

June 3

I made no entry last night. The angel was talking to
me, and when that was finished I drowsed off immediately on a cot that I have moved into the kitchen so as
to be near them.

I had never been strongly impressed by the evidence
for extrasensory perception. It is fortunate my mind was
able to accept the novelty, since to the angel it is clearly
a matter of course. Her tiny mouth is most expressive
but moves only for that reason and for eating—not for
speech. Probably she could speak to her own kind if she
wished, but I dare say the sound would be outside the
range of my hearing as well as of my understanding.

Last night after I brought the cot in and was about to
finish my puttering bachelor supper, she climbed to the
edge of the box and pointed, first at herself and then at
the top of the kitchen table. Afraid to let my vast hand
take hold of her, I held it out flat and she sat in my
palm. Camilla was inclined to fuss, but the angel looked

over her shoulder and Camilla subsided, watchful but no longer alarmed.

The table top is porcelain, and the angel shivered. I folded a towel and spread a silk handkerchief on top of that; the angel sat on this arrangement with apparent comfort, near my face. I was not even bewildered. Possibly she had already instructed me to blank out my mind. At any rate, I did so, without conscious effort to that end.

She reached me first with visual imagery. How can I make it plain that this had nothing in common with my sleeping dreams? There was no weight of symbolism from my littered past; no discoverable connection with any of yesterday's commonplaces; indeed, no actual involvement of my personality at all. I saw. I was moving vision, though without eyes or other flesh. And while my mind saw, it also knew where my flesh was, slumped at the kitchen table. If anyone had entered the kitchen, if there had been a noise of alarm out in the henhouse, I should have known it.

There was a valley such as I have not seen (and never will) on Earth. I have seen many beautiful places on this planet—some of them were even tranquil. Once I took a slow steamer to New Zealand and had the Pacific as a plaything for many days. I can hardly say how I knew this was not Earth. The grass of the valley was an earthly green; a river below me was a blue-and-silver thread under familiar-seeming sunlight; there were trees much like pine and maple, and maybe that is what they were. But it was not Earth. I was aware of mountains heaped to strange heights on either side of the valley— snow, rose, amber, gold. Perhaps the amber tint was unlike any mountain color I have noticed in this world at midday.

Or I may have known it was not Earth simply because

her mind—dwelling within some unimaginable brain smaller than the tip of my little finger—told me so.

I watched two inhabitants of that world come flying, to rest in the field of sunny grass where my bodiless vision had brought me. Adult forms, such as my angel would surely be when she had her growth, except that both of these were male and one of them was dark-skinned. The latter was also old, with a thousand-wrinkled face, knowing and full of tranquility; the other was flushed and lively with youth; both were beautiful. The down of the brown-skinned old one was reddish-tawny; the other's was ivory with hints of orange. Their wings were true membranes, with more variety of subtle iridescence than I have seen even in the wings of a drag-onfly; I could not say that any color was dominant, for each motion brought a ripple of change. These two sat at their ease on the grass. I realized that they were talk-ing to each other, though their lips did not move in speech more than once or twice. They would nod, smile, now and then illustrate something with twinkling hands.

A huge rabbit lolloped past them. I knew (thanks to my own angel's efforts, I supposed) that this animal was of the same size of our common wild ones. Later, a blue-green snake three times the size of the angels came flowing through the grass; the old one reached out to stroke its head carelessly, and I think he did it without interrupting whatever he was saying.

Another creature came, in leisured leaps. He was monstrous, yet I felt no alarm in the angels or in myself. Imagine a being built somewhat like a kangaroo up to the head, about eight feet tall, and katydid-green. Really, the thick balancing tail and enormous legs were the only kangaroo-like features about him: the body above the massive thighs was not dwarfed but thick and square; the arms and hands were quite humanoid: the head was round, manlike except for its face—there was only a single nostril and his mouth was set in the vertical; the eyes were large and mild. I received an impression of high intelligence and natural gentleness. In one of his manlike hands two tools so familiar and ordinary that I knew my body by the kitchen table had laughed in startled recognition. But, after all, a garden spade and rake are basic. Once invented—I expect we did it ourselves in the Neolithic Age—there is little reason why they should change much down the millennia.

This farmer halted by the angels, and the three conversed a while. The big head nodded agreeably. I believe the young angel made a joke; certainly the convulsions in the huge green face made me think of laughter. Then this amiable monster turned up the grass in a patch a few yards square, broke the sod and raked the surface smooth, just as any competent gardener might do—except that he moved with the relaxed smoothness of a being whose strength far exceeds the requirements of his task. . . .

I was back in my kitchen with everyday eyes. My angel was exploring the table. I had a loaf of bread there and a dish of strawberries and cream. She was trying a bread crumb; seemed to like it fairly well. I offered the strawberries; she broke off one of the seeds and nibbled it but didn't care so much for the pulp. I held up the great spoon with sugary cream; she steadied it with both hands to try some. I think she liked it. It had been most stupid of me not to realize that she would be hungry. I brought wine from the cupboard; she watched inquiringly, so I put a couple of drops on the handle of a spoon. This really pleased her: she chuckled and patted her tiny stomach, though I'm afraid it wasn't awfully good sherry. I brought some crumbs of cake, but she indicated that she was full, came close to my face, and motioned me to lower my head.

She reached me until she could press both hands against my forehead—I felt it only enough to know her hands were there—and she stood so a long time, trying to tell me something.

It was difficult. Pictures come through with relative ease, but now she was transmitting an abstraction of a complex kind: my clumsy brain really suffered in the effort to receive. Something did come across. I have only the crudest way of passing it on. Imagine an equilateral triangle; place the following words one at each corner— "recruiting," "collecting," "saving." The meaning she wanted to convey ought to be near the center of the triangle.

I had also the sense that her message provided a partial explanation of her errand in this lovable and damnable world.

She looked weary when she stood away from me. I put out my palm and she climbed into it, to be carried back to the nest.

She did not talk to me tonight, nor eat, but she gave a reason, coming out from Camilla's feathers long enough to turn her back and show me the wing stubs. The protective sheaths have dropped off; the wings are rapidly growing. They are probably damp and weak. She was quite tired and went back into the warm darkness almost at once.

Camilla must be exhausted, too. I don't think she has been off the nest more than twice since I brought them into the house.

June 4

Today she can fly.

I learned it in the afternoon, when I was fiddling

about in the garden and Judy was loafing in the sunshine she loves. Something apart from sight and sound called me to hurry back to the house. I saw my angel through the screen door before I opened it. One of her feet had caught in a hideous loop of loose wire at a break in the mesh. Her first tug of alarm must have tightened the loop so that her hands were not strong enough to force it open.

Fortunately I was able to cut the wire with a pair of shears before I lost my head; then she could free her foot without injury. Camilla had been frantic, rushing around fluffed up, but—here's an odd thing—perfectly silent. None of the recognized chicken noises of dismay: if an ordinary chick had been in trouble she would have raised the roof.

The angel flew to me and hovered, pressing her hands on my forehead. The message was clear at once: "No harm done." She flew down to tell Camilla the same thing.

Yes, in the same way. I saw Camilla standing near my feet with her neck out and head low, and the angel put a hand on either side of her scraggy comb. Camilla relaxed, clucked in the normal way, and spread her wings for a shelter. The angel went under it, but only to oblige Camilla, I think—at least, she stuck her head through the wing feathers and winked.

She must have seen something else, then, for she came out and flew back to me and touched a finger to my cheek, looked at the finger, saw it was wet, put it in her mouth, made a face, and laughed at me.

We went outdoors into the sun (Camilla too), and the angel gave me an exhibition of what flying ought to be. Not even Schubert can speak of joy as her first free flying did. At one moment she would be hanging in front of my eyes, radiant and delighted; the next instant she would be a dot of color against a cloud. Try to imagine something that would make a hummingbird seem a bit dull and sluggish.

They do hum. Softer than a hummingbird, louder than a dragonfly.

Something like the sound of hawk-moths—*Heinmaris thisbe,* for instance: the one I used to call Hummingbird Moth when I was a child.

I was frightened, naturally. Frightened first at what might happen to her, but that was unnecessary; I don't think she would be in danger from any savage animal except possibly Man. I saw a Cooper's hawk slant down the invisible toward the swirl of color where she was dancing by herself; presently she was drawing iridescent rings around him; then, while he soared in smaller circles, I could not see her, but (maybe she felt my fright) she was again in front of me, pressing my forehead in the now familiar way. I knew she was amused and caught the idea that the hawk was a "lazy character." Not quite the way I'd describe *Accipiter Cooperi,* but it's all in the point of view. I believe she had been riding his back, no doubt with her speaking hands on his terrible head.

And later I was frightened by the thought that she might not want to return to me. Can I compete with sunlight and open sky? The passage of that terror through me brought her back swiftly, and her hands said with great clarity: "Don't ever be afraid of anything— it isn't necessary for you."

Once this afternoon I was saddened by the realization that old Judy can take little part in what goes on now. I can well remember Judy running like the wind. The angel must have heard this thought in me, for she stood a long time beside Judy's drowsy head, while Judy's tail thumped cheerfully on the warm grass. . . .

In the evening the angel made a heavy meal on two or three cake crumbs and another drop of sherry, and we had what was almost a sustained conversation. I will write it in that form this time, rather than grope for anything more exact. I asked her, "How far away is your home?"

"My home is here."

"Thank God!—but I meant, the place your people came from."

"Ten light-years."

"The images you showed me—that quiet valley—that is ten light-years away?"

"Yes. But that was my father talking to you, through me. He was grown when the journey began. He is two hundred and forty years old—our years, thirty-two days longer than yours."

Mainly I was conscious of a flood of relief: I had feared, on the basis of terrestrial biology, that her explosively rapid growth after hatching must foretell a brief life. But it's all right—she can outlive me, and by a few hundred years, at that. "Your father is here now, on this planet—shall I see him?"

She took her hands away—listening, I believe. The answer was: "No. He is sorry. He is ill and cannot live long. I am to see him in a few days, when I fly a little better. He taught me for twenty years after I was born."

"I don't understand. I thought—"

"Later, friend. My father is grateful for your kindness to me."

I don't know what I thought about that. I felt no faintest trace of condescension in the message. "And he was showing me things he had seen with his own eyes, ten light-years away?"

"Yes." Then she wanted me to rest a while; I am sure she knows what a huge effort it is for my primitive brain to function in this way. But before she ended the conversation by humming down to her nest she gave me this, and I received it with such clarity that I cannot be mistaken: "He says that only fifty million years ago it was a jungle there, just as Terra is now."

June 8

When I woke four days ago the angel was having breakfast, and little Camilla was dead. The angel watched me rub sleep out of my eyes, watched me discover Camilla, and then flew to me. I received this: "Does it make you unhappy?"

"I don't know exactly." You can get fond of a hen, especially a cantankerous and homely old one whose personality has a lot in common with your own.

"She was old. She wanted a flock of chicks, and I couldn't stay with her. So I—" Something obscure here: probably my mind was trying too hard to grasp it— " . . . so I saved her life." I could make nothing else out of it. She said "saved."

Camilla's death looked natural, except that I should have expected the death contractions to muss the straw, and that hadn't happened. Maybe the angel had arranged the old lady's body for decorum, though I don't see how her muscular strength would have been equal to it—Camilla weighed at least seven pounds.

As I was burying her at the edge of the garden and the angel was humming over my head, I recalled a thing which, when it happened, I had dismissed as a dream. Merely a moonlight image of the angel standing in the nest box with her hands on Camilla's head, then pressing her mouth gently on Camilla's throat, just before the hen's head sank down out of my line of vision. Probably I actually waked and saw it happen. I am somehow unconcerned—even, as I think more about it, pleased. . . .

After the burial the angel's hands said, "Sit on the grass and we'll talk. . . . Question me. I'll tell you what I can. My father asks you to write it down."

So that is what we have been doing for the last four days. I have been going to school, a slow but willing pupil. Rather than enter anything in this journal (for in the evenings I was exhausted), I made notes as best I could. The angel has gone now to see her father and will not return until morning. I shall try to make a readable version of my notes.

Since she had invited questions, I began with something which had been bothering me, as a would-be naturalist, exceedingly. I couldn't see how creatures no larger than the adults I had observed could lay eggs as large as Camilla's. Nor could I understand why, if they were hatched in an almost adult condition and able to eat a varied diet, she had any use for that ridiculous, lovely, and apparently functional pair of breasts. When the angel grasped my difficulty she exploded with laughter—her kind, which buzzed her all over the garden and caused her to fluff my hair on the wing and pinch my ear lobe. She lit on a rhubarb leaf and gave a delectably naughty representation of herself as a hen laying an egg, including the cackle. She got me to bumbling helplessly—my kind of laughter—and it was some time before we could quiet down. Then she did her best to explain.

They are true mammals, and the young—not more than two or at most three in a lifetime averaging two hundred and fifty years—are delivered in very much the human way. The baby is nursed—human fashion—until his brain begins to respond a little to their unspoken language; that takes three to four weeks. Then he is placed in an altogether different medium. She could not describe that clearly, because there was very little in my educational storehouse to help me grasp it. It is some gaseous medium that arrests bodily growth for an almost indefinite period, while mental growth continues. It took them, she says, about seven thousand years to perfect this technique after they first hit on the idea: they are never in a hurry. The infant remains under this delicate and precise control for anywhere from fifteen to thirty years, the period depending not only on his mental vigor but also on the type of lifework he tentatively elects as soon as his brain is knowing enough to make a choice. During this period his mind is guided with unwavering patience by teachers who—

It seems those teachers know their business. This was peculiarly difficult for me to assimilate, although the fact came through clearly enough. In their world, the profession of teacher is more highly honored than any other—can such a thing be possible?—and so difficult to enter that only the strongest minds dare attempt it. (I had to rest a while after absorbing that.) An aspirant must spent fifty years (not including the period of infantile education) in merely getting ready to begin, and the acquisition of factual knowledge, while not understressed, takes only a small proportion of those fifty years. Then—if he's good enough—he can take a small part in the elementary instruction of a few babies, and if he does well on that basis for another thirty or forty years, he is considered a fair beginner. . . . Once upon a time I lurched around stuffy classrooms trying to insert a few predigested facts (I wonder how many of them *were* facts?) into the minds of bored and preoccupied adolescents, some of whom may have liked me moderately well. I was even able to shake hands and be nice while their terribly well-meaning parents explained to me how they ought to be educated. So much of our human effort goes down the drain of futility, I sometimes wonder how we ever got as far as the Bronze Age. Somehow we did, though, and a short way beyond.

After that preliminary stage of an angel's education is finished, the baby is transferred to more ordinary surroundings, and his bodily growth completes itself in a very short time. Wings grow abruptly (as I have seen), and he reaches a maximum height of six inches (our measure). Only then does he enter on that lifetime of two hundred and fifty years, for not until then does his body begin to age. My angel has been a living personality for many years but will not celebrate her first birthday for almost a year. I like to think of that.

At about the same time that they learned the principles of interplanetary travel (approximately twelve million years ago) these people also learned how, by use of a slightly different method, growth could be arrested at any point short of full maturity. At first the knowledge served no purpose except in the control of illnesses which still occasionally struck them at that time. But when the long periods of time required for space travel were considered, the advantages became obvious.

So it happens that my angel was born ten light-years away. She was trained by her father and many others in the wisdom of seventy million years (that, she tells me, is the approximate sum of their *recorded* history), and then she was safely sealed and cherished in what my superamoebic brain regarded as a blue egg. Education did not proceed at that time; her mind went to sleep with the rest of her. When Camilla's temperature made her wake and grow again, she remembered what to do with the little horny bumps provided for her elbows. And came out—into this planet, God help her.

I wondered why her father should have chosen any combination so unreliable as an old hen and a human being. Surely he must have had plenty of excellent ways to bring the shell to the right temperature. Her answer should have satisfied me immensely, but I am still compelled to wonder about it. "Camilla was a nice hen, and my father studied your mind while you were asleep. It was a bad landing, and much was broken—no such landing was ever made before after so long a journey: forty years. Only four other grownups could come with my father. Three of them died en route and he is very ill. And there were nine other children to care for."

Yes, I knew she'd said that an angel thought I was good enough to be trusted with his daughter. If it upsets me, all I need do is look at her and then in the mirror. As for the explanation, I can only conclude there must be more that I am not ready to understand. I was worried about those nine others, but she assured me they were all well, and I sensed that I ought not to ask more about them at present. . . .

Their planet, she says, is closely similar to this. A trifle larger, moving in a somewhat longer orbit around a sun like ours. Two gleaming moons, smaller than ours —their orbits are such that two-moon nights come rarely. They are magic, and she will ask her father to show me one, if he can. Their year is thirty-two days longer than ours; because of a slower rotation, their day has twenty-six of our hours. Their atmosphere is mainly nitrogen and oxygen in the proportions familiar to us; slightly richer in some of the rare gases. The climate is now what we should call tropical and subtropical, but they have known glacial rigors like those in our world's past. There are only two great continental land masses, and many thousands of large islands.

Their total population is only five billion. . . .

Most of the forms of life we know have parallels there —some quite exact parallels: rabbits, deer, mice, cats.

The cats have been bred to an even higher intelligence than they possess on our Earth; it is possible, she says, to have a good deal of intellectual intercourse with their cats, who learned several million years ago that when they kill, it must be done with lightning precision and without torture. The cats had some difficulty grasping the possibility of pain in other organisms, but once that educational hurdle was passed, development was easy. Nowadays many of the cats are popular storytellers; about forty million years ago they were still occasionally needed as a special police force, and served the angels with real heroism.

It seems my angel wants to become a student of animal life here on Earth. I, a teacher!—but bless her heart for the notion, anyhow. We sat and traded animals for a couple of hours last night. I found it restful, after the mental struggle to grasp more difficult matters. Judy was something new to her. They have several luscious monsters on that planet but, in her view, so have we. She told me of a blue sea snake fifty feet long (relatively harmless) that bellows cow-like and comes into the tidal marshes to lay black eggs; so I gave her a whale. She offered a bat-winged, day-flying ball of mammalian fluff as big as my head and weighing under an ounce; I matched her with a marmoset. She tried me with a small-sized pink brontosaur (very rare), but I was ready with the duck-billed platypus, and that caused us to exchange some pretty smart remarks about mammalian eggs; she bounced. All trivial in a way; also, the happiest evening in my fifty-three tangled years of life.

She was a trifle hesitant to explain these kangaroo-like people, until she was sure I really wanted to know. It seems they are about the nearest parallel to human life on that planet; not a near parallel, of course, as she was careful to explain. Agreeable and always friendly souls (though they weren't always so, I'm sure) and of a somewhat more alert intelligence than we possess. Manual workers, mainly, because they prefer it nowadays, but some of them are excellent mathematicians. The first practical spaceship was invented by a group of them, with some assistance. . . .

Names offer difficulties. Because of the nature of the angelic language, they have scant use for them except for the purpose of written record, and writing naturally plays little part in their daily lives—no occasion to write a letter when a thousand miles is no obstacle to the speech of your mind. An angel's formal name is about as important to him as, say, my Social Security number is to me. She has not told me hers, because the phonetics on which their written language is based have no parallel in my mind. As we would speak a friend's name, an angel will project the friend's image to his friend's receiving mind. More pleasant and more intimate, I think—although it was a shock to me at first to glimpse my own ugly mug in my mind's eye. Stories are occasionally written, if there is something in them that should be preserved precisely as it was in the first telling; but in their world the true storyteller has a more important place than the printer—he offers one of the best of their quieter pleasures: a good one can hold his audience for a week and never tire them.

"What is this 'angel' in your mind when you think of me?"

"A being men have imagined for centuries, when they thought of themselves as they might like to be and not as they are."

I did not try too painfully hard to learn much about the principles of space travel. The most my brain could take in of her explanation was something like: "Rocket—then phototropism." Now, that makes scant sense. So far as I know, phototropism—movement toward light—is an organic phenomenon. One thinks of it as a response of protoplasm, in some plants and animal organisms (most of them simple), to the stimulus of light; certainly not as a force capable of moving inorganic matter. I think that whatever may be the principle she was describing, this word "phototropism" was merely the nearest thing to it in my reservoir of language. Not even the angels can create understanding out of blank ignorance. At least I have learned not to set neat limits to the possible.

(There was a time when I did, though. I can see myself, not so many years back, like a homunculus squatting at the foot of Mt. McKinley, throwing together two handfuls of mud and shouting, "Look at the big mountain *I* made!")

And if I did know the physical principles which brought them here, and could write them in terms accessible to technicians resembling myself, I would not do it.

Here is a thing I am afraid no reader of this journal will believe: These people, as I have written, learned their method of space travel some twelve million years ago. But this is the first time they have ever used it to convey them to another planet. The heavens are rich in worlds, she tells me; on many of them there is life, often on very primitive levels. No external force prevented her people from going forth, colonizing, conquering, as far as they pleased. They could have populated a Galaxy. They did not, and for this reason: they believed they were not ready. More precisely: *Not good enough.*

Only some fifty million years ago, by her account, did they learn (as we may learn eventually) that intelligence without goodness is worse than high explosive in the hands of a baboon. For beings advanced beyond the level of Pithecanthropus, intelligence is a cheap commodity—not too hard to develop, hellishly easy to use for unconsidered ends. Whereas goodness is not to be achieved without unending effort of the hardest kind, within the self, whether the self be man or angel.

It is clear even to me that the conquest of evil is only one step, not the most important. For goodness, so she tried to tell me, is an altogether positive quality; the part of living nature that swarms with such monstrosities as cruelty, meanness, bitterness, greed, is not to be filled by a vacuum when these horrors are eliminated. When you clear away a poisonous gas, you try to fill the whole room with clean air. Kindness, for only one example: one who can define kindness only as the absence of cruelty has surely not begun to understand the nature of either.

They do not aim at perfection, these angels: only at the attainable. . . . That time fifty million years ago was evidently one of great suffering and confusion. War and all its attendant plagues. They passed through many centuries while advances in technology merely worsened their condition and increased the peril of self-annihilation. They came through that, in time. War was at length so far outgrown that its recurrence was impossible, and the development of wholly rational beings could begin. Then they were ready to start growing up, through millennia of self-searching, self-discipline, seeking to derive the simple from the complex, discovering how to use knowledge and not be used by it. Even then, of course, they slipped back often enough. There were what she refers to as "eras of fatigue." In their dimmer past, they had had many dark ages, lost civilizations, hopeful beginnings ending in dust. Earlier still, they had come out of the slime, as we did.

But their period of deepest uncertainty and sternest

self-appraisal did not come until twelve million years ago, when they knew a Universe could be theirs for the taking and knew they were not yet good enough.

They are in no more hurry than the stars. She tried to convey something, tentatively, at this point, which was really beyond both of us. It had to do with time (not as I understand time) being perhaps the most essential attribute of God (not as I was ever able to understand that word). Seeing my mental exhaustion, she gave up the effort and later told me that the conception was extremely difficult for her, too—not only, I gathered, because of her youth and relative ignorance. There was also a hint that her father might not have wished her to bring my brain up to a hurdle like that one. . . .

Of course, they explored. Their little spaceships were roaming the ether before there was anything like Man on this earth—roaming and listening, observing, recording; never entering nor taking part in the life of any home but their own. For five million years they even forbade themselves to go beyond their own Solar System, though it would have been easy to do so. And in the following seven million years, although they traveled to incredible distances, the same stern restraint was in force. It was altogether unrelated to what we should call fear—that, I think, is as extinct in them as hate. There was so much to do at home!—I wish I could imagine it. They mapped the heavens and played in their own sunlight.

Naturally, I cannot tell you what goodness is. I know only, moderately well, what it seems to mean to us human beings. It appears that the best of us can, with enormous difficulty, achieve a manner of life in which goodness is reasonably dominant, by a not too precarious balance, for the greater part of the time. Often, wise men have indicated they hope for nothing better than that in our present condition. We are, in other words, a fraction alive; the rest is in the dark. Dante was a bitter masochist, Beethoven a frantic and miserable snob, Shakespeare wrote potboilers. And Christ said, "My Father, if it be possible, let this cup pass from me."

But give us fifty million years—I am no pessimist. After all, I've watched one-celled organisms on the slide and listened to Brahms' Fourth. Night before last I said to the angel, "In spite of everything, you and I are kindred."

She granted me agreement.

June 9

She was lying on my pillow this morning so that I could see her when I waked.

Her father has died, and she was with him when it happened. There was again that thought-impression that I could interpret only to mean that his life had been "saved." I was still sleep-bound when my mind asked, "What will you do?"

"Stay with you, if you wish it, for the rest of your life." Now, the last part of the message was clouded, but I am familiar with that—it seems to mean there is some further element that eludes me. I could not be mistaken about the part I did receive. It gives me amazing speculations. After all, I am only fifty-three; I might live for another thirty or forty years. . . .

She was preoccupied this morning, but whatever she felt about her father's death that might be paralleled by sadness in a human being was hidden from me. She did say her father was sorry he had not been able to show me a two-moon night.

One adult, then, remains in this world. Except to say that he is two hundred years old and full of knowledge, and that he endured the long journey without serious ill effects, she has told me little about him. And there are ten children, including herself.

Something was sparkling at her throat. When she was aware of my interest in it she took it off, and I fetched a magnifying glass. A necklace; under the glass, much like our finest human workmanship, if your imagination can reduce it to the proper scale. The stones appeared similar to the jewels we know: diamonds, sapphires, rubies, emeralds, the diamonds snapping out every color under heaven; but there were two or three very dark-purple stones unlike anything I know—not amethysts, I am sure. The necklace was strung on something more slender than cobweb, and the design of the joining clasp was too delicate for my glass to help me. The necklace had been her mother's, she told me; as she put it back around her throat I thought I saw the same shy pride that any human girl might feel in displaying a new pretty.

She wanted to show me other things she had brought, and flew to the table where she had left a sort of satchel an inch and a half long—quite a load for her to fly with, but the translucent substance is so light that when she rested the satchel on my finger I scarcely felt it. She arranged a few articles happily for my inspection, and I put the glass to work again. One was a jeweled comb; she ran it through the down on her chest and legs to show me its use. There was a set of tools too small for the glass to interpret; I learned later they were a sewing kit. A book, and some writing instrument much like a metal pencil: imagine a book and pencil that could be used comfortably by hands hardly bigger than the paws of a mouse—that is the best I can do. The book, I understand, is a blank record for her use as needed.

And finally, when I was fully awake and dressed and we had finished breakfast, she reached in the bottom of the satchel for a parcel (heavy for her) and made me understand it was a gift for me. "My father made it for you, but I put in the stone myself, last night." She unwrapped it. A ring, precisely the size for my little finger.

I broke down, rather. She understood that, and sat on my shoulder petting my ear lobe till I had command of myself.

I have no idea what the jewel is. It shifts with the light from purple to jade-green to amber. The metal resembles platinum in appearance except for a tinge of rose at certain angles of light. . . . When I stare into the stone, I think I see—never mind that now. I am not ready to write it down, and perhaps never will be; anyway, I must be sure.

We improved our housekeeping later in the morning. I showed her over the house. It isn't much—Cape Codder, two rooms up and two down. Every corner interested her, and when she found a shoe box in the bedroom closet, she asked for it. At her direction, I have arranged it on a chest near my bed and near the window, which will be always open; she says the mosquitos will not bother me, and I don't doubt her. I unearthed a white silk scarf for the bottom of the box; after asking my permission (as if I could want to refuse her anything!) she got her sewing kit and snipped off a piece of the scarf several inches square, folded it on itself several times, and sewed it into a narrow pillow an inch long. So now she had a proper bed and a room of her own. I wish I had something less coarse than silk, but she insists it's nice.

We have not talked very much today. In the afternoon she flew out for an hour's play in the cloud country; when she returned she let me know that she needed a long sleep. She is still sleeping, I think; I am writing this downstairs, fearing the light might disturb her.

Is it possible I can have thirty or forty years in her

company? I wonder how teachable my mind still is. I seem to be able to assimilate new facts as well as I ever could; this ungainly carcass should be durable, with reasonable care. Of course, facts without a synthetic imagination are no better than scattered bricks; but perhaps my imagination—

I don't know.

Judy wants out. I shall turn in when she comes back. I wonder if poor Judy's life could be—the word is certainly "saved." I must ask.

June 10

Last night when I stopped writing I did go to bed but I was restless, refusing sleep. At some time in the small hours—there was light from a single room—she flew over to me. The tensions dissolved like an illness, and my mind was able to respond with a certain calm.

I made plain (what I am sure she already knew) that I would never willingly part company with her, and then she gave me to understand that there are two alternatives for the remainder of my life. The choice, she says, is altogether mine, and I must take time to be sure of my decision.

I can live out my natural span, whatever it proves to be, and she will not leave me for long at any time. She will be there to counsel, teach, help me in anything good I care to undertake. She says she would enjoy this; for some reason she is, as we'd say in our language, fond of me. We'd have fun.

Lord, the books I could write! I fumble for words now, in the usual human way: whatever I put on paper is a miserable fraction of the potential; the words themselves are rarely the right ones. But under her guidance—

I could take a fair part in shaking the world. With

words alone. I could preach to my own people. Before long, I would be heard.

I could study and explore. What small nibblings we have made at the sum of available knowledge! Suppose I brought in one leaf from outdoors, or one common little bug—in a few hours of studying it with her I'd know more of my own specialty than a flood of the best textbooks could tell me.

She has also let me know that when she and those who came with her have learned a little more about the human picture, it should be possible to improve my health greatly, and probably my life expectancy. I don't imagine my back could ever straighten, but she thinks the pain might be cleared away, possibly without drugs. I could have a clearer mind, in a body that would neither fail nor torment me.

Then there is the other alternative.

It seems they have developed a technique by means of which any unresisting living subject whose brain is capable of memory at all can experience a total recall. It is a by-product, I understand, of their silent speech, and a very recent one. They have practiced it for only a few thousand years, and since their own understanding of the phenomenon is very incomplete, they classify it among their experimental techniques. In a general way, it may somewhat resemble that reliving of the past that psychoanalysis can sometimes bring about in a limited way for therapeutic purposes; but you must imagine that sort of thing tremendously magnified and clarified, capable of including every detail that has ever registered on the subject's brain; and the end result is very different. The purpose is not therapeutic, as we would understand it: quite the opposite. The end result is death. Whatever is recalled by this process is transmitted to the receiving mind, which can retain it and record any or all of it if such a record is desired; but to the subject who recalls it, it is a flowing away, without return. Thus it is not a true "remembering" but a giving. The mind is swept clear, naked of all its past, and, along with memory, life withdraws also. Very quietly. At the end, I suppose it must be like standing without resistance in the engulfment of a flood tide, until finally the waters close over.

That, it seems, is how Camilla's life was "saved." Now, when I finally grasped that, I laughed, and the angel of course caught my joke. I was thinking about my neighbor Steele, who boarded the old lady for me in his henhouse for a couple of winters. Somewhere safe in the angelic records there must be a hen's-eye image of the patch in the seat of Steele's pants. Well—good. And, naturally, Camilla's view of me, too: not too unkind, I hope—she couldn't help the expression on her rigid little face, and I don't believe it ever meant anything.

At the other end of the scale is the saved life of my angel's father. Recall can be a long process, she says, depending on the intricacy and richness of the mind recalling; and in all but the last stages it can be halted at will. Her father's recall was begun when they were still far out in space and he knew that he could not long survive the journey. When that journey ended, the recall had progressed so far that very little factual memory remained to him of his life on that other planet. He had what must be called a "deductive memory"; from the material of the years not yet given away, he could reconstruct what must have been; and I assume the other adult who survived the passage must have been able to shelter him from errors that loss of memory might involve. This, I infer, is why he could not show me a two-moon night. I forgot to ask her whether the images he did send me were from actual or deductive memory. Deductive, I think, for there was a certain dimness about them not present when my angel gives me a picture of something seen with her own eyes.

Jade-green eyes, by the way—were you wondering?

In the same fashion, my own life could be saved. Every aspect of existence that I ever touched, that ever touched me, could be transmitted to some perfect record. The nature of the written record is beyond me, but I have no doubt of its relative perfection. Nothing important, good or bad, would be lost. And they need a knowledge of humanity, if they are to carry out whatever it is they have in mind.

It would be difficult, she tells me, and sometimes painful. Most of the effort would be hers, but some of it would have to be mine. In her period of infantile education, she elected what we should call zoology as her lifework; for that reason she was given intensive theoretical training in this technique. Right now, I guess she knows more than anyone else on this planet not only about what makes a hen tick but about how it feels to be a hen. Though a beginner, she is in all essentials already an expert. She can help me, she thinks (if I choose this alternative)—at any rate, ease me over the toughest spots, soothe away resistance, keep my courage from too much flagging.

For it seems that this process of recall is painful to an advanced intellect (she, without condescension, calls us very advanced) because, while all pretense and self-delusion are stripped away, there remains conscience, still functioning by whatever standards of good and bad the individual has developed in his lifetime. Our present knowledge of our own motives is such a pathetically small beginning!—hardly stronger than an infant's first effort to focus his eyes. I am merely wondering how much of my life (if I choose this way) will seem to me altogether hideous. Certainly plenty of the "good deeds" that I still cherish in memory like so many well-behaved cherubs will turn up with the leering aspect of greed or petty vanity or worse.

Not that I am a bad man, in any reasonable sense of the term; not a bit of it. I respect myself; no occasion to grovel and beat my chest; I'm not ashamed to stand comparison with any other fair sample of the species. But there you are: I *am* human, and under the aspect of eternity so far, plus this afternoon's newspaper, that is a rather serious thing.

Without real knowledge, I think of this total recall as something like a passage down a corridor of myriad images—now dark, now brilliant; now pleasant, now horrible—guided by no certainty except an awareness of the open blind door at the end of it. It could have its pleasing moments and its consolations. I don't see how it could ever approximate the delight and satisfaction of living a few more years in this world with the angel lighting on my shoulder when she wishes, and talking to me.

I had to ask her of how great value such a record would be to them. Very great. Obvious enough—they can be of little use to us, by their standards, until they understand us; and they came here to be of use to us as well as to themselves. And understanding us, to them, means knowing us inside out with a completeness such as our most dedicated and laborious scholars could never imagine. I remember those twelve million years: they will not touch us until they are certain no harm will come of it. On our tortured planet, however, there is a time factor. They know that well enough, of course. . . . Recall cannot begin unless the subject is willing or unresisting; to them, that has to mean willing, for any being with intellect enough to make a considered choice. Now, I wonder how many they could find who would be honestly willing to make that uneasy journey into death, for no reward except an assurance that they were serving their own kind and the angels?

More to the point, I wonder if I would be able to achieve such willingness myself, even with her help?

When this had been explained to me, she urged me again to make no hasty decision. And she pointed out to me what my thoughts were already groping at—why not both alternatives, within a reasonable limit of time? Why couldn't I have ten or fifteen years or more with her and then undertake the total recall—perhaps not until my physical powers had started toward senility? I thought that over.

This morning I had almost decided to choose that most welcome and comforting solution. Then the mailman brought my daily paper. Not that I needed any such reminder.

In the afternoon I asked her if she knew whether, in the present state of human technology, it would be possible for our folly to actually destroy this planet. She did not know, for certain. Three of the other children have gone away to different parts of the world, to learn what they can about that. But she had to tell me that such a thing has happened before, elsewhere in the heavens. I guess I won't write a letter to the papers advancing an explanation for the occasional appearance of a nova among the stars. Doubtless others have hit on the same hypothesis without the aid of angels.

And that is not all I must consider. I could die by accident or sudden disease before I had begun to give my life.

Only now, at this very late moment, rubbing my sweaty forehead and gazing into the lights of that wonderful ring, have I been able to put together some obvious facts in the required synthesis.

I don't know, of course, what forms their assistance to us will take. I suspect human beings won't see or hear much of the angels for a long time to come. Now and then disastrous decisions may be altered, and those who believe themselves wholly responsible won't quite know why their minds worked that way. Here and there, maybe an influential mind will be rather strangely nudged into a better course. Something like that. There may be sudden new discoveries and inventions of kinds that will tend to neutralize the menace of our nastiest playthings. But whatever the angels decide to do, the record and analysis of my not too atypical life will be an aid: it could even be the small weight deciding the balance between triumph and failure. That is fact one.

Two: my angel and her brothers and sisters, for all their amazing level of advancement, are of perishable protoplasm, even as I am. Therefore, if this ball of earth becomes a ball of flame, they also will be destroyed. Even if they have the means to use their spaceship again or to build another, it might easily happen that they would not learn their danger in time to escape. And for all I know, this could be tomorrow. Or tonight.

So there can no longer be any doubt as to my choice, and I will tell her when she wakes.

July 9

Tonight* there is no recall—I am to rest a while. I see it is almost a month since I last wrote in this jour-

---

* At this point Dr. Bannerman's handwriting alters curiously. From here on he used a soft pencil instead of a pen, and the script shows signs of haste. In spite of this, however, it is actually much clearer, steadier, and easier to read than the earlier entries in his normal hand. —BLAINE.

nal. My total recall began three weeks ago, and I have already been able to give away the first twenty-eight years of my life.

Since I no longer require normal sleep, the recall begins at night, as soon as the lights begin to go out over there in the village and there is little danger of interruption. Daytimes, I putter about in my usual fashion. I have sold Steele my hens, and Judy's life was saved a week ago; that practically winds up my affairs, except that I want to write a codicil to my will. I might as well do that now, right here in this journal, instead of bothering my lawyer. It should be legal.

> TO WHOM IT MAY CONCERN: I hereby bequeath to my friend Lester Morse, M.D., of Augusta, Maine, the ring which will be found at my death on the fifth finger of my left hand; and I would urge Dr. Morse to retain this ring in his private possession at all times, and to make provision for its disposal, in the event of his own death, to some person in whose character he places the utmost faith.
>
> (Signed) David Bannerman*

Tonight she has gone away for a while, and I am to rest and do as I please until she returns. I shall spend the time filling in some blanks in this record, but I am afraid it will be a spotty job, unsatisfactory to any readers who are subject to the blessed old itch for facts. Mainly because there is so much I no longer care about. It is troublesome to try to decide what things would be considered important by interested strangers.

---

* In spite of superficial changes in the handwriting, this signature has been certified genuine by an expert graphologist.
—BLAINE.

Except for the lack of any desire for sleep, and a bodily weariness that is not at all unpleasant, I notice no physical effects thus far. I have no faintest recollection of anything that happened earlier than my twenty-eighth birthday. My deductive memory seems rather efficient, and I am sure I could reconstruct most of the story if it were worth the bother: this afternoon I grubbed around among some old letters of that period, but they weren't very interesting. My knowledge of English is unaffected; I can still read scientific German and some French, because I had occasion to use those languages fairly often after I was twenty-eight. The scraps of Latin dating from high school are quite gone. So are algebra and all but the simplest propositions of high-school geometry: I never needed 'em. I can remember thinking of my mother after twenty-eight, but do not know whether the image this provides really resembles her; my father died when I was thirty-one, so I remember him as a sick old man. I believe I had a younger brother, but he must have died in childhood.*

Judy's passing was tranquil—pleasant for her, I think. It took the better part of a day. We went out to an abandoned field I know, and she lay in the sunshine with the angel sitting by her, while I dug a grave and then rambled off after wild raspberries. Toward evening the angel came and told me it was finished. And most interesting, she said. I don't see how there can have been anything distressing about it for Judy; after all, what hurts us worst is to have our favorite self-deceptions stripped away.

As the angel has explained it to me, her people, their cats, those kangaroo-folk, Man, and just possibly the

* Dr. Bannerman's mother died in 1918 of influenza. His brother (three years older, not younger) died of pneumonia, 1906.   —BLAINE.

cats on our planet (she hasn't met them yet) are the only animals she knows who are introspective enough to develop self-delusion and related pretenses. I suggested she might find something of the sort, at least in rudimentary form, among some of the other primates. She was immensely interested and wanted to learn everything I could tell her about monkeys and apes. It seems that long ago on the other planet there used to be clumsy, winged creatures resembling the angels to about the degree that the large anthropoids resemble us. They became extinct some forty million years ago, in spite of enlightened efforts to keep their kind alive. Their birth rate became insufficient for replacement, as if some necessary spark had simply flickered out; almost as if nature, or whatever name you prefer for the unknown, had with gentle finality written them off. . . .

I have not found the recall painful, at least not in retrospect. There must have been sharp moments, mercifully forgotten, along with their causes, as if the process had gone on under anesthesia. Certainly there were plenty of incidents in my first twenty-eight years that I should not care to offer to the understanding of any but the angels. Quite often I must have been mean, selfish, base in any number of ways, if only to judge by the record since twenty-eight. Those old letters touch on a few of these things. To me, they now matter only as material for a record which is safely out of my hands.

However, to any persons I may have harmed, I wish to say this: you were hurt by aspects of my humanity which may not, in a few million years, be quite so common among us all. Against these darker elements I struggled, in my human fashion, as you do yourselves. The effort is not wasted.

It was a week after I told the angel my decision before she was prepared to start the recall. During that week she searched my present mind more closely than I should have imagined was possible: she had to be sure. During that week of hard questions I dare say she learned more about my kind than has ever gone on record even in a physician's office; I hope she did. To any psychiatrist who might question that, I offer a naturalist's suggestion: it is easy to imagine, after some laborious time, that we have noticed everything a given patch of ground can show us; but alter the viewpoint only a little—dig down a foot with a spade, say, or climb a tree branch and look downward—it's a whole new world.

When the angel was not exploring me in this fashion, she took pains to make me glimpse the satisfactions and million rewarding experiences I might have if I chose the other way. I see how necessary that was; at the time it seemed almost cruel. She had to do it, for my own sake, and I am glad that I was somehow able to stand fast to my original choice. So was she, in the end; she has even said she loves me for it. What that troubling word means to her is not within my mind: I am satisfied to take it in the human sense.

Some evening during that week—I think it was June 12—Lester dropped around for sherry and chess. Hadn't seen him in quite a while, and haven't since. There is a moderate polio scare this summer, and it keeps him on the jump. The angel retired behind some books on an upper shelf—I'm afraid it was dusty—and had fun with our chess. She had a fair view of your bald spot, Lester; later she remarked that she liked your looks, and can't you do something about that weight? She suggested an odd expedient, which I believe has occurred to your medical self from time to time—eating less.

Maybe she shouldn't have done what she did with those chess games. Nothing more than my usual blundering happened until after my first ten moves; by that time I suppose she had absorbed the principles and she took over, slightly. I was not fully aware of it until I saw Lester looking like a boiled duck: I had imagined my astonishing moves were the result of my own damn cleverness.

Seriously, Lester, think back to that evening. You've played in stiff amateur tournaments; you know your own abilities and you know mine. Ask yourself whether I could have done anything like that without help. I tell you again, I didn't study the game in the interval when you weren't here. I've never had a chess book in the library, and if I had, no amount of study would take me into your class. Haven't that sort of mentality—just your humble sparring partner, and I've enjoyed it on that basis, as you might enjoy watching a prima-donna surgeon pull off some miracle you wouldn't dream of attempting yourself. Even if your game had been away below par that evening (O don't think it was), I could never have pinned your ears back three times running, without help. That evening you were a long way out of *your* class, that's all.

I couldn't tell you anything about it at the time—she was clear on that point—so I could only bumble and preen myself and leave you mystified. But she wants me to write anything I choose in this journal, and somehow, Lester, I think you may find the next few decades pretty interesting. You're still young—some ten years younger than I. I think you'll see many things that I do wish I myself might see come to pass—or I would so wish if I were not convinced that my choice was the right one.

Most of those new events will not be spectacular, I'd guess. Many of the turns to a better way will hardly be recognized at the time for what they are, by you or anyone else. Obviously, our nature being what it is, we shall not jump into heaven overnight. To hope for that would be as absurd as it is to imagine that any formula, ideology, theory of social pattern, can bring us into Utopia. As I see it, Lester—and I think your consulting room would have told you the same even if your own intuition were not enough—there is only one battle of importance: Armageddon. And Armageddon field is within each self, world without end.

At the moment I believe I am the happiest man who ever lived.

July 20

All but the last ten years now given away. The physical fatigue (still pleasant) is quite overwhelming. I am not troubled by the weeds in my garden patch—merely a different sort of flowers where I had planned something else. An hour ago she brought me the seed of a blown dandelion, to show me how lovely it was—I don't suppose I had ever noticed. I hope whoever takes over this place will bring it back to farming: they say the ten acres below the house used to be good potato land—nice early ground.

It is delightful to sit in the sun, as if I were old.

After thumbing over earlier entries in this journal, I see I have often felt quite bitter toward my own kind. I deduce that I must have been a lonely man—much of the loneliness self-imposed. A great part of my bitterness must have been no more than one ugly by-product of a life spent too much apart. Some of it doubtless came from objective causes, yet I don't believe I ever had more cause than any moderately intelligent man who would like to see his world a pleasanter place than it ever has been. My angel tells me that the pain in my back is due to an injury received in some early stage of the world war that still goes on. That could have soured me, perhaps. It's all right—it's all in the record.

She is racing with a hummingbird—holding back, I think, to give the ball of green fluff a break.

Another note for you, Lester. I have already indicated that my ring is to be yours. I don't want to tell you what I have discovered of its properties, for fear it might not give you the same pleasure and interest that it has given me. Of course, like any spot of shifting light and color, it is an aid to self-hypnosis. It is much, much more than that, but—find out for yourself, at some time when you are a little protected from everyday distractions. I know it can't harm you, because I know its source.

By the way, I wish you would convey to my publishers my request that they either discontinue manufacture of my *Introductory Biology* or else bring out a new edition revised in accordance with some notes you will find in the top left drawer of my library desk. I glanced through that book after my angel assured me that I wrote it, and I was amazed. However, I'm afraid my notes are messy (I call them mine by a poetic license), and they may be too advanced for the present day—though the revision is mainly a matter of leaving out certain generalities that ain't so. Use your best judgment: it's a very minor textbook, and the thing isn't too important. A last wriggle of my personal vanity.

July 27

I have seen a two-moon night.

It was given to me by that other grownup, at the end of a wonderful visit, when he and six of those nine other children came to see me. It was last night, I think—yes, must have been. First there was a murmur of wings above the house; my angel flew in, laughing; then they were here, all about me. Full of gaiety and colored fire, showing off in every way they knew would please me. Each one had something graceful and friendly to say to me. One brought me a moving image of the St. Lawrence seen at morning from half a mile up—clouds— eagles; now, how could he know that would delight me so much? And each one thanked me for what I had done.

But it's been so easy!

And at the end the old one—his skin is quite black, and his down is white and gray—gave the remembered image of a two-moon night. He saw it some sixty years ago.

I have not even considered making an effort to describe it—my fingers will not hold this pencil much longer tonight. Oh—soaring buildings of white and amber, untroubled countryside, silver on curling rivers, a glimpse of open sea; a moon rising in clarity, another setting in a wreath of cloud, between them a wide wandering of unfamiliar stars; and here and there the angels, worthy after fifty million years to live in such a night. No, I cannot describe anything like that. But, you human kindred of mine, I can do something better. I can tell you that this two-moon night, glorious as it was, was no more beautiful than a night under a single moon on this ancient and familiar Earth might be—if you will imagine that the rubbish of human evil has been cleared away and that our own people have started at last on the greatest of all explorations.

July 29

Nothing now remains to give away but the memory of the time that has passed since the angel came. I am to rest as long as I wish, write whatever I want to. Then I shall get myself over to the bed and lie down as if for sleep. She tells me that I can keep my eyes open: she will close them for me when I no longer see her.

I remain convinced that our human case is hopeful. I feel sure that in only a few thousand years we may be able to perform some of the simpler preparatory tasks, such as casting out evil and loving our neighbors. And if that should prove to be so, who can doubt that in another fifty million years we might well be only a little lower than the angels?

LIBRARIAN'S NOTE: As is generally known, the original of the Bannerman Journal is said to have been in the possession of Dr. Lester Morse at the time of the latter's disappearance in 1964, and that disappearance has remained an unsolved mystery to the present day. McCarran is known to have visited Captain Garrison Blaine in October, 1951, but no record remains of that visit. Captain Blaine appears to have been a bachelor who lived alone. He was killed in line of duty, December, 1951. McCarran is believed not to have written about nor discussed the Bannerman affair with anyone else. It is almost certain that he himself removed the extract and related papers from the files (unofficially, it would seem!) when he severed his connection with the FBI in 1957; at any rate, they were found among his effects after his assassination and were released to the public, considerably later, by Mrs. McCarran.

  The following memorandum was originally attached to the extract from the Bannerman Journal; it carries the McCarran initialing.

Aug. 11, 1951

The original letter of complaint written by Stephen Clyde, M.D., and mentioned in the accompanying letter of Captain Blaine, has unfortunately been lost, owing perhaps to an error in filing.

Personnel presumed responsible have been instructed not to allow such error to be repeated except if, as, and/or when necessary.

C. McC.

On the margin of this memorandum there was a penciled notation, later erased. The imprint is sufficient to show the unmistakable McCarran script. The notation read in part as follows: *Far be it from a McC. to lose his job except if, as, and/or*—the rest is undecipherable, except for a terminal word which is regrettably unparliamentary.

STATEMENT BY LESTER MORSE, M.D., DATED
  AUGUST 9, 1951

On the afternoon of July 30, 1951, acting on what I am obliged to describe as an unexpected impulse, I drove out to the country for the purpose of calling on my friend Dr. David Bannerman. I had not seen him nor had word from him since the evening of June 12 of this year.

I entered, as was my custom, without knocking. After calling to him and hearing no response, I went upstairs to his bedroom and found him dead. From superficial indications I judged that death must have taken place during the previous night. He was lying on his bed on his left side, comfortably disposed as if for sleep but fully dressed, with a fresh shirt and clean summer slacks. His eyes and mouth were closed, and there was no trace of the disorder to be expected at even the easiest natural death. Because of these signs I assumed, as soon as I had determined the absence of breath and heartbeat and noted the chill of the body, that some neighbor must have found him already, performed these simple rites out of respect for him, and probably notified a local physician or other responsible person. I therefore waited (Dr. Bannerman had no telephone), expecting that someone would soon call.

Dr. Bannerman's journal was on a table near his bed, open to that page on which he has written a codicil to his will. I read that part. Later, while I was waiting for others to come, I read the remainder of the journal, as I believe he wished me to do. The ring he mentions was on the fifth finger of his left hand, and it is now in my possession. When writing that codicil Dr. Bannerman must have overlooked or forgotten the fact that in his formal will, written some months earlier, he had appointed me executor. If there are legal technicalities involved, I shall be pleased to cooperate fully with the proper authorities.

The ring, however, will remain in my keeping, since that was Dr. Bannerman's expressed wish, and I am not prepared to offer it for examination or discussion under any circumstances.

The notes for a revision of one of his textbooks were in his desk, as noted in the journal. They are by no means "messy"; nor are they particularly revolutionary except insofar as he wished to rephrase, as theory or hypothesis, certain statements that I would have supposed could be regarded as axiomatic. This is not my field, and I am not competent to judge. I shall take up the matter with his publishers at the earliest opportunity.*

So far as I can determine, and bearing in mind the results of the autopsy performed by Stephen Clyde,

---

* LIBRARIAN'S NOTE: But it seems he never did. No new edition of *Introductory Biology* was ever brought out, and the textbook has been out of print since 1952.

M.D., the death of Dr. David Bannerman was not inconsistent with the presence of an embolism of some type not distinguishable on post mortem. I have so stated on the certificate of death. It would seem to be not in the public interest to leave such questions in doubt. I am compelled to add one other item of medical opinion for what it may be worth:

I am not a psychiatrist, but, owing to the demands of general practice, I have found it advisable to keep as up to date as possible with current findings and opinion in this branch of medicine. Dr. Bannerman possessed, in my opinion, emotional and intellectual stability to a better degree than anyone else of comparable intelligence in the entire field of my acquaintance, personal and professional. If it is suggested that he was suffering from a hallucinatory psychosis, I can only say that it must have been of a type quite outside my experience and not described, so far as I know, anywhere in the literature of psychopathology.

Dr. Bannerman's house, on the afternoon of July 30, was in good order. Near the open, unscreened window of his bedroom there was a coverless shoe box with a folded silk scarf in the bottom. I found no pillow such as Dr. Bannerman describes in the journal, but observed that a small section had been cut from the scarf. In this box, and near it, there was a peculiar fragrance, faint, aromatic, and very sweet, such as I have never encountered before and therefore cannot describe.

It may or may not have any bearing on the case that, while I remained in his house that afternoon, I felt no sense of grief or personal loss, although Dr. Bannerman had been a loved and honored friend for a number of years. I merely had, and have, a conviction that after the completion of some very great undertaking, he had found peace.

William Tenn

"WILL YOU WALK A LITTLE FASTER?"

. . . And then there is the alien civilization that wants what we've got and is calmly preparing to take it. This usually involves such technological advances as flying saucers, hydrogen bombs, and other items which are by now such common topics of contemporary chitchat that as science-fiction devices they have become somewhat stale.

But this flying-saucer tale, in which you are asked to "walk a little faster" (said Lewis Carroll's whiting to the snail), is much too unusual a dish, with definitely too peculiar a type of alien inhabitant, not to be included in this collection.

A careful reading of this story will tend to convince you that its author is not above harboring some suspicions as to the level of the social I.Q. of the human race. In this belief you are probably right, for he has placed us in as nasty a situation as you could possibly imagine.

THIS is a good story, all right. This is almost *too* good a story. But, dammit, I should be ashamed of myself for telling it.

Or *should* I? If Forkbeard was right about us, my misplaced idealism has been getting in the way of the biggest chunk of fame and fortune that a poor slob of a scrivener can expect in this world. If he was right, the others haven't been keeping their mouths shut. While I've been practically starving—

Why, for all I know, there is a cow on the White House lawn this very moment! . . .

Last August, to be exact, I was perspiring over an ice-cold yarn that I never should have started in the first place, when the doorbell rang.

I looked up and yelled, "Come in! Door's open!"

The hinges squeaked a little, the way they do in my place. I heard feet slap-slapping up the long entrance corridor that makes the rent on my apartment a little lower than most of the others in the building. I couldn't recognize the walk as belonging to anyone I knew, so I waited with my fingers on the typewriter keys and my face turned to the study entrance.

After a while, the feet came around the corner. A little man, not much more than two feet high, dressed in a green knee-length tunic, walked in. He had a very large head, a short, pointed red beard, a long, pointed green cap, and he was talking to himself. In his right hand he carried a golden pencil-like object; in his left, a curling strip of what seemed to be parchment.

We considered each other for a bit, in the course of which my lower jaw began to drop faster and faster, giving every sign of an earnest intention to part company forever with the rest of my head.

"Now, you," he said with a guttural accent, pointing both the beard and the pencil-like object at me, "now, you must be a writer."

I closed my mouth carefully around a lump of air. Somehow, I noted with interest, I seemed to be nodding.

"Good." He flourished the pencil and made a mark at the end of a line halfway down the scroll. "That completes the enrollment for this session. Come with me, please."

He seized the arm with which I had begun an elaborate gesture. Holding me in a grip that had all the resilience of a steel manacle, he smiled benevolently and walked back down my entrance hall. Every few steps he walked straight up in the air, and then—as if he'd noticed his error—calmly strode down to the floor again.

"What—who—" I said, stumbling and tripping and occasionally getting walloped painfully by the wall. "You wait, you—who—*who*—"

"Please do not make such repetitious noises," he admonished me. "You are supposed to be a creature of civilization. Ask intelligent questions if you wish, but *only* when you have them properly organized."

I brooded on that while he closed the door of my apartment and began dragging me up the stairs. His heart may or may not have been pure, but I estimated his strength as being roughly equivalent to that of ten. I felt like a flag being flapped from the end of my own arm.

"We're going up?" I commented tentatively as I was swung around a landing.

"Naturally. To the roof. Where we're parked."

"Parked, you said?" I thought of a helicopter, then of a broomstick. These things just don't happen to a guy, I told myself. Not a guy like me—not in a run-down neighborhood like mine. Maybe in places like Hollywood, or Washington, D.C., or Paris —

Mrs. Flugelman, who lives on the floor above, came out of her apartment with a canful of garbage. She opened the door of the dumb-waiter and started to nod good morning at me. She stopped when she saw my friend.

"That's right: parked. What you call our flying saucer." He noticed Mrs. Flugelman staring at him and jutted his beard at her as we went by. "Yes, I said flying saucer!" he spat.

Mrs. Flugelman walked back into her apartment with the canful of garbage and closed the door behind her very quietly.

Maybe the stuff I write for a living prepared me for such experiences, but—somehow—as soon as he told me that, I felt better. Little men and flying saucers—they seemed to go together. Just so halos and pitchforks didn't wander into the continuity.

When we reached the roof, I wished I'd had time to grab a jacket. It was evidently going to be a breezy ride.

The saucer was about thirty feet in diameter and, colorful magazine articles to the contrary, had been used for more than mere sightseeing. In the center, where it was deepest, there was a huge pile of boxes and crates lashed down with crisscrossing masses of gleaming thread. Here and there in the pile was the unpackaged metal of completely unfamiliar machinery.

Still using my arm as a kind of convenient handle to the rest of me, the little man whirled me about experimentally once or twice, then scaled me accurately end over end some twenty feet through the air to the top of the pile. A moment before I hit, golden threads boiled about me, cushioning like an elastic net and tying me up more thoroughly than any three shipping clerks. My shot-putting pal grunted and prepared to climb aboard.

Suddenly, he stopped and looked back along the roof. "Irngl!" he yelled in a voice like two ocean liners arguing. "Irngl! *Bordge modgunk!*"

There was a tattoo of feet on the roof so rapid as to be almost one sound, and an eight-inch-high replica of my strong-arm guide—minus the beard—leaped into the craft. Young Irngl, I decided, *bordge modgunking.*

His elder stared at him suspiciously, then walked back slowly in the direction from which he had run.

He halted and shook a ferocious finger at the youngster. Beside me, Irngl cowered.

Just behind the chimney was a cluster of television antennas. But the dipoles of these antennas were no longer parallel: some had been carefully braided together; others had been tied into delicate and perfect bows. Growling ferociously, shaking his head so that the pointed red beard made like a metronome, the old man untied the knots and smoothed the dipoles out to careful straightness with his fingers. Then he bent his legs slightly at their knobby knees and performed one of the most spectacular standing broad jumps of all time.

And, as he hit the floor of the giant saucer, we took off. Straight up.

When I'd recovered sufficiently to regurgitate my larynx, I noticed that old Redbeard was controlling the movement of the disk beneath us by means of an egg-shaped piece of metal in his right hand. After we'd gone up a goodly distance, he pointed the egg south and we headed that way.

Radiant power, I wondered? Not much information had been volunteered. *Of course,* I realized suddenly: I hadn't asked any questions! Grabbed from my typewriter in the middle of the morning by a midget of great brain and muscle—I couldn't be blamed: few men in my position would have been able to put their finger on the nub of the problem and make appropriate inquiries. *Now,* however—

"While there's a lull in the action," I began breezily enough, "and as long as you speak English, I'd like to clear up a few troublesome matters. For example . . ."

"Your questions will be answered later. Meanwhile, you will shut up." Golden threads filled my mouth, and I found myself unable to open it. Redbeard stared at me as I gurgled impotently. "How hateful are humans!" he said, beaming. "And how fortunate that they are so hateful!"

The rest of the trip was uneventful, except for a few moments when the Miami-bound plane came abreast of us. People inside pointed excitedly, seemed to yell, and one extremely fat man held up an expensive camera and took six pictures very rapidly. Unfortunately, I noticed, he had neglected to remove the lens cap.

The saucer skipper shook his metal egg, there was a momentary feeling of acceleration—and the airplane was a disappearing dot behind us. Irngl climbed to the top of what looked like a giant malted-milk machine and stuck his tongue out at me. I glared back.

It struck me then that the little one's mischievous quality was mighty reminiscent of an elf. And his pop—the parentage seemed unmistakable by then—was like nothing other than a gnome from Germanic folklore. Therefore, didn't these facts mean that—that—that—

I let my brain have ten full minutes, before giving up. Oh, well, sometimes that method works: reasoning by self-hypnotic momentum, I call it.

I was cold, but otherwise quite content and looking forward to the next development with interest. I had been selected, alone of my species, by this race of aliens for some significant purpose.

I couldn't help hoping, of course, that the purpose was not vivisection.

We arrived, after a while, at something huge: another vehicle, very much like ours but many, many times larger (what you might call a flying platter or soup tureen) poised on an invisible pillar of force several miles high. I suspected that a good distance down, under all those belly-soft clouds beneath it, was the state of South Carolina. I also suspected that the clouds were artificial.

Our entire outfit entered through an oversized porthole in the bottom. It wasn't until much later that I understood the big porthole was really an air lock. Somehow, I had never expected an outer air lock to be transparent.

Since the flying soup tureen had a cover, so to speak, we found ourselves in a hollow disk close to a quarter of a mile in diameter. Flying saucers stacked with goods and people—both long and short folk—were scattered up and down its expanse between great masses of glittering machinery.

Evidently I was wrong about having been selected as a representative sample. There were lots of us, human men and women, all over the place—one to a flying saucer. It was to be a formal meeting between the representatives of two great races, I decided.

Only why didn't our friends do it with the U.N.? Then I remembered Redbeard's comment on humanity. . . .

On my right, an Army colonel, with a face like a keg of butter, was chewing on the pencil with which he had been taking short, hastily scrawled notes. On my left, a tall man in a gray sharkskin suit flipped back his sleeve, looked at his watch, and expelled his breath noisily, impatiently. Up ahead, two women were leaning toward each other at the touching edges of their respective saucers, both talking at the same time and both nodding vehemently as they talked.

Each of the flying saucers also had at least one equivalent of my red-bearded pilot. I observed that while the females of this people had beards too, they were exactly one-half as motherly as our women. But they balanced, they balanced. . . .

Abruptly, the image of a little man appeared on the

ceiling. His beard was pink and it forked. He pulled on each fork and smiled down at us.

"To correct the impression in the minds of many of you," he said, chuckling benignly, "I will paraphrase your great poet, Shakespeare. I am here to bury humanity, not to praise it."

A startled murmur broke out all around me. *"Mars,"* I heard the colonel say. "Bet they're from Mars. H. G. Wells predicted it. Dirty little, red little, Martians. Well, just let them try!"

"Red," the man in the gray sharkskin suit repeated, staring at him anxiously. *"Red?"*

"Did you ever—" one of the women started to protest. "Is that a way to begin? No manners! A real foreigner."

"However," Forkbeard continued imperturbably from the ceiling, "in order to bury humanity properly, I need your help. Not only yours, but the help of others like you who, at this moment, are listening to this talk in ships similar to this one and in dozens of languages all over the world. We need your help—and, knowing your peculiar talents so well, we are fairly certain of getting it!"

He waited until the next flurry of fist-waving and assorted imprecations had died down; he waited until the anti-Negroes and the anti-Jews, the anti-Catholics and the anti-Protestants, the Anglophobes and the Russophobes, the vegetarians and the fundamentalists in the audience all had identified him colorfully with their peculiar concepts of the opposition.

Then, once relative quiet had been achieved, we got the following blunt tale, rather contemptuously told.

There was an enormous and complex galactic civilization surrounding our meager nine-planet system. This civilization, composed of the various intelligent species throughout the Galaxy, was organized into a peaceful federation for trade and mutual advancement.

A special bureau in the Galactic Federation was in charge of new arrivals on the intellectual scene. Thus, quite a few millennia ago, the bureau had visited Earth to investigate tourist accounts of a remarkably ingenious animal that had lately been noticed wandering about and handling its affairs with a definite amount of self-consciousness. The animal having been certified as intelligent and possessed of a high cultural potential, Earth was closed to tourist traffic, and sociological specialists began the customary close examination.

"And, as a result of this examination"—the forked pink beard smiled gently down from above—"the specialists discovered that what you call the human race was nonviable. That is, while the individuals composing it had strongly developed instincts of self-preservation, the species as a whole was suicidal."

"Suicidal!" I found myself breathing with the others.

"Quite. This is a matter on which there can be little argument from the more honest among you. High civilization is a product of communal living, and Man, in groups, has always tended to wipe himself out. In fact, a large factor in the growth of what little civilization you do experience has been due to rewards derived from the development of mass-destructive weapons."

"We have had peaceful, brotherly periods," a hoarse voice said on the opposite side of the ship.

The large head shook slowly from side to side. The eyes, I saw suddenly and irrelevantly, were all black iris. "You have not. You *have* occasionally developed an island of culture here, an oasis of cooperation there, but these have inevitably disintegrated upon contact with the true standard-bearers of your species—the warrior races. And when, as happened occasionally, the warrior races were defeated, the conquerors in their turn became warriors, so that the suicidal strain was once more rewarded and became even more dominant. Your past is your complete indictment; and your present—your present is about to become your executed sentence. But enough of this peculiar bloody nonsense—let me return to *living* history."

He went on to explain that the Federation felt a suicidal species should be allowed to fulfill its destiny unhampered. In fact, so long as overt acts were avoided, it was quite permissible to help such a creature along to the doom it desired—"Nature abhors self-destruction even more than a vacuum. The logic is simple: both cease almost as soon as they come into existence."

After the Federation sociologists had extrapolated the probable date on which humanity might be expected to extinguish itself, the planet was assigned to the inhabitants of an Earth-like world for the use of such surplus population as they might then have. These were the red-beards.

"We sent representatives here to serve as caretakers, so to speak, of our future property. But about nine hundred years ago, when your world still had six thousand years to run, we decided to hurry the process a bit, as we were experiencing a rising index of population on our own planet. We therefore received full permission from the Galactic Federation to stimulate your technological development into an earlier suicide. The Federation stipulated, however, that each advance be made the moral responsibility of an adequate representative of your race; that he be told the complete truth of the situation. This we did: We would select an individual to be the discoverer of a revolutionary technique or scientific principle; then we would explain both the value of the technique and the consequences to his species in terms of accelerated mass destruction."

I found it hard to continue looking into his enormous eyes. "In every case"—the booming rattle of the voice had softened perceptibly—"in every case, sooner or later, the individual announced the discovery as his own, giving it to his fellows and profiting substantially. In a few cases, he later endowed great foundations which awarded prizes to those who advanced the cause of peace or the brotherhood of man. This resulted in little beyond an increase in the amount of currency being circulated. Individuals, we found, always chose to profit at the expense of their race's life expectancy."

Gnomes, elves, kobolds! Not mischievous sprites— I glanced at Irngl sitting quietly under his father's heavy hand—nor the hoarders of gold, but helping Man for their own reasons: teaching him to smelt metals and build machinery, showing him how to derive the binomial theorem in one part of the world and how to plow a field more efficiently in another.

To the end that humanity might perish from the Earth . . . a little sooner.

"Unfortunately—ah, something has developed."

We looked up at that, all of us—housewives and handymen, soldiers and stockholders, preachers and professional entertainers—looked up from the tangle of our reflections and prejudices, and *hoped*.

As S-Day (S for suicide, of course) drew nigh, those among the kobolds who intended to emigrate filled their flying saucers with possessions and families. They scooted across space in larger craft, such as the one we were now in, and took up positions in the stratosphere, waiting to assume title to the planet as soon as its present occupants used their latest discovery—nuclear fission—as they had previously used ballistics and aeronautics.

The more impatient wandered down to survey home-sites. They found to their annoyance that an unpleasant maggot of error had crawled into the pure mathematics of extrapolated sociology. Humanity should have wiped itself out shortly after acquiring atomic power. But— possibly as a result of the scientific stimulation we had been receiving recently—our technological momentum had carried us past uranium-plutonium fission and up to the so-called hydrogen bomb.

Whereas a uranium-bomb Armageddon would dispose of us in a most satisfactory and sanitary fashion, the explosion of several hydrogen bombs, it seems, will result in the complete sterilization of our planet, as the result of a subsidiary reaction at present unknown to us. If we go to war with this atomic refinement, Earth will not only be cleansed of all present life forms but will also become uninhabitable for several million years to come.

Naturally, the kobolds view this situation with understandable unhappiness. According to Galactic Law, they may not intervene actively to safeguard their legacy.

Therefore, they would like to offer a proposition— Any nation which guarantees to stop making hydrogen bombs and to dispose of those it has already made —and the little red-beards have, they claim, satisfactory methods of enforcing these guarantees—such a nation will be furnished by them with a magnificently murderous weapon. This weapon is extremely simple to operate and is so calibrated that it can be set to kill, instantaneously and painlessly, any number of people at one time, up to a full million.

"The advantage to any terrestrial military establishment of such a weapon over the unstable hydrogen bomb, which is not only very expensive and random in its effects but must be transported physically to its target," the genial face on the ceiling commented, "should be obvious to all of you! And, as far as we are concerned, anything that will dispose of human beings on a wholesale basis, while not damaging—"

At this point, there was so much noise that I couldn't hear a word he was saying. For that matter, I was yelling quite loudly myself.

"—besides the injury of useful and compatible life forms—"

"Ah-h," screamed a deeply tanned stout man in a flowerful red sports shirt and trunks, "whyn't you go back where you came from?"

"Yeah!" someone else added wrathfully. "Can't yuh see yuh not wanted? Shut up, huh? Shut *up!*"

"Murderers," one of the women in front of me quavered. "That's all you are—murderers trying to kill inoffensive people who've never done you any harm. Killing would just be too good for you."

The colonel was standing on his toes and oscillating a portentous forefinger at the roof. "We were doing all right," he began apoplectically, then stopped to allow himself to un-purple. "We were doing *well* enough, I can tell you, without—without—"

Forkbeard waited until we began to run down.

"Look at it this way," he urged in a wheedling voice. "You're going to wipe yourselves out—*you* know it, *we* know it, and so does everybody else in the Galaxy. What difference can it possibly make to you whether you do it one way or another? At least by our method you confine the injury to yourselves. You don't damage the highly valuable real estate—to wit, Earth—which will be ours after you've ceased to use it. And you go out with a weapon which is *much* more worthy of your destructive propensities than any you have used hitherto, including your pride and joy, the atomic bomb."

He paused and spread knobbed hands down at our impotent hatred. "Think of it—*just think of it:* a million deaths at one plunge of a lever! What other weapon can make that claim?"

Skimming back northward with Redbeard and Irngl, I pointed to the flying saucers radiating away from us through the delicate summer sky. "These people are all fairly responsible citizens. Isn't it silly to expect them to advertise a more effective way of having their throats cut?"

There was a shrug of the green-wrapped shoulders. "With any other species, yes. But not you. The Galactic Federation insists that the actual revelation of the weapon to humanity as a whole must be made by a fairly intelligent representative of your own species, in full possession of the facts, and after he or she has had an adequate period to reflect on the consequences of disclosure."

"And you think we will, eh? In spite of everything?"

"Oh, yes," the little man told me with tranquil assurance. *"Because* of everything. All of you have been selected with a view to the personal advantage each would derive from the revelation. Sooner or later, one of you will find the advantage so necessary and tempting that the inhibiting scruple will disappear; eventually, all of you would come to it. As Shulmr pointed out, each member of a suicidal race contributes to the destruction of the whole even while attentively safeguarding his own existence. Disagreeable creatures, but fortunately short-lived!"

"I take it that more than one nation has the hydrogen bomb?"

"Quite correct. You *are* an ingenious race. Now, if you wouldn't mind stepping back onto your roof? We're in a bit of a hurry, Irngl and I, and we have to disinfect after. . . . Thank you."

I watched them disappear upward into a cloud bank. Then, walking around a television dipole tied in a hangman's noose that Irngl's father had overlooked, I trudged downstairs.

For a while, I was very angry. Then I was glum. Then I was angry again. I've thought about it a lot since August.

I've read some recent stuff on flying saucers, but not a word about the superweapon we'll get if we dismantle our hydrogen bombs. Only trouble is, if someone else has blabbed, how would I know about it?

That's just the point. Here I am a writer, a science-fiction writer, no less, with one of the hottest yarns since Noah drove the first nail into the ark. Besides, and by no means incidentally, it is also a highly *salable* story.

Well, it happens that I need money badly right now; and it further happens that I am plumb out of plots. How long am I supposed to go on being a sucker?

Somebody's probably told by now. If not in this country, in one of the others. And I *am* a writer, and I have a living to make. And this is fiction, and who asked you to believe it anyhow?

Only—only—I did intend to leave out the signal. The signal, that is, by which a government can get in touch with the kobolds, can let them know it's interested in making the trade, in getting that weapon. I did intend to leave out the signal.

But I don't have a satisfactory ending to this story. It needs some sort of tag-line. And the signal makes a perfect one. Well—it seems to me that if I've told *this* much—and probably, anyhow—

The signal's the immemorial one between man and kobold: Leave a bowl of milk outside the White House door.

Katherine MacLean

PICTURES DON'T LIE

About all that can safely be said about this little scorpion of a tale is: "Oh, don't they!"

THE man from the *News* asked, "What do you think of the aliens, Mr. Nathen? Are they friendly? Do they look human?"

"Very human," said the thin young man.

Outside, rain sleeted across the big windows with a steady, faint drumming, blurring and dimming the view of the airfield where *They* would arrive. On the concrete runways the puddles were pockmarked with rain, and the grass growing untouched between the runways of the unused field glistened wetly, bending before gusts of wind.

Back at a respectful distance from the place where the huge spaceship would land were the gray shapes of trucks, where TV camera crews huddled inside their mobile units, waiting. Farther back in the deserted, sandy landscape, behind distant sandy hills, artillery was ringed in a great circle, and in the distance across the horizon bombers stood ready at airfields, guarding the world against possible treachery from the first alien ship ever to land from space.

"Do you know anything about their home planet?" asked the man from the *Herald*.

The *Times* man stood with the others, listening absently, thinking of questions but reserving them. Joseph R. Nathen, the thin young man with the straight black hair and the tired lines on his face, was being treated with respect by his interviewers. He was obviously on edge, and they did not want to harry him with too many questions at once. They wanted to keep his good will. Tomorrow he would be one of the biggest celebrities ever to appear in headlines.

"No, nothing directly."

"Any ideas or deductions?" the *Herald* persisted.

"Their world must be Earthlike to them," the weary-looking young man answered uncertainly. "The environment evolves the animal. But only in relative terms, of course." He looked at them with a quick glance and then looked away evasively, his lank black hair beginning to cling to his forehead with sweat. "That doesn't necessarily mean anything."

"Earthlike," muttered a reporter, writing it down as if he had noticed nothing more in the reply.

The *Times* man glanced at the *Herald,* wondering if he had noticed, and received a quick glance in exchange.

The *Herald* asked Nathen, "You think they are dangerous, then?"

It was the kind of question, assuming much, that usually broke reticence and brought forth quick facts—when it hit the mark. They all knew of the military precautions, although they were not supposed to know.

The question missed. Nathen glanced out the window vaguely. "No, I wouldn't say so."

"You think they are friendly, then?" said the *Herald,* equally positive on the opposite tack.

A fleeting smile touched Nathen's lips. "Those I know are."

There was no lead in this direction, and they had to

get the basic facts of the story before the ship came. The *Times* asked, "What led up to your contacting them?"

Nathen answered, after a hesitation, "Static. Radio static. The Army told you my job, didn't they?"

The Army had told them nothing at all. The officer who had conducted them in for the interview stood glowering watchfully, as if he objected by instinct to telling anything to the public.

Nathen glanced at him doubtfully. "My job is radio decoder for the Department of Military Intelligence. I use a directional pickup, tune in on foreign bands, record any scrambled or coded messages I hear, and build automatic decoders and descramblers for all the basic scramble patterns."

The officer cleared his throat but said nothing.

The reporters smiled, noting that down.

Security regulations had changed since arms inspection had been legalized by the U.N. Complete information being the only public security against secret rearmament, spying and prying had come to seem a public service. Its aura had changed. It was good public relations to admit it.

Nathen continued, "In my spare time I started directing the pickup at stars. There's radio noise from stars, you know. Just stuff that sounds like spatter static, and an occasional squawk. People have been listening to it for a long time, and researching, trying to work out why stellar radiation on those bands comes in such jagged bursts. It didn't seem natural."

He paused and smiled uncertainly, aware that the next thing he would say was the thing that would make him famous—an idea that had come to him while he listened, an idea as simple and as perfect as the one that came to Newton when he saw the apple fall.

"I decided it wasn't natural. I tried decoding it."

Hurriedly, he tried to explain it away and make it seem obvious. "You see, there's an old intelligence trick, speeding up a message on a record until it sounds just like that, a short squawk of static, and then broadcasting it. Undergrounds use it. I'd heard that kind of screech before."

"You mean they broadcast at us in code?" asked the *News*.

"It's not exactly code. All you need to do is record it and slow it down. They're not broadcasting at us. If a star has planets, inhabited planets, and there is broadcasting between them, they would send it on a tight beam to save power." He looked for comprehension. "You know, like a spotlight. Theoretically, a tight beam can go on forever without losing power. But aiming would be difficult from planet to planet. You can't expect a beam to stay on target, over such distances, more than a few seconds at a time. So they'd naturally compress each message into a short half-second- or one-second-length package and send it a few hundred times in one long blast to make sure it is picked up during the instant the beam swings across the target."

He was talking slowly and carefully, remembering that this explanation was for the newspapers. "When a stray beam swings through our section of space, there's a sharp peak in noise level from that direction. The beams are swinging to follow their own planets at home, and the distance between there and here exaggerates the speed of swing tremendously, so we wouldn't pick up more than a *bip* as it passes."

"How do you account for the number of squawks coming in?" the *Times* asked. "Do stellar systems rotate on the plane of the Galaxy?" It was a private question; he spoke impulsively from interest and excitement.

The radio decoder grinned, the lines of strain vanishing from his face for a moment. "Maybe we're intercepting everybody's telephone calls, and the whole Galaxy is swarming with races that spend all day yacking at each other over the radio. Maybe the human type is standard model."

"It would take something like that," the *Times* agreed. They smiled at each other.

The *News* asked, "How did you happen to pick up television instead of voices?"

"Not by accident," Nathen explained patiently. "I'd recognized a scanning pattern, and I wanted pictures. Pictures are understandable in any language."

Near the interviewers, a senator paced back and forth, muttering his memorized speech of welcome and nervously glancing out the wide, streaming windows into the gray, sleeting rain.

Opposite the windows of the long room was a small raised platform flanked by the tall shapes of TV cameras and sound pickups on booms, and darkened floodlights, arranged and ready for the senator to make his speech of welcome to the aliens and the world. A shabby radio sending set stood beside it without a case to conceal its parts, two cathode television tubes flickering nakedly on one side and the speaker humming on the other. A vertical panel of dials and knobs jutted up before them, and a small hand-mike sat ready on the table before the panel. It was connected to a boxlike, expensively cased piece of equipment with "Radio Lab, U. S. Property" stenciled on it.

"I recorded a couple of package screeches from Sagittarius and began working on them," Nathen added. "It took a couple of months to find the synchronizing signals and set the scanners close enough to the right time to even get a pattern. When I showed the pattern to the Department, they gave me full time to work on it, and an assistant to help. It took eight months to pick out the color bands and assign them the right colors, to get anything intelligible on the screen."

The shabby-looking mess of exposed parts was the original receiver that they had labored over for ten months, adjusting and readjusting to reduce the maddening rippling plaids of unsynchronized color scanners to some kind of sane picture.

"Trial and error," said Nathen, "but it came out all right. The wide band spread of the squawks had suggested color TV from the beginning."

He walked over and touched the set. The speaker bipped slightly and the gray screen flickered with a flash of color at the touch. The set was awake and sensitive, tuned to receive from the great interstellar spaceship which now circled the atmosphere.

"We wondered why there were so many bands, but when we got the set working and started recording and playing everything that came in, we found we'd tapped something like a lending-library line. It was all fiction, plays."

Between the pauses in Nathen's voice, the *Times* found himself unconsciously listening for the sound of roaring, swiftly approaching rocket jets.

The *Post* asked, "How did you contact the spaceship?"

"I scanned and recorded a film copy of *The Rite of Spring,* the Disney-Stravinsky combination, and sent it back along the same line we were receiving from. Just testing. It wouldn't get there for a good number of years, if it got there at all, but I thought it would please the library to get a new record in.

"Two weeks later, when we caught and slowed a new

batch of recordings, we found an answer. It was obviously meant for us. It was a flash of the Disney being played to a large audience, and then the audience sitting and waiting before a blank screen. The signal was very clear and loud. We'd intercepted a spaceship. They were asking for an encore, you see. They liked the film and wanted more. . . ."

He smiled at them in sudden thought. "You can see them for yourself. It's all right down the hall where the linguists are working on the automatic translator."

The listening officer frowned and cleared his throat, and the thin young man turned to him quickly. "No security reason why they should not see the broadcasts, is there? Perhaps you should show them." He said to the reporters reassuringly, "It's right down the hall. You will be informed the moment the spaceship approaches."

The interview was very definitely over. The lank-haired, nervous young man turned away and seated himself at the radio set while the officer swallowed his objections and showed them dourly down the hall to a closed door.

They opened it and fumbled into a darkened room crowded with empty folding chairs, dominated by a glowing bright screen. The door closed behind them, bringing total darkness.

There was the sound of reporters fumbling their way into seats around him, but the *Times* man remained standing, aware of an enormous surprise, as if he had been asleep and wakened to find himself in the wrong country.

The bright colors of the double image seemed the only real thing in the darkened room. Even blurred as they were, he could see that the action was subtly different, the shapes subtly not right.

He was looking at aliens.

The impression was of two humans disguised, humans moving oddly, half dancing, half crippled. Carefully, afraid the images would go away, he reached up to his breast pocket, took out his polarized glasses, rotated one lens at right angles to the other, and put them on.

Immediately, the two beings came into sharp focus, real and solid, and the screen became a wide, illusively near window through which he watched them.

They were conversing with each other in a gray-walled room, discussing something with restrained excitement. The large man in the green tunic closed his purple eyes for an instant at something the other said and grimaced, making a motion with his fingers as if shoving something away from him.

Mellerdrammer.

The second, smaller, with yellowish-green eyes, stepped closer, talking more rapidly in a lower voice. The first stood very still, not trying to interrupt.

Obviously, the proposal was some advantageous treachery, and he wanted to be persuaded. The *Times* groped for a chair and sat down.

Perhaps gesture is universal; desire and aversion, a leaning forward or a leaning back, tension, relaxation. Perhaps these actors were masters. The scenes changed: a corridor, a parklike place in what he began to realize was a spaceship, a lecture room. There were others talking and working, speaking to the man in the green tunic, and never was it unclear what was happening or how they felt.

They talked a flowing language with many short vowels and shifts of pitch, and they gestured in the heat of talk, their hands moving with an odd lagging difference of motion, not slow, but somehow drifting.

He ignored the language, but after a time the difference in motion began to arouse his interest. Something in the way they walked . . .

With an effort he pulled his mind from the plot and forced his attention to the physical difference. Brown hair in short, silky crew cuts, varied eye colors, the colors showing clearly because their irises were very large, their round eyes set very widely apart in tapering, light-brown faces. Their necks and shoulders were thick in a way that would indicate unusual strength for a human, but their wrists were narrow and their fingers long and thin and delicate.

There seemed to be more than the usual number of fingers.

Since he came in, a machine had been whirring and a voice muttering beside him. He turned from counting their fingers and looked around. Beside him sat an alert-looking man wearing earphones, watching and listening with hawklike concentration. Beside him was a tall streamlined box. From the screen came the sound of the alien language. The man abruptly flipped a switch on the box, muttered a word into a small hand microphone, and flipped the switch back with nervous rapidity.

He reminded the *Times* man of the earphoned interpreters at the U.N. The machine was probably a vocal translator and the mutterer a linguist adding to its vocabulary. Near the screen were two other linguists taking notes.

The *Times* remembered the senator pacing in the observatory room, rehearsing his speech of welcome. The speech would not be just the empty pompous gesture he had expected. It would be translated mechanically and understood by the aliens.

On the other side of the glowing window that was the stereo screen the large protagonist in the green tunic was speaking to a pilot in a gray uniform. They stood in a brightly lit canary-yellow control room in a spaceship.

The *Times* tried to pick up the thread of the plot. Already he was interested in the fate of the hero, and liked him. That was the effect of good acting, probably, for part of the art of acting is to win affection from the audience, and this actor might be the matinee idol of whole Solar Systems.

Controlled tension, betraying itself by a jerk of the hands, a too quick answer to a question. The uniformed one, not suspicious, turned his back, busying himself at some task involving a map lit with glowing red points, his motions sharing the same fluid, dragging grace of the others, as if they were under water or on a slow-motion film. The other was watching a switch, a switch set into a panel, moving closer to it, talking casually— background music coming and rising in thin chords of tension.

There was a close-up of the alien's face watching the switch, and the *Times* noted that his ears were symmetrical half circles, almost perfect, with no earholes visible. The voice of the uniformed one answered—a brief word in a preoccupied, deep voice. His back was still turned. The other glanced at the switch, moving closer to it, talking casually, the switch coming closer and closer stereoscopically. It was in reach, filling the screen. His hand came into view, darted out, closed over the switch—

There was a sharp clap of sound and his hand opened in a frozen shape of pain. Beyond him, as his gaze swung up, stood the figure of the uniformed officer, un-moving, a weapon rigid in his hand, in the startled position in which he had turned and fired, watching with widening eyes as the man in the green tunic swayed and fell.

The tableau held, the uniformed one drooping, looking down at his hand holding the weapon which had killed, and music began to build in from the background. Just for an instant, the room and the things within it flashed into one of those bewildering color changes that were the bane of color television—to a color negative of itself, a green man standing in a violet control room, looking down at the body of a green man in a red tunic. It held for less than a second; then the color-band alternator fell back into phase and the colors reversed to normal.

Another uniformed man came and took the weapon from the limp hand of the other, who began to explain dejectedly in a low voice while the music mounted and covered his words and the screen slowly went blank, like a window that slowly filmed over with gray fog.

The music faded.

In the dark, someone clapped appreciatively.

The earphoned man beside the *Times* shifted his earphones back from his ears and spoke briskly. "I can't get any more. Either of you want a replay?"

There was a short silence until the linguist nearest the set said, "I guess we've squeezed that one dry. Let's run the tape where Nathen and that ship radio boy are kidding around CQing and tuning their beams in closer. I have a hunch the boy is talking routine ham talk and giving the old radio count—one-two-three-testing."

There was some fumbling in the semidark and then the screen came to life again.

It showed a flash of an audience sitting before a screen and gave a clipped chord of some familiar symphony. "Crazy about Stravinsky and Mozart," remarked the earphoned linguist to the *Times,* resettling his earphones. "Can't stand Gershwin. Can you beat that?"

He turned his attention back to the screen as the right sequence came on.

The *Post,* who was sitting just in front of him, turned to the *Times* and said, "Funny how much they look like people." He was writing, making notes to telephone his report. "What color hair did that character have?"

"I didn't notice." He wondered if he should remind the reporter that Nathen had said he assigned the color bands on guess, choosing the colors that gave the most plausible images. The guests, when they arrived, could turn out to be bright green with blue hair. Only the gradations of color in the picture were sure, only the similarities and contrasts, the relationship of one color to another.

From the screen came the sound of the alien language again. This race averaged deeper voices than human. He liked deep voices. Could he write that?

No, there was something wrong with that, too. How had Nathen established the right sound-track pitch? Was it a matter of taking the modulation as it came in, or some sort of heterodyning up and down by trial and error? Probably.

It might be safer to assume that Nathen had simply preferred deep voices.

As he sat there, doubting, an uneasiness he had seen in Nathen came back to add to his own uncertainty, and he remembered just how close that uneasiness had come to something that looked like restrained fear.

"What I don't get is why he went to all the trouble of picking up TV shows instead of just contacting them," the *News* complained. "They're good shows, but what's the point?"

"Maybe so we'd get to learn their language, too," said the *Herald.*

On the screen now was the obviously unstaged and genuine scene of a young alien working over a bank of apparatus. He turned and waved and opened his mouth in the comical O shape which the *Times* was beginning to recognize as their equivalent of a smile, then went back to trying to explain something about the equipment, in elaborate, awkward gestures and carefully mouthed words.

The *Times* got up quietly, went out into the bright white stone corridor, and walked back the way he had come, thoughtfully folding his stereo glasses and putting them away.

No one stopped him. Secrecy restrictions were ambiguous here. The reticence of the Army seemed more a matter of habit—mere reflex, from the fact that it had all originated in the Intelligence Department—than any reasoned policy of keeping the landing a secret.

The main room was more crowded than he had left it. The TV camera and sound crew stood near their apparatus, the senator had found a chair and was reading, and at the far end of the room eight men were grouped in a circle of chairs, arguing something with impassioned concentration. The *Times* recognized a few he knew personally, eminent names in science, workers in field theory.

A stray phrase reached him: "—reference to the universal constants as ratio—" It was probably a discussion of ways of converting formulas from one mathematics to another for a rapid exchange of information.

They had reason to be intent, aware of the flood of insights that novel viewpoints could bring, if they could grasp them. He would have liked to go over and listen, but there was too little time left before the spaceship was due, and he had a question to ask.

The hand-rigged transceiver was still humming, tuned to the sending band of the circling ship, and the young man who had started it all was sitting on the edge of the TV platform with his chin resting in one hand. He did not look up as the *Times* approached, but it was the indifference of preoccupation, not discourtesy.

The *Times* sat down on the edge of the platform beside him and took out a pack of cigarettes, then remembered the coming TV broadcast and the ban on smoking. He put them away, thoughtfully watching the diminishing rain spray against the streaming windows.

"What's wrong?" he asked.

Nathen showed that he was aware and friendly by a slight motion of his head.

"*You* tell me."

"Hunch," said the *Times* man. "Sheer hunch. Everything sailing along too smoothly, everyone taking too much for granted."

Nathen relaxed slightly. "I'm still listening."

"Something about the way they move . . ."

Nathen shifted to glance at him.

"That's bothered me, too."

"Are you sure they're adjusted to the right speed?"

Nathen clenched his hands out in front of him and looked at them consideringly. "I don't know. When I turn the tape faster, they're all rushing, and you begin to wonder why their clothes don't stream behind them, why the doors close so quickly and yet you can't hear them slam, why things fall so fast. If I turn it slower, they all seem to be swimming." He gave the *Times* a considering sideways glance. "Didn't catch the name."

Country-bred guy, thought the *Times*. "Jacob Luke, *Times*," he said, extending his hand.

Nathen gave the hand a quick, hard grip, identifying

the name. "Sunday Science Section editor. I read it. Surprised to meet you here."

"Likewise." The *Times* smiled. "Look, have you gone into this rationally, with formulas?" He found a pencil in his pocket. "Obviously, there's something wrong with our judgment of their weight-to-speed-to-momentum ratio. Maybe it's something simple, like low gravity aboard ship, with magnetic shoes. Maybe they *are* floating slightly."

"Why worry?" Nathen cut in. "I don't see any reason to try to figure it out now." He laughed and shoved back his black hair nervously. "We'll see them in twenty minutes."

"Will we?" asked the *Times* slowly.

There was a silence while the senator turned a page of his magazine with a slight crackling of paper and the scientists argued at the other end of the room. Nathen pushed at his black hair again, as if it were trying to fall forward in front of his eyes and keep him from seeing.

"Sure." The young man laughed suddenly, talked rapidly. "Sure we'll see them. Why shouldn't we, with all the government ready with welcome speeches, the whole Army turned out and hiding over the hill, reporters all around, newsreel cameras—everything set up to broadcast the landing to the world. The President himself shaking hands with me and waiting in Washington—"

He came to the truth without pausing for breath.

He said, "Hell, no, they won't get here. There's some mistake somewhere. Something's wrong. I should have told the brass hats yesterday when I started adding it up. Don't know why I didn't say anything. Scared, I guess. Too much top rank around here. Lost my nerve."

He clutched the *Times* man's sleeve. "Look. I don't know what—"

A green light flashed on the sending-receiving set. Nathen didn't look at it, but he stopped talking.

The loud-speaker on the set broke into a voice speaking in the aliens' language. The senator started and looked nervously at it, straightening his tie. The voice stopped.

Nathen turned and looked at the loud-speaker. His worry seemed to be gone.

"What is it?" the *Times* asked anxiously.

"He says they've slowed enough to enter the atmosphere now. They'll be here in five to ten minutes, I guess. That's Bud. He's all excited. He says holy smoke, what a murky-looking planet we live on." Nathen smiled. "Kidding."

The *Times* was puzzled. "What does he mean, murky? It can't be raining over much territory on Earth." Outside, the rain was slowing and bright-blue patches of sky were shining through breaks in the cloud blanket, glittering blue light from the drops that ran down the windows. He tried to think of an explanation. "Maybe they're trying to land on Venus." The thought was ridiculous, he knew. The spaceship was following Nathen's sending beam. It couldn't miss Earth. "Bud" had to be kidding.

The green light glowed on the set again, and they stopped speaking, waiting for the message to be recorded, slowed, and replayed. The cathode screen came to life suddenly with a picture of the young man sitting at his sending set, his back turned, watching a screen at one side that showed a glimpse of a huge dark plain approaching. As the ship plunged down toward it, the illusion of solidity melted into a boiling turbulence of black clouds. They expanded in an inky swirl, looked huge for an instant, and then blackness swallowed the screen. The young alien swung around to face the camera, speaking a few words as he moved, made the O of a smile again, then flipped the switch and the screen went gray.

Nathen's voice was suddenly toneless and strained. "He said something like break out the drinks, here they come."

"The atmosphere doesn't look like that," the *Times* said at random, knowing he was saying something too obvious even to think about. "Not Earth's atmosphere."

Some people drifted up. "What did they say?"

"Entering the atmosphere, ought to be landing in five or ten minutes," Nathen told them.

A ripple of heightened excitement ran through the room. Cameramen began adjusting the lens angles again, turning on the mike and checking it, turning on the floodlights. The scientists rose and stood near the window, still talking. The reporters trooped in from the hall and went to the windows to watch for the great event. The three linguists came in, trundling a large wheeled box that was the mechanical translator, supervising while it was hitched into the sound-broadcasting system.

"Landing where?" the *Times* asked Nathen brutally. "Why don't you do something?"

"Tell me what to do and I'll do it," Nathen said quietly, not moving.

It was not sarcasm. Jacob Luke of the *Times* looked sideways at the strained whiteness of his face and moderated his tone. "Can't you contact them?"

"Not while they're landing."

"What now?" The *Times* took out a pack of cigarettes, remembered the rule against smoking, and put it back.

"We just wait." Nathen leaned his elbow on one knee and his chin in his hand.

They waited.

All the people in the room were waiting. There was no conversation. A bald man of the scientist group was automatically buffing his fingernails over and over and inspecting them without seeing them; another absently polished his glasses, held them up to the light, put them on, and then a moment later took them off and began polishing again. The television crew concentrated on their jobs, moving quietly and efficiently, with perfectionist care, minutely arranging things that did not need to be arranged, checking things that had already been checked.

This was to be one of the great moments of human history, and they were all trying to forget that fact and remain impassive and wrapped up in the problems of their jobs, as good specialists should.

After an interminable age the *Times* consulted his watch. Three minutes had passed. He tried holding his breath a moment, listening for a distant approaching thunder of jets. There was no sound.

The sun came out from behind the clouds and lit up the field like a great spotlight on an empty stage.

Abruptly, the green light shone on the set again, indicating that a squawk message had been received. The recorder recorded it, slowed it, and fed it back to the speaker. It clicked and the sound was very loud in the still, tense room.

The screen remained gray, but Bud's voice spoke a few words in the alien language. He stopped, the speaker clicked, and the light went out. When it was plain that nothing more would occur and no announcement was to be made of what was said, the people in the room turned back to the windows and talk picked up again.

Somebody told a joke and laughed alone.

One of the linguists remained turned toward the loud-speaker, then looked at the widening patches of blue sky showing out the window, his expression puzzled. He had understood.

"It's dark," the thin Intelligence Department decoder translated, low-voiced, to the man from the *Times*. "Your atmosphere is *thick*. That's precisely what Bud said."

Another three minutes. The *Times* caught himself about to light a cigarette and swore silently, blowing the match out and putting the cigarette back into its package. He listened for the sound of the rocket jets. It was time for the landing, yet he heard no blasts.

The green light came on in the transceiver.

Message in.

Instinctively, he came to his feet. Nathen abruptly was standing beside him. Then the message came in the voice he was coming to think of as Bud. It spoke and paused. Suddenly the *Times* knew.

"We've landed." Nathen whispered the words.

The wind blew across the open spaces of white concrete and damp soil that was the empty airfield, swaying the wet, shiny grass. The people in the room looked out, listening for the roar of jets, looking for the silver bulk of a spaceship in the sky.

Nathen moved, seating himself at the transmitter, switching it on to warm up, checking and balancing dials. Jacob Luke of the *Times* moved softly to stand behind his right shoulder, hoping he could be useful. Nathen made a half motion of his head, as if to glance back at him, unhooked two of the earphone sets hanging on the side of the tall streamlined box that was the automatic translator, plugged them in, and handed one back over his shoulder to the *Times* man.

The voice began to come from the speaker again.

Hastily, Jacob Luke fitted the earphones over his ears. He fancied he could hear Bud's voice tremble. For a moment it was just Bud's voice speaking the alien language, and then, very distant and clear in his earphones, he heard the recorded voice of the linguist say an English word, then a mechanical click and another clear word in the voice of one of the translators, then another as the alien's voice flowed from the loudspeaker, the cool single words barely audible, overlapping and blending like translating thought, skipping unfamiliar words yet quite astonishingly clear.

"Radar shows no buildings or civilization near. The atmosphere around us registers as thick as glue. Tremendous gas pressure, low gravity, no light at all. You didn't describe it like this. Where are you, Joe? This isn't some kind of trick, is it?" Bud hesitated, was prompted by a deeper official voice, and jerked out the words.

"If it is a trick, we are ready to repel attack."

The linguist stood listening. He whitened slowly and beckoned the other linguists over to him and whispered to them.

Joseph Nathen looked at them with unwarranted bitter hostility while he picked up the hand mike, plugging it into the translator. "Joe calling," he said quietly into it in clear, slow English. "No trick. We don't know where you are. I am trying to get a direction fix from your signal. Describe your surroundings to us if at all possible."

Nearby, the floodlights blazed steadily on the television platform, ready for the official welcome of the aliens to Earth. The television channels of the world had been alerted to set aside their scheduled programs for an unscheduled great event. In the long room the people waited, listening for the swelling sound of rocket jets.

This time, after the light came on, there was a long delay. The speaker sputtered and sputtered again, building to a steady scratching through which they could barely hear a dim voice. It came through in a few tinny words and then wavered back to inaudibility. The machine translated in their earphones.

"Tried . . . seemed . . . repair . . ." Suddenly it came in clearly. "Can't tell if the auxiliary blew, too. Will try it. We might pick you up clearly on the next try. I have the volume down. Where is the landing port? Repeat. Where is the landing port? Where are you?"

Nathen put down the hand mike and carefully set a dial on the recording box and flipped a switch, speaking over his shoulder. "This sets it to repeat what I said the last time. It keeps repeating." Then he sat with unnatural stillness, his head still half turned, as if he had suddenly caught a glimpse of answer and was trying with no success whatever to grasp it.

The green warning light cut in, the recording clicked, and the playback of Bud's face and voice appeared on the screen.

"We heard a few words, Joe, and then the receiver blew again. We're adjusting a viewing screen to pick up the long waves that go through the murk and convert them to visible light. We'll be able to see out soon. The engineer says that something is wrong with the stern jets, and the captain has had me broadcast a help call to our nearest space base." He made the mouth O of a grin. "The message won't reach it for some years. I trust you, Joe, but get us out of here, will you?— They're buzzing that the screen is finally ready. Hold everything."

The screen went gray and the green light went off.

The *Times* considered the lag required for the help call, the speaking and recording of the message just received, the time needed to reconvert a viewing screen.

"They work fast." He shifted uneasily and added at random, "Something wrong with the time factor. All wrong. They work *too* fast."

The green light came on again immediately. Nathen half turned to him, sliding his words hastily into the gap of time as the message was recorded and slowed. "They're close enough for our transmission power to blow their receiver."

If it was on Earth, why the darkness around the ship? "Maybe they see in the high ultraviolet—the atmosphere is opaque to that band," the *Times* suggested hastily as the speaker began to talk in the young extra-Terrestrial's voice.

That voice *was* shaking now. "Stand by for the description."

They tensed, waiting. The *Times* brought a map of the state before his mind's eye.

"A half circle of cliffs around the horizon. A wide muddy lake swarming with swimming things. Huge, strange white foliage all around the ship and incredibly huge, pulpy monsters attacking and eating each other on all sides. We almost landed in the lake, right on the soft edge. The mud can't hold the ship's weight, and we're sinking. The engineer says we might be able to blast free, but the tubes are mud-clogged and might blow up the ship. When can you reach us?"

The *Times* thought vaguely of the Carboniferous era. Nathen obviously had seen something he had not.

"Where are they?" the *Times* asked him quietly.

Nathen pointed to the antenna position indicators. The *Times* let his eyes follow the converging imaginary lines of focus out the window to the sunlit airfield, the empty airfield, the drying concrete and green waving grass where the lines met.

Where the lines met. The spaceship was there!

The fear of something unknown gripped him suddenly.

The spaceship was broadcasting again. *"Where are you? Answer if possible! We are sinking! Where are you?"*

He saw that Nathen knew. "What is it?" the *Times* asked hoarsely. "Are they in another dimension or the past or on another world or what?"

Nathen was smiling bitterly, and Jacob Luke remembered that the young man had a friend in that spaceship. "My guess is that they evolved on a high-gravity planet with a thin atmosphere, near a blue-white star. Sure, they see in the ultraviolet range. Our sun is abnormally small and dim and yellow. Our atmosphere is so thick it screens out ultraviolet." He laughed harshly. "A good joke on us, the weird place we evolved in, the thing it did to us!"

"Where are you?" called the alien spaceship. "Hurry, please! We're sinking!"

The decoder slowed his tumbled, frightened words and looked up into the *Times'* face for understanding. "We'll rescue them," he said quietly. "You were right about the time factor, right about them moving at a different speed. I misunderstood. This business about squawk coding, speeding for better transmission to counteract beam waver—I was wrong."

"What do you mean?"

"They don't speed up their broadcasts."

"They don't—?"

Suddenly, in his mind's eye, the *Times* began to see again the play he had just seen—but the actors were

moving at blurring speed, the words jerking out in a
fluting, dizzying stream, thoughts and decisions passing
with unfollowable rapidity, rippling faces in a twisting
blur of expressions, doors slamming wildly, shatteringly,
as the actors leaped in and out of rooms.

No—faster, faster—he wasn't visualizing it as rapidly
as it was, an hour of talk and action in one almost in-
stantaneous "squawk," a narrow peak of "noise" inter-
fering with a single word in an Earth broadcast! Faster
—faster—it was impossible. Matter could not stand
such stress—inertia—momentum—abrupt weight.

It was insane. "Why?" he asked. "How?"

Nathen laughed again harshly, reaching for the mike.
"Get them out? There isn't a lake or river within hundreds of miles from here!"

A shiver of unreality went down the *Times'* spine.
Automatically and inanely, he found himself delving in
his pocket for a cigarette while he tried to grasp what
had happened. "Where are they, then? Why can't we
see their spaceship?"

Nathen switched the microphone on in a gesture that
showed the bitterness of his disappointment.

"We'll need a magnifying glass for that."

THE DISTANT FUTURE: *Epilogue*

FINALLY, there are those stories that assume that Man has lived out his allotted time—whether short or long, ended violently or peacefully, is not always stated —and has disappeared. Then along come visitors from another civilization to dig in the ruins and see what they can find. There are many well-known variations on this theme, most of them grim and gloomy on the subject of the low survival value of Modern Man.

However, our single example of the post-Homo-sapiens tale blithely disregards all that. . . .

Anthony Boucher

THE GREATEST TERTIAN*

*Pardon is requested for closing this otherwise solemn
and semiscientific collection of stories with the following piece of charming burlesque on the scholarly efforts
of a superior, posthuman race. No editor in possession
of his nonsenses could ever turn down so gravely hilari-
ous and so portentously sly a piece as this.*

*This little item was originally written for a proposed
volume of Sherlock Holmesiana planned by The Illus-
trious Clients, the Indianapolis Section of The Baker
Street Irregulars. That volume is yet to appear, but here
is what would have undoubtedly been its pièce de ré-
sistance. According to Mr. Boucher, "The Greatest
Tertian" is—so far as he knows—the only s.-f. treatment
of Sherlock Holmes. Which is, of course, another sheerly
unavoidable reason for including it in this anthology.*

ONE of the outstanding characteristics of the culture of
the third planet from the Sun is, as I have stressed
earlier, the tendency toward onomatolatry, the worship
of great names all but divorced from any true biographical or historical comprehension.

Many of these names, employed with almost magical
significance, must be investigated in later chapters; they
include (to give approximate phonetic equivalents)

* Excerpt from Rom Gul's *Tertian History and Culture*. Translated by Anthony Boucher. 12 vols. Kovis, 4739.

Linkn, Mamt, Ung Klsam, Staln, Ro Sflt (who seems to have appeared in several contradictory avatars), Bakh, Sokr Tis, Mi Klan Jlo, Me Uess-tt, San Kloss, and many others, some of them indubitably of legendary origin.

But one name appears pre-eminently in every cultural cache so far investigated. From pole to pole and in every Tertian language, we have yet to decipher any cultural remains of sizable proportion that do not contain at least a reference to what must have been unquestionably the greatest Tertian of all time: Sherk Oms.

It is well at this point to settle once and for all the confusion concerning the two forms of the name: Sherk Oms and Sherk Sper. A few eccentric scholars, notably Shcho Raz in his last speech before the Academy*, have asserted that these names represented two separate individuals; and, indeed, there are small items in which the use of the two forms does differ.

Sherk Sper, for instance, is generally depicted as a writer of public spectacles; Sherk Oms as a pursuer of offenders against society. Both are represented as living in the capital city of the *nation*† of In Glan under the unusual control of a female administrator; but the name of this female is generally given, in accounts of Sherk Sper, as Li Zbet; in accounts of Sherk Oms, as Vi Kto Rya.

The essential identity of these female names I have explained in my *Tertian Phonology***. The confusion

* See my refutation in *Academy Proceedings*, 2578: 9, 11/76.
† For a full discussion of this extraordinary word, meaning a group of beings feeling themselves set apart from, and above, the rest of the same type of beings (a peculiarly Tertian concept), *vide infra*, Chapter 127.
** Pp. 1259 ff.

of professions is more apparent than real; the fact of the matter is that Sherk Oms (to use the more widespread of the two forms) was both a writer and a man of action and tended to differentiate the form of his name according to his pursuit of the moment.

Clinching evidence exists in the two facts that:

(1) While we are frequently told that Sherk Oms wrote extensively, no cultural cache has turned up any fragment of his work, aside from two accounts of his personal adventures.

(2) While we know thoroughly the literary work of Sherk Sper, no cultural cache has revealed the slightest reliable biographical material as to his life.

One characteristic, it may be added, distinguished the great Sherk under both names: his love for disguise. We possess full details on the many magnificently assumed characterizations of Sherk Oms, while we also read that Sherk Sper was wont to disguise himself as many of the most eminent writers and politicians of his era, including Bekn, Ma Lo, Ok Sfud, and others.

Which aspect of the great Sherk was it, you may well ask, which so endeared him to all Tertians? This is hard to answer. Aside from religious writings, there are two items which we are always sure of discovering in any Tertian cultural cache, either in the original language of In Glan or in translation: the biographical accounts* of the crime-hunter Sherk Oms, and the *plays* (to use an untranslatable Tertian word) of Sherk Sper.

Both contributed so many phrases to the language that it is difficult to imagine Tertian culture without them:

The dog did nothing in the nighttime (a proverb

* Principally by Wa Tsn, though also by Start, Pa Mr, Smit, Dr Leth, etc.

equivalent to our: While nature rests, the wise chudz sleeps).

Friends, Romans, countrymen, lend me your ears (indicating the early Tertian development of plastic surgery).

The game is a foot (a baffling reference, in that no cultural cache has yet yielded evidence of a sport suitable to monopods).

To bee or not to bee (an obvious reference, though by Sherk Sper, to Sherk Oms' years of retirement).

Difficult though it is to estimate the relative Tertian esteem for the Master in his two guises, we certainly know, at least, from our own annals, which aspect of the great Sherk would in time have been more valuable to the Tertians—and it was perhaps a realization of this fact that caused the dwellers in Ti Bet to address their prayers to him in the form: *Oms mani padme Oms**.

The very few defeats which Sherk Oms suffered were, as we all know, caused by us. Limited as even he was by the overconventional pattern of Tertian thought, he was quite unable to understand the situation when our advance agent Fi Li Mor was forced to return to his house for the temporospatial rod that Wa Tsn thought to be a rain shield. Our clumsy and bungling removal of a vessel for water transport named, I believe, A Li Sha was still sufficiently alien to perplex him; and he never, we must thank the Great Maker, understood what we had planted on his Tertian world in what he thought to be a matchbox.

But in time, so penetrating a mind as he reveals under both guises would have understood; and more than that, he might have developed methods of counterattack. We owe our thanks to the absurd brevity of the Tertian life

* The meaning of the middle words is lost.

span that he, considered long-lived among his own people, survived fewer than a hundred orbital cycles of the third planet.

If Sherk Oms, most perceptive and inventive of Tertians, had still been living, the ultimate conquest of the third planet by the fourth might well have been foiled, and his planet might even today still swarm with pullulating Tertians, complete with their concepts of *nations, wars,* and *races**, rather than being the exquisitely lifeless playground for cultural researchers which today it offers to us, the inhabitants of that neighboring planet which, as best our phoneticists can make out, the Tertians knew as Marz.

* For these peculiarly Tertian words, again see Chapter 127.